ALSO BY ELLE KENNEDY

The GRAHAM EFFECT

a novel

ELLE KENNEDY

Bloom *books*

Published by Bloom Books, an imprint of Sourcebooks
P.O. Box 4410, Naperville, Illinois 60567-4410
(630) 961-3900
sourcebooks.com

Cataloging-in-Publication data is on file with the Library of Congress.

Printed and bound in the United States of America.
WOZ 10 9 8 7 6 5 4

PROLOGUE
GIGI

Is he famous or something?

SIX YEARS AGO

WHEN I WAS LITTLE, ONE OF MY DAD'S FRIENDS ASKED ME WHAT I wanted to be when I grew up.

I proudly replied, "Stanley Cup."

My four-year-old self thought the Cup was a person. In fact, what I gleaned from all those adult conversations going on around me is that my dad personally knew Stanley Cup (met him several times, actually), an honor bestowed to only the most elite group. Which meant Stanley, whoever this great man was, had to be some kind of legend. A phenom. A person one must aspire to be.

Forget turning out like my dad, a measly professional athlete. Or my mother, a mere award-winning songwriter.

I was going to be Stanley Cup and rule the fucking world.

I can't remember who burst my bubble. Probably my twin brother, Wyatt. He's an unrepentant bubble burster.

The damage was done, though. While Wyatt got a normal nickname from our dad when we were kids—the tried and true "champ"—I was dubbed Stanley. Or Stan, when they're feeling lazy. Even Mom, who pretends to be annoyed with all the obnoxious nicknames spawned in the hockey sphere, slips up sometimes. She asked Stanley to pass her the potatoes last week at dinner. Because she's a traitor.

This morning, another traitor is added to the list.

"Stan!" a voice calls from the other end of the corridor. "I'm popping out to pick up coffee for your dad and the other coaches. Want anything?"

I turn to glare at my father's assistant. "You promised you'd never call me that."

Tommy gives me the courtesy of appearing contrite. Then he throws that courtesy out the window. "Okay. Don't shoot the messenger, but it might be time to accept you're fighting a losing battle. You want my advice?"

"I do not."

"I say you embrace the nickname, my beautiful darling."

"Never," I grumble. "But I will embrace 'my beautiful darling.' Keep calling me that. It makes me feel dainty but powerful."

"You got it, Stan." Laughing at my outraged face, he prompts, "Coffee?"

"No, I'm good. But thanks."

Tommy bounds off, a bundle of unceasing energy. During the three years he's been my dad's personal assistant, I've never seen the man take so much as a five-minute break. His dreams probably all take place on a treadmill.

I continue down the hall toward the ladies' change rooms, where I quickly kick off my sneakers and throw on my skates. It's 7:30 a.m., which gives me plenty of time to get in a morning warm-up. Once camp gets underway, chaos will ensue. Until then, I have the rink all to myself. Just me and a fresh sheet of beautiful, clean ice, unmarred by all the blades that are about to scratch it up.

The Zamboni is wrapping up its final lap when I walk out. I inhale my favorite smells in the world: The cool bite of the air and the sharp odor of rubber-coated floors. The metallic scent of my freshly sharpened skates. It's hard to describe how good it feels breathing it all in.

I hit the ice and do a couple of slow, lazy laps. I'm not even participating in this juniors camp, but my body never lets me veer from my routine. For as long as I can remember I've woken up early for my own private practice. Sometimes I assign myself simple drills. Sometimes I just glide aimlessly. During the hockey season, when I have to attend actual practices, I take care not to overexert myself with these little solo skates. But this week I'm not here to play, only to help my dad. So there's nothing stopping me from doing a full sprint down the wall.

I skate hard and fast, then fly behind the net, make that tight turn, and accelerate hard toward the blue line. By the time I slow down, my heart is pounding so noisily that for a moment it drowns out the voice from the home bench.

"…to be here!"

I turn to see a guy about my age standing there.

The first thing I notice about him is the scowl.

The second thing I notice is that he's still astoundingly good-looking despite the scowl.

He has one of those attractive faces that can sport a scowl without a single aesthetic consequence. Like, it only makes him hotter. Gives him that rugged, bad-boy edge.

"Hey, did you hear me?" His voice is deeper than I expect. He sounds like he should be singing country ballads on a Tennessee porch.

He hops out the short door, his skates hitting the ice. He's tall, I realize. He towers over me. And I don't think I've ever seen eyes that shade of blue. They're impossibly dark. Steely sapphire.

"Sorry, what?" I ask, trying not to stare. How is it possible for someone to be this attractive?

His black hockey pants and gray jersey suit his tall frame. He's kind of lanky, but even at fifteen or sixteen, he's already built like a hockey player.

"I said you're not supposed to be here," he barks.

Just like that, I snap out of it. Oh, okay. This guy's a dick.

"And you're supposed to be?" I challenge. Camp doesn't start until nine. I know for a fact because I helped Tommy photocopy the schedules for everyone's welcome packages.

"Yes. It's the first day of hockey camp. I'm here to warm up."

Those magnetic eyes sweep over me. He takes in my tight jeans, purple sweatshirt, and bright pink leg warmers.

Lifting a brow, he adds, "You must have mixed up your dates. Figure skating camp is next week."

I narrow my eyes. Scratch that—this guy's a huge dick.

"Actually, I'm—"

"Seriously, prom queen," he interrupts, voice tight. "There's no reason for you to be here."

"Prom queen? Have you ever seen yourself in the mirror?" I retort. "You're the one who looks like he should be voted prom king."

The irritation in his expression sparks my own. Not to mention that smug gleam in his eyes. It's the latter that cements my decision to mess with him.

He thinks I don't belong here?

And he's calling me *prom queen*?

Yeah…kindly screw yourself in the butt, dickface.

With an innocent look, I tuck my hands in my back pockets. "Sorry, but I'm not going anywhere. I really need to work on my spins and loop jumps, and from what I can see"—I wave a hand around the massive empty rink—"there's plenty of room for both of us to practice. Now if you'll excuse me, this prom queen really needs to get back to it."

He scowls again. "I only called you that because I don't know your name."

"Ever consider just asking my name then?"

"Fine." He grumbles out a noise. "What's your name?"

"None of your business."

He throws his hands up. "Whatever. You want to stay? Stay. Knock yourself out with your loops. Just don't come crawling to me when the coaches show up and kick your ass out."

With that, he skates off, sullying my pristine ice with the heavy marks of his blades. He goes clockwise, so out of spite I move counterclockwise. When we pass each other on the lap, he glares at me. I smile back. Then, just because I'm a jerk, I bust out a series of sit spins. In my one-legged crouch, I hold my free leg in front of me, which means it's directly in his path on his second lap. I hear a loud sigh before he cuts in the other direction to avoid me.

Truth is, I did indulge in some figure skating as a kid. I wasn't good enough—or interested enough—to keep at it, but Dad insisted I'd benefit from the lessons. He wasn't wrong. Hockey is all about physical plays, but figure skating requires more finesse. After only a month of learning the basics, I could already see major improvements in my balance, speed, and body positioning. The edge work I honed during those lessons made me a better skater. A better hockey player.

"Okay, seriously, get out of the way." He slices to a stop, ice shavings ricocheting off his skates. "It's bad enough I'm stuck sharing the ice with you. At least have some fucking respect for personal space, prom queen."

I rise out of the spin and cross my arms. "Don't call me that. My name is Gigi."

He snorts. "Of course it is. That's such a figure skater name. Let me guess. Short for something girly and whimsical like…Georgia. No. Gisele."

"It's not short for anything," I reply coolly.

"Seriously? It's just Gigi?"

"Are you really judging my name right now? Because what's your name? I'm thinking something real bro-ey. You're totally a Braden or a Carter."

"Ryder," he mutters.

"Of course it is," I mimic, starting to laugh.

His expression is thunderous for a moment before dissolving into aggravation. "Just stay out of my way."

When his back is to me, I grin and stick my tongue out at him. If this jerk is going to intrude on my precious early morning ice time, the least I can do is get on his very last nerve. So I make myself as invasive as possible. I pick up speed, arms extended to my sides, before executing another series of spins.

Damn, figure skating is fun. I forgot how fun.

"Here we go, now you're about to get it," comes Ryder's snide voice. A note of satisfaction there too.

I slow down, registering the loud echo of footsteps beyond the double doors at the end of the rink.

"Better skedaddle, Gisele, before you piss off Garrett Graham."

I skate over to Ryder, playing dumb. "Garrett who?"

"Are you shitting me right now? You don't know who Garrett Graham is?"

"Is he famous or something?"

Ryder stares at me. "He's hockey royalty. This is his camp."

"Oh. Yeah. I only follow figure skaters."

Flipping my ponytail, I glide past him. I want to get one last move in, mostly to see if I still remember any of the stuff I learned during my lessons.

I pick up speed. Find my balance. I don't have a toe pick because I'm wearing hockey skates, but this jump doesn't need to kick off the pick. I enter on a turn, gaining momentum as I take off from the edge of my skate and rotate in the air.

The landing is atrocious. My body isn't properly aligned. I also overrotate, but somehow manage to save myself from falling on my face. I wince at my total lack of grace.

"Gigi! What the hell are you doing? You trying to break your ankle out there?"

I turn toward the plexiglass, where my father stands about

twenty feet away, frowning deeply at me. He's wearing a baseball cap and T-shirt with the camp logo on it, a whistle around his neck and foam coffee cup in one hand.

"Sorry, Dad," I call out, sheepish. "I was just messing around."

I hear a choked noise. Ryder sidles up to me, those blue eyes darkening.

I tip my head to flash him an innocent smile. "What?"

"Dad?" he growls under his breath. "You're Garrett Graham's kid?"

I can't help laughing at his indignation. "Not only that, but I'm helping with your shooting drills today."

His eyes narrow. "You play hockey?"

I reach over to pat his arm. "Don't worry, prom king, I'll go easy on you."

Hockey Kings Transcript

Original Air Date: 07/28

© **The Sports Broadcast Corporation**

Jake Connelly: Speaking of unmitigated disasters, I guess this is a perfect segue to our next segment. Massive news coming out of the college hockey world: the Briar/Eastwood merger. Talking about your alma mater here, G.

Garrett Graham: My kid goes there too. Keeping it in the family, you know?

Connelly: On a scale of one to ten—one being catastrophe and ten being the apocalypse—how bad is this?

Graham: Well. It's not great.

Connelly: I believe we call that an understatement.

Graham: I mean, yes. But let's unpack this. Setting aside the fact that it's unprecedented—two D1 men's ice hockey programs merging into one? Unheard of. But I suppose there could be some advantages. Chad Jensen is looking at a superteam here. I mean, Colson and Ryder on one roster? Not to mention Demaine, Larsen, and Lindley? With Kurth in the crease? Tell me how this team isn't unstoppable.

Connelly: On paper, absolutely. And I'm the first person to give credit where credit's due. Chad Jensen is the most decorated coach in college hockey. Twelve Frozen Four forays and seven wins during his tenure at Briar. He holds the record for championship wins—

GRAHAM: Does your father-in-law pay you to be his hype man? Or you do it for free to score approval points?

CONNELLY: Says the man who won three of those seven championships under Jensen.

GRAHAM: Yeah, all right. So we're both biased. All jokes aside, Jensen is a miracle worker, but even he can't erase decades of bitter rivalry and hostility. Briar and Eastwood have battled it out in their conference for years. And suddenly these boys are expected to play nice?

CONNELLY: He's got a tough job ahead of him, that's for sure. But like you said, if they manage to make it work? Come together as one team? We could be seeing some magic happen.

GRAHAM: Either that, or these guys are going to kill each other.

CONNELLY: Guess we're about to find out.

CHAPTER ONE
GIGI

Slutty bad-boy dick magic

A HOCKEY PLAYER ISN'T JUST SOMEONE WHO PLAYS HOCKEY.

Someone who plays hockey shows up at the rink an hour before a game, throws their skates on, pounds out three periods, changes back into their street clothes, and scampers on home.

A hockey player lives and breathes hockey. We're always training. We pour our time into it. We show up two hours before practice to hone our game. Mental, physical, and emotional. We strengthen, condition, push our bodies to their limits. We dedicate our lives to the sport.

Playing at a collegiate level requires a staggering commitment, but it's a challenge I've always been eager to meet.

A week before classes start at Briar University, I'm back to my usual early-morning routine. The offseason is great because it lets me spend more time with friends and family, sleep late, indulge in junk food, but I always welcome the start of a new season. I feel lost without my sport.

This morning I'm running drills in one of the two rinks at Briar's performance center. Just a simple shooting exercise where I accelerate on a turn and slap the puck at the net, and while I chide myself every time I miss, there's nothing like the sound of a puck striking the boards in an empty arena.

I keep at it for about an hour, until I notice Coach Adley by the home bench gesturing at me. I'm sweating through my practice jersey as I skate toward him.

One corner of his mouth quirks up. "You shouldn't be here."

I slide my gloves off. "Says who?"

"Says the NCAA rules regarding offseason practices."

I grin. "Regarding *official* practices led by the coaching staff. This is just me free skating on my own time."

"You know you don't have to push yourself this hard, G."

"Wow," I tease. "Are you saying you want me to perform to less than my abilities?"

"No, I want you to keep some gas in the tank for—" He stops, chuckling. "You know what? Nothing. I keep forgetting I'm talking to a Graham. You're your father's daughter."

My spark of pride is dampened slightly by a teeny sting of resentment. When you have a famous parent, you tend to spend a lot of your time in their shadow.

I knew when I started playing, I would be forever compared to my father. Dad is a living legend, no other way around it. He holds so many records, it's impossible to keep track of them anymore. Dude played in the pros until he was forty years old. And even at forty, he kicked ass that last season. He could've kept playing another year or two easy, but Dad's smart. He retired on top. Just like Gretzky, who he's constantly being likened to.

That little aggrieved pang is one I need to rein in. I know that. If there's anyone you want to be compared to, it's one of the greatest athletes of all time. I think maybe I'm just scarred from the misogynistic caveats that come with all the compliments I've received over the years.

She played really well…for a girl.

Her stat lines are impressive…for a woman.

Nobody tells a male hockey player that he played amazingly well for a man.

The truth of the matter is, men and women's hockey are two vastly different beasts. Women have fewer opportunities to keep playing after college, the professional league has fewer viewers, drastically lower salaries. I get it—one NHL game probably draws a gazillion more viewers than all women's hockey games combined. The men deserve every dime they are paid and every opportunity given to them.

It just means I need to capitalize on every opportunity granted to me as a female player.

And *that* means?

The Olympics, baby.

Making Team USA and winning Olympic gold has been my goal since I was six years old. And I've been working toward it ever since.

Coach opens the bench door for me. "Is your dad still coming this year to pimp out his camp?"

"Yeah, sometime this week. He needs some recovery time first. We just got back from our annual Tahoe trip last week."

Every year my family spends the month of August in Lake Tahoe, where we're joined by close friends and family. It's a revolving door of visitors all summer.

"This year some of Dad's former Boston teammates made an appearance, and let's just say there were a lot of hungover men passed out on our dock every morning," I add with a grin.

"God help that lake." Adley is fully aware of the trouble Dad and his teammates are capable of. He used to be an assistant coach for the Bruins when Dad played for them. In fact, Dad is the one who poached Tom Adley to head up the women's program at Briar.

Even if I wanted to escape my father's shadow, it's his name outside on the building. The Graham Center. Thanks to his donation, the girls' program received a complete revamp about ten years ago. New facilities, new coaching staff, new recruiters to find the best talent out of high school. For years the program had been a pale comparison of the men's, until Dad injected new life into it. He said he wanted me to have a solid program to land in if I decided to attend Briar when I got older.

If.

Ha.

Like I was going anywhere else.

"What are you doing here today anyway?" I ask Coach on our way down the tunnel.

"Jensen asked me to help out with his training camp."

"Oh shit, that starts today?"

"Yes, and do me a favor and tell the girls to keep it down. This is a closed practice. If Jensen sees any of you, I'm pleading ignorance."

"What do you mean, the girls—"

But Coach is already disappearing around the corner toward the coaching offices.

I get my answer when I enter the locker room to find a couple of my teammates congregated there.

"Hey G, you sticking around to watch the shit show?" Our team captain, Whitney Cormac, grins at me from her perch on the bench.

"Hell yes. I wouldn't miss it. But Adley says we need to remain inconspicuous, otherwise Jensen will freak."

Camila Martinez, a fellow junior, snorts loudly. "I think Jensen'll be too busy trying to wrangle those frothing pit bulls to notice a few of us lurking in the stands."

I take my toiletries out of my locker. "Let me grab a quick shower, and I'll see you guys out there."

I leave the girls in the change area and duck into the showers. As I dunk my head under the warm spray, I wonder how on earth the men's team is going to survive the Briar/Eastwood merger. This is such a huge seismic shift in the program, and it happened so fast that a lot of the players were caught unprepared.

Eastwood College was our rival for decades. Last month, they went under. As in, the whole university shut down. Turns out, enrollment was down to the dregs, and basically the only thing keeping the school afloat was a few of its athletic programs, particularly men's hockey. It was a sure thing Eastwood would close its doors, and all those athletes would be shit out of luck. And then Briar U came in clutch, swooping in to save the day and bailing them out like a boss. Which means Eastwood is now part of Briar, a development that brings more than a few changes.

Their campus in Eastwood, New Hampshire, an hour's drive north of Boston, has officially been dubbed Briar's Eastwood Campus. Full-time classes are still offered up there, but to streamline things, all the athletic facilities were shut down, those buildings scheduled to be repurposed.

And, of course, most importantly: Eastwood men's hockey has been absorbed into Briar men's hockey.

Coach Chad Jensen now has the very unenviable task of taking two huge rosters and condensing them into one. A lot of the guys who were starters at both schools are going to lose their slots.

Not to mention they all hate one another's guts.

I'm not missing this for the world.

I finish my shower and then change into faded jeans and a tank top. I brush my wet hair into a ponytail and slather some moisturizer on my face because the air in the arena always dries out my skin.

My teammates wait for me in the stands. They wisely chose to avoid the benches, instead sitting to the left of the penalty boxes and several rows up. Close enough that we'll be able to overhear any smack talk, but discreet enough that we can hopefully avoid Coach Jensen's notice.

Whitney scoots over so I can sit beside her.

The muffled sounds of overgrown man-children in the tunnel trigger my excitement.

In front of me, Camila rubs her hands together and glances over with pure glee. "Here we go."

They emerge in clumps of twos and threes. A couple sophomores here, a few seniors there. They're wearing either black or gray practice jerseys. I notice some guys tugging on their sleeves uneasily, grimacing, as if it makes them physically ill to wear Briar's colors.

"I sort of feel bad for the Eastwood guys," I remark.

"I don't feel bad at all," Camila replies, smiling broadly. "They're going to provide us with entertainment for at least a year."

My gaze drifts to the ice. Not everyone has their helmets on yet, and a familiar face catches my eye. My heart stutters at the sight of him.

"Case is looking good," Whitney says, a knowing lilt to her voice. It's obnoxious.

"Yeah," I answer noncommittally.

She's not wrong, though. That's what makes it obnoxious. My ex-boyfriend is stupidly good-looking. Tall and fair, with pale blue eyes that warm into the shade of a summer sky when he's working the charm.

He's talking with his friend Jordan Trager. He hasn't noticed me and I'm glad for that. Last time we saw each other was back in June, although we texted a bit over the summer. He wanted to come see me. I said no. I don't trust myself around Case. The mere fact that my heart did a foolish flip just now tells me I made the right call by denying him this summer.

"Oh my God, I'm in love."

Camila pulls my attention away from Case and toward another new arrival.

Okay, wow. He's undeniably hot. Dirty-blond hair, light gray eyes, and a face that could stop traffic. He must be an Eastwood guy because I've never seen him before.

Camila is practically drooling. "I don't think I've ever been this turned on by a guy's profile."

A few of the guys are warming up now, sticks in hand, skating close to the boards. I scan the players, but don't recognize any of them.

Camila leans forward and peers below. "Which one is Luke Ryder?" she asks curiously. "I heard Jensen didn't even want him."

"Uh-huh, yes, he didn't want the number-one ranked forward in the country," Whitney says dryly. "I highly doubt that."

"Hey, boy comes with a reputation," Cami counters. "I wouldn't fault Jensen for wanting to keep his program pristine."

She has a point. We all saw what happened in the World Juniors a couple years ago, when Luke Ryder and a teammate threw down in the locker room after the USA boys took home the gold. Ryder broke the guy's jaw and landed him in the hospital. The whole incident was kept very hush-hush, or at least the motivations behind it were. It's still never been confirmed who started the fight, but considering the other player suffered the brunt of the injuries, it seems like Ryder had a score to settle.

As far as I've heard, he's kept his nose clean since, but beating the shit out of another player is something that follows you around. It's a stain on your record, no matter what your scoring stats are.

"That's him," I say, gesturing to the ice.

Luke Ryder skates over to the blond that Cami is still making starry eyes at and another guy with close-cropped dark hair. I catch a glimpse of Ryder's chiseled jawline before he slips his helmet on and turns away.

He's still as attractive as I remember. Only he's not a lanky fifteen-year-old anymore. He's a grown man, filled out and muscular. Sheer power drips off him.

I haven't seen him in person since that youth camp my dad ran five or six years ago. To this day, I still bristle when I think about the way he disparaged me. Told me I didn't belong on the ice. Assumed I was a figure skater, to boot. *And* he called me prom queen. Dick. It had definitely been fun wiping that cocky grin off his face when we ran a two-on-one drill later, and I outskated him and another boy to score on net. It's the petty little things that make me happy.

"He's fucking sexy," Whitney says.

"It's the slutty bad-boy dick magic," Cami pipes up. "Makes them hotter."

We all snicker.

"Is he a slutty bad boy?" Whitney asks.

Cami laughs and says, "Well, the bad-boy thing is pretty self-evident. Just look at him. But yeah, he's totally got a reputation for hooking up. But not, like, in a conventional way."

I poke her in the back, grinning. "What does that mean? How does one hook up unconventionally?"

"Meaning he doesn't go out of his way to get laid. Doesn't chase anyone, doesn't do the whole cocky player routine. My cousin saw him at a party last year, and she said this guy just stood there brooding in the corner the entire time. Didn't say a word to anyone all night, yet somehow there's a swarm of thirsty chicks throwing themselves at him. Boy basically has his pick of hookups."

A whistle pierces the air. On instinct, we all snap to attention and it's not even our practice.

Coach Jensen skates onto the ice, trailed by two assistant coaches and Tom Adley. He blows his whistle again. Two sharp blasts.

"Line up! I want two lines at center ice." His voice carries in the vast arena.

Helmets and face masks are slapped on, gloves readjusted as the team lines up. There are fewer guys here than I expected.

"Didn't Eastwood have a roster of almost thirty?" I ask Whitney.

She nods. "I heard he's splitting training camp into two practice groups. This is probably just the first one."

I give a wry smile when I notice how the team lines themselves up. Briar guys standing shoulder to shoulder. Eastwood guys doing the same. Ryder is between his two buddies, jaw set in a rigid line.

"All right," Jensen barks, clapping. "Let's not waste any time. We've got a lot to cover this week in order to finalize the roster. We're going to start with a basic dump-and-chase drill. Get some of that energy out, all right?"

The other coaches herd everyone into position behind one net. Because of the way they lined up previously, most of the player pairs feature one guy from Briar, one from Eastwood.

This should be fun.

"First player to get possession, I want you to take a shot on goal. Second player, I want to see you forechecking to get that puck back."

He blows the whistle again to get things going. It's one of the simplest drills there is, yet a thrill still dances through me. I love this game. Everything about hockey is pure exhilaration.

Jensen dumps the puck in the corner behind the opposite net, and the first pair races along the boards toward it. Their jerseys don't have names or numbers, so I don't know who I'm looking at.

In the second pair, though, I clock Case instantly. Not for his looks, but his trademark style, that quick release. Case Colson has the most accurate shot placement in all of college hockey. He could probably give most NHL goalies a run for their money too. There's a reason he was drafted by Tampa.

"This is way more boring than I thought," Whitney grumbles. "Where are the fireworks?"

"For real," Camila chimes in. "Let's just bail—"

No sooner do those words leave her mouth than said fireworks go off.

It starts with a hard forecheck from Jordan Trager. Just like with Case, I've watched enough Briar games to identify Trager's aggressive style. He lives and breathes the goon life. He's also a raging asshat, so when the other player starts giving the aggression back good, I know Trager's running his mouth as usual.

Before I can blink, the gloves are off.

In a real college hockey game, fighting isn't allowed. Both these dumbasses would be thrown out of the game and benched for the next one. During practice, it would normally be frowned upon and likely disciplined.

Today's practice?

Jensen lets it play out.

"Damn." Whitney hisses through her teeth when the Eastwood player takes a powerful swing at Trager, connecting with his left cheek.

Trager's cry of outrage reverberates through the rink. In the next instance the two men are locked in battle, clutching each other's jerseys while their fists fly. Loud, feral shouts of encouragement ring out from their teammates, who surge closer to the fight.

When the two players tumble to the ice, legs and skates tangled up, Cami makes a sound of alarm.

"How is Jensen not stopping this?" she exclaims.

Chad Jensen stands ten feet away, looking bored. All around him is chaos. Briar guys egging Trager on. Eastwood players cheering for their guy. I see Case try to skate forward to intervene, only to halt when Briar's captain David Demaine slaps a hand on his arm.

"Holy shit, Double-D is letting it happen too," Camila marvels.

I agree that one's kind of shocking. Demaine is as placid as they come. It's probably the Canadian in him.

It isn't until drops of red stain the sheet of white that someone finally takes charge.

My eyebrows fly up when I realize it's Ryder. His tall frame takes off in a brisk skate. Another blink of the eye, and he's hauling his Eastwood teammate away from Trager.

When Trager stands up and tries to lunge, Ryder steps between the two red-faced players. I don't know what he says to Trager, but whatever it is, it stops the guy cold.

"God, that's hot," Whitney breathes.

"Breaking up a fight?" I ask, amused.

"No, he managed to shut Trager up. Goddamn miracle right there."

"Sexiest thing anyone could ever do," agrees Cami, and we all laugh.

Trager is such a loud-mouthed, abrasive jerk. I tolerated him when I dated Case, but there were days when even tolerance was difficult. I suppose that's the one bright spot that came from our breakup. No more Trager.

Jensen blows his whistle before his commanding voice finally joins the fray. "Practice is over. Get the fuck off my ice."

"Let's get out of here too," Whitney says with a note of urgency.

I wholly agree. Jensen must know we're here, but although he didn't throw us out before, we just witnessed his practice devolve into a bloody fistfight. No way does he want an audience for the aftermath.

Without another word, the three of us scurry down the aisle. At the bottom of the bleachers, we have a decision to make. Either go toward the tunnel to the locker rooms, where the players are fleeing with their tails between their legs. Or try to exit using the double doors across the arena, where Jensen and the coaches congregate.

Rather than risk the wrath of Jensen, we make the unspoken choice to avoid the exit. We reach the tunnel entrance at the same time as a couple of Eastwood players.

Luke Ryder startles for a second when he notices me. Then his eyes narrow—those dark, dark blue eyes I've never forgotten—and one corner of his mouth tips up.

"Gisele," he mocks.

"Prom king," I mock back.

With a soft chuckle, he spares me one last look before striding off.

CHAPTER TWO
RYDER

No pets. Ever.

I'M GOING TO GO OUT ON A LIMB AND SAY WE DIDN'T MAKE THE best first impression.

I could be wrong. Maybe Chad Jensen enjoys blood and gore during his practices. Maybe he's the kind of coach who craves a *Lord of the Flies* ice battle to separate the men from the boys.

But the murder in his eyes tells me no, he's not that kind of coach.

His expression grows turbulent, more impatient, while we all scramble for a seat. Jensen only gave us five minutes to change out of our practice gear, so everyone in group one looks harried and disheveled, tucking in shirts and smoothing out hair as we file into the media room.

There are twice the number of guys in this room than there were on the ice. The second practice group was already assembled here, viewing game film with one of the assistant coaches. Everyone in group two watches the newcomers with wary expressions.

Three rows of seats home in on the huge screen that serves as the room's focal point. I won't lie, these digs are a lot nicer than the ones at Eastwood. The padded chairs even swivel.

Coach Jensen stands in the center of the room, while three stone-faced assistants lean against the wall by the door.

"Did you get that out of your system?" he inquires coldly.

Nobody utters a word.

From the corner of my eye, I see Rand Hawley rubbing the corner of his jaw. He took a nasty hit from Colson's lackey. Still, he should've known better than to let Trager push his buttons like that.

Having played against Briar these last couple of years, I'm familiar with everyone on their roster. I know most of their stats, and I know who to watch out for. Trager's always been one to keep an eye on. He has the reputation as a blustering goon and is exceptional at drawing out penalties.

He's not my biggest competitor, though. That would be… I sneak a peek at the blond junior in the front row.

Case Colson.

Really, he's the only dude in this room I need to care about. A beauty of a player. He's Briar's MVP, which means he'll undoubtedly be on the first line.

My line.

Well, unless Jensen fucks me over and puts me on the second line.

I don't know what's worse. Not playing first line…or playing on the same one as Colson. Suddenly I'm supposed to trust a Briar player to have my back? Yeah, right.

"You sure we're good here?" Coach says, still glancing around. "Nobody else wants to pull out their dick and compare sizes? Wave them around to see who the biggest man here is?"

More silence.

Jensen crosses his arms. He's a tall imposing figure with dark eyes and salt-and-pepper hair, still broad-shouldered and fit considering he must be in his sixties. He looks at least ten years younger.

Hands down, this man is the best coach in college hockey. That's probably why it stings so much, the memory that he turned me down when I wanted to come to Briar.

I had been fending off recruiters since sophomore year of high school. Even ones from Briar, my first-choice school. But come graduation, when it was time to make a choice, there wasn't a Briar scholarship on the table. I still remember the morning I swallowed my pride and asked for a phone call with Jensen. Hell, I even would've made the trip from Phoenix to Boston to talk to him in person. But he made it clear on the phone that after "careful consideration" he'd determined I wasn't a good fit for his program.

Well, joke's on him, ain't it?

Not only am I here now, but I'm the best player in this room. A first-round draft pick, for fuck's sake.

"Good. Now that the pissing contest is over, let me make myself clear. You ever disrespect my ice like that during practice, and you won't be representing this school as a member of my hockey team."

Rand, who has no filter and no idea how to read a room, decides to defend himself. "With all due respect, Coach," he says darkly, "Eastwood didn't start shit. That was all Briar."

"You *are* Briar!" Jensen rumbles.

That shuts up my teammate.

"You don't get that. You're one team now. There is no Eastwood. You are all members of the Briar men's hockey team."

Several guys shift in their seats, visibly uneasy.

"Look, this situation is not ideal, all right? This merger happened at the last minute. It didn't offer a lot of time for you to transfer to other colleges or find your place in other programs. You got fucked over," he says simply.

For a brief second, his eyes land on mine before skipping away, focusing on somebody else.

"And I promise you, I will do my best to get you on another team if you don't make this roster."

The generous offer startles me. Jensen has the rep for being an unfeeling hard-ass, but maybe he has a softer side.

"With that said, the fact remains that I've got almost sixty guys, and less than half of you will be on the final roster. Those are not good numbers." His tone is grim. "A lot of you are not going to make this team."

The silence becomes deafening. Hearing him say that, so matter-of-factly, is not a good feeling. Even for me. I'm highly confident Jensen can't screw me out of a roster slot, but even I feel a twinge of trepidation.

"So, this is how the week will play out. Because we all got screwed here, we received permission from the NCAA to run a one-week training camp to get our numbers down. At the end of this week, I'll release the final roster, as well as the list of who'll be starting in the first game. Then Coach Maran, Coach Peretti, and I will sit down and finalize the lines. Any questions so far?"

No hands go up.

"With that said, I'd like you to nominate two interim captains for the duration of training camp. Then, once the roster is set, you can either revote or stick with the two you select today."

Two?

My head lifts in surprise. I look over at Shane Lindley, my teammate and best friend. He looks intrigued as well, dark eyes gleaming. Technically, Eastwood came into this merger captainless. Ours fled after the announcement and transferred to Quinnipiac. So much for a captain going down with his ship. Briar's current captain is the French-Canadian, David Demaine.

"I believe for the sake of team unity, cocaptains is the best way to go. I want you guys to pick one player from the existing Briar roster and one from Eastwood."

"Thought you said we were one and the same," someone in the back row mutters sarcastically.

Coach's razor-sharp hearing is on point. "You are," he snaps at the griper. "But I'm also not naive enough to think that me saying those words makes it so. I'm not a fucking fairy godmother who waves a wand and then life is perfect, all right? I think the best way to bridge this gap is to have two captains, at least over the course of this week, working together to remind everyone we're all one team—"

"I nominate Colson," a swollen-lipped Trager pipes up, his tone flat. Jensen's jaw tightens at the interruption.

"I nominate Ryder," my teammate Nazzy calls out.

I smother a sigh.

Okay, this is not getting off to a good start.

It's obvious what's happening. They picked the two best players to be captain. Not necessarily the two players who *should* be captain. First, we're both juniors. Most of the seniors in this room probably deserve the nod far more than we do.

And second, I'm not goddamn captain material. Are they crazy? My personality isn't suited for leadership. I'm not here to hold hands and love everybody.

I'm the man who wants to be left the fuck alone.

Case Colson appears equally annoyed to be included in this farce. But as I look around, a sea of determined faces greets me. My Eastwood teammates have war in their eyes, several of them nodding decisively. Briar's players convey identical fortitude.

Coach sees the same thing I do on their faces. The battle lines have been drawn.

He blows out a breath. "So that's it? That's who you all want? Colson and Ryder?"

A chorus of agreement ripples through the room. This is a statement, right here. Each side wants the other to know that their player, their superstar, is in charge.

"Fucking hell," I mutter under my breath.

Shane chuckles. On my other side, Beckett Dunne snorts. I'd like to say my best friends have the whole angel/devil thing going on, where one is a dick and the other sits on my shoulder spewing kindness and compassion. I'd *like* to say that.

But they're both just assholes who take great amusement out of my misery.

"Ryder, are you good with this?" Jensen's sharp gaze finds mine.

I'm not good with it at all.

"Yeah, sure," I lie. "All good."

"Colson?" Jensen prompts.

Case glances at last season's captain. Demaine gives him a quick nod.

"If that's what the team wants," Colson mutters.

"Fine." Jensen walks over to the podium to jot something in a notebook.

God fucking help me.

And yet despite this unwanted title being foisted upon me, I can't deny I do feel relief knowing Jensen won't try to get rid of me this time.

Coach leaves his notes and walks toward the whiteboard beneath the multimedia screen, black-felt marker in hand.

"Okay, now that that's decided, there are a few more things we need to go over before training camp gets underway. Number one: What happened out there just now with group one? Un-fucking-acceptable. You hear me?"

Jensen stares directly at Jordan Trager and Rand Hawley. Then he frowns, because neither of them shows an iota of penitence. Only petulance.

"We don't fight each other at this school," he says. "Do so again at your own peril."

He turns to scribble something on the whiteboard.

NO FIGHTING

"Number two, and this is very important, so I hope you're fucking listening. I will not clean up my language for you assholes. If your delicate sensibilities can't handle a few f-bombs, then you have no business playing hockey."

He writes something else.

FUCK YOU

Shane snickers quietly.

"Number three: Every year or so, some dumbass gets the cockamamie idea that the team needs a pet. A living mascot in the form of a goat or a pig or some other godforsaken farm animal. I will no longer tolerate such ideas. Don't present them to me—your request will be denied. There was an unfortunate incident in the past, and neither I personally, nor the university itself, will place ourselves in that position again. We have been pet-free for twenty years and will remain that way for eternity. Understood?"

When nobody answers, he glares.

"Understood?"

"Yessir," everyone says.

He turns toward the board.

No Pets. Ever.

"What do you think the unfortunate incident was?" Beckett leans closer to whisper in my ear.

I shrug. Fuck if I know.

"Maybe it was a chicken and they accidentally ate it," Shane suggests.

Beck blanches. "That's dark."

"All right, that's it." Jensen claps his hands. "Group one, you fucking blew it, so you can go home. I'll see you at 9:00 a.m. tomorrow. Group two, meet me on the ice in fifteen minutes."

The room comes to life as everyone stands and shuffles along the rows toward the aisle. Jensen calls out before I reach the door. "Ryder."

I glance over my shoulder. "Sir?"

"A minute, please."

Swallowing my apprehension, I walk toward him. "What's up, Coach?"

He's quiet for moment, just studying me. It's unnerving and I resist the urge to fidget with my hands. I'm rarely intimidated by people, but something about this man makes my palms sweat. Maybe it's because I know he never wanted me here.

I fucking *hate* knowing that.

"Is this captain thing going to be a problem?" he finally asks.

I shrug. "I guess we're going to find out."

"That's not the answer I want to hear, son." He repeats himself. "Is it going to be a problem?"

"No, sir," I answer dutifully. "It won't be a problem."

"Good. Because I can't have my team at war. You need to step up and be a leader, understand?"

My self-restraint escapes me for a moment. "Are you going to give Colson the same talk?"

"No, because he doesn't need it."

"And I do? You don't even know me."

Christ, shut the hell up, I chide myself. Challenging my new coach isn't going to get me anywhere good.

"I know team unity isn't your strongest suit. I know leadership doesn't come naturally to you. We both know your former teammates selected you for your skill and not your leadership— and a choice like that only ends in disaster. With that said, I don't typically interfere with who a team picks as their captain, and I'm not going to interfere now. But I am watching you, Ryder. I'm watching carefully."

I manage to keep my palms flat to my sides when they want to curl into fists. "Thanks for the heads-up. May I go now?"

He gives a brisk nod.

I stalk out and release a heavy breath in the hallway. This entire situation is fucked. I have no idea how it's all going to play out, but judging by this morning's events, it won't be pretty.

It takes a few moments to orient myself and figure out how to leave the building. Briar's hockey facilities are larger than Eastwood's, and some of the corridors feel like a maze. Eventually I emerge into the lobby, a cavernous space with pennants hanging from the rafters and framed jerseys lining the walls. Through the wall of glass at the entrance, I spot several of my friends loitering outside.

"So that was a fun morning," Shane remarks when I join them.

"A blast," I agree.

The sun beats down on my face, so I slide my sunglasses over my eyes. When I first moved to the East Coast from Arizona after high school, I assumed Septembers in New England were chilly. I didn't expect the summer temperatures to linger on, sometimes well into the fall.

"Hopefully group two fares better than we did," Mason Hawley says with a wry smile. Mason is Rand's younger brother and, most of the time, Rand's keeper.

"Doubt it," Shane says. "There's no unclustering this fuck."

As if to prove his point, a bunch of Briar guys exit the arena and all their expressions cloud over when they spot us. They halt at the top of the steps, exchanging guarded looks. Then Case Colson murmurs something to Will Larsen, and the group strides forward.

Colson and I lock gazes. Only for a moment, before he breaks eye contact and marches past us. The group descends the front steps without acknowledging us.

"Such a warm reception," Beckett drawls at their retreating backs. His Australian accent always becomes more pronounced when he's being sarcastic. Beck's family moved to the States when he was ten. America basically beat the accent out of him, but it's always there, dancing just beneath the surface of his voice.

"Seriously, I feel so wanted here," Shane pipes up. "All these Briar rainbows and unicorns are making me fucking giddy."

"This fucking blows," Rand mutters, still watching the Briar guys. He straightens his shoulders and turns to me. "We need an emergency meeting. I'm sending a group text. Can we do it at your place?"

"The second group is still at practice," Shane points out.

Rand's already pulling out his phone. "I'll tell them to be there at noon."

Without waiting for approval, he sends out the SOS. And that's how a couple hours later, the living room of our townhouse is crammed with twenty-plus bodies.

Shane, Beckett, and I moved into this place last week. Our house in Eastwood was larger, but the pickings are slim for off-campus housing in Hastings, the small town closest to the Briar campus. Whereas I had my own bathroom before, now I share one with Beckett, who uses way too many products in his hair and clutters up all the counter space. For a fuckboy, he's actually kind of a chick.

Speaking of fuckboys, Shane is a newly anointed one, and instead of paying attention to Rand, he's texting with some girl he met at Starbucks literally an hour ago. Shane's been trying to screw his way out of a broken heart since June. Though if you ask him, the breakup was mutual.

Spoiler alert: there's no such thing.

"All right, shut up, y'all," Rand orders. He and Mason are Texas boys, each boasting a faint twang, but while Mason has that laid-back southern demeanor, his older brother is always wound up tight. "We need to talk about this roster issue."

He waits for everyone to quiet down, then looks at me.

"What?" I mutter.

"You're the captain now. You need to get the meeting going."

Leaning against the wall, I cross my arms tight to my chest. "I'd like it on the record that I didn't want to be captain and you're all assholes for doing this to me."

Shane hoots.

"Yeah, tough shit," Rand tells me, rolling his eyes. "They threw Colson's name out there. What else were we supposed to do?"

"Not pick me?" I suggest coldly.

"We had to make a statement. Put up our best against their best."

"It's not their best," Austin Pope speaks up, hesitant. The curly-haired kid stands near one of the leather armchairs with some of the other freshmen.

Rand glares at him. "What was that, rookie?"

"I'm just saying, there's no 'their best' and 'our best' anymore. We're all on the same team now."

He sounds as miserable as we all feel.

"Whatever. Can we please talk about the roster now?" Rand says impatiently.

"What about it?" Beckett asks in a bored voice. He's typing something on his phone, only half paying attention. "Jensen's gonna pick whoever he's gonna pick."

"Wow, words of inspiration right there." Our sophomore goalie snickers from his seat on the gray sectional.

"We don't actually need to be worrying, do we?" Austin looks ill now. "He can't cut all of us, right? What if he goes and cuts Eastwood in a clean sweep?"

Everyone just stares at him.

"What?" the teenager says awkwardly.

Shane grins. "You're playing in the World Juniors in a couple of months. There's no way you're not making this team, kid."

Austin possesses the rawest talent of anyone I've ever seen. Other than me, of course. Eastwood recruited him hard last year, and we were all thrilled when he accepted. Back in the spring, nobody would've guessed our entire fucking school would go under.

What pisses me off more is that only twenty-five Eastwood guys chose to migrate to Briar. Several of our other teammates, mostly the incoming seniors, jumped ship the moment it was announced. Some transferred to other colleges. Some went to the pros. A few quit the team altogether. The quitters are the ones I don't understand. True hockey players know you don't just quit when things get tough.

Shane's right, though. Austin has nothing to worry about. A lot of us don't. It's easy to guess who Jensen will gravitate toward. Shane, Beck, and Austin, almost certainly. Patrick and Nazem are sophomores, but they're two of the best skaters I've ever seen. Micah, a senior, is probably the best stickhandler playing right now.

The problem is, as I look around this room, I see more talent than open slots. Someone, no, many someones, are bound to be disappointed.

As if sensing where my thoughts went, Rand's face reddens with anger. His cheek is already showing signs of bruising, thanks to Trager.

"If I don't make this team and that fuckhead Trager does…"

"You'll make it," Mason assures his brother, but he doesn't sound entirely convinced.

"I better," Rand retorts. "And it better be Eastwood strong. All of us, and very little of them."

As the new cocaptain, I know I should stop that line of thinking. Squash it hard. Because we can't start a new season with an us-versus-them mentality.

But no matter how much Jensen wishes otherwise, it *is* us versus them. I've played with my Eastwood teammates for two years already. We're a team, and we went all the way to the Frozen Four last season. We didn't take home the trophy, but we were geared up to change that this year.

Whoever approved this merger basically took a shotgun and blasted buckshot into a team that was about to hit its peak.

"You guys don't get it," Rand growls, visibly frustrated by the lack of urgency in our teammates. "Can none of you do the math? Just here in this room alone, we have sixteen starters. That means for all of us to *remain* starters, Jensen would have to cut his entire existing lineup."

The bitterness hardening his features rubs off on some of the other guys. Faces cloud over. Annoyed murmurs travel through the room.

The hostility fuels Rand, who's already a hostile dude by default. He starts pacing, beefy shoulders tense.

"Some of us aren't going to start, you realize that, right? Do you fucking get that? We're competing for our own fucking positions—"

"You could have transferred," Beckett points out. He was

scrolling on his phone, but now raises his head to interrupt Rand's angry rambling.

Rand quits pacing. "And go where? Besides, fuck that. You want me to jump ship like our own captain? Like our pussy coach?"

He's referring to Scott Evans, our former head coach. Evans refused to work under Jensen after the merger, so he accepted a coaching job at an elite prep school in New Hampshire.

"Cool, then shut the fuck up," Shane says with a shrug. "Quit complaining and fight for your position. Prove that you belong out there."

Rand grits his teeth, and I know what he's thinking. There are at least ten dudes on the Briar side who are better than him. And it all depends on how Jensen organizes his lines too. If he values grinders and bruisers like Rand, or if he wants to stack the team with goal scorers.

"What about you?" Rand demands, suddenly fixing his scowl on me. "You really got nothing to say?"

Irritation pinches my gut. Rand and I have never been best buds. Of course, I don't think you can say I'm truly "best buds" with anyone. Even my best friends hardly know me.

My voice sounds gravelly when I address the room.

I drop my arms to my sides, shrugging. "This situation is bullshit, I get it. But like Lindley said, if you want to start, fight for it."

Rand barks out a derisive laugh. "C'mon, Ryder, you're goddamn stupid if you think it stops there. You're already a starter, sure. But what do you think happens next, bro? What, you're going to play on the same line with Colson, and you think he's going to have your back out there? He's going to pass the puck to you instead of hogging all the glory for himself because he doesn't want to share with an Eastwood guy? This isn't just about fighting to be a starter. Because even once you're picked, you're still left competing with your own fucking teammates."

The room goes so silent you could hear a feather floating in the air.

The worst part is, Rand's not wrong.

No matter which way you slice this, we're all screwed.

CHAPTER THREE

GIGI

It was just a kiss

MY DAD'S BEEN DOING HIS *HOCKEY KINGS* SHOW FOR A FEW YEARS now. It first aired a year after he retired, but that wasn't his original retirement plan. Initially, TSBN offered him a nine-figure deal—and yes, I said nine—to be a sportscaster. But several months before he was slated to start, he and another recent retiree, Jake Connelly, did a guest spot on ESPN to commentate on that year's Stanley Cup Finals. That one measly episode drew the highest ratings the network had seen in years. TSBN instantly saw dollar signs and realized Dad was better suited doing commentary than calling games. They pitched *Hockey Kings* to Dad and Connelly, and the rest is ratings history.

The two of them discuss all things hockey. NHL, college, international. There's even some high school content. Everything's on the table and the viewers love it. My favorite part, though, is the segment titles. The producers like to get creative with them. They also have serious hard-ons for alliteration.

Which is why tonight's C-block topic had a title card with the words *BRUTAL BRIAR BLOODBATH* on it. Apparently, news of this morning's scuffle made it all the way to the big sports networks.

"A little melodramatic, don't you think?" I ask my dad when he calls me a couple of hours after he goes off the air. "It was, like, the least bloody brawl I've ever seen. A handful of blood drops, tops."

"Hey, gotta get those views somehow. Blood sells in hockey."

"You host a show with Jake Connelly, the most beautiful man in the world. Trust me, you're going to get the views."

"Nope, nope, nope," he groans. "You know how I feel when you talk about Connelly's stupid looks. It triggers my crippling inferiority."

I snort out a laugh.

"What is it with you and your mother thinking that guy is handsome? He's average, at best."

"Oh, he's definitely not average."

"Agree to disagree."

Chuckling to myself, I pull a pair of sweatpants out of my dresser drawer. I'm going down the hall to Whitney's room tonight to watch a movie.

"Have you spoken to your brother today?" Dad asks.

"No. He texted last night, just some silly meme, but other than that, nothing in a few days. Why? Is he AWOL again?"

My twin has a habit of losing track of his surroundings when he's writing music. His phone is constantly dead too. Which means Mom is constantly worrying and then texting me to find out if I've heard from Wyatt.

"No, no, he's around. I talked to him this morning. He doesn't have any gigs lined up, so he's thinking he might come home for a few weeks."

Unlike myself, Wyatt doesn't attend college. He announced that decision to our parents the morning after our high school graduation, despite having been accepted into three of the best schools in the country, including Juilliard. He sat them down, all business (or as businesslike as one can look in ripped jeans and a threadbare T-shirt) and told them college had nothing to offer him, his path was music, and don't bother talking him out of it, please and thank you.

Three weeks later, he moved to Nashville. And he's not even a country music guy. His style lends itself more toward a folksy rock-pop mix—I don't think I could accurately pin it down. All I know is, he's good. Incredible, actually. He inherited the musician gene from Mom.

But the thing that sucks most about my brother? He also inherited *Dad's* talent. Dude can play hockey too. And play it well.

He just doesn't *want* to.

My brain can't wrap itself around that. Who wouldn't want to play hockey?

What the hell's wrong with him?

"Anyway, I was thinking, if he does come home, maybe you can make it back too. Next weekend or the weekend after?"

"Yeah, I could probably swing it. Our season opener isn't for a few weeks."

"How did the men look, by the way? This morning, I mean."

"I have no idea. Like I said before, they were two minutes into a drill before Jordan went off on one of the Eastwood guys. Luke Ryder finally broke it up."

"That Ryder has a bad attitude. I have no idea how he'll fare under a coach like Jensen, who has no patience for that crap."

"Honestly, I can't see how any of them are going to fare well."

"If you're worried about Case not making the team, don't. There's no doubt he'll start."

"Nope, wasn't worried about that at all, but nice segue. Is the fishing expedition beginning now?"

"Who's fishing?" Dad says innocently. "But I mean, since you brought it up…"

I roll my eyes at the phone. "We're not back together, if that's what you want to know. I know you're obsessed with him, but you need to move on, my friend."

"I'm not obsessed with him," my father protests. "I just like the guy. I thought he was good for you."

I thought so too.

Until he went and cheated on me.

But my dad doesn't know that. We're a tight-knit family, but there are certain things I draw the line at when it comes to sharing. I don't discuss my sex life. I don't tell them how many drinks I might imbibe at a party, or if I take a hit of an occasional joint.

And I certainly don't talk about how the guy I was madly in love with kissed someone else the night after I told him I loved him. Nope.

"Anyway, I gotta go now," I say before Dad can grill me some more. "Movie night with Whitney and Cami."

"All right. Say hi to them. Love you, Stan."

"I will. Love you too."

I end the call just as a text from Case pops up on the screen. His ears must've been burning.

CASE:

> Can we please talk?

I stare at the message. My thumbs hover over the keypad, but I can't bring myself to type a response.

I know I should. It was easy to dodge his texts and calls over the summer, but now that we're both back on campus, it'd probably behoove us to clear the air. Yet at the same time, I don't know what there is to say anymore. We're broken up. I'm not interested in getting back together, and I'm not ready to be best friends with him again.

CASE:

> I should probably add—I'm at your door.

For fuck's sake. He's taken the decision out of my hands, and I'm a bit annoyed as I stomp toward my door and throw it open.

Sure enough, Case is there at the threshold wearing sweatpants, a black hoodie, and a backward baseball cap. He bites his lip when he sees my displeased expression.

"I know. I'm a dick. I shouldn't just show up here."

"No, you shouldn't," I agree.

"Also, I should give this back." He holds out the key card required to gain entry into Hartford House.

I quickly snatch it from him. Shit. I forgot he even still had it.

"But now that I'm here…" He casts that familiar smile that usually melts my heart into goo.

Tonight it's only half goo, because I'm mad at him for showing up uninvited.

"I only need five minutes." At my reluctance, he implores me with those pale blue eyes. "Please?" he says huskily.

I open the door wider. "Fine. But I'm on my way out. Whitney's waiting for me."

"I'll be quick," he promises.

He walks into the common area, his tall muscular frame dominating the modest space. I have a two-bedroom suite in Hartford House, one of the nicer dorms at Briar. It's also one of the oldest buildings, almost entirely covered in ivy, and since it was built before the university started maximizing every square foot of space, the rooms and suites are much bigger than those in other dorms. Hartford is located on the very edge of campus, right near all the running trails, which is perfect for me—a few times a week I'm able to wake up and get a quick run in before practice. I've never been a gym girl. I like being outdoors, even in the winter.

Rather than immediately diving into emotional territory, Case starts us off with a safe topic, sliding both hands in his pockets.

"This morning was brutal," he tells me. "I know you guys were watching."

"Yeah. It looked tense. Did Jensen give you shit afterwards?"

"Oh yeah." He grimaces. "And then he named me cocaptain."

Surprise flutters through me. "Really? Why didn't he just keep Demaine as captain?"

"Oh, he didn't pick. The guys did. And it gets even better—Jensen says we need *two* captains to try to unite the team or whatever. Which is fucking garbage. Nobody's uniting shit." Bitterness splashes off every word. "Anyway, the other captain they picked? Luke Ryder."

My eyebrows soar. "Are you kidding? They voted *him* captain? That dude's got the personality of a cactus."

Case snickers. "Accurate assessment."

Several seconds of silence tick by, and I brace myself for the change of subject. I feel it coming the way I always know when it's going to rain. I'm a barometer for rain and awkward conversations.

"I've really missed you."

His grief-stricken confession hangs between us. My heart can't handle it when he says things like that.

I bite the inside of my cheek. "Case..."

"I know I have no right to say that. I just...I miss you. I can't help it." He hesitates. "Do you miss me at all?"

He gives me that earnest expression, and it's another hit to my already aching heart. It sucks because Case is a genuinely good guy. He wasn't being malicious when he did what he did. I truly don't believe he meant to hurt me. He made a mistake.

No, corrects the sharp voice in my head. He didn't make a mistake. He made a choice.

"G?" he prompts.

"Of course I miss you," I answer, because I've never been able to lie to him. "But that doesn't change the fact that we broke up."

That brings a stricken look to his face.

Letting out a defeated breath, Case walks to the black leather couch my roommate's parents bought for us when they realized the prior sofa we were using had come from a garage sale in Hastings. Mya's parents are...*snobs* is putting it nicely. But they're snobs with great taste.

Case sinks onto the couch and drops his head in both palms.

It takes all my willpower not to go over there and wrap my arms around him. I've always hated seeing Case upset. It's just such an unnatural state for him. He's generally a positive person, taking everything in stride. And like I said, he's a good guy. With a truly good heart. That makes it impossible to hate him.

Finally, he lifts his head. "I want you back. Please, baby." His voice cracks slightly. "I hate not being with you."

Little fissures form in the armor I've erected around my heart.

"I know you hate this too," he pleads. "Being apart. Like this summer, not being with you? It was brutal. Just fucking unbearable."

Yes and no. I did miss him this summer. I'm not going to deny that. But I also wasn't crying myself to sleep and composing lovelorn messages in my Notes app, paragraph after paragraph about how much he hurt me and what it would take for us to be together again.

The truth is, I don't know if it's even possible. I'm not a cold or rigid person. My friends tell me I forgive way too easily. And I *have* forgiven Case, truly.

But I also can't forget what he did.

"You cheated on me," I remind him. My tone is flat.

"It was just a kiss," he says miserably.

A rush of anger and indignation heats my throat before I can stop it. I open my mouth, but he's quick to speak before I can.

"I know, I get it. We don't agree on what cheating is. I don't think what I did is exactly cheating—"

"You made out with someone else! That's not 'just a kiss,' Case. And it's cheating."

"It was stupid, okay? I fully acknowledge I fucked up."

This is the same fight we had in June after he confessed what he'd done. The same fight we kept having when he tried to win me back. I'm sick of it.

"You want to get back together, and yet you won't even admit that what you did was cheating."

"It was a mistake." His features become strained when he clocks my inflexible expression. "All right. I cheated. Okay? I cheated, and I've regretted it every second of every day since it happened. I was drunk, and freaking out because it was getting so serious with us, and I...freaked out," he repeats, hanging his head in shame.

I feel awkward standing there in front of him, so I walk over to sit down. I keep a couple feet of distance between us, but he turns, shifting his body so he's angled toward me. His legs are so long that one of his scuffed-up sneakers grazes my socked foot.

"You told me you would think about it," he reminds me in a soft voice. "About trying again."

I release a weary sigh. "I did think about it. But like I told you the last time we texted, I don't want to get back together."

His face falls. When he reaches for my hand, I let him take it. He laces his fingers through mine. His hand feels so familiar. Warm and dry, the pads of his long fingers callused.

He implores me with his eyes. "Please. I just want to prove that I'm not messing around here or playing games. I made a mistake and I own it. But the only thing I need you to know right now, the thing that matters most, is that I love you."

My heart flutters at that. He has no idea how long I'd waited for him to say those words. The entire year and a half we were together, in fact. I fell for Case so fast, but I forced myself not to say it too early, afraid to scare him off. And then, when I finally uttered those three words for the first time, he didn't say them back. Sure, he was suddenly throwing them around *after* he kissed someone else. But the night I said *I love you*, he didn't say *I love you too*.

The reminder turns the fluttering of my heart into a deep sting.

"You're skeptical," Case says, eyeing me.

"I don't know what I am. I...can't give you any answers. We broke up."

He nods slowly. Runs a hand through his golden hair, drawing my attention to the strong line of his jaw. Any girl would take one look at that perfect face and throw herself at him, tell him, *Yes, of course I'll take you back!*

But I'm not so quick to let him back in. Not after everything that happened.

"Okay. I understand," Case says after a long silence. "I'll get out of your way then."

Guilt trickles through me. I squeeze his hand before he can pull away.

"Hey," I assure him. "I'm still your friend. You know if you ever need me, ever, all you have to do is call, right?"

"I know, and I'm always here for you too." He tugs me to my feet. "C'mon, I should go. And you've got Whitney waiting for you."

At the door, Case lets go of my hand and holds out his arms. I can't resist stepping into them. Letting him wrap them around me in a hug that feels like home.

For a moment I'm tempted to tilt my head up. To let his lips come down on mine and just lose myself in his kiss.

But then I think about his lips on somebody else's, and the urge dies.

CHAPTER FOUR
GIGI

Is it Carl?

EARLY THE NEXT MORNING, I HIT THE RINK FOR A SOLO SKATE, ducking out just as the men's team arrives for their second day of training camp. Then I manage to squeeze a run in afterward but keep it short because it's more humid outside than I expect. On my way back to the dorms, I get a phone call from my twin, and soon I've got Wyatt whining in my ear about our mom, who didn't appropriately fawn over the new song he sent her. I guess she didn't love the arrangement, but the way he's ranting, you'd think she told him to forsake music altogether and get a job in pharmaceutical sales.

I slow to a jog, enjoying having the campus all to myself. Once classes start on Monday, Briar will be buzzing with life. The cobblestone paths will be teeming with students and faculty, the wrought-iron benches crammed with bodies. There'll be people sitting in the quad for as long as the weather permits. Blankets strewn on the grass while students throw Frisbees and footballs around. Even when the weather changes, the campus will still be beautiful. A blanket of snow, frost in the trees. I love every season in New England. This place is in my blood.

It's in my brother's blood too, and yet Wyatt has had trouble staying still his whole life. He's always had a serious case of wanderlust. Always convincing our dad to take us on epic trips in the offseason. Surfing and zip-lining in Costa Rica. Hiking in South America. Scuba diving in the Maldives. He and Dad are super close, but (as much as he'd deny it) Wyatt's actually a huge mama's boy.

Which is why I laugh and cut him off midrant. "Okay, can we just stop with the fake outrage? We both know you're going to do what she suggests in the end."

"That's not true," he argues.

"Really? So you're not going to adjust the bridge of the song then?"

"If I do change the bridge, it'll be because I feel like I should, not because Mom said so."

"Uh-huh. Sure. Keep telling yourself that, champ." I loudly cough out the words, *"Mama's boy."*

"I am not a mama's boy." The outrage is back.

"Isn't your profile pic a photo of you and Mom?"

"Yeah, from the Grammys," he growls. "Who wouldn't use a picture of themselves at the Grammys?"

I wouldn't. But that's also because I have no interest in throwing on a fancy gown and getting my picture taken at award shows. I could've gone with them to the ceremony last year—Mom wrote an album for a new indie rock trio that was nominated for several Grammys—but that's more Wyatt's scene than mine.

"Whatever. *Clearly* I'm not going to get any support from my beloved sister."

"Beloved," I echo with a snort. "That's rich."

I reach the front doors of Hartford House and stop to tie a shoelace that's come undone.

"Anyway, I gotta go now," I tell him after I hop to my feet. "I've got a ton of plans today."

"Later, traitor."

I'm on the road not long after, driving to my best friend's place in town to take advantage of the sunny, humid morning.

Diana lives in a new apartment complex called Meadow Hill, which is inaptly named because it's neither in a meadow nor on a hill. Hastings, Massachusetts, comprises mostly flat residential streets, little parks, and wooded trails. Still, I love this new housing development. White-railed balconies overlook a massive landscaped courtyard that features a huge pool and rows of lounge chairs with red-and white-striped umbrellas. It's heavenly.

Instead of her voice crackling over the intercom outside her lobby, I hear it wafting down from her balcony.

I look up to find her waving at me. "Don't bother coming up! I'm heading down! Meet you at the pool!"

I shift my oversized beach bag to my other shoulder and follow the flower-lined path toward the rear of the property. I'm shocked to find the pool area devoid of people. Not a single soul there.

Diana dashes out the back doors in denim shorts and a bright pink bikini top. Her platinum blond hair is in a high ponytail that swings from side to side as she bounds toward me.

If there's one word to describe Diana Dixon, it's *firecracker*. Barely over five feet, she possesses a scary amount of energy, a flair for the dramatic, and a complete and total lust for life. She's one of my favorite people in the world.

"Where is everyone?" I demand when she reaches me. I gesture at the empty pool. "How is nobody taking advantage of this sunshine?"

"People have jobs, Gigi. Not everyone can be ladies of leisure like you and I."

That makes me laugh. She's right. I keep forgetting this isn't college housing. Actual adults live here. Diana's the youngest of the tenants, in fact.

During freshman year, she roomed with me and Mya in a triple suite, but at the end of second semester, her aunt passed away and left Diana this apartment. I was bummed to see her go, but really, I don't blame her for fleeing the dorms. She's a homeowner now, with her own private space and a mortgage completely paid for by her late aunt's estate.

I suppose I could've been in a similar position—my parents offered to rent or buy me an off-campus apartment when I started at Briar. But the idea didn't sit right with me. They already pay my tuition; I passed on a scholarship because it felt wrong taking an opportunity away from someone who might not be able to afford an Ivy, when I come from a wealthy family.

On the same token, I don't want extra perks thanks to my rich parents. Living in the dorms is cheaper than off campus because everything's included, so if my parents were already going to fund my entire college experience, I feel better not accepting any more money than needed.

"I hope you brought sunscreen, 'cause I'm all out."

I lift the corner of my bag. "I got you covered, babe."

"You always do."

We lay our towels on two loungers. I brought spray-on sunscreen with me, so we take turns with the can, spraying ourselves while the sun beats down on our heads.

"How was cheer practice this morning?" I ask her. "Is that new chick still angling for your job?"

Diana's a flyer on the cheerleading team. The top girl, or at least she was last year when they came in second at nationals. Yesterday she texted me she was worried she might lose that position to some new freshman dynamo whose high school team won the last four high school national championships.

"Margo? Donesies," Diana says flatly. Her eyes convey regret rather than relief. "She tore her ACL at practice this morning. Our trainer says she's out for the whole year."

I whistle in dismay. "Shit. That's brutal."

Injuries are a fact of life for student athletes, but sometimes it's easy to forget how fickle the human body can be. One minute you're vying for top girl, the next you're sidelined for an entire cheer season.

"Yeah, I feel bad for her."

Kicking off my sandals, I grab my bottle of water and sit at the edge of the concrete pool deck. The water is warmer than I expect when I dip my feet in.

I glance over my shoulder. "Are you still dating both those guys?"

Diana ditches her flip-flops and comes to join me. "Oh, plot twist. It's three now."

"Jesus. That kind of multitasking would make me break out in hives."

She heaves an exaggerated sigh. "Yes. It's starting to be a bit much. You have to help me decide who to pick."

"Can't we date them all?"

"We have been! I've been trying to narrow it down from two to one for the last few weeks, and instead, I just ended up *adding* one to the list! But I'd like to start getting naked, so it's time to pick. I can only give one of them my flower."

I choke midsip of my water. "Yes, your treasured flower."

Diana's no virgin, but she's picky as hell about who she sleeps with. She also likes to make me laugh by using the most absurd language to describe sex and body parts.

Her green eyes dance playfully. "Anyway, I need your help. Help me decide."

"All right, let's hear it. One of them is the guy from your squad, right? The stunt guy? What was his name again? Actually, I can't remember either of their names. Wow. My memory sucks."

"Nope, I'm not reminding you. I don't want to bias you. Because the third guy has a really bad name."

"What! What is it! Please tell me. Is it Roger? Biff? Is it Carl?"

"I'll tell you at the end. After you pick."

"You're such a tease. Okay. Suitor A. The cheerleader."

She nods. "He's so athletic. So dedicated. Really funny. Cocky but not arrogant. Sex appeal galore. Only con is that he sings everything."

"Like he sings a lot of songs?"

"No." She groans. "He *sings everything*. Like, 'I a-am go-ing to chew-ooh some guuuum nowwww!'"

Her musical rendition has me keeling over in laughter. "Oh my God. I love him."

"It's legit one of the most obnoxious things I've ever experienced in my life. Suitor B is an actual musician and he doesn't sing nearly as much."

"Oh, I remember the musician. He wrote you that song and tried to rhyme *Diana* with *banana*." I firmly shake my head. "No love song should have the word *banana* in it. Also, your family's from Savannah. Missed opportunity right there."

"He's not a great rhymer," she concedes. "He's also not very funny. He doesn't get my jokes and he's super intense."

"The intensity is a musician thing."

"I know, but I like a good sense of humor in a guy."

"Is Suitor C funny?"

"Oh my gosh, yes. And he's sort of dorky. He's a physics student. Really smart, but not condescending. Super sweet. He's not my usual type, but we bumped into each other at the Coffee Hut last week, and I was oddly attracted to him."

"Con?"

"Sort of insecure. He constantly asks about my exes, but then gets pissy when I answer any of his questions."

"That's annoying, but at least he's not singing the questions."

"Very good point. Oh, he's also a bit older," she reveals.

"How much older?"

"Six years. He's twenty-six. He's doing his masters."

I purse my lips, thinking it over. "All right. Based on the available data, I'm between Suitor A and C. I guess it all depends on whether you want a cocky cheerleader or a sweet academic. If it were me, I'd probably take a chance on the academic. It'd be a nice change of pace for you. And I bet he's going to be good in bed. I have a feeling."

"Intriguing. All right. Decision made! Suitor C it is."

At that, she slides off the deck and plops herself into the pool. She instantly submerges, dunking her head in the water before popping up and shaking her ponytail like a wet dog. I get sprayed and start laughing.

"You're evil," I accuse, but the cool droplets do feel nice on my face. Actually, screw it. I adjust the strings of my bikini bottoms and then jump into the water too.

It's heaven. Cold and refreshing, a nice antidote to the thickening humidity and relentless sun.

I float on my back for a few moments before remembering something very important. "Hey, wait, what's Suitor C's name? Spill."

Diana does a slow butterfly stroke toward me. Stalling.

"*Is it Carl?*"

She releases a defeated sigh. "Percival."

My jaw drops. "And he's only twenty-six? What kind of parents do that to their kid? Does he at least go by Percy?"

"He doesn't love Percy, but maybe I can wear him down." She starts floating beside me, laughing to herself. "You know what? I don't even care. I like Percival. He's the one I want."

We spend the next hour in the pool, floating and treading water and chatting about nothing. Then we spend another hour getting some sun, until my growling stomach becomes too difficult to ignore.

"Damn, G, keep that thing down." Diana looks over and grins.

"I can't help it. I'm starving."

"Want to order some lunch?"

"I can't. I'm meeting Will in town. Actually..." I sit up and stick my hand in my bag to search for my phone. "I should check the time."

"You know how I feel about this Will thing," Diana chastises. "You have no business hanging out with your ex-boyfriend's friends."

"He was my friend first." I check the screen. "Shit. It's almost one. I need to start heading out soon. Wanna join us?"

"Nah. I want to run through some of the choreography we learned at practice this morning. You should come back tonight, though. There's this new reality channel on TV, and they released a roster of shows, and some of them are batshit. It's amazing."

"Oh my God, have you watched *Fling or Forever*? My mom and I are obsessed with it."

"Yes," she blurts out, and we proceed to spend about fifteen minutes discussing the best but also the worst dating show on the planet. The kind of crack that makes you feel bad about yourself after you realize you wasted ten hours of your life on it.

Eventually I have to cut us off so I can go inside and change for lunch.

———

Diana's not the only one who chides me about remaining close with Case's friends. I've heard it from almost everyone in my life, and their warnings flutter in the back of my mind as I walk into Sue's, the restaurant where I'm meeting Will Larsen.

In my defense, I really *was* friends with Will long before I started dating Case. He's Boston-born like me, and we attended the same high school. Went out a few times too, before we realized you can't find two more platonic people than us. Like, zero chemistry.

Will is the one who introduced me to Case freshman year, and the one who convinced me to go on a date with him. Having played hockey my entire life, I always shied away from dating hockey players. Mostly because I know what they're like.

As in, notorious fuckboys.

Hmm, so really, when you think about it...this is all Will's fault.

"Hey," I greet him, giving him a hug as he rises from the table.

He smacks a kiss on my cheek, then flashes his perfect white smile. Will has those boy-next-door looks that women can't resist.

"Hey. Look," he says, holding up a laminated page. "New menus."

"Shocker." This place revamps their menu about once a month. It's like the owners can't decide what kind of restaurant they want to be.

"They got rid of all those artisan sandwiches," Will tells me. "I'm bummed. I liked those."

"Aw, they were great." I skim the latest menu, frowning. "There's a lot of sushi on here now. This alarms me."

Will snickers. "Maybe they can rename the place Sue's Sushi."

"No, it should be Sue's Super Sushi Shop. Say that five times."

"And then they could start serving soup and change it to Sue's Super Sushi and Soup Shop."

"Oh, even better."

We continue to scan the menu options. I sort of feel bad for the owners. They've been struggling to stay afloat since they opened two years ago. Meanwhile, their biggest competitor, Della's Diner, always has a line out the door. Della's has been around forever, though, a beloved landmark in this town. My mom waited tables there when she went to Briar.

Will and I settle on burgers and fries, because that seems safer than ordering sushi from an establishment that only last week called itself an all-day breakfast place.

"You have that charity game this week, right?" Will asks while we wait for our meals.

I nod. "Thursday. Want to come root for us?"

"If I'm not too exhausted from training camp, then definitely."

"How's the new team gelling?"

"Oh, perfectly. You know, like oil and water. Blending right up."

I laugh. "That bad?"

"Worse. Those Eastwood guys all have humongous chips on their shoulders."

"Yes, I'm sure it's one-sided," I say dryly.

Will stubbornly shakes his head. "I'm just saying, they're in our house. They could afford to be nicer."

"See, that's the problem. You're calling it your house. Like they don't belong."

"Well, they *don't* belong," he grumbles. But he's smiling now, a tad rueful. "Point taken. Maybe it's not one-sided. But anyway, yeah, it's only the second day of camp and everyone is ready to kill each other. No way we're even making the playoffs this season, let alone going all the way."

I reach over and pat his forearm. "Don't worry. At least *one* Briar hockey program will win the Frozen Four this year. The women will get it done for you, sweetie."

"Aw, thanks."

The waitress comes over with our drinks, and Will takes a long sip of his soda before dropping a bomb.

"Miller's transferring."

"What? Since when?"

Miller Shulick is another Briar player, and a damn good one, playing on the second line last year. He's also a really sweet guy. His only flaw, really, is being best friends with Jordan Trager.

"Since this morning," Will says glumly. "Coach secured him a spot at Minnesota Duluth."

"That's a good program."

"Yeah. He'll go from being top ten here to top three there. Definitely an upgrade. It's just a bummer to see him go. We're throwing a thing for him Friday night. Barbecue, booze. Maybe sit around the firepit. You down?"

"Yeah, for sure." I like Miller. I'm sad he's leaving. "That *is* a bummer. Why can't Trager be the one transferring?"

"Because we can't have nice things."

I snort. Even Jordan's teammates can't stand him.

"Anyway, tell your girls about Miller's party. The more, the merrier. Is Mya back yet from wherever she's been jet-setting?"

My roommate, Mya, is my other best friend at school. Her dad is the ambassador to Malta, her mom an heiress to a shipping empire, so Mya spends her summers sunbathing on yachts in the Med or staying in fancy European villas. Which is funny, because as snooty as her parents are, she's the least pretentious person you'll ever meet.

"You know her, she doesn't show up until the day before classes start. Diana's in town, though."

"Cool. Bring 'er to the party."

I lift a brow. "Are you inviting any of the new guys?"

"The fuck do you think?"

"I take that as a no."

"Of course it's a no. That would be rubbing salt in Miller's wounds."

The waitress arrives with our food. After we thank her, Will takes a bite of his cheeseburger, chewing for what seems like forever.

When he speaks again, I realize he was trying to find the most nonchalant way to ask his next question.

"So what's going on with you and CC?"

His attempt at nonchalance fails horribly.

Laughing, I pop a french fry in my mouth. "And there it is."

"What?"

"The Case interrogation. What, you think I really believed you just called me up out of the blue and invited me to lunch?"

"We have lunch together all the time," protests Will.

"Sure, but this particular lunch just *happens* to fall the day after I tell Case we're not getting back together? Very suspicious."

"Purely coincidence." He winks at me.

"Uh-huh. I'm sure."

"I swear."

He takes another bite of his burger and chews extra slow again. He watches me, waiting for me to fill the silence. But I don't. I simply munch on my fries and pretend not to notice his growing impatience.

"Okay, you gotta give me something here," he blurts out. "What the hell am I supposed to tell my boy?"

"Ha, I knew it! He totally put you up to this."

"Come on, you know he's sorry, G. He feels like total shit about everything."

I swallow my growing frustration. "I know you're only looking out for him, but can we please change the subject?"

I search the table for ketchup and realize the waitress forgot to bring it. Instead of trying to flag her down, I take advantage of the perfect way out of this conversation.

I rise from my chair. "Just gonna grab some ketchup from the counter."

I'm so focused on placing distance between me and Will's questions that I don't pay attention to my surroundings. I reach the counter at a brisk pace and slam into none other than Luke Ryder.

CHAPTER FIVE
RYDER

Carma with a C

GARRETT GRAHAM'S DAUGHTER IS HOT. SHE WAS HOT WHEN I met her six years ago, and she's even hotter now. Her eyes widen after she bodychecks me. Big gray eyes, reminiscent of an overcast sky. But they're not muted or plain. They're vibrant, as if that sky is crackling with electricity in anticipation of thunder and lightning.

Her long brown hair is arranged in a side braid that falls over one slender shoulder. She tucks a loose strand that's fallen out of her braid behind her ear. Recovering from her surprise, she gives me a half smile.

"Hey," she says.

I lift a brow. "I was wondering how long it would take for you to work up the nerve to talk to me."

Gigi rolls her eyes at me. "I didn't need to gather my courage. Just haven't had an opportunity."

That's bullshit. We passed each other in the corridor outside the locker rooms this morning, and she barely acknowledged me. Granted, she was with one of her coaches, but she totally saw me. I also find it interesting that although the women's practice schedule hasn't even been set yet, Gigi still wakes up at ungodly hours to skate and run her own private drills. She did the same thing at the camp she helped her father run.

"Anyway, I'm pretty sure I said hi to you in the hall today," she points out.

"You nodded."

"That's the same thing as hi."

"Is it?" I mock.

"I don't know." She sounds frazzled. "Why do you care so much if I greet you properly?"

"I don't care in the slightest."

"Then why did you bring it up?"

"I'm already regretting it."

She stares at me. "I forgot how magical your personality is."

Sighing, I head for the other end of the counter, where I was instructed to wait for my food. I'm picking up takeout for me and the guys. We could've had it delivered, but it's a nice day, so I decided to walk. Well, originally I planned to drive, but my Jeep's been making some concerning clunking noises lately. It was already on its last legs back in Eastwood, but sometime during the two-hour drive to Hastings, it also decided it didn't feel like accelerating when I shifted gears. Swear to God, if the transmission's going, I'm going to be pissed. I can't afford to get it fixed right now.

Gigi requests a bottle of ketchup from the teenage girl at the counter. While she waits, she looks over at me. "I hear it's not going well at practice."

I smirk. "Going pretty well for me. I'm cocaptain."

"Cocaptain of a team in shambles. Impressive." She smiles sweetly.

"Here you go, hon." The girl returns and holds out a glass ketchup bottle to Gigi.

"Thank you." She glances at me again. "Amazing chatting with you as always, prom king."

"Gisele."

She struts back to her table, and I can't help checking her out. She's wearing denim shorts that cling to a round perky ass. The denim is frayed, strands of whitish-blue thread tickling her firm, tanned thighs. She's not a tall woman, maybe five-four, but her legs appear endless in those tiny shorts. They're all muscle too, and shapely, a testament to her training. It's hot that she plays hockey. Female athletes are a massive turn-on.

The flicker of desire fizzles when I notice who she's sitting with.

I still don't know the names of every single Briar player, but I do know the good ones. Will Larsen's one of those. And I guess as far as assholes go, he's not as bad as his teammates.

"Order for Ryder?"

A man in a white apron appears holding two takeout bags.

"Thanks," I say, accepting the bags.

I'm leaving the restaurant when my phone buzzes with a call. I grab it from the back pocket of my cargo shorts. It's an unfamiliar number, so I let the call go to voicemail.

The walk home takes me down Main Street and through a series of quaint, well-maintained parks. Hastings is a tremendous step up from Eastwood. My former town was very industrial, with a lot of strip malls and nothing too exciting to look at. Hastings, on the other hand, resembles a town from an old-timey postcard. Gaslit lampposts and mature trees line the streets, and strings of lights and banners hang overhead on Main Street, advertising a summer jazz festival that recently finished. The storefronts are shiny and clean, the main strip full of small shops and boutiques, coffee shops, and a handful of bars and restaurants.

I cut down a winding path past a wooden gazebo, then emerge from the park onto the sidewalk. I notice whoever called left a voicemail, so I key in my password to listen to it.

"*Hello, this message is for Luke Ryder. This is Peter Greene with the Maricopa County Attorney's office. I'm calling in regard to your father's parole hearing. If you could call me back at your earliest convenience—*"

I delete the message before he's even finished reciting his phone number.

Yeah, fuck that.

I walk faster, passing a lady pushing a stroller. She takes one look at me and ducks her head. I'm wearing cargo shorts and a T-shirt, nothing remotely frightening. But maybe it's my expression at hearing the words *parole hearing* that's scaring her off.

When I get home, Shane's right where I left him. Mowing the lawn, shirtless. Across the street, a few girls congregate on their porch pretending to casually chat with one another while their gazes are glued to Shane's glistening muscles. I'd bet every dollar I made working construction this summer that one of those girls will be at our place tonight. All of them, if Beckett decides to show his face out here.

Sometimes living with Beckett gets a little loud. That headboard banging keeps you awake a lot. Shane's quieter with his conquests, but he does have them. Frequently, now that he's single.

"Oh, sweet. I'm starving." Shane turns off the mower and comes striding toward me.

We leave his fan club behind and go inside, where Beckett is loading the dishwasher in the kitchen. Shane grabs plates from the cupboard while I open the takeout bags.

"Hey, so I invited a few of the neighbors over," Beckett says.

I smother a snort. Of course he did. I was crazy to think he *hadn't* already made moves on the chicks across the street.

As it turns out, the three girls who ring our doorbell later that night are all nursing students, which leads to plenty of very unfunny doctor and nurse jokes from Beckett. And yet the chicks eat it up, because Beck has that effect on women.

One of them has her sights set on me, though. Her name is Carma—*with a C,* she makes sure to tell us—and she's a tall pretty girl with shoulder-length black curls and unabashed hunger in her dark eyes. She's on me from the moment she enters the house, flirting hard, turning up the charm. At first, I'm sort of indifferent, just nodding along, but two beers later, I find myself receptive to her advances.

When she leans in close and whispers, "Wanna go upstairs?" in my ear, I can't deny the offer is tempting.

Last time I hooked up was a month ago, when I went to visit Beckett in Indianapolis for a weekend. We hit up a few bars, and I ended up going home with a hot bartender in her late twenties. Fun night.

In the month since, however, I was tasked with finding us a house in Hastings, working twelve-hour days on a construction site, and now, this disastrous training camp.

Meaning my dick could definitely use some TLC.

So I leave my beer on the kitchen counter and shrug. "Let's go."

CHAPTER SIX
RYDER

No kiss goodbye?

I SLEPT THROUGH MY ALARM.

Fucking hell.

I hurl myself out of bed like a rocket, taking half the comforter with me. Carma whimpers in her sleep from the heat loss. Her bare legs and pink panties now exposed, she curls over and tucks her knees up.

I don't typically do sleepovers, especially during the season, but we were both pretty exhausted last night, and I felt bad telling her she couldn't crash. I did make it clear I had to be up at six, but Carma shrugged it off. Said if she was still asleep when I got up, don't wake her. Just lock up, and she'd leave through the back door.

I fly into the bathroom, wondering how the fuck I managed to sleep through my alarm. Since I got to Briar, I've been setting the alarm for six to be at the rink for seven. I always go early to train, even though practice doesn't technically start till nine. Carma and I didn't even stay up that late. We crashed around midnight.

I'm so pissed at myself right now. It takes fifteen minutes to drive to campus. I won't even have time to eat breakfast. Goddamn it.

Why didn't the others wake me? They usually leave around eight. They would've seen my Jeep in the driveway.

Furiously brushing my teeth, I scroll one-handed on my phone to call Shane.

"Yo," he answers. "Where are you?"

"At home. Why didn't you guys wake me?"

"I don't know. We figured you were taking a day off from your overachiever routine and showing up to practice at a normal time like a normal person."

Ha. He calls it overachieving. I call it being a hockey player.

"I slept through my alarm. I'm on my way now, though. Can you have a coffee waiting for me in the locker room so I can chug it while I gear up?"

"Anything for you, darling."

I return to my room, where I dress quietly while Carma continues to sleep. She's wormed her way back under the comforter and cocooned herself in it.

Since she asked me not to wake her, I leave her in my bedroom and take the stairs two at a time. I lock the front door and throw myself into the driver's seat a moment later.

When I turn the key in the ignition, the Jeep doesn't start.

Mother.

Fucker.

Not now.

I cannot fucking deal with this right now.

I waste about five minutes of precious time trying to start the engine, but the vehicle is dead as a doornail. I then release a series of expletives that would horrify even the filthiest of mouths.

Back in my bedroom, I'm done catering to Carma's beauty sleep.

"Hey." I shake her awake. "Do you have a car?"

She blinks drowsily. "Yeah…why?"

Relief pours into me. Oh, thank fuck. "I need you to drive me to practice. Please."

"But it's so early."

"No, it's late. I should have been there at seven, but I slept through my alarm."

"I changed it," she says groggily.

I freeze in place. "What?"

"I changed the alarm on your phone. You said your practice was at nine, so I don't know why you had to set the alarm for six—"

"Because I go for seven," I snap, practically vibrating from the anger that surges through me. "I can't believe you changed my fucking alarm."

And then, right on cue, to add insult to injury, my phone alarm starts blaring.

She reset the damn thing to eight thirty.

"*Eight thirty?*" I growl. "Are you kidding me right now? It takes fifteen minutes just to drive there. How am I supposed to suit up and be on the ice at nine—" I stop talking.

Jesus fucking Christ. There's no point even arguing right now.

I exhale a long, calming breath.

"My car won't start," I say flatly. "I need a ride. I would've gone with my roommates, but they left already."

"Please don't be mad at me." She's wide awake now and jumping out of bed. "I didn't realize it was such a big deal."

It's difficult not to snap at her. Who randomly sleeps over at a hookup's house and then changes his alarm? I'm close to exploding again. So I ignore her while she gets dressed and call Shane back.

"Hey," I say urgently. "I'm going to be late. Try to cover for me with Jensen if you can. Tell him my car broke down."

"I told you that Jeep was going to fuck you over one day."

Sure, it was the Jeep that fucked me over.

I've never been late for practice a day in my life. And while I hate being reliant on anyone other than myself, there are zero drivers available on any of the ride apps, so I have no choice but to catch a ride with Carma. Luckily, the fire I light under her ass does its job. She and I are jogging out the door and across the street to her driveway less than five minutes later.

Carma unlocks her little red hatchback. "All right, big boy. Get in."

She gives me a teasing little grin, and it does nothing to abate my internal rage.

I dive into the car and direct her to the two-lane road toward the Briar campus. Within minutes I'm twitching with impatience. She's driving five miles over the speed limit, so the rational part of my brain knows I can't ask her to go any faster than that. She's already speeding. But goddamn it, if it were me, I'd be risking a hundred tickets to make it on time.

I drum my fingers against the center console, hitting the imaginary gas with my foot and dying inside the entire drive to campus. Carma tries making conversation and I diligently ignore her. I'm scared of what I might say.

It's five minutes to nine when we pull into the parking lot of the Graham Center. There's zero chance I'll be dressed and on the ice before Coach blows his whistle. That's just a fact. Hopefully the car-broke-down excuse will suffice, but Jensen's been giving us serious grief since camp started. He's on the verge of cutting any of us at any time. I wouldn't put it past him to dump even me, the cocaptain, for the crime of tardiness.

Carma puts the car in park. I unbuckle my seat belt and reach for the door handle.

"What, no kiss goodbye?"

I'm too pissed to even look at her. "I have to go."

"Seriously? We spent the night together and you can't spare two more seconds to kiss me goodbye?"

If only to avoid any more delay, I dutifully lean in for a kiss. To my sheer annoyance, she doesn't leave it as a peck. Next thing I know, she's climbing into the passenger side and onto my lap, arms around my neck, tongue prodding through my surprised lips.

"*Carma,*" I caution against her mouth, curling a firm hand over her waist to try to move her off me.

She starts kissing my neck, and my anger boils over. Because this is my career we're talking about. Jensen is watching me. My NHL draft team is watching me. If I want to play in the pros and succeed there, I can't be making out with some girl while the rest of my teammates are warming up for practice.

"Thank you for the ride," I say tightly. "Now move."

All right, that was harsh.

But the last thread of my patience has snapped like a cheap elastic band. First she changes my alarm, and now she won't let me get out of the car?

I'm done here.

I manage to open the door and get myself out from under her. I jump out, lunging forward just as my peripheral vision catches another flash of movement. For a second I think it's Carma getting out of the car, but my step stutters when I notice the man clicking his key fob to lock a black Range Rover two spaces over.

It's Garrett Graham.

For a moment I'm rendered both speechless and motionless. I stand there as the hockey legend struts toward me with a travel mug in hand. I haven't seen him since the hockey camp I was invited to attend as a teenager.

He glances at the red hatchback with Carma still behind the wheel. Then he scowls at me, and I know without a doubt that he saw her in my lap.

Fuck.

Fuck fuck *fuck*.

Can this day get any worse?

"Morning skate starts at nine, doesn't it, Mr. Ryder?"

Yes, apparently it can get worse.

"I know. I'm running late. I had car trouble." I wince as the excuse leaves my mouth.

"Looks like some serious car trouble," Garrett says with a bite to his tone. His frown hasn't abated.

He matches my pace up the concrete walkway toward the entrance.

"My car broke down in the driveway," I find myself explaining, like some desperate attempt to win his approval. "So I had to catch a ride this morning. But my driver didn't see the urgency in getting me here on time."

"Not really her responsibility, now is it?" Lifting a brow, he stalks through the front doors.

I give up.

On my mad race down the hall, I wonder what Graham is even doing here. Maybe he's here to see his daughter.

The empty locker room is an accusation. A slap in the face. I can barely stomach myself as I strip out of my clothes and throw on my pads and practice uniform. Everyone else is on the ice, where they should be. And I'm here like a fucking idiot. All because I wanted to get laid last night. I already have a target on my back. From Jensen, from Colson and his guys, from the NHL. And now my idol thinks I can't get to practice on time.

Fuck my life.

I leave my phone on the mahogany shelf in my locker and sit on the bench to lace up my skates. A minute later, I walk down the rubber-coated pathway on my skate guards and emerge into the rink, where I'm relieved to find practice isn't underway yet.

Relief courses through me. Thank fuck. Guys are still warming up, while Coach Jensen stands at the benches talking to Graham, who's sipping from his travel mug.

Saved by Garrett Graham. If he weren't here distracting Coach, I probably would've been sent home.

Shane skates toward me. "You okay?"

For all the ways he can be a jackass, he's also a good friend.

"Yeah." I pause. "Carma shut off my alarm."

He grimaces. "Well, I guess that neighborly relationship is over."

I can't help but chuckle. He nailed that one right on the head.

"Dude, what the hell?" Hugo Karlsson, one of our senior d-men, skates up to us. He looks concerned too. "Everything okay?"

See? I want to shout to Graham. All these guys know me. I'm never late. The fact that they're all concerned means this is an anomaly.

Except who am I kidding? Rare or not, I still messed up. I took her upstairs last night. Let her crash in my bed when I knew I had to be up early. I was thinking with my dick. Which I don't do very often, to be honest. Don't get me wrong, I get laid. I like to fuck. But I'm the one who let a random hookup turn into a problem.

Shane and I do a few laps. I breathe in, trying to center myself. At one point Beckett comes up alongside me. "What happened?" he asks.

"Carma," I reply.

"Karma always comes for you, mate."

"You're not funny usually, and you're especially not funny this morning."

He merely chuckles and skates off.

My gaze drifts back to the benches. My hackles raise when I notice Colson is there now, laughing at something Graham said.

"Best buds over there," I mutter to Shane.

Shane leans in, lowering his voice. "I heard Colson and Trager talking in the locker room earlier. Turns out Colson used to date Graham's daughter."

I try to disguise my interest. But yeah…that is certainly interesting. Wonder how Colson fucked that one up.

Still, however things ended with him and Gigi, Case clearly remains in her father's good graces.

Unlike me.

A piercing whistle slices through the crisp air.

"Gather around," Coach orders.

I don't miss the way everyone's gazes dart toward Graham as we line up in front of the two men. The man is an actual superstar. The best player to ever come out of Briar, which says a lot because

Briar's produced plenty of other legends. John Logan. Hunter Davenport. This year alone, there are eight draft picks in this rink. Eight. Briar's an elite hockey program, with only the cream of the crop.

"I'm sure this man needs no introduction, but this is Garrett Graham. He'll be helping me lead practice today."

A ripple of excitement travels through the group.

"Are you fucking kidding me?" Patrick Armstrong blurts out.

Coach glares at him.

"Oh, sorry," Patrick says hastily. "I mean, are you kidding me? No f-bomb."

"Since when do I give a fuck about your language?" Coach says. "I care about the interruption. Shut up." He jabs a finger at Patrick, who instantly shuts up.

"Now, this isn't simply the case of an alumnus wanting to kill some time, relive his glory days," Coach explains. "You want to tell them why you're here?"

Graham takes a step forward. "Hey, nice to see you all. I'm not sure how familiar any of you guys are with my foundation, but we work with a lot of charities to raise funds for various causes. We also run a few junior hockey camps. There's one in particular that I head up with Jake Connelly."

More excited murmurs ring out. Connelly is another legend. Not Briar-produced, but a legend just the same.

"About three years ago, we started the Hockey Kings juniors camp. It runs for one week every August. And every year we pick two NCAA players to help us coach the camp."

This is the first I've heard of it. But I realize why that is when he continues.

"I always pick one Briar player, and Connelly picks one guy from Harvard." Garrett makes a gagging noise. "You can't account for taste."

A few guys snicker.

"I'll be keeping an eye on all of you during the season, you know, to scope you out. Scout who I think would be a good fit to coach with us. Last year Case helped us out."

I notice Shane rolling his eyes.

Lucky Colson. Guess that's what happens when you bang the man's daughter.

"Year before that was David." Graham nods toward Demaine. "With that said, I never choose the same guy twice, so, sorry, you two. You're shit out of luck this year. The rest of you, it's fair game. Do your thing today, practice as usual, and anyone who's interested, just leave your name with Coach."

I imagine every single guy other than Colson and Demaine will be writing their name on that list. Even the rich ones who go jet-setting with their folks in the summer will undoubtedly make the trek back for that one week. We're talking about running a camp with two of the greatest players of all time. Anyone who's serious about hockey will want to be there, myself included.

I know from personal experience what it's like to learn directly under Garrett Graham. He and I didn't spend much one-on-one time that week six years ago, only a couple solo sessions, but I learned more in those five days from him than in all my years playing hockey combined. Graham possesses innate, almost otherworldly instincts when it comes to this sport.

"All right, enough talk." Jensen claps his hands. "We're going to set up two three-on-three corner drills. I want to see you fighting over that puck. We're going to run them simultaneously on either end of the rink. Garrett on one end, me on the other. Graham, pick your men."

Garrett scans the thirty or so faces in front of him. "I'll take Larsen, Colson, and Dunne. Facing against Trager, Coffey, and Pope."

My stomach sinks. So it's like that, huh?

Jensen assigns me to his group, which is something, I suppose. While everyone scatters to get in position, I skate over to Garrett.

"Hey," I hedge, feeling awkward as hell. "I just wanted to say it's an honor to have you here. Learning from someone of your caliber is invaluable to all of us."

Awesome. I might as well pull the man's pants down and kiss his ass for real instead of proverbially.

His half smile tells me he knows exactly what I'm doing.

"If you think a couple compliments are going to make me forget what I saw out in the parking lot, they won't. It'll take a lot more than that."

"I know. I just…I do want you to know that's not who I am. I'm never late. Well, clearly not never. But this was the first time," I amend. "And I hope you can overlook this morning's screwup, because I'm an excellent player, and I really would like to be considered for this opportunity."

He gives me a long, discomfort-inducing once-over. Finally, he speaks. "My choice isn't based solely on who's an excellent player, kid. This is about a lot more than stat sheets. It's about leadership. And from what I've seen so far, you might be lacking greatly in that quality."

CHAPTER SEVEN
RYDER

Fuck the laws of physics and fuck you

"THERE'S NO SUCH THING AS NO-HOLDS-BARRED TIME TRAVEL. There has to be rules. Because at the end of the day, you can't resolve the grandfather paradox," Beckett is arguing from the other end of the couch. "You just can't."

Shane shifts his gaze from the TV to Beck. "Is that when you go back in time to bang your grandfather?"

"No, it's when you murder him, dumbass. That means your dad isn't going to be born, therefore eliminating your own conception. But if you weren't born, then how can you be there standing over your granddad's corpse? You can't exist and also not exist. That's the paradox. And that's why we need rules to reconcile—"

"Dude. You need to face the facts. Time travel doesn't exist. The laws of physics forbid it."

"Fuck the laws of physics and fuck you."

Beckett gets very passionate about this shit.

"Ryder, back me up here."

"Huh?" I lift my head to find Shane watching me. I scowl. "What are you two babbling about now?"

"What bug crawled up your ass today?" Beck asks in amusement. "You've been brooding over there for, like, the last hour."

"Are you still sulking about the Garrett Graham thing?" Shane laughs.

"Yes," I mumble. "Because I'm fucked."

It's been a full day since Graham showed up at our practice and gave me the verbal equivalent of a spanking, and I haven't been able to move past it. Coaching at his hockey camp would be invaluable. Given the chance, I'd show up every day like a sponge and absorb every drop of knowledge those two legends have to offer.

"You're not fucked," Beckett assures me.

"He said I lack leadership qualities. That's basically saying he's not picking me for his camp. Ergo, I'm fucked."

And all because of a chick.

See? This is why I don't do girlfriends.

Okay, to be fair, that's not entirely the reason. It's not like I've specifically avoided relationships all these years in fear that one day a woman I had casual sex with would purposely shut off my alarm after I pass out so that we could sleep in and then my hockey idol would catch us kissing in the car when I'm late for practice—

"You were voted cocaptain," Shane points out, interrupting my chaotic train of thought. "If leadership's what he's looking for, then he can't exactly say you don't have it."

"I'm cocaptain of a team where half the dudes loathe each other. Doing a great job so far," I crack. During this morning's practice, Rand and Trager almost ripped each other's heads off again.

"Your phone is blowing up," Beck says, glancing at the coffee table that's littered with our phones and their beer bottles.

"I know. It's Carma. She's been messaging all day to apologize."

I messaged back once to say I had a good time the other night, but that after yesterday morning, it's clear our schedules don't align and I'd like to focus on hockey, please and thank you. Apparently, she thinks if she keeps apologizing, somehow those sentiments will change.

Shane grins knowingly. "Zero chance for a repeat, huh?"

I swear that guy can read my mind sometimes. Although it's common sense, I suppose. You don't fuck with a man's hockey schedule. The end.

I blow out a breath, my frustration rising again.

"See, mate, this is why my theory of time travel is the supreme one," Beckett says. "In my model, you would be able to go back in time and order yourself not to go upstairs with her. Like I always say, when Carma closes a door, Destiny opens the window."

"Let it go," Shane pleads. "She doesn't even spell it the same way."

"Spelling is overrated. So anyway, if time and space are linear—"

Shane points his index finger at him. "One more word on the subject and I will literally dump this beer over your head."

"You're no fun, mate."

Shane turns back to me. "Also, I realized the solution to your Garrett Graham problem is staring you right in the face."

I perk up. "Yeah?"

He gives me a broad, satisfied smile. "Gigi Graham."

My brows knit in question. "What about her?"

"Bro. The man's daughter *goes to your school.* You've got a built-in contact. You should talk to her."

"And say what?"

He shrugs. "Ask her to put in a good word for you."

"Yeah…unlikely."

Shane eyes me suspiciously. "Why, what did you do to her?"

Beckett chuckles into his beer.

"I didn't do shit."

"So just being yourself then."

That gets a loud snort from Beck.

"Whatever." I push off the couch and get to my feet. "I'm going upstairs."

I leave them to their devices and head to my room, where I heave myself on the bed and grab my laptop.

Just like I did yesterday when I got home from the rink, I search for more details about Graham and Connelly's juniors camp. But I've already exhausted that well, so I conduct a different search. Thanks to Shane, I've got Gigi on the brain now.

I pull up some of her highlights, but they're few and far between. College hockey isn't televised the way the NHL is, and *women's* college hockey is nearly impossible to find. I do manage to locate one game from last season, a playoffs matchup between Briar and Yale. One of the local sports networks aired it in its entirety and thankfully someone uploaded it.

At one point, the camera pans to a sophomore Gigi on the bench. As she leans forward, watching her teammates kill a penalty, the intensity in her gray eyes pours off the screen and heats my blood. I can't help but wonder what she's like in bed. If she harnesses that same intensity.

There's something fiercely sexy about her. Something so hot about the way she's out there playing one of the most physical sports there is. Body checking isn't allowed in women's hockey, but that doesn't take away from the strength you need to play this sport. Besides, it ends up becoming a cerebral battle. Far more tactical. I think about what it would take to neutralize my opponent without contact, how I'd create turnovers, and I realize I'd have to adjust my entire game.

Without the roughness and the players getting bashed into the boards, the game itself stands out. And Gigi plays it well. Her skill level is insane. There's beauty in the way she moves. Her stick-handling is fucking gorgeous.

By the third period, Briar is ahead by three goals, and Gigi's line is done for the night. The camera pans over to the Briar bench. She has her helmet off, dark hair in a sweaty ponytail. Unaware of the camera on her, she undoes the elastic band to slip it onto her wrist, and her hair tumbles down her shoulders in long loose waves.

It's then I realize that my dick is hard.

Luckily, a knock sounds on my door before I commit a first and jerk off to a women's hockey game.

"Yo." Shane pops in without waiting for permission.

I close my laptop and set it beside me on the mattress. "Yeah?"

"The women's team has an exhibition game tonight. Briar versus Providence. It's in Newton." He names an area about an hour's drive, west of downtown Boston.

"So?"

"So you should go."

"Why?"

"To talk to Gigi Graham, dumbass."

Before I can object, a set of keys sails toward me.

I catch them on instinct, nearly getting stabbed by the unicorn key chain Shane's little sister gave him for his birthday in April. The guy has a real soft spot for that kid. It's kind of sweet. Which of course didn't stop Beckett from buying a pink stuffed unicorn this summer and leaving it on Shane's pillow one night when he knew Shane was having a chick over.

"I'm even gracious enough to let you take my Mercedes."

"I don't need your pity Mercedes, rich boy."

"Cool. We'll ask the tow truck dude to grab your Jeep from the garage and have him tow you there while you sit in the driver's seat and pretend to steer."

"Fuck off."

This Jeep situation *is* a problem, though. The mechanic texted this morning and said the transmission needs to be replaced. I have no idea where I'll scrape together the cash to pay for it. I don't have wealthy parents to pay my bills like Shane, and I hate dipping into my meager savings. I also hate borrowing money from friends.

But I guess I'm not above borrowing their cars.

Watching me pocket his keys, Shane starts to laugh. "Make sure you grovel hard. Maybe get on your knees," he advises. "Chicks like it when you're on your knees."

I roll my eyes. "I'm not going there to eat her out."

"Maybe you should. She's hot."

He's not wrong. But if I'm going to drive all the way there to see Gigi, it's not sex I want.

Still chuckling, he claps my shoulder when I reach the doorway. "Go get her, champ."

CHAPTER EIGHT

GIGI

Use your words

WITHIN THREE SECONDS OF THE PUCK DROPPING, I DISCOVER Providence College came here to murder us.

It's supposed to be a friendly exhibition. Yes, it's played under regular conditions. We're dressed in full gear, utilizing the lineups we'll use during the real season. But it's an unspoken rule that you don't push yourself one hundred percent in these exhibitions. Why risk getting injured for a game that doesn't even count? Just give the crowd a good show. All ticket proceeds go to a children's cancer charity, and during intermissions, the kids whose parents purchased the more-expensive-tier tickets are pulled along in little sleds on the ice. It's supposed to be cute and fun.

Instead, I'm literally in a primal struggle for my life.

The Providence girls apply pressure from go. They swarm past the blue line like hyenas. Our goalie, Shannon, is the carcass. Or rather, she's still alive, but she's injured and they smell her blood. They fire bullets at her while our defensemen race to try to bail her out.

Finally, my teammate liberates the puck from our zone only to get called for icing. Fuck. Now the face-off is to the left of our net.

We're five minutes into the first period, and I'm sweating like I exited a steam bath at the gym.

The rival center grins at me. "Having fun yet?" she taunts.

"It's a fucking charity game, Bethany," I growl, crouching in preparation. "Calm your tits."

She tsks under her breath, while the ref gets in position.

"Come on, Graham. You should always bring your A game, no matter the circumstances."

Bullshit. They're trying to prove something. What, I don't know. We're not even bitter rivals, the way Eastwood and Briar used to be. It's supposed to be a goddamn fun evening. They're ruining it.

The crowd screams when Bethany wins the face-off. She snaps a pass off to her right winger, who shoots and scores.

First blood goes to Providence.

It isn't until I get back to the bench that the puzzle pieces fall together.

Cami looks at me and hisses, "The coaches from Team USA are here."

I freeze. "What? Seriously?"

"Yeah, Neela just heard it from one of the refs."

I turn to our teammate Neela for confirmation before realizing she's on the ice fighting for her own life. Providence is not going easy on us.

Instead, I search the stands for Alan Murphy, Team USA's head coach. It's a futile exercise. One of my pet peeves is in movie scenes where there's a huge audience, thousands of people in the stands, and somehow the hero or heroine manages to lock eyes with one specific person, the whole crowd disappearing as they maintain this very deliberate eye contact.

Lies. You can't see anything out here. Only a sea of indistinguishable faces.

"Why are they here?" I demand.

"I don't know. Maybe they're involved with the charity?"

Or maybe they're here to do some scouting.

Shit, and we're playing like garbage out there.

The knowledge lights a fire under my ass. Adley shouts for a changeup, and I wait until my teammates reach the boards before I jump out the door.

My skates touch the ice just as Whitney passes me the puck. Providence is on their own shift change. It's the worst possible timing for them, giving me the perfect opportunity to make a play. Badly timed shift changes can make or break a hockey game, and this is the first mistake the other team has made since the game started.

I waste no time capitalizing on their error and the breakaway it provides me. The air hisses past my ears as I fly toward the opposing net. One defenseman attempts to catch me and can't. I outskate her, then outmaneuver her counterpart as I wind my arm back and take a shot.

Goal.

I hear the thunderous roar of the crowd. The loud tapping of sticks against the boards, my teammates' seal of approval, echoes through the packed arena. Camila skates by and smacks my arm.

"*Yes*, baby!" she crows, and then we make another shift change, and the second line takes over.

When the buzzer goes off to indicate the end of the first period, we're tied 1–1.

The second period is as high intensity as the first. It's a battle of the defense, both offenses getting shut down hard. I'm tangled up multiple times behind the Providence net. It's my least favorite place to be. I'm smaller than a lot of other players, which makes it hard to win battles behind the net. I don't have the shoulders for it. My dad always makes fun of my dainty shoulders.

Luckily, I'm fast, so I can usually get myself out of jams. Rather than battle, I try to pass to Cami at the point, only for it to be intercepted. The next thing I know, we're chasing them again. The rest of the third period is like that. Deep pressure. High speeds.

Providence leads us 2–1 all the way until the last forty seconds, when Neela makes a play behind the net. Unlike me, she thrives back there. She keeps their goalie distracted, then manages to get the puck in front of the net, directly into Whitney's waiting stick for a one-timer.

The charity organizers whisper to Coach Adley that they don't want this ending in a tie, so we hold a tiebreaker shootout that Briar handily wins because nobody can outshoot me. Nobody.

And just like that, we win the charity game, a.k.a. the Death Match.

"Jesus Christ," I groan on the walk to the locker room. "That was ridiculous."

All my teammates appear equally exhausted.

"I thought I was in shape!" Neela squawks. "Like, I've been lifting hard in the offseason. My arms feel like jelly." She lifts them up, then lets them drop down like wet noodles.

Coach strides into the locker room before everyone starts to change.

"That was some damn good hockey," he tells us, looking around in admiration. Then he rolls his eyes. "Although I'm not sure which part of 'Save your energy for our season opener' you didn't understand," he finishes, referring to the speech he gave before the game began.

"You know us, we leave nothing out there on the ice," Whitney chirps.

He sighs. "Someone told you Brad Fairlee was in the stands, I presume?"

"Yup," she says, and everyone laughs.

Everyone except me. Because my blood has run cold.

Brad Fairlee?

Anxiety tugs at my belly, twisting into a knot. "What happened to Alan Murphy?" I blurt out.

"He's out," Adley says. "The higher-ups are saying medical reasons. They're being hush-hush about it, but I think he might've suffered a heart attack or several."

"Jeez, is he okay?" asks Whitney.

"I believe he's still in the hospital, but that's all I know. USA Hockey gave the job to Brad Fairlee, their offensive coordinator. He's good. Well-deserved promotion." Adley heads for the door. "All right. Get dressed. I'll see you on the bus."

Everyone starts talking amongst themselves again as girls drift toward the showers. My nervous energy only intensifies while I shower the sweat and exhaustion away. I don't wash my hair, just throw it up in a wet topknot, get dressed, and hurry out of the locker room.

I want to find Brad Fairlee, but I'm not sure what to say to him. We haven't spoken in a few years. I suppose I could pretend I'm asking about his daughter, Emma, but depending on how much she's told her dad, he might see through that ruse. Because I don't give a flying hoot how Emma Fairlee is doing.

Still, I can't just let the head coach of the national team leave this building without at least trying to gauge where his head is at. I should have heard something by now. That is, I should have heard something *if* they were considering me for the team. I know one girl from Wisconsin was already asked to train with them, so they must be in the process of finalizing their roster. They have to; all the big games are coming up, like the 4 Nations Cup in November and the USA-Canada Rivalry game in February. And then next February is the biggest game of all. The Olympics.

God. I fucking want this.

I don't ask for a lot of things. I was never one of those spoiled girls who asked Daddy for ponies and demanded an elaborate Sweet Sixteen party. Granted, Wyatt and I spent our sixteenth birthdays watching our dad win Game Seven of a critical playoff series. His team didn't win the Cup that year, but it's still pretty cool to spend your birthday in the owners' box at TD Garden.

This, though. I *want* it. Want it so bad I can taste it.

To my surprise, there's no need to hunt Fairlee down like a bomb-sniffing dog. He calls out my name the moment I enter the lobby.

"Mr. Fairlee, hey," I call back, trying to tamp down my eagerness. "It's been a long time."

"It has," he agrees. "What is it now? Three years?"

"About that."

I close the distance between us, my hockey bag slung over my shoulder.

Mr. Fairlee isn't a tall man, but he's built like a tank, with a barrel chest and thick neck. He played hockey in his youth, but didn't find much success in the pros, mostly because of his height. Eventually he went into coaching, where he *did* find success. A lot more of it now, apparently.

"Congratulations on the win."

"I wasn't expecting such a competitive game," I answer ruefully.

He nods. "Good job on that shootout."

"Thanks. And I hear congratulations are in order for you too. Coach Adley told us you were named head coach of Team USA."

Pride fills his eyes. "Yes, thank you. I'm looking forward to heading up the team. Winning some medals."

"Sounds great…" I pause, hoping he'll fill that space. Praying he'll tell me something, anything, any hint about where he's at in terms of building a team.

But he says nothing.

Awkwardly, I go on. "I mean, I guess it goes without saying, but I would love to be considered for the roster."

Another nod. "Of course. We're looking at several players right now. There's a really dynamic group of college players this year."

Bullshit.

I swallow the word, trying not to bristle. I am by no means arrogant, but I know every single player in NCAA hockey, including the new crop of freshmen. Some rookies are showing potential, but for the most part there are only a few standout players among all the D1 programs. And I'm definitely in the top ten, if not five.

"Well, that's good to hear. I don't know how many college players typically make the roster, but—"

"About thirty, forty percent," he supplies.

That shuts me up.

Damn. That's a brutal stat. Considering the size of the roster, if there are only a few open slots, that means he'll be choosing two, *maybe* three college players.

"Like I said," he continues after he notices my expression, "we're looking at several players, but of course, you're one of them. Your talent is undeniable, Gigi. Sure, there are minor issues to work on, but that applies to everyone."

"What issues?" I ask a little too quickly then realize it might sound like I'm offended by the criticism. So I hurry on to add, "I'd love any pointers you might have for me. I always want to improve my game."

He purses his lips. "It's the same issue you've always had. You're not effective behind the net."

This time I do bristle, because he's acting as if this "issue" is some Achilles' heel that's been plaguing me for years, holding me back from having any success. That's nonsense. Every player has their strengths and weaknesses.

"That's great feedback, thanks. I'll talk to Coach Adley about that." Then, because I know it'll be conspicuous if I don't ask about her, I force myself to inquire, "How is Emma doing, by the way? She's at UCLA, right?"

"She's doing well. Really thriving on the West Coast. She landed a small role in a pilot."

"Cool," I lie.

It bothers me to hear good things are happening for her, and I hate that streak of pettiness. I don't like thinking of myself as petty.

"I'll tell her you asked about her."

Please don't, I think.

But the slight edge to his voice tells me he wasn't going to pass my regards along anyway. Yeah…she totally poisoned this well.

"Well, it was good to see you, Gigi. I see someone else I need to speak to."

He pats my arm. Then, to my utter horror, he marches toward Bethany Clarke, the captain of the Providence team.

Is this a joke? Bethany might have played a good game today, but she's nowhere near the caliber of player that I am. It's like a slapshot to the face. My throat is tight with jealousy and resentment as I stalk outside. I still feel cold even as I step into the humid air.

I'm halfway down the front steps when I hear my name again.

"Gigi, wait."

I look over my shoulder to find Luke Ryder loitering at the bottom of the staircase, off to my left. He walks toward me, long legs encased in faded denim. He's also sporting a black T-shirt and a Bruins cap with the brim down low, nearly shielding his eyes.

A wrinkle appears in my forehead as I descend the rest of the way to meet him on the sidewalk. "What are you doing here?"

He shrugs.

"Use your words, Ryder."

I'm not in the mood for his caveman conversational style right now. Brad Fairlee's dismissal of me still burns like battery acid in my blood.

Ryder lifts his hat and runs one hand over his hair to smooth it before shoving the cap back down. The move draws my attention to his right wrist and the bracelet there. Woven from black and gray string, like those friendship bracelets at island resorts that the locals try to scam you into buying. It's old and frayed, as if he's been wearing it for ages.

"Just checking out your game."

"All right. Weird. But okay." I eye him, bemused. "Did you enjoy it?"

His shoulder begins to move in a shrug, but then he sees my face and stops himself.

"It was more dramatic than I expected," he says drolly. "Also didn't need to go to shootout."

"You think it should have ended in a tie?"

"No, I mean just what I said—it didn't need to go to shootout. You could have won the game for your team in the third."

"You know, most people would compliment me on the fact that I won that shootout," I point out.

"Is that what you need from people? To be told what a good girl you are?"

His mocking words send a bolt of heat directly between my legs.

Wow.

Okay.

I didn't expect my body to react like that. And I don't love that it did. Especially since I should be angry right now. He literally just told me I'm the reason we went to a shootout in the first place.

"I'm not sure if you missed it," I say tightly, "but the pressure they had on us was nuts."

Ryder doesn't answer.

"What?" I grumble.

Still nothing.

I drop my hockey bag on the pavement, and it lands with a thud. Crossing my arms over my chest, I shoot him a dark glare. "Go on. Tell me your thoughts."

He meets my eyes. "You panic behind the net."

The censure slices into me like a dull knife.

Normally I would gently take that in, absorb the criticism, and view it as constructive, not let it cut me this deeply. But he's echoing Fairlee's sentiments, and that's the last thing I need right now.

Now I have two men telling me I suck behind the net?

"When you're under pressure in their zone and there's no other option, you should automatically be moving the puck to the back of the net," Ryder says when I don't respond. "Instead, you panic and try for poor passes and get intercepted. Like you did in the third."

I think I like him better when he doesn't talk.

My jaw clenches so tight that my molars begin to throb. Ignoring his blunt assessment of my suckiness, I unhinge my jaw to ask, "Why are you really here?"

His dark-blue eyes flicker with what appears to be discomfort. I expect him to stall, or not answer at all, but he surprises me by being direct. "Your father was at our practice yesterday."

"So?"

Ryder adjusts the brim of his cap again. "He said he runs a Hockey Kings camp every summer. I was hoping—"

"Oh, for fuck's sake." I know exactly where this is going and it chafes me to no end. "Seriously? You too?"

"What?"

I pick up my bag and throw the strap over my shoulder. "Do you know how many dudes have hit me up over the years just to get close to my father? This isn't my first rodeo."

I shake my head, swallowing the rising animosity. I will say, at least Ryder is upfront about it. He's not trying to take me to dinner, where he'll hold my hand and whisper sweet words to me and *then* ask for the favor.

Despite my best efforts, that bitter feeling surfaces. I was already in a bad mood before he ambushed me, and now I feel a thousand times worse.

"I knew you were a dick, but this is next level. You show up here, insult my game, and then want to use me to get to my dad?"

He gives his trademark shrug.

"What?"

"Like you haven't been using him too?"

I stiffen. "What's that supposed to mean?"

"We practice in a building called the Graham Center." He laughs without much humor. "If that's not nepotism in action, I don't know what is."

My cheeks are scorching. I know they're turning redder by the second. "Are you implying I couldn't get into Briar on my own merit?"

"I'm saying you're good, but I'm sure it doesn't hurt what your last name is."

I struggle to calm myself. Breathing deep.

Then I say, "Fuck you."

And walk away, because I'm thoroughly done with this conversation. I won't even entertain it.

He doesn't follow me, and I'm seething when I climb onto the team bus a minute later.

Ryder's wrong. My last name isn't why Briar—and half a dozen other big hockey schools—begged me to attend. They wanted me because I'm good. No, because I'm great.

I *know* I am.

But that doesn't stop the dam of insecurity from bursting open and a flood of doubt from seeping into my blood.

CHAPTER NINE

GIGI

Full carpet

I'M STILL ENGULFED BY A DARK THUNDERCLOUD WHEN I GET HOME a couple of hours later. Then I spot the two huge suitcases in the middle of the common area, and my spirits lift.

"Oh my God," I shriek. "Are you home?"

Mya Bell appears in the doorway flashing her brilliant white smile.

"I have arrived!" she yells in very dramatic, Diana-esque fashion.

And then we're throwing our arms around each other in one of those dorky hugs where you're also kind of dancing and wobbling so hard you almost fall over.

"What are you doing here?" I ask happily. "I wasn't expecting you until Sunday."

"I got bored in Manhattan. Plus my mother was driving me crazy. I needed some peace and quiet."

"Damn, she must've been extra insufferable if you, of all people, are craving silence."

Mya is not, and I repeat, not a quiet person. This isn't to say she's obnoxiously loud. She's just talkative.

"Mom decided she wants to find me a husband or a wife, and I have no say in the matter," Mya explains, rolling her eyes.

"Really? How are you supposed to get married and become an OR superstar at the same time? I feel like it can only be one or the other right now." Mya's a biology major on the med-school track. She wants to be a surgeon.

"Exactly. I can't focus on a stupid spouse when I'm staying awake for thirty-six hours straight on my surgical residency. But you try telling my mother that. She spent half the summer grilling every diplomat we ran into about whether they had any single children. She's even compiling a dossier of candidates."

"At least she's come around to the wife part."

When Mya came out as bisexual to her parents our freshman year of college, it took her mom a while to wrap her head around it. Mostly because she thought that meant she'd never have grandchildren to buy ponies for. Mya finally had to sit her mother down and explain that if she did end up with a woman, there were plenty of reproductive options available to same-sex couples these days. That seemed to appease Mrs. Bell.

"True," Mya answers. "But I swear to God, I don't need my mother setting me up with anyone. Have you met her? She's the biggest snob on the planet. She'll marry me off to some uptight heiress or a prince who wears pinkie rings."

Mya proceeds to regale me with stories from her family's summer travels. We crack open a bottle of red wine and sit on the couch to catch up. At first I'm entertained, but soon my mind returns to the events of this evening, until I'm preoccupied and feeling hostile again.

Fuck Brad Fairlee and fuck Luke Ryder. So what if my pass was intercepted tonight? And so what if—

"What," Mya says in amusement, jolting me from my thoughts, "my story about this nude Greek dinner party isn't doing it for you?"

"No, it's hilarious. Sorry. My mind drifted for a second, and I started stewing again. I was in the worst mood before I saw your gorgeous face."

"One, I need you to keep the compliments coming because my mother basically reduced my self-esteem to ashes this summer. And two, what are we stewing about?"

"Emma Fairlee. My old friend from high school."

"Ahh, the betrayer."

"Yes." I laugh at her phrasing, but there's a twinge of pain there too, because if you told me senior year of high school that Emma and I wouldn't be friends come graduation, I would've said you were crazy.

Mya stretches her impossibly long legs and rests them on the coffee table. "So why are we thinking about Evil Emma?"

"Well, actually, I'm thinking more about her dad. I found out tonight that Mr. Fairlee is Team USA's new head coach."

"Oh shit. And she poisoned Daddy against you?"

"I don't know. I haven't spoken to her or anyone in that family, really, since graduation. But I can't imagine she would have anything nice to say about me. She's been slandering me on social media for three years now."

At first it was overtly aggressive posts about how awful, selfish, and evil my entire family and I were. Eventually it became veiled "thoughts" and ambiguous quotes that were clearly directed at me and my various personality flaws.

Which is juvenile as fuck, but the problem with Emma is she hates being ignored. She always has to be the center of attention, which is great when you're a teenager and partying, and you have this fun, vivacious friend who throws herself headfirst into adventure and drags you along for the ride.

But the moment you're not serving her and feeding her ego, she turns on you.

"Anyway, I'm worried he's not going to give me a fair shot," I admit, chugging nearly half my glass. The wine sluices to the pit of my stomach and swirls there uneasily. "They're still selecting players and finalizing the roster and..." I lick a drop off my bottom lip. "I don't know, I'm nervous. I have a bad feeling about this."

"You shouldn't. You're literally the number one female hockey player in the world."

"Okay, that's an overstatement."

"Top three," she amends. "Globally."

"Top ten. Nationally."

"All right, top five globally," she says with an airy wave. "You're telling me this asshole isn't going to choose one of the best players for his team?"

"That's not how it works."

"Then how does it work?"

I mull it over because it's hard to explain. The selection process is almost deliberately vague.

"The coaches don't select players based only on objective criteria. They look at past performances in any national events, which I don't have. They look at who they think would work well together as a team. Sometimes they might hold tryouts, but your previous performance is way more relevant than a bunch of drills." I try to sum it up in simpler terms. "Essentially, any time I step out onto the ice, I'm trying out for the national team."

And not making a good impression, apparently. At least according to Brad Fairlee.

I make a frustrated noise. "Whatever. I can't talk about this anymore."

Sliding off the couch, I fling myself onto the soft shag carpet, where I stretch out on my back and groan loudly.

"Uh-oh," Mya sighs.

I open my eyes to find her peering down at me. Her expression is a mixture of amusement and concern.

"What?" I grumble.

"You need to get laid."

"No, I don't. I'm fine."

"You are not. I've been back for an hour, and I was already seeing the signs before you went full carpet. With that said, lying on the carpet is always the last straw."

"Stop. I do not lie on the carpet that often."

"You totally do. This happens every time you max out your stress levels or get too overwhelmed. Then after carpet time, you get super crabby and start snapping at me for trivial shit like drinking from your monogrammed water bottle. And then Case comes over and bangs you, and you go back to being sweet little Gigi."

"I don't think I've ever been sweet."

"Fine, I'll concede that. But don't even try to argue the rest. You have a very predictable horniness cycle. And the second you get laid, suddenly you're less crabby and our carpet is spared."

"I don't like you."

"When was the last time you had a release?"

I open my mouth triumphantly—

"With a human male and not your hand," she interrupts before I can speak.

I sigh in defeat. "Not since Case."

"So, what, end of May? As in almost four months ago?"

"Four months is not a long time to go without sex," I protest.

"Not for most people. But for stressed-out stress cases like you? It's an eternity."

I refuse to give her the satisfaction, but…she's not wrong. Regular sex is one of the reasons I prefer relationships. People always brag about how easy it is to go out and find a one-night stand. But who truly wants to have that *every* night? A perpetual string of one nights or regular sex with one guy I love? I'll pick the latter every time.

"Should we sign you up for a dating app?"

I sit and lean against the couch. "No. I hate those things. And you know I hate casual sex."

"Well, it's either that or get back with Case." She leans forward and refills her glass. "Is that an option?"

"It is not."

Speaking of Case, he calls when I'm getting ready to shower

later. I want to wash my hair for real after half-assing it in the locker room earlier.

My fingers hover over the "accept" button. I almost don't answer, but habit takes over.

That, and I can't deny I miss the sound of his voice sometimes.

"How'd the game go?" Case asks.

Ducking out of my private bath, I fall onto the edge of my bed and into old patterns of venting to Case. "It was brutal. We need to watch out for Providence this season."

"You sore?"

"Sore and a bit bruised, but nothing a good ice bath tomorrow can't fix."

"Or a warm bath now." His voice, soft and slow like molasses, drifts into my ear. "I could come over and join you if you want company."

I'm...tempted.

A shiver dances through me at the thought of being naked with Case, pressed up against his body while he strokes my hair and kisses my neck.

Mya's right. I'm so hard up right now.

Which is why I hurry to end the call. "No," I say lightly, "I'm all good. Just gonna shower and then go to bed."

"I'm here, G. You know that, right? I'm always going to be here."

But he wasn't there. Not when it mattered.

So how am I supposed to believe he's here now?

Ugh, I don't have the mental bandwidth for this right now. I take a shower, then brush and blow-dry my hair before crawling into bed. Lying there, though, sleep eludes me. I'm antsy and—fine, maybe in need of release. So when 1:00 a.m. rolls around and I'm still wide awake, I bite my lip and slide my hand between my legs.

Is that what you need from people? To be told what a good girl you are?

Before I can stop it, Luke Ryder's gravelly voice slides into my head. Once again my core clenches, my body whispering, *Yes, call me a good girl.*

My fingers brush my clit, a fleeting caress, before I realize who I'm throbbing for.

Just like that, my arousal dies. I'm not allowed to touch myself thinking about the jerk who showed up at my game today, listed all my issues as a player, and then insinuated I don't deserve to play D1 hockey.

Nepotism in action, my ass.

Fuckhead.

It takes forever to fall asleep, and even after I do, it's not at all restful. I toss and turn and wake up feeling tired.

Because of that, I struggle during my morning run, which Mya joins me for because I desperately need the company. She attempts to distract me from the gloomy mood that still hasn't lifted, but it's not until we walk back to Hartford House from the trails that she starts finding success, drawing genuine laughter out of me.

Which, of course, promptly fades the second I spot Ryder waiting for us at the front entrance.

Holding a bouquet of daisies.

CHAPTER TEN
GIGI

International Eat an Apple Day

"I'm just saying, you can't keep calling yourself a prince when Malta abolished the monarchy in the seventies. Like, bro, your family sells doors and windows now. I don't care that once upon a time you were distantly related to the fucking queen—" Mya stops talking when she notices Ryder. Then she spies the little bouquet of white and yellow flowers. "Oh, wow. Okay. I'm here for this."

At our approach, Ryder straightens his broad shoulders and takes a step forward. He's sporting the same outfit combo as yesterday, jeans and a black T-shirt, but no baseball cap this time. His dark hair is tousled, and he shoves his free hand through it.

"Hi," he says brusquely.

"Hi," I answer. My tone has a chill to it.

Silence falls. We eye each other. I'm suspicious. He's expressionless.

"Hi!" Mya chirps.

I totally forgot she was here.

"Ryder, this is Mya," I say hastily. "My roommate."

He nods in greeting.

She looks him up and down, and from the slight curve to her full Cupid's bow lips, I can tell she likes what she sees.

He's still holding the daisies but makes no move to give them to me. For a moment I wonder if maybe they're for somebody else.

"Can we talk?" he asks.

"Oh, for sure," Mya answers. Then she clocks his expression and realizes, "Oh, you mean you and Gigi alone. Damn it, I really wanted to know what this was about."

"I'll fill you in," I promise.

She grins and walks past us toward the dorm, where she scans her key card to get inside.

"I have one question," I tell Ryder once we're alone.

"What is it?"

"Did you actually bring me flowers?"

"Yes," he mutters.

I have to bite my lip to stop from laughing. I've never seen anyone look more disgusted with their own behavior.

"Look, we both know you're a dick, but that's just your personality, kiddo. You didn't have to degrade yourself by bringing me apology flowers."

He gives me a slight smirk. "Who says they're apology flowers? Maybe they're celebration flowers."

"Uh-huh. Really. What are we celebrating?"

He pulls his phone out of his back pocket and unlocks it. He scans the screen for a moment, and from my vantage point, it looks like he's consulting a calendar app.

"It's International Eat an Apple Day." He lifts his gaze. "Seemed like something we should celebrate."

I stare at him. "You're making that up."

He turns the screen toward me. Sure enough, on the list of international holidays, International Eat an Apple Day is actually a thing.

"I really like apples," he says, carelessly smug.

"You know, I think I like this Ryder. I had no idea you were so quirky."

"I am not quirky," he growls.

"Then why are we celebrating your love of apples?"

He thrusts the bouquet at me. "Just take the fucking things."

An unwitting smile springs free. I put him out of his misery and accept the daisies.

"I do love flowers," I inform him. "Not as much as I love butterflies, but pretty close."

Ryder sighs.

"What?" My tone is defensive.

"You like flowers and butterflies? Just when I was starting to think you were cool."

"Well, what do *you* like?" I challenge.

"Not those things."

"Funny, coming from the guy who spent his whole morning picking I'm-sorry flowers for a girl."

"I didn't spend the whole morning. It took like one minute. I stole them out of my neighbor's planter."

"Oh my God."

"And they're not I'm-sorry flowers," he grumbles.

"Mm-hmm."

"Because I'm not sorry." He flicks up one eyebrow. "I spoke the truth."

I glower at him. "How would you feel if I ambushed you after one of your games and then stood there and listed everything you're bad at?"

"That's not what I did. You asked for my thoughts."

"You didn't have to answer."

"Don't ask things you don't want the answer to," he counters.

"You know, I liked it better when you didn't talk at all."

That actually gets me a smile.

Damn it. It's my fault. I'm the one who made him smile. And now I'm graced with that stupid smile, and it's a killer one. I remember what Camila said about how he stands against the wall at parties and women flock to him, and now I get why he has no shortage of options.

"Look, if this were an apology, hypothetically speaking, I guess I might acknowledge that I can be too blunt sometimes."

"No!" I say in shock.

"Not that anyone's ever complained about that."

"Oh no, I'm sure everyone loves it."

He narrows his eyes. "This was a bad idea."

"No," I push. "I'm enjoying your hypothetical apology. So, let's say, hypothetically, you were too blunt and made someone feel like shit by saying they were only playing hockey for Briar because of nepotism…go on."

His expression sobers. "I didn't mean that. The nepotism comment was out of line."

I think he's being sincere. He might be a jerk, but I'm not sure he's cruel.

Then again, I hardly know him.

"It wasn't my intention to make you feel like shit. When it comes to hockey, I'm honest. I'm always refining my own game, working on my weaknesses. Guess I forgot not everyone wants that kind of advice." He pauses, features pained. "And I'm sorry for implying that your dad is the reason you are where you are. I watched that game. You were phenomenal."

Despite the rush of warmth his compliment elicits, I can't stop a flicker of doubt. "Are you just saying that so I don't feel shitty again?"

"I don't just say things."

I'm starting to suspect how true that is.

"Well, thanks. I guess I appreciate that." Grudgingly, I add, "You're a very good player too."

"I didn't say you were very good. I said you were phenomenal."

"And I said you're very good."

He snickers under his breath. "Anyway." He gestures to the bouquet in my hand. "That's my peace offering. Shane said chicks like daisies and they don't give the wrong idea."

"What's the wrong idea? That you're trying to get with me? Or that you're sucking up to me so I'll put in a good word for you with my dad? That's why you showed up at the game yesterday, isn't it?"

"Yes," he says honestly. "But you made your stance clear on that, so I'm not going to ask again. That's not who I am." He shrugs. "All right. I'll get out of your hair now."

He starts to walk away.

"I want the advice," I blurt out.

Ryder turns to give me a wry look. "I'm not falling for that one again, Gisele."

"No, I mean it. I was in a trash mood yesterday, and that's the only reason I snapped at you. Usually, I'm like you. Always perfecting my game." I meet those intense blue eyes. "If you were to give me any advice, what would it be?"

He hesitates, scraping his hand through his hair again.

"Please. What do I need to do behind the net?"

"Stop being so eager to get out of there," he finally answers. "If you learn how to master that space and make effective use of it, the scoring opportunities are endless."

"High-risk, high reward?"

He nods. "Gain an offensive position behind the net, and you force both the goalie and opposing defense to focus on that space. And when their focus is there, they can't keep track of who's out front."

I gulp down my frustration. "I lose control of the puck back there, though. The space is too tight."

"Like I said, learn to master it. Sometimes you get lucky and draw both their d-men to you. If they have shit communication, they both might try to cover you, and now you've got one or more of your teammates wide open in prime position to score." He shrugs. "Do with that what you will."

He takes off walking again, leaving me in front of my dorm holding the bouquet.

I gaze down at the daisies and rub my thumb over one silky white petal. They really are pretty. I don't even care if he stole them. Then I look at Ryder's retreating back, those defined arms, the confidence of his stride.

"Ryder," I find myself calling out.

He turns. "Yeah?"

An idea forms in the back of my mind. Burrowing and wiggling forward until it's at the forefront and I'm walking toward him.

He slides his hands in his pockets, waiting for me to reach him.

"I have an offer to make you," I announce.

Amusement flickers through his eyes. "What kind of offer?"

"Well, maybe more of a quid pro quo. You help me; I help you."

The glimmer of humor sharpens into a glint of interest.

"My dad's hockey camp... He's super picky about who he picks for assistant coach. And I'm not going to lie—his impression of you isn't the greatest. I don't know if that's a recent thing or what. I do know he's been watching you for years, though. He follows all the good college players."

His expression clouds over. "So you're saying he's for sure not giving me the coaching slot."

"I'm not saying that. But he did mention he thinks you have a bad attitude. So, yeah, I could probably put in a good word for you. About your leadership or whatever. He and I speak on the phone all the time, and I'm going home next weekend for a visit. If you want, I'll talk you up every time. Well, maybe not every time or he'll get suspicious. But I'll tell him we're friends and make sure he knows you'd be a solid choice." I offer a shrug. "My opinion means a lot to him."

Ryder eyes me expectantly. "What do you want in return?"

"Help me iron out some of those issues behind the net. Maybe we can have a few sessions together. One-on-one." I grin at him. "Hey, I could probably teach you a thing or two as well."

"I don't doubt it. You got moves."

"See? This would be beneficial for both of us then. You work with me, I work for you. Win-win." I meet his gaze. "You interested?"

He contemplates it for so long, I wonder if he's going to turn me down. Which would be stupid and make utterly no sense because—

"I'm down," he says gruffly. "Text me the time and place for our first session, and I'll be there."

He strides off for real this time, leaving me staring after him. And wondering what I've signed myself up for.

BRIAR UNIVERSITY MEN'S ICE HOCKEY

STARTING ROSTER

PLAYER	POSITION	YEAR
Case Colson	Forward (C)	JR
Luke Ryder	Forward (C)	JR
Will Larsen	Forward	JR
David Demaine	Defense	SR
Shane Lindley	Forward	JR
Beckett Dunne	Defense	JR
Tristan Yoo	Forward	FR
Austin Pope	Defense	FR
Joe Kurth	Goalie	SR
Matt Tierney	Defense	JR
Tim Coffey	Defense	SR
Nick Lattimore	Forward	JR
Nazem Talis	Forward	SOPH
Todd Nelson	Goalie	SOPH
Micah Kucher	Forward	SR
Jim Woodrow	Defense	SOPH
Jordan Trager	Forward	JR
Rand Hawley	Defense	SR
Hugo Karlsson	Defense	SR
Patrick Armstrong	Forward	SOPH
Mason Hawley	Forward	SOPH

CHAPTER ELEVEN
RYDER

Chad Jensen, drama queen

GIGI TEXTS LATER THAT NIGHT ASKING IF TOMORROW WORKS FOR our first private session. It's weird seeing her name on my phone. Or maybe it's weird seeing it as "Gigi." She's been Gisele in my head for years now. I feel like my phone should probably reflect that, so I pull up her contact info and change the name, chuckling to myself because I know how much this would annoy her if she knew.

ME:

Tomorrow works for me. But we have to clear the ice time with Jensen or Adley to see when we can use the rink.

GISELE:

Actually, I have a more private place for us to practice. You cool going somewhere else? Has to be at night, though. After 8.

ME:

Got it. You need me to be your dirty little secret.

GISELE:

It sounds so shady when you say it like that.

ME:

Doesn't make it any less true.

She's typing again. I'm sure some explanation for why she can't be seen fraternizing with the enemy. I send a follow-up before she can respond.

ME:

Is it cool if Beckett tags along? Have some drills in mind but we need a third, preferably a d-man.

The dots disappear, then return.

GISELE:

Fine. If you think it'll help.

ME:

Don't worry, I'll make sure he keeps our dirty secret to himself. Won't tarnish your good girl reputation.

GISELE:

I'll message you tomorrow to confirm the details.

GISELE:

Delightful chatting with you as always!

I grin, grabbing a beer from the fridge. I twist the cap off and join my friends in the living room. It's Friday night, but nobody made any plans to go out. Shane's on the couch with a dark-haired cheerleader in his lap. He met her on the quad earlier while she and some friends were suntanning topless on the grass. Now her tongue is mining for gold in his mouth. When I enter the room, they don't even notice me.

Beckett sits in the armchair, playing a video game. His eyes twinkle when he notices where mine are focused. He nods toward the couple. "I keep asking to tag in, but…"

I chuckle and settle on the other end of the sectional from the kissing couple, mindlessly watching Beckett shoot zombies on the screen. He loses the level when the horde traps him against a chain-link fence, then sets down the controller and reaches for his phone. He checks the screen.

"Still no lists," he says.

I nod. Training camp wrapped up this morning, but the final roster still hasn't been released. Jensen said there'd be two lists: the full roster, and the nineteen or so starters he plans to dress for our first game.

I'm worried about some of my Eastwood teammates. There'll be guys who won't make the cut, and that's going to be a tough pill for them to swallow.

"I assumed it would be emailed at the end of the day," Beckett says. "Like, regular business hours."

I lift my beer to my lips and take a swig. "Maybe the asshole likes the drama."

Beck snorts. "Right. Chad Jensen, Drama Queen."

A soft moan sounds from the end of the couch. Shane has his hand up the cheerleader's shirt.

"Yo," Beckett tells them. "Take it somewhere else."

Shane pries his lips off hers. His eyes are a bit hazy, but there's an unmistakable gleam of humor. "Says the biggest exhibitionist I know," he taunts at Beck.

"Fine, I'll own that."

"Besides, it's not like you're not enjoying the show."

"Of course I'm enjoying it," Beckett groans. "Kara, what are you doing over there with this asshole? I'm clearly the better man here."

Shane's hookup partner slides off his lap and settles beside him. I notice him do some strategic rearranging, as if we all haven't seen it before. Dude's been making a sport out of hooking up since his girlfriend dumped—sorry, *mutually* dumped his ass.

He throws his arm around Kara's shoulders and reaches for the IPA on the coffee table. "Still no list?" he says, also checking his screen.

My phone dings, and both guys lean forward.

"Is that it?" Shane demands.

"Jesus Christ. Relax. No, it's just Owen."

OWEN MCKAY:

Got time to chat?

I'm about to text back, then think *Fuck it* and decide to give him a call.

"Be right back." I'm already dialing Owen as I duck out of the living room.

I walk barefoot toward the glass sliding doors in the kitchen. It's early September and the sun has already set, but it's still warm outside. The houses on this street have decent-sized backyards, and I sit on the top step of our small cedar deck. Shane's parents bought us a patio set to put out here, but we've been too lazy to assemble everything, so the table is still in its box in the garage, the chairs covered in plastic wrap.

Voices drift toward me from several houses down. Mostly male voices, with a few female ones in the mix. Loud guffaws of laughter intermingle with a pop-rock song whose lyrics I can't make out. Sounds like someone's having a party down there.

"Hey," I say when Owen picks up.

"Hey," his familiar voice slides into my ear. "How you doing?"

"Good, brother. You?"

"Busy as hell lately. I got suckered into a bunch of OTAs and it's been eating up my schedule since July."

Offseason team activities. I know the lingo. And I will say, it is kind of sick that I know an actual superstar in the form of NHL powerhouse Owen McKay. This must be how Gigi feels.

Sometimes I watch his games and wonder what the hell I'm doing wasting time in college. Owen went to play for Los Angeles right out of high school at the age of eighteen. As a rookie he didn't see a lot of ice time, but during his sophomore season, watch out. He's been playing for four years now, each season more explosive than the last.

Owen's the one who talked me into sticking to the college route. He knew how important it was to me to get an education, so when I was vacillating, debating whether I should go pro after high school and follow in his footsteps, he reminded me of the education goals I'd set for myself.

I think it was the right call. I don't know how well I would have done in the pros at eighteen years old, as demonstrated by my childish postgame performance in the Worlds. Luckily, I still got drafted despite that incident. Dallas has the rights to me, and I'm excited to head down there after graduation.

Apparently, Dallas is also the subject of this call.

"So, listen, I spoke to Julio Vega last night. He was at the golf tournament the team was playing in. Pulled me aside after the trophy ceremony and brought up your name."

My back tenses. "What did he say?"

There's a beat.

"What?" I press.

"He mentioned the Worlds. Made a point to say that the higher-ups are watching you."

I wince.

Fuck. I hate hearing that. Julio Vega is Dallas's new general manager. The franchise recently made the change, and I had a call with him a couple of weeks ago. I thought it went well, but now it turns out my behavior at the World Juniors is going to follow me until the end of time.

I let out a breath. "This shit is going to haunt me forever, man. And the worst part is, I never lose my temper. You know that."

"Trust me, I know." He chuckles. "You're like the iceman. Stoic to the core. Klein must have crossed a serious line for you to lose it on him like that…"

Michael Klein is the teammate whose jaw I broke in the Worlds. He had to get it wired shut after what I did to it.

But I haven't told anybody what was said in that locker room, and I don't plan to.

"Yeah, yeah, I know," he says when I don't respond. "It's in the past and therefore forbidden from being discussed."

Owen likes to mock my "It's in the past" motto, the phrase I tend to throw out when someone tries forcing me to talk about shit I don't want to talk about. It particularly annoys women. Or people with sunshine and rainbows in their backgrounds—they're incapable of understanding why I want to keep that door latched and locked.

Behind that door is nothing but darkness and pain. Who wants to trudge through that filth? To ruminate and rehash? Best to always keep the door shut.

"Anyway, I wanted to give you the heads-up," Owen says. "I promised you I'd keep my ears open."

"No, I really appreciate it." I change the subject. "You looking forward to this season?"

"Damn straight. Can't wait to get back out there. How about you? Everything good at Briar?"

"Fuck no. Training camp sucked. Lots of passive-aggressive

bullshit, and other times just plain aggressive, no passive about it."
I pause. "Garrett Graham showed up to our practice this week. Of
course it happened to be the one time I was late."

"Late?" Owen sounds surprised. "That's not like you."

"The Jeep's dead. Transmission gave out on me. It's sitting at a
garage in Hastings now because I've got no money to fix it, so I've
got Shane chauffeuring me."

"I'll transfer you some cash."

"No—" I start to object.

"Bro, I showed you my contract. I can afford it. Besides, I'm
investing in future talent here. I can't have my protégé not making it
to practice on time."

There's no use arguing. Owen's more stubborn than I am. "You
really don't have to. But thank you, I appreciate that. I'll pay you
back."

"I don't want you to."

The door slides open behind me.

"Dude," Shane orders. "Inside. Now."

"I gotta go," I tell Owen. "Something's brewing."

"All right, keep in touch."

"Yeah. Later."

I go inside and realize that sometime when I was on the phone,
the email from Jensen landed in our inboxes.

In the living room, I find several new arrivals in the form of
fellow forward Nick Lattimore, his girlfriend, Darby, and the
Hawley brothers. I used to think Rand was the one who dragged his
younger brother around everywhere, until I realized Mason mostly
tags along to keep his older brother in check.

The triumph in Rand's eyes tells me it's good news.

Shane starts rattling off names, and relief hits me when I hear
both my best friends made the list. Well, of fucking course they did.
Jensen would be an idiot to sideline a solid defenseman like Beckett
or a right winger with as much power as Shane. Rand, Mason, and

Nick all made it too. And Colson and I have been named official captains, no longer interim.

"Dude, we won," Rand tells me.

I frown at him. "What do you mean *won*?"

"The starters list. Eleven of us. Nine of them."

Shane continues to skim the list, head down. "I mean, in terms of starters, yeah. But the final tally is about sixty percent existing Briar players, forty percent Eastwood."

"Dude, who cares who's riding the pine?" Rand counters. "Eastwood dominates the ice. That's all that matters. Right, Ryder?"

I shrug, distracted. I'm studying the list on my own phone now. Jensen made the right calls here. Solid choices, all around. And the fact that we do outnumber the starters shows he wasn't picking favorites.

"I guarantee *someone* cares about riding the pine." Shane's hookup partner, Kara, joins the conversation, her expression wry. "They're probably super pissed right now. And talk about terrible timing—the list shows up right in the middle of Miller's goodbye party? Brutal."

"Miller?" Rand echoes blankly.

"Miller Shulick. He's transferring?" She gives us an amused look. "You know they live like five houses down, right?"

"You're fucking kidding me. You guys are neighbors?" Rand looks like he discovered there is a herpes outbreak on our street.

"I had no idea," Shane says.

"Case, Miller, and Jordan live in the corner house at the end of this street," Kara reveals. "Well, Miller not for much longer. He's moving out on Sunday."

"How do you know all this?" Rand demands.

"I used to date Jordan."

"Trager?" He's flabbergasted.

She nods.

"That asshat? What's wrong with you?"

She glares at Rand. "Wow. Dick much?"

He ignores that.

But she's not wrong. Dude's a raging dickhead.

Case in point: "I think we should go over there," Rand says gleefully.

"Come on, man," Nick speaks up, looking annoyed. "We're not going to their house to gloat."

"Yeah, that's mean," agrees his girlfriend.

I'm surprised when Beckett takes a different position. "Maybe it's not a terrible idea."

"Seriously?" Shane gapes at him. "You want to gloat?"

"No, obviously not that part." Beckett rolls his eyes. "I just mean, maybe it won't hurt to make a peace offering. Bring them a case of beer or something. Wish Miller goodbye. It is kind of shitty he's transferring."

"You just want to party," Shane accuses.

Our buddy grins. "I mean, that too." He looks at Kara. "Everyone swears Briar's party scene is fire, but I haven't seen it yet."

"Classes haven't even started," she protests. "Greek Row is basically a ghost town right now. Trust me, once everyone's back on campus, you'll see."

"Well, until then, I vote we walk down the street and extend the olive branch in the form of booze and weed," Beckett says.

Everyone looks toward me. I don't know how I feel about this unsolicited crown that's been placed on my head.

"I'm not making decisions for you assholes," I say irritably, and Darby laughs in delight. "Do whatever you want to do."

Rand is already texting our other teammates. "I'll get the rest of the guys over," he says.

Right.

Because this sounds like a stellar idea.

CHAPTER TWELVE
GIGI

Sweetie. You're Briar hockey.

"I'M GONNA MISS YOU, G." MILLER SHULICK THROWS HIS ARM around me and rests his head in the crook of my neck.

We're in the living room of the townhouse, carving out our own little spot on the couch while the party rages all around us. Well, it's not quite a rager yet—Trager still has his shirt on. Once that comes off (which is often accompanied by him bellowing and beating his chest like Tarzan), it usually means it's time to go.

Maybe tonight will end up being more low-key, though. The party is already suffering the strains of Chad Jensen's email. For the past forty minutes, most of the guys have been bitching about the final roster. At least ten dudes here didn't make the cut, and a few of them were so bummed they didn't bother sticking around. They hugged Miller goodbye and glumly left the party. I feel for them.

Across the room, I spot Case standing with Whitney. He holds a plastic cup full of watered-down keg beer, sipping from it as Whitney chats with him about something. Every few seconds, his light-blue eyes flit in my direction.

"Aw, I'm gonna miss you too, Shu. Are you sure about this Minnesota thing?" I speak in his ear so he can hear me over the loud rock song blasting from the speakers.

"They won the Frozen Four last year. Of course I'm sure." He shrugs ruefully. "Besides, change is good. I'm looking forward to the fresh start."

I've always appreciated that about Miller. How adaptable he is. I don't love change, personally. I prefer stability. Once I feel comfortable with something—a place, a person, a routine—I want it to last forever.

I hate that it never does.

"G, come have a drink with us," Case calls.

Miller tugs me to my feet. "Come on. I need a refill and you need a fill." He gestures to his empty cup, then my empty hands.

I grin.

We dodge four of his teammates who stumble into the room reeking of pot. The party is half indoors, half out. When we were outside earlier, the number of joints being passed around was astounding. But I guess the guys are allowed to let loose this weekend, considering the week Jensen put them through.

Case abruptly swivels from the doorway as we approach, and at first, I think he's purposely turning his back to me. Then I become aware of a commotion at the front door. Trager is arguing with someone.

Miller and I exchange a look. "That doesn't sound good," he says.

I trail him to the hall and...nope, not good. A bunch of hockey players crowd the porch. Eastwood players, to be precise. Beckett Dunne, the blond hottie whose social media Camila has been drooling over since she saw him at practice, holds a twenty-four case of locally brewed lager.

Someone turns down the music, and now I can clearly hear every word being exchanged.

"Seriously, we come in peace." Beckett's gray eyes convey sincerity.

"Well, take your peace and get the fuck out of here," Trager snaps.

"Relax," Case interjects, placing a firm hand on Trager's arm. He steps forward to address the newcomers. "Hey," he says warily. "What's up?"

I peer past Beckett's big shoulders to get a better look at who else decided to brazenly crash this party. I don't know why, but my gaze seeks out only Ryder. I suppose because he's their leader, and I want to know where he stands on all this. I glimpse him at the edge of the porch, leaning against the railing, looking bored. Seems about right.

"Like we told your boy, we're here to extend the olive branch," Beckett tells Case.

"And like I said," growls Trager, "fuck off."

Shane Lindley steps forward, annoyance in his eyes. I've been doing my research too this week, and I'm starting to recognize individual Eastwood guys. Lindley is tall, dark, and handsome, where Dunne is tall, fair, and equally handsome.

"Look, we know you guys saw the list. We're just here because going forward, we need to be one team, you know? I'm not sure how you do it here at Briar, but at Eastwood, we won as a team, we lost as the team, and we partied as a team."

"Same here," Case answers, albeit grudgingly.

"C'mon, C," Trager says darkly. "We're not partying with these guys." He glares at the interlopers. "You fucking outnumber us in starters."

"You outnumber us in total," one of the Eastwood guys snaps back.

It's the same guy Jordan fought the first day of camp. I think his name is Rand, and I get the feeling he's the Eastwood version of Jordan. Same rude scowl. Same crimson cheeks tinged with rage. Like Trager, he's a live wire, liable to explode at any time.

"That doesn't count," Trager mutters. "You stole our goddamn slots."

"You know what?" Lindley sounds bored now. "Forget this shit. Enjoy the rest of your evening, ladies."

"No, wait," Case tells them. "Just come in. There's plenty of booze to go around."

I try to mask my surprise. I half expected Case to send them away, if only to avoid the potential disaster. Inviting these Eastwood guys to the party is…dangerous.

But it's happening, and Whitney glances at me in delight as eight or so new hockey players trudge into the house.

"This should be fun," she murmurs.

Ryder takes up the rear of the group. Clad in jeans and a gray hoodie. Completely expressionless, even as his blue eyes conduct a sweep of his surroundings. I can tell he's entirely aware of everything going on around him. Not quite a live wire like his teammate, but always on the ready.

"Gisele," he drawls, nodding.

Case narrows his eyes. "Don't push it," he warns Ryder.

Ryder merely smirks and saunters past him toward the kitchen.

I give Case a wary look. "Sure this is a good idea?"

"Guess we're about to find out."

It doesn't stop with the eight new bodies. More Eastwood guys trickle in, along with a bunch of my teammates. Camila arrives in a bodycon red dress on the arm of some guy from the basketball team, only to pout when she realizes Beckett Dunne is here and she can't flirt with him in front of her date.

I text Diana and Mya to see if they want to come. Mya has other plans. Diana passes because she's watching *Fling or Forever* and apparently just applied a charcoal and smashed pea mask as part of a new beauty routine. I choose not to comment on the charcoal-and-peas part. I think one of my favorite things about Diana is how much she loves her own company. That's rare these days.

I sip on a watery beer and chat with Miller and Whitney, all the while on guard. I don't trust this. These boys have been battling it out for roster slots all week. The lingering antagonism hangs in the air like the radiation cloud after a nuclear bomb. Even as they drink, dance, and pass joints around, there's still a distinct separation between the two factions.

For at least two hours, the waters remain calm. When it gets too stuffy inside, I go outside for some air. Although they have no permit for it, someone's gotten the fire going at the very edge of the backyard. The firepit is much too close to the fence. If my mother saw this, she'd have a heart attack.

When the wind changes direction, I'm suddenly hit with a face full of smoke that makes my eyes water. I edge backward until my shoulders hit a hard wall.

I turn in surprise and realize it's Ryder's chest.

Jesus Christ. This guy is pure muscle.

"Sorry," I say.

"All good." He gestures to the guy beside him. "You know Shane, right?"

"Not officially." I stick out my hand. "I'm Gigi."

Shane's handshake lingers, as does his seductive gaze. "Short for Gisele, right?"

I snatch my hand back and glower at Ryder. "Actually, no. Not at all. Prom king over here is just an ass."

Shane starts to laugh. "Aw, look at that," he says to his friend. "You two have your own inside jokes. How adorable."

Ryder glares at him.

"Lindley!" someone shouts from the firepit. "Need your lighter."

"And that's my cue," he says cheerfully. He winks at me. "Nice seeing you, Gisele."

"Look what you've started," I accuse Ryder.

"I refuse to believe your name isn't short for something," is his response.

"It's really not. Blame my father. He's the one who named me. Mom was in charge of my brother's name, and she picked a normal one."

For a moment, Ryder contemplates the orange-red embers

dancing in the air. Then he glances over. "You looking forward to our secret session tomorrow?"

"Why do you have to make it sound so dirty?"

He tips his head. "I'm not doing that at all. I think this might be a you problem."

God. Maybe he's right. I went full carpet and now I have sex on the brain twenty-four/seven. I got myself off twice last night after watching one of the couples on *Fling or Forever* bang in the Sugar Suite. Stupid reality show with all those stupid oiled-up hotties.

I don't know what compels me to remain beside him. I could walk away. Go join Case and Miller, whose heads I see in the kitchen window. Or find Whitney and Cami, who've been swallowed up into the bowels of the party.

But I stay outside. Staring at the fire with Ryder.

"That thing's a fucking hazard," he remarks, eyeing the pit. "One gust of wind and that fence goes up in flames."

"You sound like my mom. She's been watching this firefighter show on TV, and now all she talks about is fire safety. Dad thinks it's 'cute.'" I use air quotes. "My brother and I think she might be going insane. She bought a roll-down rope ladder for our top floor 'just in case.' And it comes with this pet basket you can use to lower your dogs down. And I was like, dude, no way Dumpy and Bergeron are willingly getting into that fucking thing. You're better off trying to fling them out the window into the pool."

Ryder stares at me.

"What?"

"Your dogs are named Dumpy and Bergeron?"

"Yes. Got a problem with that?"

"Sort of."

I roll my eyes. "Take it up with my father. We've already established he's a bad namer."

"About that... How's my endorsement going?"

"Haven't spoken to him today. But don't worry, I'll be showering you with praise next time we talk."

A burst of laughter sounds from the firepit. I glance over, astounded to discover someone was brave enough to cross the Eastwood-Briar divide. It's none other than Will, who's now chilling with Shane, Beckett, and two others whose names I don't know. He chortles at something Shane said, but the good humor dies fast. Will is midchuckle when one of his friends forcibly drags him away from the Eastwood players.

Ryder notices the same thing, rumbling under his breath.

"So how is this ever going to work, cocaptain?" I can't help but taunt. "Because it seems like you've got a serious stalemate happening. No one's budging."

"You're budging," he points out.

"I'm not part of this."

"Sure, you are. You're Briar hockey."

"Sweetie. *You're* Briar hockey."

He cringes.

I laugh in sheer delight. "Aw, you just hate to hear that, don't you? I kind of like knowing how much it pains you to be here. Why didn't you transfer?" I ask curiously.

Before he can answer, loud shouts spill out from the open back doors of the house.

Yeah.

That was bound to happen. Surprised it took this long.

I hurry inside to find a full-blown fistfight has broken out in the living room between—who else?—Trager and that guy Rand. They're going at it hard, and once again nobody does a goddamn thing to stop them.

"You still think it's funny?" Trager spits out as he slams his knuckles into Rand's cheek.

Rand's head rears back, but he barely misses a step. He lunges at Trager, and the two men go tumbling onto the hardwood floor. I hear a sickening crunch of bone on bone when Rand lands a blow that triggers an eruption of blood from Trager's nostrils. Cheers break out all around us, drowning out the music that's still blaring in the room.

"What are they fighting about?" I hiss at Camila, who appears beside me, her face creased with concern.

"The Eastwood guy made some joke about Miller transferring because he's too much of a pussy to stick around to see if he'd make the roster, and Jordan just lost it."

On the floor, Trager now straddles Rand, peering down at him with a bloody smile. His eyes are bright and feral.

"You wanna talk about the roster? Eastwood is shit. Jensen only put you on the roster because he fucking feels bad that your school went under."

"We're better than all of you combined," Rand sneers half a second before Jordan's fist smashes into his mouth.

I push my way forward and seek out Case. "Come on, Case. Stop this," I urge.

"I don't know," he says grimly. "Maybe they need to get it out of their systems."

But I can tell it's more than that. These guys are going to beat each other to death if they're not stopped. And I'm not nearly as entertained by this fight as some of the other partygoers, many of whom are shouting and egging it on, several actually filming it.

"Fucking prick," Rand roars, managing to roll himself out from Jordan's grip and get up. "Y'all are a bunch of entitled Ivy League assholes."

"Not my fault you're goddamn poor," Jordan grunts out, lurching to his feet.

"Fuck you." Rand launches himself at Trager again.

Abandoning Case, I grab Ryder's arm instead. He's so tall I have to tip my head back to meet his eyes. Dark blue and deadly.

"Stop this?" I say softly.

Case realizes who I'm talking to and his expression flashes with disapproval. But he had his chance to put an end to this. He said no.

Ryder looks at me for a moment. Then he lets out a breath and takes a step forward. Completely unfazed when a fist flies past his cheekbone.

"*Enough.*"

One word. Deep. Commanding.

It succeeds in stopping Rand cold. Ryder shoves his teammate's chest. "Get your shit together, Hawley."

Rand is breathing hard. Blood drips from his split eyebrow in a sticky line down one side of his face. I wince. Trager doesn't look much better. His nose is swollen, bloody, and likely broken.

But while Rand has been reined in thanks to Ryder, Trager remains a loose cannon. He shoots forward again, and now one of his teammates, Tim Coffey, decides he's going to be the hero.

"Dude, *stop*," Coffey orders, grabbing Trager's arm.

But Trager is still a wild beast. He pushes Coffey off him.

Hard enough that Coffey loses his balance and crashes into the coffee table, which collapses under his weight and breaks apart like a house of cards. Wood splinters fly in all directions, table legs creaking and snapping, and then a cry of pain as Coffey lands awkwardly on the floor.

Directly on his wrist.

CHAPTER THIRTEEN
GIGI

Date night

I WAKE UP THE NEXT MORNING TO A STRONGLY WORDED EMAIL from the head of the athletics department.

In two terse lines, it states that my presence, along with every single member of the hockey program, is required at the Graham Center at 1:00 p.m. sharp. Any player who doesn't show up better have a doctor's note or be dead. I assume Chad Jensen added that last part himself because it's very Jensen-esque.

Thanks to donations from former students like my father, the Briar Hockey complex is basically its own little kingdom on campus. We have our own gym and training center full of PT and weight rooms, saunas, hot and cold tubs. Two huge media rooms, two rinks, enormous locker rooms.

And a large auditorium where today's emergency meeting is being held to discuss the events of last night.

The entire coaching staff of both the men's and women's programs stand on the stage, while their respective players fill the first three rows of cushy seats. Near the podium is a tall willowy woman in a white pantsuit. Her entire vibe screams public relations.

Coach Jensen looks like he wants to murder everyone in the

room, including his own colleagues. He approaches the microphone at the podium and gets things going in a brisk, irritated voice.

"I would like to congratulate each and every one of you for ruining my Saturday plans with my granddaughter. She's ten years old and recently developed an affinity for tiger sharks, and she cried when I told her I couldn't take her to the aquarium today. Everyone, give yourselves a round of applause for making a ten-year-old girl cry."

Beside me, Cami smothers her laughter with the sleeve of her hoodie.

"In other news," he announces. "Tim Coffey's out for at least four weeks with a sprained wrist. He'll miss the entire preseason and likely several games."

Jensen punctuates this with a glare at our team doctor, as if he's the one who sprained Coffey's wrist. To his credit, Dr. Parminder doesn't even flinch. Tim Coffey does, however. In the front row, the freckle-faced senior hangs his head in shame. I heard he spent half the night in the emergency room getting X-rays.

"I won't bother telling you how stupid and irresponsible you all were last night. I get it, I was young once. I enjoyed a good party in my days. I won't lecture you about the drinking—underage drinking for many of you." He shoots a pointed look at the lowerclassmen. "I won't even go too hard on the fighting. But to the bonehead who decided to film the fight and post it online?"

He does a slow clap, which triggers another wave of silent giggles from Camila.

"Congratulations, bonehead—you've scared the boosters." Shaking his head in disgust, Jensen stalks away from the podium.

My own coach takes his place. Adley clears his throat and addresses the auditorium.

"What Chad is trying to say is, we're dealing with some very concerned boosters and alumni at the moment. Donors," he says meaningfully. "In case you need reminding, donations are what pay for this state-of-the-art facility. They're what keep your locker rooms stocked with top-of-the-line equipment. They're what gets you several televised games a year—you see any other D1 programs receiving that perk? This school offers the most elite program on the East Coast, but that doesn't just happen by chance. We might attract the talent, but we need the money to develop it. And now, thanks to last night's events, we've got boosters calling and emailing to ask why our program is in shambles. Why our own players are breaking each other's wrists and how will that help us make it to the playoffs, let alone win any championships."

My fearless, smart-ass captain thrusts her hand in the air.

Coach Adley notices and nods in her direction. "Yes, Whitney?"

"I want it on the record that the women's team had nothing to do with yesterday's fight, and we did not bring shame upon this house."

A few titters echo in the cavernous room.

"Noted," Adley says. "However, that doesn't change the fact that we're in damage control mode. And this requires a concentrated effort on the part of both our programs."

Adley nods toward the white-pantsuit lady, who takes over.

"Good afternoon. My name is Christie Delmont, and I'm the executive vice president of marketing and public relations for Briar University."

Why do job titles sound so made up these days?

For the next ten minutes, Delmont lays down the law and lists all the sins we're no longer allowed to commit. No fighting or visible hostility in public. No filming anything if hostility does arise. We're not to conduct any interviews or release any statements without prior approval from her or the athletic department, but she has arranged for a glowing profile of the new Briar/Eastwood team that will run in all the Boston newspapers.

"You will shower praise on your teammates," she tells the men, her tone brooking no argument. "I expect to see the most flattering, effusive ass-kissing in your individual interviews. Not even a whiff of animosity. From this point forward, you all love and adore each other."

She flips to the next page of the small stack she's set on the dais. "Pacifying the boosters is our main objective right now. They've sent me a list of upcoming fundraising and publicity events. I'll be enlisting many of you to participate, and in the case of the Briar alumni benefit in December, you'll be responsible for organizing several elements, including the silent auction."

She glances at her papers again, then lifts her head and searches the crowd.

"Gigi Graham and Luke Ryder?" she calls in question. "Can you raise your hands so I can see you?"

Uneasiness washes over me. At first I consider slouching in my seat and hiding, but Cami pokes me in the side, forcing me to raise my hand. In the row ahead of us, Ryder does the same. His reluctant body language reflects mine.

"If either of you have plans tonight, cancel them," Christie Delmont says sternly. "There's a charity gala in Boston organized by Leesa Wickler, whose family is one of our largest donors. You two will attend as representatives of Briar University and your respective hockey programs."

"Date night," I hear one of the dudes chortle.

I'm sorry, what? They can't just force me to start attending galas against my will, can they?

And why are they sending Ryder, of all people? I can easily guess why they want me. As Ryder enjoys pointing out, my last name is Graham. That carries a lot of weight.

But why the hell are they recruiting the most antisocial asshole I know to represent Briar at an event that requires smiling and shaking hands?

I wait until we're dismissed before pulling Coach Adley aside to get some answers. I observe Ryder doing the same with Jensen.

From his unhappy expression, it looks like Jensen isn't giving him any.

Adley admits he doesn't know why Ryder was picked but confirms the reason for my selection.

"I know you hate this kind of stuff, but the boosters love your dad," he says, sounding apologetic. "I'm sorry. I know you would've preferred to be left out of this."

"All good," I lie. "Happy to do my part."

But I'm battling a mix of resentment and irritation as I leave the auditorium.

"G, you okay?"

I find Case in the hall, concern etched into his handsome face. He's in sweatpants and a Briar hoodie, his blond hair rumpled as if he was running his hand through it while waiting for me.

"Yeah, I'm good."

"This Ryder thing is BS. Want me to talk to Jensen and see if he'll send me instead?"

"No. It's fine. Really," I add when I note his skepticism. "I don't want to make any waves."

We fall into step together, heading down the hall toward the lobby.

"I don't want you hanging around that guy," Case grumbles.

Then I probably shouldn't mention I was planning on seeing Ryder tonight regardless. We had plans to practice, before Jordan Trager decided it was more important to break poor Tim's wrist. Now we'll have to reschedule, thanks to stupid Trager.

"I'll be fine," I assure him.

And you're not my boyfriend anymore, I want to add. He doesn't get a say any longer about who I spend time with.

We reach the lobby, where I bid him goodbye because my teammates are waiting for me by the doors.

"Gigi," Case says before I can walk away. "Put me out of misery. Please."

Unhappiness lodges in my throat. "I…can't. We're not together anymore, Case. I don't want to be."

He looks so frustrated and upset that it triggers a rush of guilt, but I force myself to ignore it and keep walking.

Later that night, I drive to Hastings to pick up Ryder for the booster gala. The email from the Briar PR lady stated the dress code as semiformal to black tie.

A.k.a. the kind of fashion extremes that give me anxiety.

Does that mean some women will be wearing dress pants and a nice blouse while others are in sequined cocktail gowns?

What kind of gala is this?

I split the difference when dressing and picked a little black dress to wear tonight. Hair down, minimal makeup save for a bold pop of red lipstick. I even made an effort to get a French tip manicure after the meeting today, which is essentially flushing money down the toilet because my fingers will only be banged up again when practice officially starts next week.

I climb the porch steps on my high heels and ring the doorbell, wondering what a one-hour drive to Boston with Ryder in my passenger seat will be like. The man barely speaks. And while I'm usually okay with comfortable silences among friends and family, I get antsy with awkward ones. I might have to throw on one of my meditation playlists. Try to zone him out.

The door swings open and a familiar face greets me, a pair of playful eyes. Shane smiles at the sight of me, then groans when he notices what I'm wearing.

"Oh, that's nice. Can I be your date tonight instead?"

"Call it a date again and I'll punch you in the nuts," I say sweetly.

"Don't threaten me with a good time." He flashes a cheeky grin and I'm momentarily distracted. Those dimples are dangerous.

He opens the door wider for me. "Come in. I need you to settle something for us."

"Settle what? And for whom?" I gaze past his broad shoulders, but he seems to be alone.

He takes my hand and tugs me inside. Amused, I follow him into the living room, which, of course, looks like a typical man cave. Huge sectional, two leather armchairs, a massive TV, and a lot of beer bottles on the coffee table. Despite the cluttered table, the room is neat and tidy, so they're not complete heathens, I guess.

Beckett Dunne, sprawled on the chaise part of the couch, greets me with his own set of killer dimples. "Graham," he says as if we're old friends.

"Where's Ryder?" I ask.

"He'll be down in a minute," answers Shane. "You gotta settle this first."

"Fine. I'll play along. What am I settling?"

Shane slides his hands in the rear pockets of his jeans and rocks back on his heels. "Which pickup line you would respond better to."

"You're practicing pickup lines? Classy."

"We're not practicing. We're trying to determine which one of us is right. Spoiler alert: it's me."

"I kind of have a feeling you're both wrong," I say helpfully.

"Nah," Beckett drawls.

Those dimples again. God help the women on the receiving end of these pickup lines. I have to admit, even I'm not immune. I find them both attractive. If I was in the market for another hockey player boyfriend, either of them would do. Lookswise, anyway. Personalities are yet to be determined.

"I'm saying you go charming," Shane explains. "Be a little witty."

"You think your line is witty?" Beckett hoots.

Shane ignores him. "It's fucking witty," he assures me.

I turn to Beckett. "And you?"

"I think you take the direct approach. We—the chick and

I—we both know what the other one wants. Your line needs to reflect that."

I can't deny I am intrigued. "All right, let's hear them."

Shane grabs a full bottle of beer from the table and holds it out to me.

"Oh, I'm not drinking. I'm driving."

"You don't have to drink it. Just hold it. Get in character."

I laugh as he shoves the bottle in my hand and ushers me to the center of the room, where he proceeds to set the scene like the director of a community theater production.

"Okay, you're at the club, right? There's, like, a sick R&B song playing or whatever. You're vibing."

I start bopping my head to nonexistent music.

He stares at me in dismay. "Oh no. I'm not approaching you if that's how you're dancing."

I stare back. "Do you want me to play your game, or can I go find Ryder and be on my way—"

"Fine, let's continue. You ready?"

"I guess so?"

I don't know what it is about hockey players, but I find that all of them are insane. Sexy but insane.

Shane moves to the doorway, cracks his knuckles, and then fully commits to his character by striding toward me exuding sheer confidence. He casts that smile again. Tucks one hand in his pocket, all cool-like.

"Hey," he says.

"Hey," I play along.

"I'm Shane."

"Gigi."

"Tell me something, Gigi." He slants his head. "Are you an organ harvester? Because you've stolen my heart."

Dead silence crashes over the room.

Then I keel over with laughter.

Due to my hysterics, I nearly drop the beer bottle on the carpet. Beckett plucks it from my hand before it tips over.

Chuckling, he glances at his friend. "See?"

"Yes, see? She's laughing. I'm in." Shane narrows his eyes at me. "Right?"

"Well…"

"Come on, Gisele. You know that got you."

"I mean. I don't know what it did to me, but…" I take a breath, tamping down another wave of giggles. "What's yours?" I ask Beckett.

He hands me the bottle back. "Do the weird head-bopping thing again."

I oblige.

Beckett comes at me with an equally confident gait. Fuck, these guys are sure of themselves.

"Hi," he says.

"Hi."

He bites the corner of his lip. "I kind of want to fuck you. Do you want to fuck me?"

My jaw hits the floor.

I close it, then open it.

Finally, I find my voice. "I…think I might be impressed."

He smiles seductively. "Do you want to get out of here?"

"Yes," I answer, a bit winded. "I think I do."

"Oh, fuck this," Shane complains. "No way in a million years would you react that way."

I mull it over. "I might if I wanted to sleep with him."

"Mine made you laugh."

"It did," I relent, "but if we're both there for sex"—I nod toward Beckett—"I think he's my man."

He beams at me. "I knew I liked you, Graham."

"Am I interrupting?"

I suddenly notice Ryder in the doorway.

My breath hitches, because…wow. He cleans up nice. He's

wearing black trousers and a gray suit jacket over a black dress shirt. No tie, top button undone. His face is clean shaven, but his dark hair still has that tousled bad-boy look to it.

I try to ignore how good he looks. "Your friends are trying to get me into bed," I explain.

He shrugs. "Pick Shane. He just got dumped and needs the pity fuck."

Shane flips up his middle finger. To me, he says, "I didn't get dumped. Like I keep telling these assholes, it was a mutual breakup."

"Oh, sweetie. There's no such thing as a mutual breakup," I say frankly. "Ever."

Beckett snorts out a laugh. "See, mate? She gets it."

"You ready to go?" Ryder asks me.

"Yeah, let's do it."

As I walk toward him, I don't miss the way his sapphire-blue eyes drag slowly along the length of my body.

"What?" I say, self-conscious.

He shifts his gaze away. "Nothing. C'mon. Let's go."

CHAPTER FOURTEEN
GIGI

Primed

Ryder and I exit the house in silence. I check him out again, wanting to tell him he looks good, but he hasn't complimented my appearance, so I say nothing.

"This is me," I say, pointing to the white SUV parked at the curb.

I get in the driver's seat. He gets in the passenger side. We buckle up. His silence drags on as I start the engine.

Finally, I glance over at him. "Look, I know you're going to talk a mile a minute during the car ride, so I implore you, give my ears a bit of a rest sometimes, all right?"

He snorts.

"All right, Luke, off we go."

"Don't call me that," he mutters.

"Isn't it your name?" I roll my eyes.

"Never liked it, so I go by Ryder."

I think the name Luke is kind of hot, but the hardness of his eyes tells me this isn't a subject to tease him about. So I just shrug and put the car in drive.

"Did Jensen say why he picked you for this terrible gig?" I ask curiously.

"He didn't pick me. The PR lady did." He continues with a trace of sarcasm. "She thinks *number one draft pick* looks good on the resume when chatting up potential donors."

"Does she understand you're physically incapable of the chatting part?" I inquire politely. "Because you'd think someone would've warned her."

"You'd think."

Then, as if to prove my point, he doesn't utter another word, while I do everything in my power to change that.

I try discussing the roster Jensen picked. I complain about how we're stuck going to this thing. I tell him about my upcoming class schedule. Meanwhile, he communicates in grunts, sighs, and shrugs, and a short list of facial expressions ranging in emotion. One look conveys sheer boredom—that's his go-to. The other is...not quite disdain, but sort of confusion-tinged disbelief, like, *Are you still talking to me?*

Eventually I give up. I scroll through my playlists and pick a track. Within seconds, a familiar, soothing voice washes over me.

"*The call of the Canadian wilderness came to me when I was a young man, barely old enough to drink and yet plenty old to traverse a robust and often brutal landscape in hopes of self-discovery.*"

Ryder's head shifts toward the driver's seat. I see it from the corner of my eye.

"*An aural experience as diverse as it was evocative, I lost myself in the rush of a creek, the heavy crunch of a moose paw against a tangle of undergrowth, the sweet song of the golden-crowned kinglet in the distance. It was enough to rob me of breath. And now...let me take you there.*"

The track begins, a flap of wings (I assume belonging to the golden-crowned kinglet) fluttering out of the speakers. Soon, the symphony of the wilderness fills the car.

We're about ten minutes in before Ryder speaks.

"What the fuck is this?"

"*Horizons with Dan Grebbs,*" I tell him.

He stares at me. "You say that as if I'm supposed to know what or who that is."

"Oh, Dan Grebbs is amazing. He's a nature photographer from South Dakota who ran away from home at sixteen. He rode the railroads for a while, traveling the country and playing the guitar, taking pictures. Then one day he impulsively traded in his guitar for a field recorder and bought passage on a ship heading for South America. He caught the travel bug and has been all over the world ever since, working on his soundscapes. He's recorded so many different albums. This is his wilderness series."

"Jesus Christ."

"What do you have against the wilderness? Is it too good for you?"

"Yes, the wilderness is too good for me. That's exactly what I was thinking."

I fight a smile and lower the volume. "I use these tracks for meditation. A way to quiet my head when it all gets too loud. Life," I clarify, even though he hadn't asked what I meant. "You must know what I'm talking about. The hockey world can be so loud. Sometimes you just need to quiet it. Try to ease some of that pressure, you know?"

He looks over again, so I treat it as permission to continue.

"There's so much pressure, all the time." I swallow. "And the worst part is, I know I place most of it on myself. It's…this need to be the best. All the fucking time. Hey, how much do you charge per hour for your therapy services, by the way? And thank you for not asking me how it makes me feel. I went to this therapist once and that's literally all she asked the entire time. *How does it make you feel? And how does* this *make you feel? What about that, how did* that *make you feel?*"

"Do you ever stop talking?" Ryder asks me.

"Do you ever start talking?" I ask him.

He sighs.

"Dan Grebbs it is."

I turn up the volume, and that's all we listen to for the remaining forty-minute drive into the city. The lilting calls of loons and mournful wolf cries transform the car into something bigger than the both of us.

As I follow the GPS directions, I realize we're going to be driving within two miles of my own house in Brookline. The suburb, which is surrounded by Boston on three sides, is probably the most affluent neighborhood in Massachusetts. At the very top of the list, at least.

I'm almost embarrassed to admit it when I say, "I grew up three blocks from here."

The twinkling lights of the country club come into view. This club is one of the oldest in the state. Sprawling hills and twenty-seven award-winning holes make up the lush grounds. The golf course looks gorgeous in the darkness, with the historical clubhouse all lit up among the backdrop of a vast inky sky.

"Let me guess, your family has a membership to this place," Ryder mutters.

"No, but they tried hard to court us when I was about fourteen," I answer with a rueful smile. "Mom was, like, *Let's give it a shot. Who knows, we might love it.* So we spent an entire afternoon trying it out. Dad hates golf and tennis, so he played squash and discovered he hated that more than those other two combined. He stole the racket and took it home and burned it in our fireplace. Mom was annoyed when they told her the dress code for women was only white or pastels. And it was the furthest thing from mine and Wyatt's scene. We did some skeet shooting, and Wyatt got pissed because I outshot him, so he stomped off and tried to score weed from one of the kitchen workers." I chuckle to myself. "That's the day we discovered we're not a country club family."

I pull into the majestic circular drive and stop behind a BMW in the valet line. At the valet station, I hand my keys to the young man in the white polo shirt and khakis. He opens the door for me, and I realize too late that I didn't bring any cash to tip the valets. Ryder has us covered, though, slipping the kid a ten-dollar bill.

I raise my eyebrows at him. "Big spender," I murmur when the car disappears.

He shrugs. "These poor guys basically survive on tips. Least I could do."

We walk through the arched entryway toward the ornate front doors.

Ryder tugs on his collar, ill at ease. "What now?"

"Now we mingle."

"Kill me," he begs.

"How do you feel about murder-suicide? I could easily kill you, but I don't think I can kill myself, so you'll need to murder me and then take care of yourself. Is that something you're comfortable doing?"

He looks at me. "Forget I said anything."

We enter the fancy lobby, side by side but with two feet of distance between us. It smells like money in here. Looks like it too, thanks to the mahogany-paneled walls and white marble floors. We provide our names at the table tucked away on one end of the lobby, then follow the discreet easel-set signs toward the main ballroom. There, we're surrounded by a sea of people in tuxedos and gowns.

Semiformal, my ass. Clearly everyone went the black-tie route.

Every single woman we pass scopes Ryder out. That's usually the case with tall gorgeous men, but it's also the vibe he gives off. The men here are all slick, wealthy professionals. They're businessmen, lawyers, doctors. Whereas Ryder... There's something primal about him. It's the barely contained power of his body. The way he walks. The intensity in his eyes. The way his expression conveys that he doesn't give a fuck about anyone and couldn't be bothered to be here. That bad-boy energy sucks you in every time. Women are drawn to it. Most men are too.

"Gigi Graham!" A stocky man in a crisp suit and graying hair at his temples appears in our path.

I vaguely recognize him but can't remember his name.

"Jonas Dawson," he says in introduction. "My firm represents your father's foundation."

"Oh, right." I pretend to recall this fact. "Good to see you again, Mr. Dawson."

Five more steps and we're intercepted by another stranger who thinks they're my best friend.

"Gigi, so nice to see you!" a heavyset woman booms, clasping both my hands in hers. "Brenda Yarden, Bruins' head office. We met last year at your father's jersey number retirement event?"

"Of course." I feign recollection of this too. I gesture to Ryder. "This is Luke Ryder. Cocaptain of the Briar men's team."

"Good to meet you." Yarden gives his hand a quick shake before turning back to me. "We're hearing murmurs about the Hall of Fame, and we cannot be more excited. What's your father thinking about it all?"

"I mean, that's up to the selection committee," I remind her. "Not sure Dad has any say about whether he's nominated."

The next ambush involves a trio of male boosters who interrogate us about whether Chad Jensen expects to win the Frozen Four this year. I don't know why they think I can speak for Jensen, nor can I offer many details about the men's team because I don't actually play on it. But Ryder is no help, so I talk out of my ass for about ten minutes before they mercifully move along.

For the next hour, we shuffle around the ballroom like mindless robots, while I pretend to care about the boosters and what they're saying to me. I'm the only one touting the program, so my voice hurts by the time we manage to find a quiet moment for the two of us.

I grab two skinny flutes of champagne from a server in a black uniform with a red bow tie.

Ryder starts, "I don't want one—"

"It's not for you," I grumble.

I chug the first glass in front of the amused waiter and place the empty on his tray. Once he's gone, I sip the second flute.

"Easy, partner," Ryder warns.

"Partner? Is that what this is? A partnership? Because from where I'm standing, I'm the one who's been doing all the Briar hyping. PS you're driving home because I plan to have at least, oh, ten more of these."

"I told Jensen I wasn't good at this shit."

"Yeah, and you're even worse than you made yourself out to be. Would it kill you to smile?" I peer at him over the rim of my glass. "I've seen you do it, so I know your face is capable of arranging the muscles in that way."

He narrows his eyes.

I spot another small group of donors making their way toward us. Pure, single-minded purpose.

"Oh God, no," I moan. "I just need five minutes of peace and quiet."

"C'mere." Ryder grabs my champagne flute and deposits it on the tray of a passing waitress, then takes my hand.

The next thing I know, he's whisking me across the ballroom toward the stage. There's a curtained area on either side of it, blocking off the two sets of steps leading up to the wings. I blink, and suddenly we're tucked behind the curtains. Enveloped in darkness.

"Better?"

His rough voice tickles my ear.

I gulp, my pulse speeding at the realization that Ryder and I are standing in the dark, scant inches apart.

"This wasn't what I had in mind," I murmur over my pounding heart.

"Yeah, well. Best I could do."

I draw a breath, falling silent for a moment. The music in the ballroom is muffled now, not only because of the barrier provided by the curtain, but because my heartbeat continues to thunder against my rib cage. The scent of him surrounds me. Woodsy and spicy, with a note of leather I find odd because he's not wearing leather. It's deliciously masculine. I probably shouldn't enjoy it as much as I do.

"I don't get you," I confess.

"Nothing to get." He shrugs, and the action causes his shoulder to nudge mine.

"Seriously, I can't figure out if this grumpy Mr. Silent thing is an act. Some cool persona you put on."

"Sounds like a lot of effort."

"Exactly, and that's why I'm leaning toward it being genuine. That you really are just this grumpy, dangerous—"

"Dangerous, huh?" he cuts in. A soft rasp.

My eyes are adjusting to the darkness. I note that his are heavy-lidded, slitted as he looks me up and down. One side of his mouth lifts mockingly.

"Do you feel like you're in danger right now, Gigi?"

"Should I?"

"No." He chuckles. Low and smoky.

"Well, then I don't."

Something dangerous is happening, though. A strange thread of awareness traveling between us. Or maybe that's a natural conse-quence of being in the dark with an incredibly hot guy. Ryder eases a bit closer. Still watching me.

"What?" I ask self-consciously.

"You look nice." His voice is gruff.

Surprise flickers through me. "What?"

"I should have said it earlier when you showed up. That was rude of me."

"Since when do you care about being rude?"

"I don't."

A laugh slips out. "Well. Thanks, I guess. You look nice too."

Another beat of silence.

"Do you think we can hide in here forever?" I ask hopefully.

"No. Eventually somebody's gonna pry you out of here so they can rave about how amazing your father is."

"I hate this, you know." I tip my head to look at him. "Whatever you think about me and my last name, I don't use it to get ahead. I never have. Hell, I would legally change it if I knew it wouldn't break my dad's heart. But it would kill him. And, really, it's not his fault he's the greatest hockey player of all time. He deserves all the love and accolades."

"But...you hate this," he prompts.

I bite my bottom lip. "Yes. I hate these events with a passion. I've never enjoyed myself at a single one. Like, I'd literally rather be anywhere else."

"You used to go out with Colson, yeah?"

"Yes...?"

The query comes out of left field, but he's quick to connect it to the topic at hand.

"Did he ever come with you to these things?"

"Sometimes." I shift awkwardly. It feels weird to discuss Case with Luke Ryder.

"And he didn't get creative? Find ways to make these shindigs more fun for you?"

"What do you know about fun?" I can't help but tease.

He offers his trademark shrug.

"No, tell me," I push. "What would you be doing right now if you were Case? How would you make it fun?"

"If I was Colson."

"Yes."

"And you were my girl."

"Yes."

Ryder leans in, his warm breath on my ear, sending a tiny shiver through my body. "We would have been behind this curtain five minutes after we got here."

"Doing what?"

I regret the question the moment I voice it.

"Getting you primed."

My throat closes up with arousal. I struggle to swallow.

"Primed," I echo weakly. "Primed for what?"

"For me."

Oh my God.

His voice deepens. Just a hint of gravel. "I'd use my fingers probably. Yeah. I'd press my fingers inside you. Get you close. But I wouldn't let you come. Just close enough that your entire body hurts, and then I'd force you to go back out there. Watch you squirm while you talk to all those irrelevant people, until finally you're begging me to leave so I can take you home and make you come."

It's the most animated he's sounded since I met him.

I can scarcely breathe. And the lack of oxygen gets worse when his hand finds my cheek. Rough fingertips scrape along my feverish skin.

Ryder dips his head and brings his mouth close to mine. Our lips are a whisper away. My eyelids flutter closed as for one heart-stopping moment I think he's going to kiss me.

"But...I'm not Colson," he finishes, wearing the merest hint of a smile as he straightens up.

To my dismay—and disappointment I don't expect to feel—he inches the curtain aside to check if the coast is clear. Then he slides out and leaves me there feeling the exact way he just threatened to make me feel.

Squirming with need.

CHAPTER FIFTEEN
GIGI

There's always one slutty boy in every crew

RYDER:

We still on for later?

ME:

Yup. Does it still work for you guys?

RYDER:

We're good.

ME:

Thanks again for doing this.

RYDER:

Sure.

ME:

It must kill you that there isn't a decent shrugging emoji. The current one has too much emotion in it for you. It's the hand motions. Far too dramatic to accurately depict your shrugs.

RYDER:

Is it too late to cancel?

ME:

I love your quirky sense of humor! Kills me every time.

Ryder's last message is the middle finger emoji.

Yeah. That one suits him best.

It's taken us a few days to reschedule our session. Classes started on Monday, along with my official hockey practice schedule, so it was difficult to get on the same page and find a time that worked for both of us. And Beckett, I guess. He's tagging along tonight to help with Ryder's drills.

Until then, I still have some errands to run, including one that's more treat than errand: meeting my uncles at Della's Diner.

I grew up with a lot of uncles. Luckily not the creepy kind who say inappropriate things at weddings and hit on all the teenage girls.

"I hear you're single again."

Or maybe they do say inappropriate things.

"That's old news," I inform Dean Di Laurentis. "Did it arrive to you by carrier pigeon?"

"No, smart-ass. I've known for a while. We just haven't had any alone time since it happened."

I reach for my coffee. We're in a corner booth, the tabletop littered with half a dozen slices of pie because my gluttonous uncles couldn't settle on one flavor so they ordered one of each.

Uncle Logan stepped outside to take a phone call from my aunt Grace, one of my three godmothers. I've also got three godfathers, because my parents didn't want to choose between all their best friends but still had to make a decision. Although my family isn't religious, my grandparents on Mom's side insisted on a christening when Wyatt and I were born. The pictures from that day are literally ridiculous. An entire sports team of godparents standing up on that altar holding Wyatt and me as infants in our filmy white gowns.

I will say, I do love that we have a big family. Or found family, anyway. Both my parents are only children, and neither of them had massive clans growing up. An aunt here and an uncle there, hardly any cousins. My dad wasn't even speaking to his own father in the years leading to his death. Dad didn't attend the funeral. So it's really nice being surrounded by aunts, uncles, and cousins. There's always been a lot of love in my life.

Also, a lot of nosy questions.

"Is my dad forcing you to talk about this?" I ask before taking a sip of coffee.

"I mean, he brought it up, but do I look like the kinda guy who gets forced to do anything?"

Dean flashes a smile. He's got those chiseled male model looks that keep getting better with age. I've seen pictures of him from his college days and he was smokin' back then, but I think he looks even better now.

"I was surprised to hear about the breakup. You and Colson seemed like you were made for each other. Both play hockey. Both good-looking."

"Well, right, because that's all it takes to be soulmates. A shared sport and somewhat equal level of attractiveness."

"Got that sarcasm gene from your mother, I see."

"I'll take that as a compliment. But yes, Case and I are broken up, we're not getting back together, and that's all I'm going to say on that subject."

"So then you're playing the field now?"

"I mean, I wouldn't phrase it that way, but sure."

Dean's features crease with resignation. "Damn it. I really didn't want it to come to this."

"What does that mean?" I ask suspiciously.

I'm instantly on the alert. For a bunch of grown men, my dad's friends are capable of shenanigans I never anticipate.

He reaches for the messenger bag beside him on the bench. When I first saw it, I teased him about carrying a man purse. But I guess he keeps his work in it. Dean coaches the women's team at Yale, which I suppose makes him the enemy, but not entirely since they're not in our conference. If we play them in the finals, though, watch out. Uncle or not, I'll happily destroy his girls.

"Here," he says.

I almost spit out my coffee when he places a box of condoms on the table.

No, not just a box.

A very large value pack containing a staggering fifty condoms.

"What the hell is this?" I squawk. "Oh my God."

"I can't have you acting irresponsibly now that you're single. Better safe than sorry, Gigi."

"How much sex do you think I have? Nope, wait—" I hold up my index finger, my tone stern. "Don't you dare answer that."

Dean snorts. "I'm just saying… I remember college. Vividly. All the hormones. The parties. I want you to be safe, all right? And don't tell your parents I gave you these."

"Oh, trust me, I'm never speaking about this again."

"Also," he continues, cutting off a piece of the pecan pie with his fork, "before you get involved with any dude, make sure he's not the slut of the group. And if he is, get him tested. Because there's always one slutty boy in every crew."

I already regret what I'm about to ask, but curiosity wins. "Who was the slut in yours?"

"Tucker," is the instant reply.

I take another sip from my coffee mug, eyeing him over the rim. "Tucker," I echo doubtfully.

"Of course." Dean blinks innocently. "Dude knocked up a woman on a one-night stand. Can't get more promiscuous than that."

"The way he describes it, it was love at first sight with Aunt Sabrina."

"Tucker says a lot of things. Especially regarding me and my supposed ladies' man reputation." Dean winks. "Don't believe a word of it."

John Logan chooses that moment to return to the booth. He stares at the monster box of condoms. Then he glances at Dean and sighs.

"Yeah, I'm telling her father."

"Like hell you are."

Logan slides in beside me and pulls one of the pie dishes toward him. Strawberry rhubarb. I'm glad that we were able to make this quick meetup work. They both happened to be in the area today, which rarely ever happens because Uncle Dean lives in New Haven with his family.

"Can you put those away?" Logan grumbles at Dean. "Waitstaff is totally gonna get the wrong idea."

"I can't take them home with me," protests Dean. "Allie's gonna have questions."

"I will accept your condoms," I say graciously. "But only so I can put them in a big bowl and hand them out at parties."

"Good call. I'm sure it'll be much appreciated at the frat house."

Logan glances at me as he chews a bite of his pie. "You back together with Colson?"

"Oh my God. Can we please drop this subject?"

"I liked that guy," he says.

"Yeah, well, it's over. And no, I'm not dating anyone else right now. And no, I'm not going to be using this bulk box of condoms. But if I *was* going to use them, I would never tell either one of you. Ever. So…"

"Yeah, I don't want to know," Logan agrees, grinning.

The bill arrives then, and the two begin bickering about who's going to pay it. I'm pretty sure it's only like twenty bucks, and finally, I grab it myself.

"Please, let me treat my dear uncles." I offer a beaming smile. "Young people should always be kind to the elderly."

They both balk at me.

"Oh, I'm going to remember that," Dean growls.

"I'm telling your father," Logan adds.

"He knows he's old. You don't need to remind him."

I pay the check, then tuck my wallet, along with the rink keys, into my oversized leather purse.

I stare at the stupid box of condoms. After a beat of hesitation, I shove it in my bag too, mostly to show them I'm cool and carefree and don't blink at things like bulk condom purchases.

And then, before I know it, it's time to go meet Luke Ryder.

CHAPTER SIXTEEN
RYDER

Condom math

MUNSEN IS A SMALL TOWN NEAR HASTINGS. FROM WHAT I'VE HEARD, it's kind of a shithole. Yet when we pull up to the rink, it's housed in a brand-new sprawling building with walls of gleaming windows. A complete contrast to the rest of the gritty, industrial-looking town.

Beckett notices too. He whistles softly from the passenger side of my Jeep, which, thanks to Owen, I was able to get fixed. I'll pay him back, though. I don't do handouts.

Gigi's white SUV is the only other vehicle in the parking lot when we pull in. It's 9:00 p.m. and the building just closed to the public according to the hours posted online.

"You sure she doesn't mind I'm here?" asks Beckett, running a hand through his blond hair.

"I texted her earlier to confirm. All good."

"Texting with our cocaptain's ex-girlfriend. Look at you, living on the edge over here."

I roll my eyes. "Yeah, I'm not scared of Colson."

We hop out of the Jeep.

"You got to admit, a bite of forbidden fruit always tastes sweeter."

"I'm not looking to bang her. I said I'd help her behind the net. She said she'd talk me up to her dad. Win-win."

"Uh-huh. I'm sure that's all it is."

"Dude, this was your idea."

"Actually, it was Lindley's idea."

"Whatever. You cosigned it."

Gigi is opening her trunk now. She's in jeans and a tight white tank top, her dark hair arranged in a long braid down her back. She leans into the trunk and heaves out her hockey bag and a backpack. We do the same from the back of the Jeep.

"Hi," she says at our approach. She casts a slightly wary look in Beckett's direction.

He's unfazed, flashing that obnoxious Australian grin of his. The one that utilizes maximum dimples. "Looking good, Graham."

"Thanks."

"What? Not going to return the compliment?"

She snorts.

"Wow, that hurts," he says, slapping a hand over his heart in mock agony.

"Yeah, like you need me to stroke your ego."

"My ego? No. But other things…" He trails off suggestively. And where it would've sounded slimy coming from any other dude, somehow Beckett pulls it off.

Gigi giggles, confirming my suspicions that Beckett Dunne can do and say no wrong when it comes to women.

Her laughter fades when our eyes lock. She bites her lip and I wonder if she's thinking about the weekend. I know I am. For days I've been trying to make sense of the mountain of sexual tension that suddenly rose between us when we were hiding from the boosters.

When I almost kissed her.

I'm still trying to wrap my head around that one. Yes, she's hot. I spent the whole night trying not to stare at her bare tanned legs. And don't get me started on the rest of her body. Tight and sculpted. Hot enough to scald my blood.

Until the gala, though, I wasn't thinking too hard about banging her.

Now I kind of am.

"Anyway." She clears her throat. She has her bags over one shoulder, and a leather purse on the other. She slides a hand into the latter and pulls out a key ring. "Let's go in."

I raise a brow. "You got a key to this place?"

"I know a guy."

"What guy?" Beckett asks curiously.

"My uncle. He grew up here."

At the entrance, there's a small gold plaque screwed onto the outer wall that reads:

IN RECOGNITION OF JOHN LOGAN
FOR HIS GENEROUS DONATION TO BETTER
THE TOWN OF MUNSEN, MASSACHUSETTS

"Your uncle John Logan," I mumble incredulously.

"I mean, not by blood, but he's my dad's best friend. My brother and I grew up calling him Uncle Logan."

I try not to dwell on the realization that our childhoods were so drastically disparate, we may as well have been raised on two different planets. But a pang of bitterness rises nonetheless. For all she wishes her family name didn't follow her around, the truth is, it does. It opens doors for her that I could never dream of opening for myself.

My mind flashes to the fancy, well-kept neighborhood we drove through Saturday night on our way to the country club. Again, a whole other planet from where I lived as a child. First the small two-bedroom Phoenix apartment where I lived with my parents before my mother died. Then the run-down foster homes with overgrown yards and sagging chain-link fences. It's almost impossible to envision the idyllic upbringing Gigi must've had.

"Damn, I want to be you when I grow up," Beckett remarks.

"Anyway, I told Logan I needed a private place to practice, and he offered up this rink. I grabbed the keys from him earlier."

"Nice perks you got there from Daddy," I can't help but crack.

"Hey, Daddy is the reason we're here, isn't he? So I can talk you up to him?" She offers a saccharine smile. "So I've either got a famous dad who can benefit you and you don't complain about it, or I don't and you're shit out of luck. Can't have it both ways, prom king."

She has a point.

"Locker rooms are down here," she says, leading us to the end of a fluorescent-lit corridor.

Her jeans are practically painted on, and I can't help checking out her tight, perky ass. Beckett's looking too. He catches me doing it and gives me a knowing grin. I scowl at him.

We reach the men's change rooms, which are locked. Gigi stops and fumbles with her key ring. "Hold on. I'm not sure which one it is."

As she bends forward to stick the first key in the lock, her purse slides off her shoulder and down her arm. She attempts to catch it before it falls, but to no avail. The bag tumbles to the shiny floor, its contents spilling out on the way down.

A giant box of condoms lands at my feet.

Beckett and I stare at it, then exchange an amused look.

Gigi's cheeks turn a shade of red that doesn't exist in nature. She quickly kneels to collect the fallen items, shoving everything back in her purse.

"You didn't see that," she orders.

I raise a brow. "Value pack, huh? Big plans this weekend?"

"They're not mine," she says through gritted teeth.

"You're a bad liar, Gisele."

"Okay, fine, they're mine. But I acquired them against my will."

"Out of curiosity, how many rubbers do you require per session?" Beckett pipes up, grinning with delight.

She's on her feet, trying another key. This one also doesn't work.

"Goddamn it The keys are against me," she moans.

Beckett's still working through the condom math of it all. "I mean, a box of fifty, huh? Let's be ambitious and say we go three or four rounds a night. That's three or four condoms. Although I guess if it's a group thing…you know, like the three of us here—"

"Oh my God. Would you stop?"

"—then we're talking two condoms at once, three or four rounds. That means you could hypothetically go through six to eight condoms per night. Damn. We're knocking that whole box out in less than a week."

Gigi sighs and looks my way. "Is he always like this?"

"Pretty much," I confirm.

She locates the right key, and the loud breath of relief she releases makes me chuckle.

"There." She pushes open the door for us. "Go suit up."

"Should we put the condoms on now or after?" Beckett inquires.

"I hate you." She moves down the hall toward the women's locker room. "I'll meet you guys on the ice. Rink B."

In the men's room, Beckett and I change into our practice gear.

I strip off my shirt, then give him a dry look. "You're not as cute as you think, you know. And you sure as shit ain't getting a three-way out of her."

"Bullshit. She was interested."

That gives me pause.

Was she?

"Nah," I finally answer, because Gigi Graham really doesn't strike me as a threesome type of girl.

"That's a shame. The more the merrier. You know that's my motto."

I want to say he's joking, but he's not. In the two years we've known each other, the kind of debauchery I've witnessed from Beckett Dunne has been pretty extraordinary. I also never heard a bad word about him from anyone he ever hooked up with at Eastwood, so that's something, at least. Hell, most of those chicks remained in our friend group. Those good looks and Gold Coast tan provide him with a lot of leeway.

"What about you?" he asks as he sits on the opposite bench to lace up his skates.

"What about me?"

"You interested?"

I lift my head to find him grinning at me. "Sorry, brother. I think you're pretty, but I just don't feel any sparks."

"I mean, in her. Because you look interested."

I duck my head and finish lacing up. "I'm not."

"Really."

"Really," I say, because for some reason uttering the words *"Yes, I'm interested"* makes me...uneasy.

Because I'm not interested.

I don't think.

Fuck. Why am I even dwelling on this right now? That's not why we're here tonight.

The Zamboni has just concluded its final lap when we meet Gigi out on the ice. We're not wearing our full game gear, but enough padding that we can knock each other around a little if we want. Beck and I also brought some mini orange pylons, which I stack on the ledge in front of the home bench along with a few bottles of water.

"Okay," Gigi says, beaming. She skates a few circles in front of us. "I'm your willing student."

Beckett groans softly. "Don't say things like that. I can't skate with a stiffie."

Her smile only widens. "I think I've figured you out," she informs him.

"Have you?"

"Yes. You're the man who tries to disarm everyone with sex." She jerks a thumb at me. "And he's the grumpy man of few words." She shrugs. "I like knowing where I stand with people."

I do too. I suppose we have that in common. Another thing we share is the complete intensity with which we throw ourselves into our sport. The second we get down to business, Gigi's entire focus is on the task at hand. Fully and unapologetically.

"Right, so this first drill," I start gruffly. "It's all about opportunities. Versatile players know how to create scoring opportunities."

Beckett grabs the pylons and skates around to set them down. He picks a few strategic spots, one in front of the net, two at the point.

Some people gripe and complain about drills. They think nothing can ever truly prepare you for the split-second decisions and unforeseen scenarios that arise during a real game. Me, I think that's bullshit. Yes, instinct will go a long way. But practice always makes perfect.

"Beck is gonna get all up in your personal space," I warn her.

That's actually why I picked him to assist. Dunne's one of the more aggressive d-men on the team, and he knows how to make life claustrophobic for another player.

"But in this scenario, he's not the only one suffocating you. You got two other guys, or rather, women," I amend, as Beckett drops another pylon behind the net. "So if you turn and think you can just escape that way, nope. You can't. Your goal isn't to break out and score yourself. Get the puck to me, or to one of our other teammates," I say, gesturing to the various orange markers.

"Got it."

"Ready?" I glide to a random spot between the crease and the blue line.

She taps her stick on the ice. "Let's do this thing."

Grinning at her, I drop the puck and shoot it toward the boards.

Like a rocket, Gigi skates for it. Beckett is hot on her heels, practically breathing down her neck. Her stick makes contact just as he elbows her and tries to gain control of the puck.

For a moment I wonder if this is a bad idea. I'm six-five. Beck's six-two. We outmuscle her to an alarming degree. But Gigi holds her own, throwing her shoulder into it, and I hear Beck's answering grunt. As they fight for domination, I remain in position, waiting for her to make something happen.

Finally, she manages to snap the puck out, but nowhere near me or any of the pylons. The shiny black disk misses every potential stick and gets iced all the way down the boards.

"That would've been a breakaway for your opponents," I tell her when she and Beck skate out.

Gigi's cheeks are flushed behind her visor. "Not necessarily."

"My left winger would've been right there in the corner, salivating. You just made a perfect pass to him. That's not where you want to shoot."

"Hey, I'm trying. That beast was on me."

"Aw, thanks," Beckett says, looking pleased.

I roll my eyes. "All right, go again."

We run the same drill half a dozen times, and each time Gigi can't wrangle the kind of control she needs back there. Outside of that cramped space, however, she's ridiculous. The kind of elite skater that coaches drool over. Her edge work is insane. And I've seen her game tape—she's able to pluck shooting or passing opportunities out of thin air.

Except, apparently, when she's in a tight space.

"This isn't working." She sounds frazzled.

"C'mere."

She skates over to me, removing her helmet to wipe sweat off her forehead. It's inexplicably hot seeing her do that. And the sight of her braid hanging over one shoulder triggers a strange primal urge to tug on it and pull her toward me so I can slide my tongue through her frowning lips.

I snap myself out of it and try to focus.

"Beck, let's switch," I call. "I'll defend."

He skates off toward the bench, where he uncaps one of the water bottles. He chugs half of it while I brief Gigi.

"I want you to give me everything you got, all right? High pressure on me. See how I move."

Now it's the two of us battling it out, and the tension from the gala returns. My pulse quickens at her proximity, mouth running dry. Hearing her heavy breathing makes me think about how she'd sound while I'm fucking her.

She jams her stick between my skates, trying to pry the puck out. I pivot, successfully getting away from her as I twist my body. I skate out a couple of feet, pivot again, and shoot the puck straight to Beckett. He smashes it into the net.

"Oh, I hate you guys. You make it look so easy." Grudging admiration flickers across her face.

I don't switch with Beckett even though I could. I guess I enjoy having her close. I apply pressure on her, and this time she manages to get a pass off to Beckett. The speed with which the puck flies is a testament to the power of her shots. It's too fast for him to connect with his stick, and the error is his, not hers.

"That was good!" I tell her, nodding in admiration. "Really good. Let's do it again."

For the next hour, we run her hard, and even when she has trouble at first, she's quick to adapt and able to handle everything we throw at her.

"Gotta practice those deep knee bends," Beckett advises her. "And not just because they make your ass look good."

She snickers.

"It'll help you change directions faster."

She nods. After the next puck drop, she pivots so hard, it catches me by surprise, and the puck leaves her stick before I have a chance to battle for it. A perfect pass to Beckett leads to a sweet goal right in the back door.

Gigi throws her arms up in a victory post. "That's what I'm talking about, bitches."

A smile tugs on my lips. I don't let it surface, though, because I'm sure it will lead to me being made fun of for it. But I can't deny I'm proud of her progress.

"All right," she announces. "Like Coach Adley always says, let's end this shit on a high note."

We skate to the bench to drink the rest of our water.

"So you're trying to make Team USA, huh?" Beckett says.

Gigi recaps her empty bottle. "Yeah."

"I can't imagine why they wouldn't select you. You're ridiculously good. Ryder showed me some of your game tape, and you're one of the best skaters I've ever seen."

She glances at me, smirking. "You're showing people my film? That's so cute. I knew you were obsessed with me."

I roll my eyes.

We head back to the locker rooms to change into our street clothes. Beck and I don't bother showering since we're going straight home. Then we reconvene outside and walk to our cars. The parking lot is illuminated by a couple of floodlights, so it's easy to discern the gratitude shining in Gigi's slate-gray eyes.

"Thank you for this," she tells both of us, but her gaze is on me. "Let's do it again? Maybe next week?"

"Sounds good," I say brusquely.

"What are you up to this weekend?" Beckett asks her.

"Not sure yet. Why?"

"We're having people over on Friday. You should come by."

I give him a look, which he returns with a wink. I know what he's up to. Beckett is as transparent as glass. Mostly because he never tries to hide his intentions.

Gigi's still watching me, though. Contemplating. Then she shrugs and says, "Maybe," before getting into her car and driving away.

CHAPTER SEVENTEEN

GIGI

Do you want me to stop?

"I THINK WE SHOULD GO," MYA ANNOUNCES ON FRIDAY NIGHT. SHE has her bare legs up on the coffee table and is wiggling her feet to help her toenails dry. She just finished painting them a light pink that looks incredible with her skin tone. I'm too pale to pull off that shade. I look best in darker colors, like my mom.

"To the enemy party," I say dubiously.

"Well, they're your enemy, not mine. And I'm in the mood for a party. I'm bored silly. And you're horny. Let's go."

"I am not horny," I bluster.

"Liar. You were telling me and Diana all about it the other day when she came over. I have to assume your sex-drought agony has only gotten worse since then."

I glare at her.

She raises a perfectly sculpted brow.

"Fine, it's gotten worse," I grumble.

Bad enough that I actually got turned on two nights ago when Beckett Dunne was teasing me about condoms and threesomes. I feel a tingle between my legs at the memory.

"Have you ever had a threesome?" I ask Mya.

She starts to laugh. "Oh wow, someone *is* hard up for sex. Now you need two dicks? One isn't good enough?"

"Oh my God, no. Ryder's friend was teasing me about three-somes the other night. I'm just wondering." I narrow my eyes at her. "Have you?"

"No, I haven't," she answers. "Do you remember that girl I was dating freshman year? Laura? She was into that kind of shit. Group stuff, threesomes. She kept trying to convince me to create a profile for us on this app called Kink. But I don't know, I'm a one-on-one girl. I need the intimacy. I can't see how there could possibly be any level of intimacy with more than two people involved."

"I don't see it either."

"All right. I've made an executive decision. We're going to the party." She stands up. "I need to do my hair. Go put on something sexy to seduce the enemy with."

I snicker as I duck into my bedroom. I'm not planning on seduc-ing anyone, but I do choose an outfit that's...racier than usual. A black skirt that barely covers my lower thighs and a ribbed gray crop top with no bra. I debate how I feel about everyone being able to see the outline of my nipples all night, then decide to live a little.

On the drive to Hastings, our loud singalong to a very cheesy eighties song is interrupted by a call from my dad.

"Hey, Dad," I greet him. "You're on speakerphone, so don't say anything to embarrass me in front of Mya."

"I'll do my best," he promises.

"Hi, Mr. G," she chirps.

"Hey, Mya." To me, he says, "Just returning your call from earlier, Stan."

"Oh, it was nothing important. I just wanted to catch up."

"You been working hard this week?"

"God, you don't even know. Uncle Logan's letting me use his rink after hours so I can fix my issues behind the net." I pause, adopting a nonchalant tone. "Ryder's been a big help."

Mya is grinning at me. She knows about my arrangement with Ryder.

Dad is understandably suspicious. "I still don't get why you asked him instead of Case."

It's the same thing he said earlier in the week when I first dropped Ryder's name. So far, Operation Good Impression is not a smashing success.

"Because he's a better player than Case," I reply.

And I'm being honest. Case is an excellent hockey player, no doubt. He and Ryder have similar stats; they were both drafted by the NHL. But Ryder has an innate feel for the game that Case lacks.

"His instincts are incredible," I say. "He's amazing to watch."

In the passenger side, Mya signals for me to dial it down a notch.

Good call. I was going to throw in a line about what a great asset he'd make to the Hockey Kings camp, but I decide to save that for our next chat. Can't come on too strong.

"Anyway, what kind of trouble are you girls getting into tonight?" Dad asks.

"Just going to see some friends," I say, keeping it vague.

We say goodbye just as I pull up in front of Ryder's house. I park at the curb and uneasily glance toward the end of the street. Hopefully this isn't a repeat of last weekend, but with Briar crashing the party this time.

The music is blasting so loud, we can hear it from the street. On the porch, I ring the doorbell, but I already know it's a futile exercise. No one can hear it. But then the front door opens, and a pair of laughing girls tumble out. They greet us with that sheer unbridled joy only inebriated people can feel.

"Hi!" the first girl exclaims. "Oh my gosh, you two look so beautiful!"

"Stunning," the other gushes.

Drunk girls give the best compliments.

"You're sweet," I tell the total strangers.

They bound down the porch steps and stumble off to a waiting Uber, throwing themselves into the back seat.

Mya and I shrug and enter the house without an invitation. The music is even more deafening now, a hip-hop track that makes you move your hips whether you want to or not. I poke my head into the living room and spot Beckett. He's laughing with a bunch of Eastwood guys I recognize from Miller's party. I still can't remember a lot of their names. Rounding out the group are a few sorority girls wearing short skirts and Delta Nu sweaters.

Mya recognizes one of them. "Kate?" she shouts excitedly.

"Mya." The pretty dark-haired girl breaks away from the group and bounds over.

"What are you doing here?" Mya exclaims. "I thought you transferred to LSU."

"I did. I'm just home for the weekend."

From the heated look that passes between them, I deduce they're very familiar with each other.

"I was about to get a refill," Kate says, holding up an empty red cup. "You want a drink?"

"Absolutely."

Kate takes her hand, and Mya's free hand tugs on mine. But I'm intercepted by Beckett, who strides toward me in a tight T-shirt and cargo pants. Blond hair artfully tousled.

"Go. I'll meet you in the kitchen," I tell the girls.

"You came," Beckett says when he reaches me. He nods in approval.

"Yep. Here I am."

"You look…really good." I have no doubt he's noticed the beaded tips of my nipples, but his gaze doesn't linger there. It fixes on my abdomen instead.

"Fuck," he groans, eyes glazing over.

"What?"

"Those abs."

"Jealous?" I say smugly.

"Nah." He lifts the bottom corner of his T-shirt to flash his own set of chiseled abs. Not a six-pack, but a solid twelve. Jesus. "I don't know. Mine are pretty sick too."

"They're all right."

Shane Lindley wanders into the hall holding a can of beer. He looks surprised but pleased to see me. "Hey," he says, flinging his arm around my shoulder. "How'd they manage to lure you into enemy territory?"

"There was no luring involved. I was bored and decided to do you all a favor by gracing you with my presence."

He snorts. "We're honored."

Beckett lightly touches my shoulder. "Want a drink?"

"Beck, how do I change this playlist?" someone shouts from the living room.

"Hold that thought," he tells me. He winks, the tip of his tongue briefly touching his top lip. It's kind of hot.

Speaking of hot, my peripheral vision catches Ryder descending the staircase to our right. His mouth quirks, only slightly, at the sight of me.

"Gisele," he says.

"Ryder," I say.

He closes the distance between us, towering over me as always. I'm average height for a woman, yet standing next to Luke Ryder makes me feel positively tiny.

"How tall are you?" I ask curiously, craning my neck to peer up at him.

"Six-five."

Damn, he's a monster. Even has a couple of inches on my dad.

A little shiver runs through me, although I suppose I'm not the first girl to have a thing for tall strapping guys. Wait. Not that I have a thing for this one. Just, you know, the body type in general.

Right, this one does nothing for you, a voice in my head taunts.

As usual, Ryder doesn't try to fill the silence.

I shift my feet and say, "Dude, would it kill you to pull your conversational weight?"

He cocks a brow. "Says the person who got the ball rolling with the thought-provoking question of how tall I was."

"I'm just saying, you could make an effort over here. You know, *Hey, Gigi, how was your day? Do you have big plans for this weekend?*"

"How was your day? Do you have big plans this weekend?"

"Wow. Could you sound less enthused?"

"You fed me the lines. How excited can I really be about them when they're not my own?"

"Fine. Then give me your own."

He looks at me. Hot gaze raking over my body before his dark-blue eyes return to my face. "I like that top."

I don't expect the compliment, so I'm genuinely startled. "Oh," I squeak. "Thanks."

"So," Shane pipes up, and I realize I've completely forgotten his presence. "This is"—His head moves between us—"fascinating."

"What is?" I'm puzzled.

Shane nods toward Ryder. "I've never heard him speak so many words at one time. And then to punctuate it with a compliment? Did you drug him?"

"Fuck off," Ryder grumbles.

Suddenly his attention shifts. An emotion I can't discern flickers through his eyes. Then he says, "Excuse me." His voice is tight.

He walks toward the front door. The crowd parts slightly and that's when I catch a glimpse of the woman who just walked in. She's pretty. Tall and willowy, wearing skinny jeans and a corset top with her ample cleavage spilling out. Black curls tumble down her shoulders.

A desperate gleam lights her eyes before she rises on her tiptoes to whisper frantically in Ryder's ear. Next thing I know, he has his hand on the small of her back while guiding her onto the front porch where it's quieter.

Okay, then.

Beckett returns. "Hey, sorry about that. Let's grab you that drink now. Where did Ryder go?"

Grinning, Shane points toward the porch. Through the open door, I glimpse Ryder and the girl talking.

Beckett looks over and rolls his eyes.

"Who's that with Ryder?" I ask, trying not to sound overly eager for an answer.

Shane's knowing smirk tells me he knows how badly I want that answer. "That's Carma."

My brow furrows. "I don't get it. He did something to deserve something?"

"No, that's her name."

"Carma with a *C*," Beckett explains. "Feel free to make a hilarious destiny joke."

I force my gaze off Ryder. "Is she his girlfriend?"

Beckett shrugs. "She's our neighbor. They hooked up once, but I thought that was over. Who the fuck knows."

I try to ignore the knot in the pit of my stomach. I guess Ryder's off-limits.

For some unpleasant reason I'm not willing to examine, I'm more disappointed in that than I ought to be.

In the kitchen, Mya and Kate are at the counter standing very close to each other. With her hand on Mya's arm, Kate whispers something in her ear. Mya giggles in return.

When I introduce them to Beckett, I notice the approval in Mya's eyes. Yeah. He's drop-dead gorgeous, no denying it. And the kind of man who doesn't need to put in much effort to look sexy. A white T-shirt and that face. That's all it takes.

Beckett gestures to the row of liquor bottles on the kitchen table. "What are you in the mood for? I can mix you something sweet if you want a cocktail."

"Honestly, I'm the most boring drinker ever."

"I can attest to that," Mya confirms.

"Yeah? What's your poison?"

I sigh. "Scotch and soda."

"Intriguing. Are you a fifty-year-old businessman in an airport bar?"

"I know, I know. But it was the first drink I ever had with my dad," I admit. "And I kind of loved it. Either that, or a beer."

"Well, I don't think we have any scotch on hand, so beer will have to do."

He wanders over to the large cooler on the table across the room, where he fishes out two longnecks. He passes one to me. We clink bottles.

"Cheers," he says.

A few others drift toward us. Two sophomores named Patrick and Nazem. A guy named Nick who has one of those serious stay-the-fuck-away-from-me faces. But his girlfriend, Darby, makes up for it with a contagious smile and by talking a mile a minute. She seems cool.

Patrick grabs a fresh beer and twists off the cap. "Okay," he says, focusing on me. His eyes are bright, either from excitement or alcohol. He's cute, though. "Are you ready, Graham?"

"For what?"

"A thought experiment that will blow your mind."

"Oh God," sighs Darby.

I take a sip of my beer. "All right, I'll bite. Hit me."

Patrick hops up to sit on the counter, long legs dangling. "It's a regular day. A normal sunny afternoon. You're outdoors, running errands or whatever. How many owls would you need to see before you got worried?"

"Oh, that is an excellent question."

Beckett chuckles, but Darby turns to me with pleading eyes. "Please don't feed their insanity."

"What? It's an objectively great question."

"I'm just saying. You do not want to encourage it, girl."

Nick nods gravely at me. "You really don't."

"Leave her alone," Patrick grumbles at them. To me, he prompts, "So? How many?"

"Am I in the city or a rural area out in the middle of nowhere?"

"You're here. In Hastings."

I raise my bottle to my lips, giving the matter some serious consideration.

"Three," I finally answer.

Nazem, who said to call him Naz or Nazzy, jabs a finger in the air. "Explain yourself."

I take another sip first. "Okay, well, I see one owl, and I'm like, *Hey cool, an owl during the day.* Two owls, and I'm thinking, *This is kinda weird; I never see owls around here, and now I'm seeing two? Odd.* Then I see the third owl, and all my hackles are raised. At this point it's an omen and I don't fucking like it."

Mya nods in agreement. "I would've said four, but similar reasoning."

"What would you say?" I ask Patrick.

"Seven."

"Seven!" I exclaim. "If I saw seven owls in one day, I'd be packing up the car and driving to Mexico."

We talk about stupid stuff some more, until someone gets a beer pong game going in the backyard and everyone but Beckett heads outside. I might be cavorting with the enemy, but I realize I'm actually having a good time. I'm glad Mya dragged me out tonight.

In the back of my mind, I wonder what Ryder is up to. It's been a while since his "neighbor" showed up. Maybe they went upstairs. That doesn't bother me at all. Why would it.

Through the wide doorway that spills into the living room, I spot Mya and Kate on the makeshift dance floor created when somebody pushed the coffee table and armchairs aside. The hip-hop that was playing before has been replaced by sultry R&B. Mya's jam. She moves her body seductively to the beat, using Kate's lithe frame as her own personal stripper pole. Those two are unquestionably ending up in bed again tonight.

Beckett follows my gaze. "Wanna dance?"

"Nah, I'm good."

"Thank God. I hate dancing."

I can't help but laugh. "Then why'd you ask?"

"Seemed like the less sleazy way of saying I want your body pressed up against mine."

He winks, and my heart skips a beat.

I'm not afraid of the way he makes my heart react. It's a normal flip, not the entire group of gymnasts unleashed by Luke Ryder at the booster gala last week. Your heart isn't supposed to do that much gymnastics for a man. Too much anxiety isn't healthy.

Passion, whispers a little voice in my brain. *Not anxiety.*

Anxiety, I firmly tell myself.

And Beckett Dunne doesn't make me anxious.

"You're thinking too hard," he teases.

"It's a bad habit." I meet his eyes. They're a shade of gray much lighter than my own. "Maybe you should help me stop thinking."

His lips curve. "Mmm. How am I supposed to do that?"

"You seem like a creative guy. Come up with a creative solution."

Those silvery eyes gleam half a second before he cups my cheek with one hand. I'm not drunk enough to be doing this. In fact, I'm sober enough to know it's probably a terrible idea.

"Beck, toss us some more cups," Shane calls from outside. "Dumbass over here just stepped on like four of them."

"It was an accident," I hear Patrick protest.

The interruption allows me to collect my hormones and my common sense.

Beckett drops his hand, a rueful smile on his lips. "I'll be right back."

"Actually, perfect timing," I say as I watch him pull some red cups off the stack at the table. "I need to pee, anyway."

"Use the bathroom upstairs," he offers.

"Are you sure?"

"Yep. Turn left at the top of the stairs, end of the hall. That's mine and Ryder's."

"Thanks."

I set my empty bottle on the counter and dart upstairs. The music isn't as loud up here. I welcome the muffled respite, needing to clear my head. I reach the bathroom door just as the one across from it swings open and a dark-haired girl slides out of the bedroom.

"Oh, sorry," she exclaims after bumping into me.

We jump apart with awkward laughs.

"All good," I say.

I tense slightly when I realize it's Carma. I was right. They did go upstairs. I resist the urge to peer into the bedroom to see if Ryder is still in there. I imagine him adjusting his shirt. Zipping up his pants.

She notes my wary expression and quickly adds, "Don't worry, I'm allowed to be up here. I left my necklace in Ryder's room last time I was here, so I was just grabbing it." She holds up a silver pendant with a tiny silver cross dangling off it. "Anyway...have a good night."

"You too," I murmur.

I watch her go, trying to ward off the prickly sensation pinching my gut as I duck into the bathroom to pee. While I wash my hands, I stare at my reflection in the mirror. Wondering if I should have worn more makeup. I only dabbed on some concealer and lip gloss earlier. I look unnervingly plain compared to the woman I saw in the hall.

Then again, I can't look *that* bad, considering Beckett has been eye-fucking me all night. I feel a tug between my legs at the idea of doing more than eye-fucking each other. God, some release would be nice. Going solo feels good, but sometimes a girl just needs a really good dicking.

When I emerge from the bathroom, Beckett leans against the wall waiting for me.

"Hey," he says. "Thought maybe you'd gotten lost."

"Nope." I smooth out my hair before tucking it behind my ears. It's rare that I wear my hair down. Usually I keep it in a braid.

Neither of us makes a move toward the stairs. Beckett's gaze conducts a slow perusal of my body, this time lingering on my braless breasts rather than my midriff.

"You really do look incredible. Don't think I can stress that enough."

"Are you hitting on me right now?"

"Yes. Do you want me to stop?"

I slowly shake my head. "No."

He moves closer to me. Those gray eyes dancing. He's that type, I can tell. The guy who's always down for a good time. For a laugh. A screw.

"There's something about you," he says, his voice low, husky.

"Is that a line?"

"No. I don't use lines. I say what's on my mind. And there's just something about you that makes a man…" He drifts off, thoughtful.

"Makes a man what?"

"All jumbled in the head." He smiles. "I look in your eyes and kind of get lost in them." He sounds a bit sheepish now. "I know that does sound like a line, but I swear it's the truth—"

Before he can finish, I stand on my tiptoes and kiss him.

He's startled. Then I feel his lips curve against my mouth in another smile.

"Sorry," I blurt out, blushing from a pang of embarrassment. "I should have asked if I could do that. Is it okay?"

He responds by kissing me again.

The next thing I know, I'm pressed up against the wall, my hands twined around his neck, his tongue in my mouth. He's a good kisser.

A shiver dances through me when I realize he's hard. I feel him against my leg. And I'm melting into him. Warming up to the idea of throwing caution to the wind and letting myself feel good. If I'm going to hook up with anyone tonight, Beckett seems like a perfect candidate. Like someone who's not going to expect anything else or want more from me.

His tongue touches mine again, and suddenly I hear loud throat clearing.

We break apart. My pulse careens faster when I see Ryder standing at the top of the stairs.

"Sorry to interrupt." He drawls the words, yet there's a sharp edge to them. "Got a little problem."

Beckett glances over his shoulder, but Ryder's looking at me, not him.

"Your boyfriend's downstairs."

CHAPTER EIGHTEEN
RYDER

I don't get jealous

"WHERE THE HELL IS SHE?"

Colson's face is thunderous as he watches me descend the staircase. You can tell "pissed off" is not a natural state for him. He gives off a real Boy Scout vibe. Mr. Good Guy who's always smiling and taking everything in stride. Right now, though, his jaw is tighter than a drum. He blustered up the driveway a few minutes after I sent Carma on her way. With his lackey in tow, of course. When they burst inside, Trager's red face and clenched fists begged Case to unleash him on the world, but Colson kept his friend in check.

Now it appears both men are ready to explode.

"I told you I was going to get her," I answer indifferently.

I nod over my shoulder. Gigi's hurrying down the steps after me.

Relief floods Colson's eyes when he sees her. Then he notices Beckett behind her.

"What the hell? You were upstairs with him?" he snarls.

"I was using the bathroom," Gigi says.

The lie leaves her mouth smoothly, but we both know that's not what she was doing up there.

I can't explain the jolt of…something…that surges through me at the memory of finding her and Beckett up against the wall.

Fuck.

I think that something might be jealousy.

This girl is starting to get under my skin. I don't like it.

"What the hell are you doing here?" Case is oozing disapproval. "Why are you hanging out with these guys?"

"We got invited to a party," she answers with a shrug. Unruffled by his visible displeasure.

"Who's we?"

"Mya and me. What are *you* doing here?"

"We were driving back from Malone's, and I saw your car on the street. At first, I was like, *No, there's no fucking way Gigi would be here.*" Bitterness hardens his voice. "And yet here you fucking are."

Trager pipes up obnoxiously. "These assholes sprained Coffey's wrist, G," he reminds her.

"Hey, that was all you," Shane tells Trager, rolling his eyes. "You threw your man into a table. Don't put that on us."

"Your boy Hawley started it!"

I've already tuned them out. Colson has too. He's too busy frowning at Gigi.

"Go get Mya," he orders. "We're leaving."

She appears like she wants to argue. Then she releases an annoyed breath and surrenders. "One second."

She charges toward the kitchen. The music starts up again, blessedly drowning out whatever's yapping from Trager's mouth. Guy is such a douchebag.

While we wait for Gigi, Colson's attention remains firmly fixed on me. A hard glare like I'm the one responsible for this.

But as always, Beckett's dick gets us in trouble. The only surprising part of that is that Gigi Graham fell for it. She doesn't seem like the type to go for one-night stands with fuckboys.

My mood grows darker, and it was already pretty dark before Colson decided to storm into my house. Started around the time Carma also decided to show up unannounced, claiming she forgot her necklace when she was here. For all I know she had the thing stashed in her pocket when she came tonight. I know I'm a suspicious asshole, but I tend to err on the side of cynicism. Expect the worst, then be pleasantly surprised to be proven wrong. Which rarely happens.

Maybe that's not the healthiest way to live your life, but it's how I've lived mine since I was six years old. Saved me a lot of disappointment over the years.

Gigi returns a minute later. "Mya's staying," she says tersely. "Her friend Kate will drive her home."

"Let's go." Case's tone invites no argument. Harsh and unyielding.

She glances over her shoulder at Beckett and mouths, *Sorry,* when Case has his back turned.

Beckett just shrugs and grins.

Still on guard, I march to the front door and stand there, watching them trudge down the path toward the sidewalk. Trager is typing on his phone. Colson speaks in a low voice to Gigi, who looks irritated with him. They stop in front of her SUV.

I get a petty sense of satisfaction when Colson tries to open the passenger door, and she whips up her hand and evidently tells him not to get in.

Within seconds, she starts the engine and drives off. Taillights blinking.

Colson remains at the curb. As if sensing my presence, his shoulders harden, and he turns to scowl at me. I roll my eyes. He spins on his heel and stalks down the street. Home, I assume.

Just another friendly neighborly visit from my cocaptain.

"That was fun," Beckett remarks, stepping onto the porch beside me.

I shake my head at him. "Antagonizing them on purpose now? Come on, bro. Of all the chicks to get tangled up with."

"You're giving her private lessons, mate. You can't lecture me about entanglements."

My irritation only grows. "All I'm saying is, be more careful next time. What if he'd run upstairs? You were five seconds from screwing her in the hallway if I hadn't interrupted."

Beckett blinks. Then he starts to laugh.

"Oh. I see."

"What?" I mutter.

"When you said you weren't interested…it was opposite day. Got it."

I'm feeling too tense and volatile to respond. So I just grimace.

Beckett claps me on the shoulder, still chuckling. "All good, mate. I'll back off."

I want to tell him there's no need, that he can do whatever—and whoever—he wants. But those words, the go-ahead to keep pursuing Gigi, can't seem to leave my mouth.

At the end of the weekend, we get a team-wide email saying we're required to stay an extra hour after practice on Monday morning.

PR guru Christie Delmont strikes again.

The details are vague, but then again, Jensen cosigned the email, and he has a vendetta against words, so…

Shane and I step out of our respective shower stalls, towels wrapped around our waists. The Briar facilities are a massive upgrade from Eastwood. First and foremost, the smell. As in, it's almost nonexistent thanks to Briar's unrivaled air filtration system. At Eastwood, it was like stepping into an old sock factory every time you walked into the locker room. The benches left wood splinters in your ass, and the showers were mildewy. If you forgot your shower shoes, you'd have a lot more than athlete's foot to worry about. You'd risk getting your feet amputated from some flesh-eating disease.

"I'm just saying," Shane says as we head back to the main room to change. "I'm so tired of chicks asking for pictures of my dick." He heaves a sigh of exhaustion. "It's a lot of effort to take all those photos."

"Radical idea, but maybe just do it once and keep sending the same one?" Beckett suggests.

"Ha. Lazy Lance over here. That's taking the easy way out." Shane flops on the bench to roll on his socks. "Women need to feel special. If she requests a dick pic, she gets her own personal one, tailored just for her."

"Tailored just for her?" Nick Lattimore echoes. "Bro, like what are you even doing? Crafting a special scene to match each chick's personality? If she likes wildflowers, do you pose in a meadow?"

Rand keels over with laughter, slapping his knee. "Did you put a teeny pink tutu on it for Lynsey's photo?"

Shane's ex was a ballerina, and everyone busts out laughing as we visualize what Nick and Rand described. I even notice a few of the Briar guys fighting laughter. At least before their valiant leader Colson narrows his eyes at them.

The rational part of my brain recognizes how unhealthy this is for a team, these dividing lines that don't seem to be dissolving.

But the part that hates having this leadership role thrust upon me can't be bothered to try to fix it.

Once I have my shoes on, I grab my phone from my stall to check for any missed messages. My shoulders tense when I find one from Gigi.

GISELE:

> Can you do a session tomorrow night?

I know what she means, but I can't help the way my dick twitches. He's fickle and has been around long enough to know that *session* could refer to so many other things. Dirty things.

I discreetly tap out a response. Colson's two feet away at his own stall. After the way he dragged Gigi out of my house Friday night, I'd rather not poke the bear.

ME:

Yes. Same time and place?

GISELE:

Yup. I'll meet you there.

It's probably not a great idea to agree to this. But our deal is never far from my mind, the hope that she might be able to help me snag that coaching slot. I'd face Colson's wrath any day of the week for the opportunity to work under Garrett Graham and Jake Connelly.

Although if I'm being honest with myself, Case Colson isn't the reason I'm hesitant to see Gigi again.

It's getting harder and harder to convince myself that I don't want to fuck her brains out.

My stomach sinks when I enter the auditorium to find two dozen chairs arranged in a circle on the stage. Coach Jensen stands up there flanked by a man and woman in their midforties who look like the nauseating parents from a Disney Channel show. They vaguely resemble each other, though, so I think they might be siblings. They're both in khakis and matching pastel shirts, hers green, his pink, although I suspect he'd call it salmon.

"Fuck me," Shane mutters under his breath. "This looks like…"

"Team-building," I finish, and an honest-to-God shudder runs through me.

Every now and then, a coach gets a bug in his ass. That bug then crawls its way up to his brain and lays an egg that hatches into the big bright idea that his team could benefit from some goddamn bonding experiences.

We suffered through this last season at Eastwood when a new defense coordinator came on board and convinced Coach Evans it would be a fabulous idea to strengthen our team bonds. For three days we were forced to play stupid games and contort our bodies in ungodly human knot exercises.

It was my worst nightmare.

"Everyone have a seat," barks Jensen.

I can tell as each guy climbs the stage and sits down that they know precisely what this is. And nobody's happy.

Once we're all seated, Coach Jensen confirms our fears.

"Miss Delmont from the public relations department has signed us up for a team-building course that will run every Monday for the next six weeks."

Our goalie, Joe Kurth, looks like he's going to throw up. He leans forward in his chair and drops his face in his hands.

"Public relations is a scourge on society," Shane mumbles beside me.

"Now, there is nothing I hate more in this world than team-building activities," Jensen continues. "With that said, I have great news—I was informed that I personally don't have to participate, so…"

For once in his life, Jensen is positively beaming.

"I'd like to introduce you to Sheldon and Nance Laredo. Do everything they ask, or you're off the team. I'll leave you to it."

I half expect him to put some flowers in his hair and skip off the stage like a giddy schoolgirl. He chuckles all the way to the exit.

Nance Laredo steps forward with a sunny smile, waving vigorously. "We're so excited to meet y'all!"

Everyone stares back at her, stone-faced.

"Sheldon and I were told that a bunch of silly someones are having a problem with team unity." She uses that singsong tone reserved for puppies and kindergarteners.

I can already tell I'm going to hate her.

"And boy, that sure is an obstacle," Sheldon chimes in.

Yeah. I'm going to hate him too.

All my teammates continue to stare at the grinning, pastel-clad robots. Trying to make sense of them in our minds.

"Someone. Please. Please kill me now," Rand Hawley mumbles. "I'll pay you."

Several chuckles ring out. And not just from the Eastwood guys.

Patrick Armstrong shoots his hand up to get the robots' attention. "Did you see that? We don't need team unity!" He points at Rand, then Trager. "*He* laughed at *his* joke, and they hate each other. See, we're all done here. Let's go, everyone."

When asses start to rise from chairs, the Disney siblings transform into drill sergeants. They both blow the whistles hanging around their necks.

I wince at the shrill noises that pierce through the auditorium and bounce off the walls.

"Like Nance said," Sheldon says when our eardrums have recovered. "We were brought here by the university because there are real concerns about the behavior of this team."

"Real concerns," Nance echoes.

"Someone was injured because of the hostility bubbling all around you," Sheldon chastises. "We cannot let the hostility continue to bubble."

"That is a death sentence," Nance agrees.

"I mean, that's a bit dramatic," Shane says, and they both ignore him.

"The best way to break through this tension and animosity is to stop treating each other as enemies and start viewing each other as fellow human beings."

"Human beings," Nance repeats, nodding. She takes over for Sheldon. "For the next hour, we're going to do just that. Is everyone ready?"

Everyone is not. We all look at her sullenly.

"Our first activity is called Name and Thing. Grab the beanbag, Shel!"

"Why is there always a beanbag?" sighs Beckett.

Sheldon darts over to a large plastic tub containing horrors I hope never to have to see. He scoops out a pink beanbag and returns to the circle, tossing the bag back and forth between his own hands.

He looks so excited I expect urine stains to appear at the front of his khakis at some point.

"I don't want to play hockey anymore," Nazzy says solemnly, looking around. "I quit the team."

Nance laughs. "Sheldon! Looks like we found the joker in the group."

"We sure did." Sheldon sweeps his happy robot gaze over us. "This game is so easy, it barely requires explanation. But here's how it goes. When the bag is in your hands, you say your name and a thing that you like. When you're done, you toss the bag to somebody else, until everyone on the team has said their name and their thing."

"And it can be anything you like," exclaims Nance. "It can be pasta. It can be daydreaming. Anything at all, so long as you like it. Any questions?"

Someone raises his hand. A senior named Tristan.

"Why are you guys so cheerful? What kind of drugs do you take, and do they show up in drug tests?"

A wave of laughter travels through the circle.

Nance addresses the question earnestly. "I can't speak for Sheldon, but I'm cheerful because I feel cheer. And I feel cheer because I love uniting people. In fact, toss me the beanbag, Sheldon."

He throws it into her open palms.

"My name is Nance. And I like uniting people. That's my name. And that's my thing."

She throws it back to Sheldon who beams at us. "My name is Sheldon," he says. "And I like cheesecake."

"See how easy that was?" Nance is smiling so hard, it looks like her jaw's about to snap in two. "Okey dokey, let's start."

The first toss goes to a Briar guy. Boone Woodrow.

The normally quiet sophomore clears his throat. "Uh. My name's Boone but everyone calls me Woody."

"Oh, this is more fun than I thought," Sheldon interrupts,

nodding at Nance. "Share your nicknames if you have them, boys. Go on, Woody. What's your thing?"

"I, uh…" Woodrow thinks it over. "I like hockey."

Before he can lob the bag to someone else in the circle, Nance wags her finger.

"Oh, no, we can do better than that, Woody. I think it's safe to assume everyone likes hockey because you're all in this room and you're all on the hockey team."

"Yeah, Captain Obvious," Tim Coffey cracks.

Woodrow rolls his eyes. "Fine. I also like baseball. I pitch for Briar in the spring." He glances at the pastel robots for confirmation that he passed their test.

"Excellent," Sheldon says. "To the rest of you—that will be the only sports answer allowed."

"Oh, fuck you, Woody," Trager mutters. "Way to hog the one sports answer."

"Let's try to expand our horizons," Sheldon advises. "Dig a little deeper."

"All right, Woody," Nance chirps. "Bean that bag."

She should be arrested for that phrase.

Woodrow throws the beanbag to Austin Pope.

"I'm Austin." The freshman mulls for a second. "I like video games, I guess." He pitches it to Patrick Armstrong.

"Yeah. I'm Patrick, a.k.a. the Kansas Kid. I like dogs." He tosses the bag to Shane.

"Shane Lindley. I like golf, and I don't care that you said we can't pick sports. Because I like to play golf." He throws it to Beckett.

"Beckett Dunne. I like sex."

There's a wave of muffled laughter.

For some reason, his answer has the opposite effect on me. Suddenly I'm hit with the memory of Beckett's tongue in Gigi's mouth, and it brings a tight clench to my chest.

I'm not jealous, damn it.

I don't *get* jealous. Jealousy implies I care about something enough to covet it for myself, and caring is not in my wheelhouse.

"We are going to assume that as red-blooded American hockey players, you all enjoy sex," Sheldon says graciously. "Pick something else."

Beckett purses his lips. "All right. I'm into time travel."

Nance claps her hands. "Well, that's interesting! I'd love to hear more. Wouldn't everyone love to hear more?"

Will Larsen glances at Beckett, curious. "Like, talking about it? Theorizing?"

"Everything. Discussing it, digging into the theories, watching movies. Both fiction and documentary—"

"There are no documentaries about time travel because it's not real," Shane grumbles in exasperation. "How many times do we have to go over this?"

"Anyway," Beckett says, ignoring Shane. "That's what I like. Time travel."

He sends the beanbag sailing toward Will.

"Will Larsen. I would say time travel because I'm also into it. But maybe, like, sci-fi movies?" He throws the bag to Case.

"Case Colson," our cocaptain says. "I like camping."

I already know the beanbag is coming to me next. Colson even puts a little force behind it, so that it smacks into my palm.

"Luke Ryder," I mutter. "I like history documentaries. Like, about World War Two and shit."

"Psycho," Trager says.

I roll my eyes at him.

And on and on it goes, the torture, until everyone has stated their name and some stupid nonsense they like. Then Nance claps her hands and declares, "That was fantastic!"

Sheldon nods in fervent agreement. "Our next exercise is called…"

"Somebody kill me now," Trager finishes, and that gets a few laughs.

But a few laughs ain't going to cut it. I honestly don't know if this team is ever going to gel. How can it when one of its cocaptains is showing up at the other captain's house and dragging his ex-girlfriend out for daring to socialize with us? We're still the enemy to Colson, and I suspect we always will be.

So I probably shouldn't mention that I'm seeing his ex again tomorrow night.

Hockey Kings Transcript

Original Air Date: 09/23

© **The Sports Broadcast Network**

Garrett Graham: Moving away from the pros. Our producer, Zara, compiled some really cool facts about this upcoming college men's season. Turns out there are ten rosters this year that feature eight or more freshman players. The honor of having the largest freshman class goes to St. Anthony's, but Minnesota State is a close second. It should be interesting, watching all those rookies hit the ice when the season officially starts.

Jake Connelly: And the D1 programs have over one hundred and eighty NHL draft picks this year. That's incredible.

Graham: But before we take a deeper dive into this—a quick word from our new sponsor, TRN. Check out TRN's brand-new fall lineup, including *The Blessing*, a dating show where the dads call the shots. That's something Jake and I can get behind, right, Connelly?

Connelly: Damn right, G.

Graham: Make sure to check out TRN for all your reality show needs. TRN. All real. All life. All the time.

CHAPTER NINETEEN

GIGI
Beckett gets around

WE'RE ONLY A COUPLE OF WEEKS INTO THE SEMESTER, AND MY schoolwork is already piling up, so it's hard to keep up the after-hours schedule. On Tuesday Ryder and I are able to book private ice time in Munsen at six o'clock while the rink is still open to the public.

And he's insufferable from the moment we step onto the ice. I'd like to say he's just being himself, but there seems to be a lot more trash talk than usual. Hockeywise, he's giving me exactly what I asked for. Muscling me around, forcing me to step up my game. But the combination of his incessant taunting and having him in my personal space eventually causes me to snap.

"My God, you are so arrogant! Would you stop with the running commentary?"

His eyes gleam. "Get past me successfully and maybe I'll stop."

"Oh yeah, that's solid coaching. *I'm bigger than you, and I'll stop being an ass about it if you suddenly grow a foot taller and gain a hundred pounds of muscle.*"

That gets me a grin.

"Are you smiling?" I accuse.

And just like that, my annoyance melts away. Any time I manage to draw a normal human response out of Ryder instead of the grumpy looks he usually gives me, I like to nurture that delicate bud.

"No." He glowers at me.

"You were totally smiling."

"You're just imagining things."

He skates off to grab his water bottle, but not before I hear him chuckle.

"And you laughed!" I cry in delight, gliding after him. "I'm telling everyone."

"Go ahead. No one will believe you."

"I've got hidden cameras all over this rink."

"Is that so?" He looks intrigued. "Does that mean the world's going to see you begging the enemy for help?"

"I'm not begging you. We have an arrangement."

Ryder uncaps his bottle. "And when are you going to hold up your end of it, exactly?"

"Already have, smart-ass. I've brought your name up almost every time he's called. And I'm going home this weekend, so I'll talk you up even more."

"You better."

"Maybe I'll get a FaceTime in too before the weekend. Rave all about my good pal Ryder. Tell Dad how we listen to Dan Grebbs together…"

"Don't ruin my reputation like that."

"My dad likes *Horizons*," I say enticingly.

Ryder hesitates.

I hoot. "Holy shit, you would actually pretend to like my meditation music to suck up to him! You're a fraud. I will not endorse a fraud."

He lets out another bark of laughter.

"Oh my God, two laughs in less than five minutes."

Ryder lifts the bottle to his lips. My traitorous eyes admire his strong throat working as he takes a long drink of water.

I know I have no business asking my next question, but stupid curiosity gets the better of me. "So who's this neighbor you're seeing?"

He slowly lowers the bottle and wipes the side of his mouth. "Not seeing anyone."

"Really?" I raise a brow. "So why's that Carma chick leaving jewelry in your bedroom?"

A cloud of annoyance darkens his face. "I think she lied about that. My bedroom is basically a big empty space—I would've seen a necklace if it was actually there." He offers a shrug. "We hooked up once and I told her I wasn't interested in a repeat. I think she was looking for an excuse to see me."

"Wow. Someone thinks highly of himself."

"What?"

"You really believe a woman was so devastated about you ending it that she snuck her way into your room, planted a necklace somewhere, and then pretended to find it? What if you'd gone upstairs with her to look for it?"

"I bet she would have found a way. Pulled it out of her pocket when I wasn't looking and then magically discovered it under the bed or something."

"Or—hear me out—maybe it *did* fall off when she was over and it *was* under the bed."

"Telling you, I would've noticed."

"If you say so." I roll my eyes. "I love how you think you're that good of a lay that a woman would go to extreme lengths to win your penis back."

"I am that good of a lay."

He says it dead seriously.

My heartbeat kicks up a notch. There's something very, very sexy about this man. No wonder Carma tried to come back.

I set down my water bottle and pretend my heart is thumping along at a normal clip and not careening at a breakneck pace.

"Let's do another drill?" I skate back to center ice, the chill in the air cooling my suddenly warm cheeks.

"Beckett gets around."

His abrupt remark stops me midglide.

I turn to face him. "What?"

"Just thought you should know." Ryder absently drags his stick along the ice as he skates toward me. "He's not exactly a one-woman kind of guy, and you don't seem like a multiple-man kind of girl."

I tip my chin in challenge. "Who says I'm not? Maybe I'm all about casual sex and multiple partners."

"Are you?"

After a beat, I make an irritated noise and say, "No."

He continues to appraise me, and I get lost in his eyes for a while. I can't make sense of what they're broadcasting. They're almost entirely shuttered, but through that dark-blue veil I swear I glimpse something. Not quite heat, but—

He blinks and ducks his head before I can solve the mystery.

I position myself in one of the zone face-off circles. Ryder skates into position in front of me, puck in hand. He's still watching me.

"All right, enough chatter. Drop the puck, bitch."

He snorts. "Did you really just call me bitch?"

"Yes. I'm practicing my trash talk." I stop. "Wait. I just realized I can't use it during a game. I could never call another girl a bitch, even if I secretly think she is one. That's so derogatory."

"But you can call *me* that?"

"Yes, quite easily, actually. It's alarming."

A reluctant smile lurks on his lips.

I point at him with a gloved hand. "Do it. Unleash the smile. I know you want to."

"If you don't shut up, I'm never dropping this puck," he taunts and then drops it anyway before I'm prepared.

"Hey!" I object.

My stick barely moves before he's speeding away. I chase after him, trapping him behind the net like I'm supposed to. Soon we're both breathing hard as I battle him for the puck in the cramped, narrow space. This is more strenuous than any of my workouts. I'm sweating and gasping for air by the time I manage to get out from behind the boards.

"Nice footwork there," he tells me. "Good hip work."

"Hip work."

"Yeah, you did this cool twisting move when you pivoted."

"Wow. A compliment."

"Go again?"

I nod.

Later, on our next water break, he becomes more animated than usual as we discuss ways to distract the defenders and goaltender.

"See, now the defenders have a decision to make. When to flush you out, and how to do it. Your goal is to draw them to one side of the net, try to create an opening for a backdoor play. You want them so focused on flushing you out that when it's time for them to divert their attention to one of your teammates, it's too late—they've already scored."

"I'm so much better out in the open," I admit.

"Who isn't? We all prefer having the room to rely on our speed and accuracy instead of muscles and tricks."

I grudgingly compliment him. "You're a good coach."

He shrugs.

"I mean it. You'd be a real asset to those boys at Hockey Kings if you coached there next summer. And yes, I'll be sure to keep telling my father that."

"Thanks." His voice is gruff.

We stay for another ten minutes before calling it quits. Neither of us want to overdo it now that our season openers are coming up. A comfortable silence falls between us as we trudge down the rubber walkway toward the locker rooms.

"I'm not interested in marrying your friend," I find myself saying.

He gives me a sidelong glance. "Didn't think you were."

"You made a point to tell me he's not Mr. Monogamy. Obviously that means you were super worried about it."

"Wasn't worried in the slightest."

"Jealous, then?" I mock.

His eyes narrow. "I wasn't jealous."

"Well, either way. I wasn't looking to date him. I was stressed and wanted some…naked stress-busting."

Ryder looks over again, vaguely amused.

The problem with his constant silences is, they propel me to keep babbling when I know I shouldn't.

"I miss having regular sex. I was in a relationship for almost two years, and I got used to having a regular partner, you know? It's so nice to have someone when you're stressed or need to scratch an itch. You don't have to date around, flirt, figure out if there's an attraction, worry about STIs. You can just call them up and be like, *Babe, I need to fuck your brains out*, and they're happy to oblige."

Ryder's pensive gaze doesn't leave my face.

I swallow. My throat is suddenly dry. "What?"

He shrugs. "Nothing."

"You look like you want to say something," I push.

Another shrug.

When he still doesn't speak, I sigh. "Anyway. I'm starting to feel the pressure. Our first game is coming up, and I needed a way to release the stress." I grin at him. "And he's got an Australian accent."

"Chicks do like it," Ryder says dryly.

"But it was probably a good thing we got interrupted. I would've totally been using him. And, yeah, yeah, I'm sure he would've been happy to be used. But I kind of feel bad using someone for sex." I poke him in the side. "You're welcome, by the way."

"For what?"

"For the girl talk. It's obvious you're really into this stuff, you know, sharing feelings and talking about boyfriends and girlfriends. I'm giving you what you crave. You're welcome."

He presses his lips together, and I suspect he's trying not to laugh.

We duck into our respective locker rooms, then meet outside in the parking lot fifteen minutes later, where we get into our respective vehicles. I like that he always waits for me to drive away before following suit. It's oddly gentlemanly.

Later, I eat dinner in the dining hall with Mya before Diana comes over for game night. It's a tradition we started when the three of us lived together in the freshman dorms. One night a week, we'd pick a game, usually Scrabble, and crack open some wine. Mya and Diana would then argue the entire time because they're like cats and dogs. Sometimes I think it was good that Diana moved out. They probably would have killed each other if subjected to three more years of cohabitation.

"So…I fucked Percival," Diana announces as she shakes the velvet sack of letter tiles.

Mya chokes midsip of wine. "Wait a minute. Your new man's name is Percival?" Her head swings toward me. "Did you know this?"

"Unfortunately."

Diana picks seven tiles at random before passing the little bag to Mya. "It really is unfortunate," she says glumly. "But I'm into him, so I'm pretending in my head that he has a hot name."

"Like Thunder," Mya says. "Or Blaze."

"I said a hot name, not a gladiator."

I snicker as I arrange my tiles on my letter tray. The first word that pops out at me is COCK.

Wait. I also have a Y.

COCKY.

There. Proof I don't have dicks on the brain.

Mya gets the game going by throwing down the word BEET.

"How was the sex?" she asks Diana. "I can't even imagine what a Percival would be like in bed."

"A bit intense," confesses Diana. "He held my face a lot."

"Held your face?" I echo, grinning.

"Yeah. Not aggressively or anything. He kept cupping my cheeks and looking deep in my eyes. So I kept flipping myself over and going doggy style to give all the eye contact a break, but he'd only flip me onto my back again to stare lovingly at me."

I try not to laugh. "I guess that's…romantic?"

"Sure, if it's anniversary sex. But not when you're having sex for the first time. That's supposed to be fun and wild and passionate. Not super emotional."

"I actually agree with you." Mya appears shocked by her own admission. "How is that possible? I never agree with you."

Diana laughs and tosses her platinum hair over her shoulder. "Something's definitely wrong with the universe," she agrees.

I know it's all good-natured. They do like each other. I think. If they don't, they're doing an excellent job protecting me from their mutual hatred.

The universe *must* be off-kilter, because as I examine the board trying to figure out where I can squeeze in the word COCKY, my phone buzzes with an incoming call.

From Ryder.

My heart stutters. Why is he calling me?

"One sec," I tell my friends, reaching for the phone. I swipe to answer, my tone wary. "Hello?"

I don't get a hello back, or even a normal sentence.

His rough voice fills my ear with two inexplicable words.

"Use me."

CHAPTER TWENTY

GIGI

I want it from you

HOLDING THE PHONE TO MY EAR, I WRINKLE MY FOREHEAD TO try to make sense of what Ryder is saying to me. "I'm sorry, what?"

"Use me for sex," he clarifies.

I cough loudly. A result of choking on air because I made the mistake of taking a breath right as he said that.

Use me for sex.

That's a joke.

He's joking, right?

I strangle out another cough, drawing Diana's attention. "Are you okay? Who is it?"

"Yeah, fine," I tell her, covering the mouthpiece. "Breathing is confusing sometimes."

"Why are you so weird?" she sighs, and Mya snickers.

"I need to take this. I'll be right back."

Before they can question me further, I shoot to my feet and escape to my bedroom. Once the door is firmly closed, I refocus my attention on my phone.

"Did you seriously just ask me to use you for sex?" I blurt out. My heart thuds against my ribs, palms growing damp.

"Earlier you said you wanted to use Beckett for sex. I'm offering an alternative."

As always, his deep voice carries a mocking note.

And yet I know he's being serious right now. I highly doubt Ryder calls girls out of the blue and extends bogus dirty offers.

This is legit.

"That's…not how this works," I finally manage to croak out. "Just because I wanted to get laid last weekend doesn't mean I'll fuck just anyone. Beckett and I shared an organic moment. I didn't go to the party planning to have sex with him."

"So you don't have an itch that needs scratching anymore?"

"That's not what I'm saying."

"Then you *do* still require naked stress-busting." On a raspy chuckle, he throws my own asinine descriptor back at me.

"All I'm saying is, just because I need…"

"To get fucked," he supplies.

My cheeks nearly burst into flames. I sit on the edge of my bed while my heart continues to hammer out a wild, frantic rhythm.

"…just because I need what I need," I finish, "doesn't mean I'm desperate." I bristle to myself. "I'm not interested in pity sex."

Husky laughter tickles my ear. "Gisele. Come on now."

"What?" I gulp. My throat feels tight now.

"You think I'm throwing you a pity fuck?"

"You're not?"

"No." There's a pause. "I need what I need too." Another pause. "And I want it from you."

My pussy clenches.

Hard.

His candor sends a dose of raw lust coursing through my blood. My knees are wobbling and I'm sitting down, for Pete's sake.

I swallow again. "You're being serious, aren't you?"

"Yes."

"You want to sleep together."

"Sleep, no. But I think we should fuck."

Every inch of my body feels hot and tight. It's been a while since I felt desire this potent. I don't think it's ever been this strong. Not with Case. Certainly not with Beckett last weekend.

"You said you needed release. Someone to help you with the stress. I can help. We already have a good arrangement going here," he points out. "So why not sweeten the deal?"

"I…"

My brain is close to short-circuiting. I want to laugh this off, tell him it's an interesting idea but probably not a smart one. But the words won't come out. Instead, I say something very stupid.

"I'm not sure I'm even attracted to you."

Then I almost burst out in waves of hysterical laughter because what the hell am I even saying right now? Someone hijacked my voice and is making it spew nonsense.

Of course I'm attracted to him.

Ryder goes quiet for a second. Then he says, "All right. Hold on."

There's more silence, save for some rustling noises on his end followed by the unmistakable click of a camera.

When my phone buzzes from the incoming message, I stop breathing entirely.

I'm expecting a dick pic.

I get something even better.

His bare chest, impossibly broad with more muscles than I knew existed. He's cut like stone. Abs galore. He wears a pair of low-hanging sweatpants, his thumb hooked under one corner, pulling them down even lower to provide a suggestive view of his obliques. I notice a jagged white scar on his hip, about an inch long, and wonder how he got it. I wonder what that raised, puckered skin would feel like scraping beneath my fingertips. What I'd find if I slipped my fingers under his waistband.

My mouth waters. The longer I look at the picture, the wetter I get. Everywhere.

"Well?"

The trace of amusement in his voice tells me he knows he got me speechless.

"What, no dick pic?" I say, playing it cool.

"I've actually never taken one of those."

"Liar."

"Never," he insists.

"Why not?" I'm genuinely curious. I don't think I've met a single guy my age who hasn't sent someone a picture of his penis. Usually unsolicited.

"Why do I need to?" He sounds almost bored by the question. Until his voice turns smoky. "I'd rather see the look in a woman's eyes when she sees it for the first time."

"Why? Is it super spectacular?"

"Say yes to my offer and find out."

I rub my palm over my scorching face. "Look. Prom king. You're hot," I acknowledge. "You know you are. But a ripped chest doesn't tell me if there's chemistry between us, only that you're nice to look at."

"You're trying to tell me we don't have chemistry."

His soft chuckle makes my throat run dry.

"I don't know. Maybe we don't. We haven't even kissed." I don't know why I'm fighting this so hard.

Well, I do know why.

Because the second I open this door, there'll be no turning back.

And that...scares me.

"I'm not going to agree to a sex deal with someone I haven't even kissed," I say when he doesn't respond.

"Okay. If that's how you feel."

Then he ends the call, and the only thing I feel is disbelief.

Did he seriously hang up on me?

I stare at my phone, which now displays my lock screen. He actually did.

Unless…maybe we got disconnected? I wait nearly a full minute for him to call back. But he doesn't.

I'm in a daze when I return to the living room, where Diana and Mya are debating whether *Fling or Forever* is pure trash or pure genius.

Diana, obviously, is a proponent of Team Genius.

"You get to see young hot people have sex on camera while pretending to be there for the romantic dates. And then every week, a total stranger shows up and breaks up a couple against their will, and now the *new* couple is fucking on camera and pretending to care about the dates. Are you truly telling me this isn't the best show ever made?"

"It's brain cell–killing garbage. You'll never convince me otherwise, girl."

Diana grins at my return. "What, is game night not doing it for you anymore?"

"Who was on the phone?" Mya asks curiously.

"Luke Ryder."

"Oooh, the enemy," Diana says. "What did he want?"

I'm tempted to relate the entire conversation, word for word. But I'm barely able to make sense of it myself yet, let alone hash it out with my friends.

"Just hammering out our practice schedule," I lie, taking my seat on the couch again. I reach for my Scrabble letters.

"That's still going on?" Diana doesn't sound as interested now that it's about hockey.

"Yup. I'm learning a lot from him."

We resume our game, but my head's not in it. Even after fifteen minutes pass, I'm still internally marveling over what happened.

Honestly, the sheer audacity of this man. He tells me to use him for sex, and then when I dare to think it over, he's like, *Cool, forget it?*

Who does that?

"*Beety* is not a word!" Mya screeches in outrage when Diana tries adding a Y to board.

"Sure it is."

"Use it in a fucking sentence."

"I don't like this salad because of all the beets. It's too beety."

"G, back me up here," pleads Mya.

I glance up from my tray. "I'm vetoing *beety*."

"Traitor," Diana complains.

I'm about to put down my next word when my phone buzzes again. A text this time.

RYDER:

I'm downstairs.

My heart stops. Just quits beating altogether in my chest.

A shivery sensation whispers through me. I don't know if it's adrenaline or anticipation, but I feel weak and dizzy as I abruptly shoot to my feet.

My friends look up, startled.

"I need to go downstairs," I blurt out.

They both stare at me.

"I, ah, ordered food."

I haphazardly wave my phone around as if to show them a notification from a food delivery app, except I purposely keep the screen away from their eyes. I also don't have a plan for how I'm going to explain why I don't have food upon my return. But nobody ever said I was quick under pressure. Off the ice, anyway.

"We had dinner, like, two hours ago," Mya says in confusion, but I'm already slipping into a pair of sneakers and heading for the door.

In the small lobby, I greet the security woman at the front desk, whose wary gaze is fixed on the vertical pane of glass next to the door. Beyond the window is Ryder.

"It's okay," I assure her. "I know him."

Although I don't blame her for being suspicious of the six-foot-five man in the black hoodie lurking outside the dorm.

Outside, the night air is cooler than I expect. It's almost October, though. Soon the weather will turn completely, and going outside in yoga pants and an oversized tee won't even be an option. Then I'll be longing for this barely-there chill that's puckering my nipples.

Or maybe that's Ryder's doing.

"Why are you here?" I grumble, pulling him away from the door.

We move to the edge of the path, where he shoves his hands in the front pocket of his sweatshirt and gazes down at me through heavy eyelids.

"I came to kiss you."

My mouth falls open. I stare at him for a moment.

"You...drove all the way here to kiss me."

"Yes."

"I... You..." I'm at a genuine loss for words.

Ryder shrugs. "You won't fuck someone you haven't kissed. Isn't that what you said?"

"I..." I honestly can't think straight enough to speak.

"So." Those mesmerizing blue eyes focus on my face "Are you going to let me kiss you, Gigi?"

My pulse speeds up when it registers that he called me Gigi. Not Gisele. But my actual name. Because right now, in this moment, he's not mocking me. He's not playing games. He's being sincere.

He moves closer, slipping his hands out of his pockets. His big frame encroaches on my personal space, the spicy scent of him grabbing hold of my senses. I suck in a breath and then regret it because he always smells so good and it's distracting.

"Yes or no," he says softly.

I lick my bottom lip and meet his eyes.

Then I say, "Yes."

Before I can second-guess myself, I reach up to slide my fingers through his hair and tug his head down.

Our mouths meet in the lightest of caresses. Just a taste. A tease. But our lips feel so right against each other that I can't stop myself from driving the kiss deeper. Ryder spits out a growled curse before his tongue slides through my parted lips and sends an electric current through my body.

I press myself up against him, arms looped around his neck to pull him down as low as he can go with his height. Desperate to explore his mouth. His lips are equally hungry, but not overpowering. The way his tongue touches mine is almost unbearable. I want more of it. And more of his hands, but he's not letting them wander. One rests lightly on my hip, the other cups the side of my face, his thumb absently stroking my jaw as he kisses me as if he has all the time in the world.

"Mmmm." His husky groan tickles my lips, and then the hand on my waist suddenly moves. He slides it around to squeeze my ass and bring me flush up against him so I can feel his erection.

When I whimper in response, he pulls back to reveal his slight grin. Mocking as usual.

"Did I pass the test?"

My breathing comes out in labored pants. My mind is spinning.

"I…" I drop my hands from his shoulders and take a step back. "I don't think I'm good at casual sex." I press my hands against my sides to stop them from grabbing him. I'm already craving his kiss again. "That's what you're looking for, right?"

"Yes."

Reluctance renders me with indecision. I don't know why I can't pull this trigger and simply tell him I want him.

When my hesitation drags on, Ryder runs his fingers through his hair to smooth it out. I messed up those dark strands pretty bad when I had my hands all over him.

"All right." He finally shrugs and flicks up his eyebrows. "If you change your mind, you know where to find me."

CHAPTER TWENTY-ONE
RYDER

The universe approves

"LUKE, STOP!"

I wake up Friday morning in a cold sweat. It's soaked through the T-shirt I fell asleep in last night, pasting it to my chest. The terrified voice still reverberates through the cobwebs of my barely alert brain. I banish it because the last thing I need is to start my day engulfed in darkness.

But the nightmare proves to be an omen. When I roll over in bed to grab my phone, there's a missed call from a Phoenix area code and a voicemail notification.

Fuck.

I sit up and punch in my passcode.

"Luke, this is Peter Greene, Maricopa County Attorney's office. I tried contacting you a few weeks ago. My office also reached out via email, although I'm not certain we have the correct address; the one I have on file is quite old. I understand this might be a sensitive subject for you, but we do need to discuss the hearing and—"

"Your message has been deleted."

I toss the phone on the mattress and stumble into the hall toward the bathroom to shower. I plan to be at the performance center at 8:00 a.m. today rather than 7:00. Now that classes are officially underway, I need to cut back on the extra training and not push myself so hard.

Everyone on the hockey team has only afternoon classes this semester because of our morning skate and training schedule. Beckett catches a ride to campus with me, but Shane says he'll take his own car. We leave him in the kitchen at the blender, preparing a protein shake.

On the drive, Beckett chats about some movie he watched yesterday, but I'm only half listening. My mind is preoccupied with the same damn thing that's been eating away at it for three days now.

Gigi Graham.

It's been three days since we kissed.

Or rather, since one kiss from her got my dick so hard I could barely drive home with the damn thing trying to tunnel its way out of my pants and poke the steering wheel.

I honestly thought she'd call me by now.

And I shouldn't be as disappointed as I am that she hasn't.

With our first game coming up, practices have taken on a greater sense of urgency. Jensen works us hard this morning. Afterward, we pile into the media room to watch Northeastern game tape. They'll be our first opponent of the season.

While we wait for Assistant Coach Peretti to arrive, I continue to fixate on Gigi's silence and apparent decision to pretend that wasn't the hottest kiss either of us had ever experienced.

I didn't imagine that heat. We were both so hot for each other we were liable to burst into flames.

I try to push it out of my mind as my teammates blabber around me. As usual, the former Eastwood guys take up most of the second row, while the original Briars comprise the first one.

"All I'm saying is, you can't prove wormholes don't exist," Beckett is contending, even as he texts on his phone with some chick. He's a solid multitasker when it comes to time travel and sex.

"And you can't prove they *do* exist," Nazzy says in exasperation.

"Naz. Bro. You're fighting a losing battle," Shane advises. He's also texting. He met another cheerleader at a frat party last night. Dude's plowing through the cheer team like he's trying to win nationals himself.

"I need to ask a question right now, and I need you all to promise you won't judge me," Patrick says nervously.

"Nobody is promising that," Rand informs him.

"Forget it then."

Rand chortles. "Right. Like we're letting you get away with not asking it now."

"I said forget it." Patrick stubbornly shakes his head.

"Captain?" someone prompts me.

"Cocaptain," comes Trager's snide voice from the front row, but we all ignore him.

"Ask the question," I mutter to the Kansas Kid.

"So, ah, wormholes." He hesitates, looking around the group. "Are there worms in them?"

He's greeted by pure silence. Even Will Larsen has twisted around in his seat to stare at Patrick.

"Theoretical worms?" Patrick corrects. He looks utterly lost. "Am I saying it right?"

Shane takes pity on him. "It's okay. You're really handsome."

He doesn't realize he's being insulted until after Shane has already gone back to texting his cheerleader.

"Wait. Fuck you," Patrick growls.

"There aren't any worms in them," Beckett says in a shockingly kind tone. "Basically, wormholes are these warped areas in space that connect two distant points…"

I tune them out again. I already have to deal with this at home. I'm not allowing Beckett Dunne to ruin my life on campus too.

An hour later we're dismissed, and I cross the quad toward the ancient ivy-covered building that houses all my lectures for the day.

It's only been a couple of weeks, but it didn't take long for me to determine that, academically, Briar is much tougher than Eastwood. I'm a business admin major with a minor in history, and already both disciplines are piling a mountain of work on me. I have two papers due next week, and then two more literally a week later. Fucking brutal. Maybe it's an Ivy thing.

I'm walking out of my final lecture for the day when Gigi's name pops up on my phone. My pulse quickens.

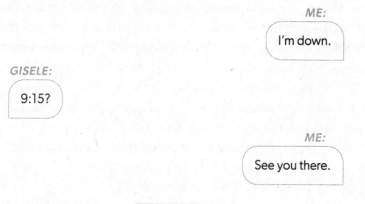

GISELE:

I know it's last minute, but do you want to do a session in Munsen tonight?

I don't think there's any innuendo there. I believe she's really asking to run drills. Yet the way my dick hardens and my ass cheeks clench, you'd think she texted me a picture of her pussy with the caption *come fuck this*.

I type a response as I walk to the parking lot.

ME:

I'm down.

GISELE:

9:15?

ME:

See you there.

The universe approves of us fucking.

This is confirmed when Gigi and I arrive at the rink and discover that the women's locker rooms are out of service. A white paper taped to the door explains there'd been a flooding issue. The faint odor of sewage reaches my nostrils as we read the sign.

Gigi shrugs and heads for the men's room, trusty keys in hand. I haven't been able to stop checking her out since we got here. Black yoga pants cling to her shapely legs and emphasize her ass. The ass I was squeezing a few nights ago. I still remember how sweet it felt in my palms, and my fingers itch to touch her again.

"How was your week?" she asks nonchalantly.

I try not to raise an eyebrow. We're playing the casual game, I see. Just ignoring the fact that she was ravenously sucking on my tongue the other night. Cool.

"Good. You?"

"Busy," she admits. "It's like every year I forget what a heavy workload it is to balance classes and hockey."

"What's your major?"

"Sports admin." She shrugs. "Kinda always thought I'd make a good agent or manager, so I picked a major that could put me on that path. How about you?"

"Business admin. Not sure what I'll do with it, though."

When we enter the change area, she slides her jean jacket off her shoulders and drops it on the bench. For a second, I think she's going to keep undressing—my libido wholeheartedly approves—but then she picks up her garment bag and heads for the adjacent shower area.

"I'll change in here," she calls over her shoulder.

Like the other times we've been here, we have the whole rink to ourselves and it's eerily silent. It doesn't feel like a real hockey arena without the soundtrack of pucks striking the boards and plexiglass. The sharp slap of a puck meeting its target can rattle the walls of a building. It's my favorite sound in the world.

It's almost impossible to focus on hockey tonight. Which is a thought I never imagined myself capable of thinking. I'm *always* focused on hockey. It's in my blood.

But tonight, my blood is burning for something else.

Gigi seems distracted too, dropping several passes she'd normally make in her sleep.

You never realize what a truly bad idea it is to play any sport while distracted until someone gets hurt.

During our next battle for the puck, Gigi lets out a cry of pain that causes my entire body to tense. I stop in my tracks.

"You okay?" I ask immediately.

She slides her gloves off, wincing as she rotates her wrist. Concern wells up inside me. Shit. If she injured herself…this could fuck up her entire season.

"C'mere."

I guide her toward the bench, where we sit down. I take her wrist in one hand and examine it with the other. I gently run my fingers over the tendons, watching her face for a reaction.

"Does this hurt?"

"No." She visibly swallows. "I think it's fine. Think I just tweaked it when we were against the boards."

I press down on another spot, still studying her. "What about this?"

"No."

"You sure?" I feel her pulse fluttering beneath the pad of my thumb now.

Gigi nods, looking relieved. "That twinge of pain I was feeling before is already gone."

She rotates the wrist again but doesn't make any move to withdraw it from my probing grasp.

"I've never actually broken a bone," she admits. "Guess I'm lucky. My brother broke his arm three different times growing up. Have you ever broken anything?"

"Do ribs count?"

"Of course."

"Then a couple different ribs, a couple different times. Other than that, it's mostly been light sprains. Ankle, wrist." I shrug. "Never broken anything important."

"I mean, ribs are pretty important." She reaches out and touches my rib cage over my sweaty jersey.

Even though she's not touching my bare skin, I feel her fingers like a cattle brand.

"You know…" She trails off thoughtfully. Gray eyes peering into me.

It makes me uncomfortable, the way she's looking at me. It's as if she's seeing something I can't. As if she knows a secret about me that even I haven't been able to decode.

Finally, she finishes that thought. "You're not actually a dick."

"Sure I am."

"Nope. It's an act. You care. You just don't want anyone to know you care. I thought you had a huge chip on your shoulder, but the rudeness is a front for something." Gigi's lips curve slightly. "Don't worry, I won't ask what. I know you won't tell me."

She continues to search my face, and I resist the urge to duck my head. I feel oddly exposed. It makes my skin itch.

"Tell me a misconception you had about me."

Her request startles me. I hadn't given it much thought, but now that I muse on it, I realize I did have some preconceived notions about her.

"I assumed you'd be cockier. Entitled," I admit.

She nods, as if expecting that.

"But you're more humble than I expected. You rarely brag about yourself, only when you're joking. Every time someone compliments you, you look pleasantly surprised, like it's the first time you've ever been complimented. And you always respond with gratitude."

Her wrist remains between my clasped hands. I can't help stroking my fingers over her pale fragile flesh.

"I've known kids of famous people before," I tell her. "I thought you'd be like them. But you're not at all like them."

Gigi's teeth sink into her bottom lip for a moment. Then she moistens both lips, locking her gaze with mine.

"Just to clarify, you're not trying to date me."

"No." I chuckle. "If you want someone to be sweet to you and take you on dates, I'm not your man. I'm not good at that stuff."

"What are you good at, then?"

That's a loaded question and we both know it.

I turn her hand over, then deliberately drag my thumb along the center of her palm. I don't miss the way she shivers.

"I'm good at making you wet," I say, hearing the rasp in my voice. "And I'll fuck you so good you'll be thinking about it for days after. It'll be the best fuck of your life."

She bites her lip again. The hazy, needy spark in her eyes nearly does me in. I almost pull her into my lap and kiss her. But she's the one hesitating. This needs to be her move to make.

And she doesn't make it.

My body cries in silent disappointment when she slowly stands up on her skates.

"Let's call it a night," she suggests. "Our heads aren't in it, and that's a recipe for injury."

I follow her back to the men's lockers, where we sit side by side on the bench to unlace our skates. Gigi removes her gear until she's in a tank top, sports bra, and boy shorts. I try not to stare.

"I'm gonna take a quick shower," she says, drifting toward the doorway across the room.

I remain on the bench, breathing through my nose. Deep, even breaths.

Christ. I want her. Never saw it coming. Totally unprepared for it. And at a loss for what to do about it.

I hear the shower start, and soon there's a layer of steam rolling toward the change room. I need to grab a shower too, so while I wait for Gigi to finish, I strip out of my practice clothes and shove them in my backpack. I'm putting the rest of my gear away when her muffled voice breaks through the sound of rushing water.

"Ryder?"

"Yeah?" I call toward the showers.

"I forgot a towel. Can you grab one and bring it to me?"

My cock turns stiffer than the hockey stick in my hand. With another deep inhalation, I lean the stick against my bag.

"Sure. One sec."

I make my way to the wall of cubbies where fresh towels are stored. Grab two off a shelf. Then I walk through the steamy air hanging like a canopy over the rows of showers. The majority of steam comes from the third stall.

Heart pounding, I stop in front of the white plastic curtain. I glimpse the tantalizing outline of her body, a blurry flash of curves and golden flesh.

I clear my throat to announce my presence, then bring the towels to the edge of the stall. "Here."

The curtain rustles.

Then it parts.

Rather than take the towels from me, Gigi stands there, fully on display for me.

She's incredible.

My breathing grows shallow as her naked body wreaks havoc on my field of vision. Perky breasts tipped with brownish-pink nipples. They're tight and puckered despite the heat of the shower. My tongue tingles with the impulse to lick them.

I tear my gaze off her tits to curb the temptation, but it only lands between her legs. An even more tempting place. She's completely bare, and now my tongue licks at my lips the way it wants to be licking her pussy.

There's an invitation in her eyes.

I leave the towels on the hook. Then I step into the stall without a word, shutting the curtain behind me. She's fully naked. I'm still in my boxer-briefs. But maybe that's a good thing, keeping a barrier between her and my aching dick.

Her gaze travels along my body in a long, heated perusal. Resting on my pecs. My abs. The very visible outline of my cock. Appreciation darkens her eyes, and damned if that doesn't bring a rush of satisfaction. I want her to like my body. I want her to use it as her own personal playground.

Neither of us speak for several long beats. Water sluices over her, droplets rolling down the valley between her perfect tits, sliding over her flat stomach, her sculpted thighs.

"Ryder," she begs, and that's all it takes.

I join her under the spray, bending down to kiss her at the same time I slip one hand between her thighs.

She gasps and I swallow the sound with my lips. Slowly backing her into the wall, I drag my knuckles over her slit. Her hips move, trying to push up against my hand. I rub her clit in a light caress, only applying pressure when she begins whimpering into my mouth.

I break the kiss and inhale a cloud of steam. It swirls all around us, droplets clinging to her full bottom lip as she stares at me beneath impossibly long eyelashes.

"More," she begs.

"More what?" A smile tickles my lips. "More of this?"

I curl my hand over her pussy.

Gigi moans.

While she rocks herself against my hand, I bend down to kiss her again. I love the way she tastes. The way she feels grinding against my hand. I hook one of her legs on my hip, opening her up more for me so I can push two fingers inside her. Her muscles clamp around them, and I damn near keel over with lust.

I need my cock in her. Christ.

Kissing her senseless, I slide my fingers in and out of her, while the heel of my palm grinds her clit. My other hand squeezes her tits, toying with the hardened buds of her nipples.

When she tries reaching between us to touch my dick, which strains against the wet material of my underwear, I chidingly nudge her eager hand away. I'm enjoying this too fucking much, and I don't want the distraction. Every fiber of my being is fixated on the sounds she's making. The uneven breaths and tiny whimpers.

She fucks my fingers in earnest now, eyes closed and chest heaving.

Some other time, I plan to spend hours playing with her, teasing her, but the urgency has reached peak levels, and suddenly the only thing I want is to make her come hard and fast.

"Let go," I whisper in her ear before dragging my tongue along the delicate tendons of her neck. "Let me feel you squeezing my fingers when you come."

A passion-drenched cry leaves her throat as she does what I ask. Gives herself over to the orgasm. To me.

I smile as she convulses with pleasure, her breaths escaping in steamy puffs. She presses her lips to my pecs, softly biting my skin and making me jerk with desire. My fingers continue to move inside her, but slower now. Her clit is swollen against my palm, her pussy slick from orgasm.

Meanwhile, I'm so painfully hard I'm surprised I'm able to remain upright. That the heavy erection in my briefs isn't tipping me right over.

"Hey, is someone in there?" a confused male voice suddenly rings out.

We jump apart.

"Cleaning staff," that same voice calls out.

Gigi's chest heaves from another deep breath. "Yeah, sorry, just finishing up in here," she calls back. "I have permission from the building owner to be here after hours. I'll be out shortly."

"Oh, all right," the cleaner says, but still sounds confused. "I'll start in the children's change rooms. Sorry to interrupt."

I'm still hard, but the moment has passed. A frantic Gigi grabs the towels I hung outside the stall, throwing one at me.

"Fuck," she mumbles under her breath. "This is so embarrassing."

"He didn't know I was in here with you. It's all good."

We towel off and hurry to the main room to get dressed. My erection hasn't subsided, not even an inch. Her lips quirk wryly when she notices me trying to slide my jeans up over it.

"Having trouble there, prom king?"

I sigh.

She throws her hair up in a messy bun, watching me for a moment. Finally, she speaks.

"I'm going home this weekend. Driving there tomorrow morning." She pauses. "I'll be back Sunday afternoon."

"My roommates will be gone all weekend too. They're hitting up some concert in Boston, and Shane said they won't be home until late Sunday night. So I'll have the house to myself."

Her eyes lower to the visible bulge in my jeans, then slide back up. "Is that your way of asking me to come over on Sunday?"

"No." I shrug. "Come over on Sunday. There—that's my way of doing it."

A smile lifts the corners of her mouth. "Okay." She meets my questioning gaze. "I'll be there."

CHAPTER TWENTY-TWO
GIGI

Don't get too invested

"I'm sorry, Henry. It was just a fling." The British host sweeps her gaze over the remaining swimsuit-clad couples strategically draped on wicker beach furniture. "The rest of you are still on the road to forever. Good night."

"Holy shit, that was intense." Wyatt is agape. "That Scottish dude seriously just waltzed into the villa and broke up Annabeth and Henry."

It's Saturday night and my family is gathered in the great room of our house in Brookline. Well, technically it's just a living room, but it's been referred to as "the great room" for as long as I can remember. Likely because of its soaring ceilings and the wall of windows. It's my favorite room in the house. I love the built-in bookcases and super comfortable sectional couches surrounding the huge stone fireplace. The room opens onto one of the many decks on the property, this one overlooking the main section of the expansive yard that houses the pool and gazebo.

On the other sectional, my mother is clicking the remote to put on the next episode, while Dad shovels a handful of popcorn into his mouth.

"I'm rooting for Mac and Samantha," he says while chewing.

"Seriously?" I demand. "Mac is such a jerk. All he does is criticize her wardrobe."

"He's only following her lead," Dad says in Mac's defense. "She's constantly complaining about his appearance. She told him his ears were small, and the poor dude was considering surgery."

"Those two are way too toxic," I argue. "I'm on Team Cam and Abby."

"Cam!" Dad balks. "Come on, Stan. He uses way too much tanning oil."

"He does," Wyatt agrees. "Looks like he crawled out of a baby oil factory explosion."

Mom howls with laughter.

"I am obsessed with this channel," I tell everyone.

"Dude. Same." Wyatt steals the last pieces of popcorn from my bowl. He devoured his own within five seconds of Mom handing it to him.

"Are you really?" I ask suspiciously. "Or are you making fun of me?"

"No, I'm into it. *Plate Pleasers*? Genius."

Mom nods in agreement. "I love those cute little judges. That one kid who never likes any of the contestants' dishes is hilarious."

"The way that little asshole scrunches up his nose," Wyatt agrees in delight. "Love it."

Bergeron suddenly hops off his dog bed and lumbers toward one set of French doors, where he stands and whines.

"Don't put the next episode on yet," I tell Mom. "Bergy needs to go out."

"I'll let him out." Wyatt heaves himself off the couch. I use the break to duck into the kitchen to pop another packet of popcorn into the microwave. While I wait for it, Dad wanders in and throws his arm around me.

"I'm so glad you're home, Stan."

I rest my head against his broad shoulder. "Me too. I needed this."

The past few days have been…intense. But I don't plan to fill my father in. Whatever's happening between Luke Ryder and me is going to stay between Luke Ryder and me. At least for the time being. Besides, even if I could make sense of it, no daughter wants to casually let her father know she's planning on having sex with someone tomorrow night.

If I go through with it.

After what happened between us in the shower, I'm a little terrified to see this through. Because the voice in my head, the one that taunted me a while ago—that it's not anxiety he instills in me, but *passion*—well, it may have been right.

And that's scary.

"Any updates about Team USA?" he asks.

I shake my head. "Nothing. But hopefully that changes after our first game. Fairlee and his staff will have to be paying closer attention then, right?"

"Presumably." Hesitation flickers through Dad's gray eyes, the same shade as mine.

"What?"

"I'm going to assume the answer to this is no, but…do you want me to give Brad a call and—"

"No," I say sharply.

He holds up his hands in surrender. "Don't worry, backing off," he says with a laugh. "I knew it would be a no. But I wanted to throw it out there. If you ever need me to put in a good word for you, you know you can just ask."

"I know," I tell him.

And we both know I'll never ask.

Not once in my life have I asked my father for favors. To use his clout or connections to help me get ahead. Every elite hockey camp I was accepted to over the years, every college offer, every award…I desperately want to believe they came to me based on merit.

Sometimes, when I'm feeling low, I let the inner critic, the cynic, rear its ugly head, whisper that maybe merit had nothing to do with it. But it's such a crushing, demoralizing feeling that I try valiantly to never listen to that voice.

"What about you?" I ask. "Given any more thought to who you're picking to help you with the camp this summer?"

"A little. I have a short list, but nothing set in stone yet." He then provides me with the perfect opening to plug Ryder. "You have any suggestions?"

I think it over, before answering in a careful tone. "Will Larsen would be a solid choice, but he doesn't like to make waves, so I don't know what kind of authority figure he'd be. I'd consider Kurth, but you know how weird goalies can be sometimes. Luke Ryder has really stepped up as cocaptain, so he'd be a good choice too."

"I don't know about Ryder. He's a great player, but he has a bad attitude. His behavior at Worlds is a cause for concern."

"He was eighteen. Anyway, like I said, he's leaning into the leadership role lately."

I'm pretty sure I'm lying right now. I haven't crashed any more Briar men's practices, but I highly doubt Ryder is leaning into anything other than wanting to be left the fuck alone.

"You're really singing Ryder's praises lately. What's up with that?"

"I told you, I've been working with him. Beckett Dunne too," I add, so he doesn't think I'm spending a bunch of alone time with Ryder, getting fingered in locker room showers.

"But you wouldn't recommend Dunne for the camp?"

"Dunne doesn't take anything too seriously. He'd treat the camp as a lark. Ryder and Larsen would step up. In my opinion."

"But between Larsen and Ryder, you'd go Ryder." That cloud of suspicion hasn't cleared from his expression.

The microwave beeps, allowing me to put my back to him as I go to refill our popcorn bowls. "Probably. But that's me. Go with whoever you think is the best fit."

The next morning, we have breakfast out on the back patio in our sweats. While my parents and I munch on our bacon and eggs, Wyatt, who inhales every meal in five seconds flat, throws a stick for the dogs. He sings them a dumb song before each throw. I'm only half paying attention to it, but it goes something like, *It's alright, it's okay, a stick's coming your way, hey-hey.* I'm surprised Dumpy is participating, but the golden lab bounds after the stick each time, actually matching our eternally wired husky's breakneck pace.

"Did you give Dumpy steroids?" I ask Dad, who snorts.

At one point, they lose the stick, and Wyatt and the dogs proceed to prowl the lawn in search of it while my brother continues to sing that stupid ditty.

"Hey, champ," Dad calls over the railing of the stone deck. "Despite what the song says, it doesn't look like a stick is coming their way, hey-hey."

"Don't lie to the dogs, Wyatt," Mom pipes up.

I keel over laughing. I love my family so much.

The lighthearted feeling in my chest wavers, however, when my phone lights up on the table. I hastily reach for it before my parents see the notification.

RYDER:

You still coming by later?

My heartbeat accelerates. Trying to play it cool so that my dad doesn't pounce, I casually drag my fingers over the keypad to type a response. Just one word. I don't need much more than that.

ME:

Yes.

CHAPTER TWENTY-THREE

GIGI

This part's easy

"OH WOW, YOU WEREN'T KIDDING."

I glance around Ryder's room in bewilderment. I was feeling nervous when I first stepped foot in here. Because, really, what am I doing alone with this guy in his bedroom? But one look at my barren surroundings, and my natural curiosity takes over.

"Are you sure you're not in the military?"

He thinks it over. "No, I'm not," he finally says.

"Was that a joke? Oh my God. You made a joke."

"Shut up."

I grin. I like poking him. It's fun. Plus there's always a fifty-fifty chance I'll be able to penetrate his grumpy jerk exterior and draw out a killer grin or two.

I continue to marvel over his bedroom. It's neat as a pin, without a single piece of clutter anywhere. Not a knickknack, not a photograph. He has a queen-sized bed. A dresser. The only things on his desk are his phone, a laptop, some textbooks, and a small stack of books. The bed is perfectly made. The floor is vacuumed and shiny. I even peek under the bed and discover there isn't a fleck of dust. He clearly cleans under there often. Now I understand why he insisted he would've seen that Carma chick's necklace and silver crucifix.

"Are you done?" he asks politely.

"Can I look in your closet?" I beg. "Please?"

He rolls his eyes. "Knock yourself out."

I open the door. Sure enough, it's organized in militant fashion. Everything hung perfectly. Very exciting color palette of black, gray, and denim.

"You want to look in my boxer drawer too?" he drawls.

That makes me blush. "Sorry, I'm being nosy. I'm just amazed by how little stuff you have."

"Stuff is overrated."

"You're so deep, Ryder. A regular old Plato."

He stretches out on the bed and picks up the remote. "You want to watch something?"

I set my beer on the nightstand. He grabbed us a couple bottles of lager when I first got here. I thought we were going to hang out in the living room, but he suggested we go upstairs. So here we are.

I'm trying not to let my gaze linger on him. His denim-encased legs stretch out in front of him, feet bare. His blue T-shirt has a surf logo on it, and suddenly I'm picturing that long powerful body crouched on a surfboard, and a tiny thrill shoots through me.

I continue wandering around the bare space. I'm wired. If I go over to the bed, I don't know what's going to happen.

Well, I do know.

And my body is primed for it. Pleading for me to move closer to him.

But my head tells me not to rush anything tonight. Just because he made me come in the shower the other night doesn't mean I shouldn't proceed with caution.

"So. Your roommates went to a concert tonight?" I lean against the dresser.

"Yeah. Some new rapper with the worst stage name known to man. No joke—his name is Vizza Billity."

"Wait, Vizza is in Boston?" I exclaim. "My roommate is obsessed with him. If I'd known, I would've stayed in the city and tried to get us tickets."

"Oh, right, I forgot. You were there this weekend."

"You did not forget. Go ahead. Just ask how it went with my parents."

"Fine. How'd it go?"

He leans back against the headboard and props one knee up, resting his beer bottle on it.

"It was good," I answer. "We binge-watched a horrible reality show. We're all addicted."

Ryder sounds dubious. "Garrett Graham watches reality shows."

"He does when we force him to." I laugh. "He got into it, though. The couple he's rooting for is so toxic. And yes, I dropped your name a bunch of times."

"What'd he say?"

I think about Dad's reluctant admission. "He said you're a great player."

Ryder narrows his eyes.

"He did," I insist. "Because you are. That's not his issue with you."

"So he has an issue with me." His broad shoulders sag a little.

"He thinks you have an attitude problem. But you already knew that."

Ryder's gaze drops to his hands. It's adorably bashful, which somehow makes him so much sexier to me. "He's not the only one. A friend in the pros told me my draft team is watching me like a hawk. Dallas has a new GM, and he's not entirely sure about me."

"Well, I mean, your reputation precedes you." I eye him pointedly. "Any chance you feel like sharing what happened at the World Juniors? Because a lot of people are curious. Including my dad."

He just looks at me. Silent.

"Yeah, what I was thinking? That was a stupid question to ask Mr. Forthcoming over here." I lift a brow. "You know, you have a really bad habit of never talking about anything important."

"That's not true. We talk about hockey all the time."

"Hockey doesn't count. And you know that's not what I mean." I reach for my lager and take a sip before setting it back on the dresser. "It wouldn't kill you to share sometimes. Even minor things. Like, for example, what you have against stuff."

"Stuff?" he echoes.

I use air quotes to repeat his earlier insight. "'Stuff is overrated.' Okay, cool—why's that? You don't like clutter? You're a neat freak? I mean, fine, it's obvious you're a neat freak. But isn't this a bit extreme? There's hardly any personal possessions in this room. Feels like a hotel room." I gesture all around us. "Come on, you gotta give me something here."

He ponders it for a moment, visibly uncomfortable.

"I moved around constantly when I was a kid," he finally answers. "Stuff got stolen a lot."

"You moved around with your family?"

"Foster care." The words are clipped, gravelly.

I soften. "Oh, I didn't know that."

He takes a drink of his beer. "Most of the homes were overcrowded. Kids would be fighting for toys, for attention. It became easier not to have anything to fight over or get stolen from me. If that makes sense." He gives his trademark shrug. "The neatness is a habit from those days too. We used to get in trouble if we didn't keep the room clean."

"Look at that," I tell him. "Do you see what's happening?"

"What?"

"We're having an actual conversation."

"Fuck. You're right. Come here."

Ryder doesn't say a lot, but when he does, it speaks volumes. Those two words—*come here*—are loaded with so much heat. His blue eyes tell me we're done talking.

I walk over and stand at the foot of the bed.

He cocks a brow. "Are you going to sit?"

"Do you want me to?"

"Yes."

My heart is pounding. Since I didn't bring a purse, I fish my phone and ID cards out of my back pocket and drop them on the nightstand. Then I join him on the mattress and sit cross-legged.

My gaze shifts to the black screen of the TV. "So are we watching something?"

"Do you want to?"

"No."

He takes a long sip of his beer. I grin when I notice the bracelet on his wrist.

"You really don't strike me as the friendship bracelet type," I say frankly.

"I'm not."

"Got it. So this is the fault of an overly sentimental BFF."

"One hundred percent. I swear, this dude cries at any movie with a dog. I figured he'd have a nervous breakdown if I cut this thing off. I'm sort of used to it now, though."

Ryder turns to place his bottle on the other night table.

"You still feeling stressed out?" His voice is gruff.

"Very much so."

I move closer to him. I put my hand on his thigh.

He glances down at it, then up at me. Slightly amused.

"My hand is on your thigh," I tell him.

"I noticed."

He smiles, and my breath hitches at the sight.

Then he chuckles. "I love how you announce your move. 'My hand is on your thigh,'" he mimics. "You know, most people would just make the move and then wait to see if it works."

"What can I say? I'm a rebel."

"Got it. So, what's the next move, rebel?" he asks with uncharacteristic playfulness.

"Ask me if you can kiss me."

His eyes grow heavy-lidded. "Can I kiss you?"

"No," I reply. "I'm not interested."

He barks out a laugh.

"Ha. See, I just did that to make you laugh."

"What's your obsession with making people laugh?"

"Not people. Only you. You're scary otherwise."

"Scary?" His voice thickens again. "Do I really scare you?"

"Sometimes. Not in that way, though," I hurry to add. "I find it unnerving when I don't know what someone's thinking."

"You wanna know what I'm thinking?"

"I'm pretty sure I know what you're thinking *now*."

I move my hand over his thigh in a slow caress.

"Yeah? And what's that?"

"You're thinking you want me to move my hand about, oh, two inches to the left."

He nods in thought. "And then what?"

"Then you want me to unzip your pants. How am I doing? Am I reading your mind?"

"Completely wrong."

My jaw drops in surprise. "Really? That's not what you're thinking?"

He inches closer and the familiar scent of him surrounds me. Woodsy and masculine.

"No, I'm thinking I want to slide my hand underneath your skirt and play with your pussy."

"Oh," I squeak.

"But first…" His face is close to mine. He's so good-looking it makes my breath catch again. "Can I kiss you?"

I nod wordlessly and his mouth covers mine. His kisses are as addictive as I remember. Slow and teasing. Deep and drugging. His lips brush over mine, and every time I try to drive the kiss deeper, he eases away slightly. My breathing grows shallow. Next thing I know, he pulls me onto his lap so I'm straddling him. My hands lock around his neck. His are around my waist, fingers stroking where the hem of my thin sweater meets the waistband of my denim skirt. He finds bare skin and my body sizzles.

This time, when I deepen the kiss, he lets me. He unleashes a soft, growly sound from the back of his throat, and it's the hottest thing I've ever heard. As my tongue slicks over his, I become aware of my phone buzzing.

"Ugh," I mumble. "I need to check that."

"No," he mumbles back, holding the side of my face to kiss me again.

"I have to. Mya took the train to Manhattan this weekend and she promised she'd text me when she got home. Want to make sure she made it back safe."

As I bend toward the nightstand for my phone, Ryder tortures me by kissing my neck, his face buried in my skin. I shiver at how good it feels.

"Let me just tell her—" I halt when I notice the screen.

CASE:

> Want to hang out tonight?

"Forget it," I say a little too fast. "It's not her."

Ryder doesn't miss the change in my tone. "Yeah? Who is it, then?"

"Someone else."

As I'm trying to shove the phone away, he peeks at the screen. Seeing the notification, he lets out a low, mocking laugh.

"Hmmm. Should we tell him?"

"Don't be an ass." Sighing, I put the phone aside.

"No, maybe we should." His voice is silky. A rasp of provocation. "Let's tell him all about how you're in my lap—" He tugs me back onto said lap, then captures my surprised squeak with another blistering kiss. He lifts his lips slightly, his breath tickling me. "Let's tell him how much you like having my tongue in your mouth."

"Who says I do?" I'm breathless, because his lips are exploring mine, his tongue teasing me into oblivion.

He breaks the kiss again. We're both breathing hard now.

"You love it," he taunts.

"You love it too," I taunt back.

"Yes, I do," he growls before our mouths collide.

It's the hottest make-out session of my life. Hungry and desperate. And just when I think my heart can't pound any faster, his hands snake their way underneath my shirt. I gasp when he lifts it up and over my head and throws it on the pristine hardwood floor. He gazes at my thin bikini bra, as if captivated by it. My nipples are poking right through the barely there material.

Ryder bites his lip. He reaches up and toys with the outline of one rigid bud. "I want you naked," he mutters.

"Then get me naked."

Without another word, he pulls my bra over my head. It joins my shirt on the floor. Next thing I know, I'm on my back and his hands are on the waistband of my skirt and panties. He drags them both down my legs. Throws those away too.

I lie there naked. Completely at his mercy. Squirming. Meanwhile, he remains fully dressed while his eyes admire my body.

"What are you doing?" I ask weakly. Impatient for him to do something.

"Looking my fill. You have no idea how incredible you are."

I swallow. I start to feel vulnerable under his heated perusal. Finally, he has mercy on me. His big capable hand glides up my stomach, along my rib cage, to cup one breast. Pleasure skitters through me. My hips arch slightly, drawing his gaze between my legs.

"So fucking nice," he murmurs. "Spread your legs. Wider. Let me see you."

It's so erotic to have him look at my most intimate place like this. He touched me in the shower, had his fingers inside me, but right now I'm a feast splayed out for him.

Visibly affected, he wrests his gaze off me. He tweaks one nipple before climbing off the bed.

"Where are you going?"

He doesn't go far, though. He gets on his knees on the floor, eyes gleaming as he slowly pulls my body toward the foot of the bed. When my ass reaches the end, he uses both hands to part my thighs. My pulse speeds up.

He curses. "You have no idea how badly I wanted to do this the other night. If we hadn't been interrupted…"

"Then what?"

"My tongue would have been inside you."

That deliciously filthy mouth lowers and he plants a long, lingering kiss between my legs. With a rough moan, he licks a hot stripe along my clit.

My hips jerk off the bed.

That makes him chuckle. His tongue toys with my clit for a moment, while one finger teases a path down my slit to my opening, which is pooling with desire.

He slips the finger inside, then peers up to smile at me. Almost feral. "Why are you so wet?"

"You know why," I gasp.

"Say it."

"Because I'm turned on. You turn me on."

There's something insanely erotic about this encounter. The sun is only now beginning to set, its leftover light streaming in through the sheer curtains. Those same shards of light play on his gorgeous face and make his blue eyes shine, the gleam of arousal more pronounced. I don't think I've ever seen a sexier sight than when he licks his lips before dipping his head again. He rumbles in appreciation when he wraps his lips around my clit and sucks gently.

As if he has all the time in the world, he teases my body, bringing me closer and closer to the edge.

I get restless, writhing on the mattress.

He lifts his head. "Are you going to come if I keep doing this? Or would you rather come while I'm fucking you?"

"Both."

His lips curve in approval. "Greedy girl."

A flush rises on my breasts. My whole chest is warm with the heat of desire. And excitement. Adrenaline. Ryder adds another finger and then thrusts both while his tongue laves my clit. He maintains that pace until I'm moaning, one hand tangling in his hair.

"Keep doing exactly that," I plead.

When the orgasm comes, it rolls through me in a hot rush. Pure bliss dances across my nerve endings and has my hips bucking, pushing me closer into his hungry mouth, my thighs locking his head in place.

He growls in approval and takes it like a champ. He's chuckling by the time I release him. "That was so hot."

I'm still gasping for air, naked and quivering, when he stands and begins to undress. He pulls his shirt off. Lets it fall. He's enormous. His height. His muscular chest. When his fingers snap open the button of his jeans, I sit up and crawl toward him on all fours.

"Holy shit, you have no idea how good you look right now." He groans and reaches for his zipper.

"Let me." And then I'm on my knees, reaching for him. I wanted to touch him so badly in the shower the other day, and he wouldn't let me. Now he's at my mercy.

I unzip his pants, slide my fingers under the waistband, and then push the jeans and boxers down his hips. A second later, his impressive dick springs up and soars toward his navel. I saw the outline of it in the shower, but now it's real, thick and heavy in my hands.

"I can't believe you just walk around with this thing in your pants," I say, feeling a bit dizzy. In a good way. He's much bigger than I'm used to, but I can't wait to feel him inside me.

He grins at me. "That's sweet of you to say."

"Aw, you used the word *sweet* in a sentence."

I start stroking him, bringing a flash of heat to his eyes.

"I think maybe you need to put that smart mouth to better use," he suggests.

"Really. Because I like using it to make fun of you."

"You might like sucking me off better."

My pulse quickens. "You know, this might be the most talkative you've ever been."

"Yeah. This part's easy," he says with a shrug.

"What part?"

"Telling you how good I want to make you feel. Telling you how good you make me feel. That's the kind of talking I'm decent at."

"Then I guess we have to do this a lot more often," I say softly. "If I want to keep you talking."

I slide off the bed and onto the floor. I take him in my mouth, infusing my senses with my first real taste of him. I love it. And I love the noises he makes. Every single sound is music to my ears. Sometimes he curses. Hisses. Groans. At one point he calls me a good girl. And it's a kink I never even knew I had.

I gaze up at him as I suck him deep.

He gazes back and says, "I want to fuck you. Are you gonna let me fuck you, Gigi?"

I whimper in response. My pussy is throbbing again. Swollen and needy. "Please."

He hauls me off my feet and leads me back onto the bed. His body is warm, powerful, as he carefully lowers it on top of me. His lips find me in a kiss, and I feel him reaching for the top drawer on the nightstand. Then he halts.

"Oh shit. I don't know if I have condoms." He peers at me, pensive. "Can I use one from your box of five hundred?"

"Fuck off." I start to laugh.

He grins.

"Do you really not have a condom?"

"No, I do. Just wanted to bring attention to your bulk condom purchases."

"I told you, it wasn't—"

He silences me with a kiss. Then grabs a condom. From a normal-sized pack. He puts it on and guides himself between my legs, and I gasp when his tip prods my opening.

"You okay?" he asks roughly.

"Yeah, just haven't done this in a while."

"I'll be gentle," he says in a tone that's anything but. His voice is pure gravel. And his body is pure power, but he stays true to his word. He eases inside me so gently that I start sweating from the anticipation.

"Jesus," he chokes out. "Yes. You feel amazing."

Very slowly, he pushes himself deeper. Inch by inch, until he's buried inside me. His size is daunting. I don't think I've ever felt so full. I sense his control, the care with which he seats himself fully, trying not to hurt me. I can feel his shoulders quivering.

I stroke my nails over his sinewy flesh. "I'm pretty sure I was promised the best fuck of my life," I remind him, and he chokes out a laugh.

Then his mouth is at my ear as he whispers, "Anything you want, Gisele."

He starts off slow. A drawn-out tempo that's utter torture. Sliding in and creeping out, while my inner muscles spasm trying to trap him inside.

"Greedy," he whispers again.

"So greedy," I murmur, then moan when he thrusts back in.

It's the kind of sex that makes your breath catch in tormented anticipation because the tempo is agonizing.

"Can you come just from this?" His hips are moving. His mouth is busy. Lips exploring my neck. Teeth digging into my shoulder while he cups my breast, kneading, playing with the tightened nipple.

"Probably no," I admit. "I need to touch my clit."

"Yeah, do it. Let me watch."

He shifts positions, rising on his knees. And while I miss the warmth of his chest on mine, there's nothing hotter than the sight of him lodged inside me while he peers down at me.

"Do it," he urges. "Show me."

I bring my hand between my legs. Slowly, I rub the pads of my fingers over the swollen bundle of nerves that's damn near ready to detonate.

His hands curl around the fronts of my thighs as his hips flex and retreat. He's watching himself fuck me. Watching me touch myself.

"Is that how you make yourself come when you're alone?"

I nod.

"Just the clit? No fingers?"

"Not usually."

"What if I came over and helped you sometime? Fucked you with my fingers while you rubbed your clit."

"What about...?" It's getting difficult to breathe. "Why not your dick?"

"That too. I'll give you any part of me you want. If it gets you off, it's yours."

"I like this Ryder," I say, moaning when he slides forward. "The Ryder who talks like this. I like these words."

Smiling faintly, he pulls his hips back, then thrusts into me again. Each time he does that, he hits a sweet spot deep inside, bringing me closer and closer to the edge.

The position provides both of us with a perfect view of his dick sliding in and out of me.

"You take me so good," he says in approval.

The urgency building in my core becomes unbearable. I lift my hips, grinding against him.

"Gonna make me come if you keep doing that," he warns.

I smile up at him. "Is that a threat?"

At that, he coils forward, his body fully covering mine again as his hips move faster. The change of angle is exactly what I need to find my bliss. With his pelvis deliciously scraping my clit and his cock plunging deep, the orgasm starts in my core and ignites my entire body.

"Oh my God, Ryder, don't stop," I beg, digging my fingernails into his back as I shudder from release.

He's not far behind, groaning hoarsely into my neck. His thrusts become more and more erratic until he finally presses himself in deep and trembles as he comes.

I'm pretty sure I just had the best sex of my entire life.

CHAPTER TWENTY-FOUR
RYDER

Dirty little secret

I'M PRETTY SURE I JUST HAD THE BEST SEX OF MY ENTIRE LIFE.

It takes a while for my heartbeat to regulate. Gigi is curled up beside me. Her fingers dance over my chest, stroking carelessly. Sucking in a breath, I cover her hand with mine, lacing our fingers together. It's not a standard move in my arsenal. In fact, it's one I would normally avoid at all costs. But it feels nice, so I don't question why I did it.

I wait for her to start talking. To start asking questions. In my experience, this is when women want to talk. When the dopamine is still surging through their bloodstream, all those feel-good emotions flooding their system.

But Gigi doesn't say anything.

"Something on your mind?" I say gruffly.

Fucking hell.

I initiated a conversation.

Willingly.

What is happening and how do I stop this? Why can't I stop this? I've never been interested in digging deeper with the women in my bed, but I'm a bit eager for a glimpse into Gigi's head.

"Just thinking about this Team USA thing," she admits. Her

fingertips play with my knuckles. "My dad offered to speak to the head coach on my behalf."

"I assume you said no."

I feel her body tense. "Obviously."

The more I get to know her, the more apparent it is that she's desperate to separate herself from her father. To stand on her own merit.

She relaxes a moment later. "Sorry. That sounded harsh. It's just…" Her sigh warms my chest. "That nepotism comment you made a while ago is constantly in the back of my mind now. It eats at me."

A pang of guilt tugs at me. "I'm sorry. I should never have said that."

"It's always been a fear of mine. I think you just made me face it. And I hate facing it."

"Yeah, I hear you. Facing things sucks."

She lifts her head to grin at me. But the humor doesn't last. She settles back, her soft hair brushing my chin.

"I also hate that I'm in this position in the first place. I hate wondering whether Brad Fairlee is purposely denying me the opportunity. People keep telling me what a good coach he is. Impartial. I want to believe he gave me that criticism because he genuinely wants me to improve my game and not because he's trying to keep me off the team."

My forehead creases. "Why would he do that?"

"I have history with his daughter. We were best friends growing up."

When Gigi's fingers stiffen, I slowly loosen each one, pressing her palm flat my chest.

"Did you get in a fight or something?" I ask.

"You could say that. She got involved with my brother senior year, even after I warned her that Wyatt was never going to commit. He didn't want a girlfriend. Still doesn't, three years later. But Emma did that delusional girl thing where they pretend they're okay with no strings. Or maybe it's not delusional—maybe they actually convince themselves of it, but then they have sex a couple times and start planning the wedding. Either way, Wyatt bailed the second she tried to wrangle a commitment out of him, and she went scorched earth on his ass. Spreading rumors about him at school. Telling people how awful he was."

Sorrow and contempt mingle in her voice. "Emma and I were inseparable since the second grade, and she took a match to our friendship and lit it on fire. Spread rumors about me too. Posted really embarrassing stuff online, things I'd told her in confidence, screenshots of old chats where I admitted my boyfriend Adam wasn't that great in bed."

"Damn," I marvel. Women have truly mastered the art of social media warfare.

"So then Adam broke up with me. And started dating Emma, of course. Our mutual friends all pulled away from her because they'd seen her nasty side. She started commenting on other people's posts with snarky comments about me and Wyatt and everyone who bailed on her. Or posting her own passive-aggressive bullshit." Her voice becomes harder now. Angry. "Honestly, all that shit was minor. Juvenile. I don't care that she tried to make me choose between her and Wyatt. Or that she slandered me afterward. Stole my boyfriend. It's that she had the audacity to try to hurt my mom."

"How'd she do that?" I roll onto my side so I can see her face. Her gray eyes are on fire.

"It was a couple months after graduation. My mom was out of town recording an album with some artist, I can't remember who. And Wyatt had just taken off on a road trip with friends. So Dad and I were fending for ourselves that summer."

I'm not sure where this is going, but it doesn't sound good.

"Emma called me under the guise she wanted to patch up our friendship. And because of our history, I agreed to hear her out. But I was running a kid's hockey camp that week and wasn't done till later in the day. I guess I mentioned on the phone that it was only Dad and me at the house, although I don't remember how it came up. I told her to come by later if she still wanted to talk." Gigi laughs in amazement. "Instead, this girl shows up at my house when I'm at camp and sneaks in using the spare key. Then she gets naked, drapes herself on my parents' bed, and tries to seduce my dad when he walks in."

"Are you serious?"

"Yup." Gigi sounds livid. "For a while afterward, we were all afraid she would throw out crazy accusations, make a false claim that he tried to do something to her. She seemed unstable enough to do that. But I think even Emma's not foolish enough to spread that level of hate. All her lies and rumors were always just shy of actually destroying anyone's life. Mostly petty gossip."

Gigi sits up, still naked. My eyes flit to her bare breasts, and although my dick twitches slightly, the mood is too somber for anything more than a twitch right now.

"Can I tell you a secret?" she says, biting her lip.

"Sure?"

"I loathe her."

I snort. "I mean, I don't blame you."

"I've never said that out loud."

"Really? You couldn't say you hate her even after she exposed all your secrets on the internet? Feels like major betrayal in girl world."

"It is. But I still always tried to take the high road. Find some compassion. Her mother abandoned her when she was twelve. Her father spoiled her to make up for that." Gigi sighs. "My parents raised me to try to see the best in people. I always try not to drag them."

"She dragged you. You're allowed to be pissed."

"That's what my friends say. It drives them nuts that I don't want to sit around and trash Emma. It's not that I forgive her or feel any goodwill toward her—I trash her plenty in my head. But I never say it out loud. I feel like I'm not...allowed to be hateful."

I'm curious to understand that. "Because it's bad for your own well-being?" I ask. "Or because of some toxic positivity bullshit that says you must be nice to everyone, even those who don't deserve it?"

She shifts uneasily. "I've never really thought about why. I guess it feels like I'm not allowed to."

"Why not?"

"Because I have all these opportunities in my life. I'm not some victim. I've had it so good up until now. It feels selfish to bitch about my problems."

"It's not selfish, it's natural. I'm allowed to get pissed when people piss me off, no matter how many or how few problems I have in my life. That chick Carma? She switched off my alarm the night she stayed over and made me late for practice. Dead to me now."

Gigi grins at me. "That's harsh."

"You don't owe people your forgiveness."

"You forgive for yourself, not for them." She sounds distraught now. "That's why it upsets me. What does it say about me that I'm perfectly okay holding on to the hatred?"

"If it's not harming you, who cares?"

"I want to be a good person."

"Who says you're not?"

She lies down beside me again, growing quiet. Once again, her fingers drag over my abs. With each absentminded downstroke, her elbow nudges my penis. It rests heavy on my leg, only semihard, but the more contact is made, the less semi it gets.

Gigi eventually notices.

"Who would've thought," she marvels in amusement. "Deep conversations get your dick hard."

"No. *You* get my dick hard by rubbing it during deep conversations."

She slides into a seated position again, her long hair falling forward as she peers down at me. "Can I tell you another secret?"

The mischief in her eyes triggers a spark of heat in my groin.
"Hmmm?"

"I want you again."

"Can't get enough, huh?" I mock. I like it, though, that needy
glow on her face.

"I told you, I'm very stressed out." Licking her lips, she bends
over me. Her mouth comes closer, until it's millimeters from mine.
"And you promised to help."

"You're right, I did."

I reach for the strip of condoms I left on the nightstand. A
moment later, I tug her onto me so that she's straddling my thighs.
I wrap my fingers around my shaft and give it a long, slow stroke.

"Use me," I order.

A smile curves her lips.

She settles on top of me and guides my cock inside her. Suddenly
I'm surrounded by her tight heat, and my entire world is reduced to
the words *oh fuck* and *don't stop*. She rides me, head thrown back in
pleasure. It's the kind of sex that makes you sort of mindless. Her
moans are a symphony to my ears. There's something melodic about
them. Low and throaty and so sexy it makes me shake with need.

"I'm going to come," she chokes out and sinks forward, grinding
on my dick.

I can't remember my name as she milks every ounce of pleasure
out of me. She's breathless from her orgasm when I flip her over
and pound into her until I'm lost in oblivion again, this time from
scorching release.

And it doesn't end. We go at it all night. Fucking each other
senseless, coming, and then taking a rest, while she lures conversations out of me that I don't expect to be having.

Eventually, after one last mind-blowing round, our labored
breathing quiets and I become aware of voices. Shit. I didn't realize
the guys were back. I don't remember the sound of the front door
opening, or hearing Shane and Beckett in the house when I or

Gigi went to use the bathroom. But it's two in the morning now, and I've been so absorbed in Gigi Graham that for all I know, the guys have been home for hours.

"Crap," she blurts out, noticing the time herself. "I should go."

"Early practice?"

"No. I have class at ten. But I can't crash here. Your roommates…" She drifts off. The rest of that sentence is self-explanatory.

I nod. "C'mon. Let's sneak you out."

"I need to call an Uber first."

"You didn't drive?" I'm confused. She only drank one beer tonight, and that was when the sun was still out. We've only had water since then, keeping ourselves hydrated between crazy sex.

"No. I…" She guiltily avoids my questioning gaze. "I didn't want Case to see my car on your street."

Something jolts through me. Not quite jealousy. But annoying all the same.

"Right. Because this is our dirty little secret," I drawl.

Although to be fair, keeping this on the down low is probably a good idea. Our first game is this weekend. Everyone's heads need to be on it, and that includes Colson.

"No," she corrects, "because the last time he did, he stormed into your house uninvited."

"True."

I shove a pair of boxers up my hips while Gigi quietly gathers her clothes and gets dressed. After she snaps the button of her denim skirt, she turns to me in dismay. "Damn it. I have to pee again."

In that moment, I silently curse Shane, who won the three-way rock, papers, scissors match this summer to earn himself the master bedroom and its ensuite bath.

I open my door a crack and peer out into the shadow hallway. Beckett and Shane's bedroom doors are closed.

"The coast is clear," I tell her.

Gigi ducks into the hall and uses the bathroom. I continue to eye their doors while the toilet flushes and the sink faucet turns on. They remain closed.

Afterward, we sneak downstairs and creep toward the front hall. And just when I think I've successfully dodged a bullet, Shane steps out of the kitchen.

Fuck.

His dark eyes take in Gigi's disheveled hair. My boxers. The scratch marks on my chest.

And his lips twitch in humor.

"Late night?" he inquires.

Her cheeks are visibly red even in the darkness of the hall. "You didn't see this," she begs softly. "Please."

Shane appears as if he's about to make a joke, but I give him a hard look, and he offers an assurance instead.

"I saw nothing."

I walk her outside to the waiting Uber. We don't kiss good night. She's rattled now from getting caught by Shane and barely glances at me as she slides into the back seat. Red taillights wink in the dark night, the car whisking her away from me.

I return to the house, where Shane, of course, is waiting for me.

"There are so many reasons this is bad idea," he tells me.

"I know."

"Colson will murder you."

"He can try."

"Beck seemed into her too."

"Nah. He backed off that."

"Got it. So you swept right in and scooped her up." Shane rolls his eyes.

"That's not how it went down."

He studies me for long enough to make me shift in discomfort, then sighs. "Ryder. That, right there"—he points toward the front door, indicating the woman who'd just left—"is a girlfriend. And you, right here, aren't a boyfriend."

A sigh of my own lodges in my throat. "Just keep this to yourself, all right? Like you said, there's lots of reasons to keep it quiet. But the most important one is that she asked."

He studies me for another long beat. Then he nods. "Sure. You got it."

"Thanks, brother."

The next morning, Shane proves to be a man of his word.

When Beckett enters the kitchen and spots me at the counter, he arches a brow. "Didn't realize we were having a sex marathon last night."

Then his phone dings and he dips his head to read the incoming text. Chuckling to himself, he taps out what appears to be a long message in response.

Shane observes him from the other end of the counter, where he's chopping vegetables for our omelets. "Who the hell are you texting so early?"

Beck slides the phone in his pocket. "Nobody."

"Because that's not suspicious," Shane says.

"Relax. It's just a girl. And don't think I haven't noticed you dodging the subject, Ryder." He walks past me and opens the fridge. "So, sex marathon. I would've invited someone over myself if I'd known that's what we were doing."

"I didn't have anyone over," I lie.

"Bullshit. Someone was getting fucked good last night. What time did we get home?" he asks Shane. "Ten thirty? Started hearing the sex noises around then."

Christ. They were home for nearly four hours before I even noticed? Uneasiness washes over me. I don't think I've ever lost my head over a woman like that.

Ever.

I turn to grab a loaf of bread from the pantry. Stalling.

"Dude," Shane tells Beckett. "That was me."

"Really? I thought you got a BJ from that chick at the concert. You booty-called someone after we got home?"

"No. Porn, dude." He rolls his eyes as if it's obvious.

"Those sex noises were going on for like four hours." Beckett gapes at him. "You were jerking it for that long? How is your dick still attached?"

"I was doing this, ah, edging thing I keep hearing about."

"Right. I hear that's popular in the porn community," Beck says solemnly.

Shane gives him the finger. "Whatever. I'm young. I can do whatever I want with my dick. Mind your business."

"Then keep the volume down next time. There's this thing called earbuds. Invest in them."

Chuckling, Beckett goes to the stove and grabs a pan for the eggs.

Shane winks at me as I pass him, lightly punching my arm.

"You owe me," he murmurs.

CHAPTER TWENTY-FIVE
RYDER

Communication hiccups

THE NIGHT OF OUR SEASON OPENER HOME GAME, I DRIVE TO THE Graham Center with Beckett and Shane. Sitting in the back seat of Shane's Mercedes, I type on my phone and send the usual text message to our Eastwood group chat, a superstition that started last year and now we're stuck with. During the drive, a dozen notifications blast the same message.

In the locker room, Beckett attempts to defend some movie he tried forcing Shane to watch last night.

"You don't get it. The hero wasn't in the same timeline as the brother—"

"Like I told you last night, it made zero sense and I don't care to discuss it."

"And like I told *you*, you have to watch it at least three times before it makes sense—"

"What kind of time do you think I have?" Shane interrupts. "I barely have time to watch one movie once, let alone the same fucking movie three times."

"Funny coming from the bloke who watched porn for *four* hours straight last weekend. Loudly." Beckett turns toward our Eastwood buddies. "Four hours, no joke. Although, I will say, he picked something good. I'll give you that, Lindley. Not sure if it was the same chick moaning in all the clips, but she was amazing. Nice tone and pitch. She sounded really hot."

She was. She was pure fire and my body still feels the heat of her on me.

And like an ass, I haven't called her since that night.

I just…can't.

Something happened that night. I love sex as much as the next guy, but Gigi came over before the sun set and left in the wee hours of the morning. We didn't even *eat*, for chrissake. Just pounded water and each other. Longest session of my life, and it still wasn't enough by the time she left. And then, all those moments in between, where we lay there talking. Well, she did most of the talking. But I *wanted* to listen. I asked questions. I initiated.

Needless to say, this behavior cannot be repeated.

Before we hooked up, I made it clear to Gigi that all I wanted was sex. Yet, somehow, *I'm* the one who forgot that.

Until I can make sense of whatever the hell's happening in my head, I can't risk the temptation of seeing her again.

"Don't *bloke* me," Shane grumbles at Beckett, bending forward to stretch out his back. "This ain't Australia, matey."

I notice Will Larsen chuckling during their exchange, but he stops when he notices Colson frowning at him.

Once everyone is suited up, Coach Jensen comes in for his first pep talk of the season.

"Go out there and deliver." He nods, then turns toward the door.

"Wait, that's it?" Patrick blurts out.

Jensen turns around. "What? What else do you want? Do you want me to do a little dance for you?"

"I, personally, would love that," Tristan Yoo says.

A couple of titters ring out.

"I don't do speeches," Coach states firmly. "I do enough talking during practice." He looks around the locker room. "With that said—individually, every single one of you has the chops. As a team? Well, we're about to find out."

And find out we do. The game is fast-paced from the first face-off. Which is surprising because Northeastern isn't typically as strong as either Briar or Eastwood. Not only that, but from the film I've seen, their new sophomore goalie is a sieve.

And yet we can't shoot a single bullet past him.

I'm on the first line, skating with Colson and Larsen, and defensemen Demaine and Beckett. We're the strongest players on the team and should be unstoppable.

And yet.

On our next shift, we try to make something happen. The chill in the rink suffuses my face as I skate hard past the blue line. We're on the attack.

"On you," I shout to Case, whose back is to the play when the opposing defenseman goes in for the forecheck.

He completely ignores the warning and proceeds to get slammed into the boards. Luckily, he manages to win that battle and get the puck.

Beckett shouts, "Point, point," to indicate he's open. Colson ignores our defenseman and tries to be a fucking hero. He takes a shot at net, it's scooped up by our opponent, giving Northeastern a breakaway.

"What the hell was that?" Beckett shouts at Colson, utterly irate.

Beckett never loses his temper. Yet we're only in the first period and he's already snapped twice at our cocaptain. Our intrepid cocaptain who, apparently, thinks he's the only one playing out there. I remember Rand Hawley's warning at the beginning of the year about whether I can trust Colson to share with Eastwood.

Guess we have that answer now.

Coach calls for a substitution as the other team regroups behind their net. I fly back to the bench, while Shane, Austin, and the rest of the second line hits the ice. They're equally good, and equally in trouble.

As an observer from the bench, I clearly see the issue.

There's zero communication out there. At least not between anyone from Briar and formerly Eastwood. And that's a massive problem, because you're supposed to be able to rely on your teammates out there. They're your second pair of eyes. You alone can't be everywhere all at once, and during a game there are constant mini battles being fought on the ice. Your teammates are seeing plays you might not know are available to you. And they're supposed to fucking tell you.

"Golden Boys," Jensen shouts. "You're on."

Okay. I guess that's the name of our line now.

We're back on, and I win the face-off and snap a pass to Colson. When it comes to handling the puck, the guy is excellent at deception and throws off defenders left and right. He's so good at what he does. Weaving and cutting through opponents, faking a shot only to cut away and fake another one. His patience is superhuman. But even with all that skill, we can't seem to score on these damn guys.

After a dump and chase, I'm caught up behind the net fighting two Northeastern forwards. I use all the moves I've been teaching Gigi, pivoting hard and creating confusion until I hear Demaine shout, "Open slot," and get a quick pass to him.

He goes for the one-timer.

It's denied.

"Motherfucker," the French-Canadian growls as we scramble for the rebound.

The ref's whistle suddenly pierces the air.

I groan when I see Beckett took a penalty for slashing. The Briar fans scream their outrage, and then our line is off the ice and the penalty kill team takes over. Trager and Rand are both on that line. They're two of the best penalty killers in college hockey. But they're not in sync at all. They're so busy encroaching on each other's territory that they both somehow lose sight of the puck.

The Northeastern left winger easily scores, drawing first blood in the game.

Coach throws down his clipboard.

He's fuming when Trager and Rand return to the bench. "What was that?" he yells. "What in goddamn hell was that?"

You'd think they'd feel foolish enough to be shamefaced, but they're too busy glaring at each other.

"That was a garbage goal," Rand mutters when he catches me frowning at him.

I stare at him in disbelief. To even imply it was nothing but a lucky goal is insane. He and Trager screwed up and the other team capitalized on it. The end.

He sees my face and ducks his head, his own expression dark.

The buzzer signals the end of the first period. Coach reams into us in the locker room during intermission. It's well deserved, and we take it without a word. Trager looks like he's got something to say, but he blessedly keeps his obnoxious mouth shut under the face of Jensen's wrath.

But he's got plenty to say when the game resumes. After I miss a shot and return to the bench for a line change, Trager glowers at me and spits out a series of insults, ending with, "Why the fuck didn't you pass? Case was wide open."

I give him a withering glare. "I didn't see that he was wide open. I don't have eyeballs in the back of my head."

"Enough. All of you shut up." Coach's eyes are stone-cold murder.

The second period is much like the first. We're completely out of sorts. The only saving grace is that our goalie is a rock star. That starting position was well earned by Kurth. He's truly the greatest goaltender I've ever seen play outside a professional setting.

"He's incredible," Shane mutters as we watch Kurth's glove pluck another shot out of the air, and the home crowd releases a deafening roar of approval.

"Rock star," one of the Briar guys agrees in awe.

Evidently, that's the only agreement we can reach on the bench—that our goalie is saving our collective asses.

As the game nears its last seconds, we're still completely shut out by Northeastern's goalie, who typically has more holes than Swiss cheese. It's a testament not to how good he is, but to how bad we're playing.

The final buzzer blares to cheers from the small amount of Northeastern fans and a chorus of boos from the Briar crowd.

Our first game is the most dismal Briar showing in a real long time, and for a man who's not into speeches, our coach has no problem telling us that in the locker room.

"That, in all my years of coaching at this university, was the most pathetic display I've ever seen," he fumes. "And not because you lost. We've been shut out before." His harsh gaze flicks toward some of the older Briar players. "We all know what it's like to lose. But to lose like that? Because you couldn't be bothered to work together? Goddamn unacceptable."

He whips his clipboard across the room in an explosion of pages.

Jensen draws a breath. Then he exhales in a slow, even rush.

"Keep your gear on, except for your skates. Put on your shoes and go meet Coach Maran in the gymnasium."

He stalks out of the room.

We all stand there, still in full uniform and pads, still sweating from the three periods we spent skating around like chickens with our heads cut off.

Guys exchange wary looks.

"I don't like this," Patrick says uneasily. "Why can't we change and shower?"

"C'mon," Nick mutters. "Let's get this over with."

A few minutes later we enter the gymnasium, where Nazem lets out an anguished wail that bounces off the acoustics in the cavernous space.

My vision is assaulted by three unacceptable things.

Nance.

Sheldon.

And an obstacle course.

"No," Shane moans. "Please. I can't. No."

"Jensen had this set up already!" Patrick exclaims, betrayal filling his eyes. "That means he thought we were going to lose."

He's right, I realize. Which evokes a rush of acrimony, because what kind of coach has such low confidence in his team that he proactively prepares a punishment for an expected loss?

Everyone swivels toward our assistant coach in pure accusation.

"Oh, no, this was going to happen either way," Maran reveals with a shrug. "Win or lose."

"So if we won, we were still going to get punished?" Trager is outraged.

"Now, boys, this isn't punishment," Sheldon says, stepping forward with a comforting smile.

"It's a *reward*," Nance tries to reassure us. "This is soul food. We have to nourish the soul in order to reach our full growth potential."

Sheldon makes a tsking noise with his tongue. "With that said, we heard we have an itty-bitty communication problem happening here."

Assistant Coach Maran snorts.

"Luckily, we have the perfect exercise to solve this problem," Sheldon says.

Both siblings are wearing whistles and pastels again. And both look way too excited to be spending their Friday night playing communication games with a bunch of pissed-off, sweaty hockey players.

"I can't," moans the freshman who replaced Tim Coffey on the starting roster until Coffey's wrist heals. "Come on, Coach. We just played three periods of hockey. I'm so tired."

"Yep. And now you're going to complete an obstacle course," Coach Maran says cheerfully. He nods at the Laredos. "I'll leave you to it."

I clench my teeth to stop myself from hissing expletives at Maran's retreating back. This is a goddamn nightmare.

"I should've transferred schools," mutters Shane.

"Yeah, for real." Beckett sounds exhausted.

"Whatever," Trager says, stalking forward. His Converse sneakers look absurd with his uniform, though I'm sure we all look equally ridiculous. "Let's get this bullshit over with."

"All right," Nance announces, clapping her hands. "You're going to pair up now. Each pair needs to consist of one former Eastwood and Briar player. Doesn't matter how you pick your pairs, but that's the only stipulation."

Colson is standing beside me, so I look over and we exchange a tight nod. On my other side, Beckett seeks out a Briar guy and winds up with Will Larsen.

I step forward and examine the course in front of us. Three lanes wind their way from one end of the gym to the other. One side has a raised wooden platform I assume is the starting position, the other side offers a color-specific mat that must be the finish line. The lanes are color-coordinated and contain identical features. Balance beams about three feet high. Random milkcrates, painted their lane color, along with a few big black tires, are scattered on the waxed floor. Past the minefield of crates and tires is a kiddie pool with a second balance beam suspended over it, although this beam is wider and lower to the ground. Beyond that are big fake papier-mâché boulders.

"Here's how this is going to work," Nance starts, pure joy shining on her face.

I swear she gets off on this shit. She probably sits at home and fantasizes about all the team-building exercises she can torture college students with.

"One player will stand on the starting platform—this is the caller. The other player, the runner, will be blindfolded. He'll navigate the course under the guidance of his caller, who must communicate the best path forward to his runner. Callers, make sure your runners follow your designated path. Runners, you will be dodging the obstacles as well as the other players on the course at the same time. Once your partner safely reaches your color mat, he'll take off the blindfold, and the runner will become the new caller. Be warned—it is going to get loud in here. So, please, no cursing. Because I don't like to hear it. I am a lady."

"A sexy lady," Sheldon says, beaming at her.

Beckett raises a brow. "Yikes," he says, low enough they can't hear.

"Communication is key in this exercise," Nance explains to us. "As it is in nearly every aspect of our lives. Without communication, for example, our marriage would not thrive."

Now they're beaming at each other.

"Wait, what?" Patrick blurts out. "You're not brother and sister?"

Sheldon frowns at him. "We've been happily married for twenty-two years."

Patrick remains entirely unconvinced. "Come on. You're just playing around now. You're brother and sister," he insists. He turns to the group for backup. "Am I the only one who thought that?"

Shane laughs silently into the crook of his arm, broad shoulders shaking.

"In fact, one of our side gigs is marriage counseling," Sheldon tells us. "We work primarily with couples whose marriages suffer from communication hiccups. So, if any of you young men are married and need guidance…"

"I'd rather get divorced," someone says.

Several guys snort with laughter.

Nance sighs and tries to direct our attention back to the course. "Before we get started, are there any questions?"

"Are you really not brother and sister?" Nazem asks.

"Any other questions?"

CHAPTER TWENTY-SIX
GIGI

National Dessert Day

THE COMMITTEE FOR THE ATHLETIC DEPARTMENT'S DECEMBER fundraiser meets in the Briar library on Monday afternoon, after my teammates and I wrap up practice.

It's an interesting group. From the women's team, it's me, Camila, and Whitney. For the men, it's Ryder, Shane, and Beckett representing the former Eastwood side, while Will Larsen and David Demaine represent Briar. Must have been strategic on Jensen's part, who he assigned—or rather, forced into this. A loudmouth like Trager or that Rand guy would only derail all the plans. But I am surprised Case isn't here. As the other captain, he probably should be.

That's cleared up when Demaine takes his seat and says, "Colson got stuck in a meeting with his professor. He said to text him the details. He'll be here next time, though."

I try not to meet Ryder's gaze. It's been a full week since we had sex, and we haven't spoken.

Not one single word. Not one single text message. I haven't even passed him in the halls of the training facility, which makes me wonder if he's actively avoiding me.

After the first few days of radio silence, I started to get pissed.

Because, come on, I don't even deserve a *Hey, how are ya?* after a literal sex marathon?

But then the relief started trickling in, because…the truth is, I didn't know what to say to him either.

We had sex for hours that night. So many hours that I was sore for three days afterward. I even got my period four days early, as if my body was forcing a reboot after that wild night with Luke Ryder.

And the worst part is, I want him again. It scares me how badly I want him. So I've been keeping my distance.

Clearly, he and I are on the same page in that regard. He's barely looked my way since we sat down.

At the head of the table, Whitney opens her notebook and uncaps her pen. "Let's get this going," she says. "I have dinner plans."

Beside me, Camila is making eyes across the table at Beckett. He's making eyes right back. Yeah, those two make sense. They ooze sensuality.

"I printed out the email from the charity head." Whitney pulls it out and gives it a scan. "We're in charge of getting the items for the silent auction."

"Sounds exciting," Beckett says, still eyeing Camila.

She winks at him.

"So let's make a list of ideas, items we think would be good for the auction. We'll have to reach out to businesses and high-profile individuals for donations. How about this? Each of us will contact, let's say, ten businesses or people?"

"I'll create an online form where we can all input the information we gather," Will offers. "Like names, numbers, what they're offering, that sort of thing."

Whitney thanks him. "For bigger organizations, we can send a form email asking for a donation. But I always find there's better success when you ask in person. So for any local businesses, either go in yourself, or at least make a phone call." She glances at David. "Do you remember what kind of shit was up for auction last year?"

I think the two of them were involved in the previous year's fundraiser. Luckily, I managed to escape that assignment.

"I don't know," he says slowly, his French-Canadian accent so subtle you can barely hear it sometimes. "I think there was, like, a skydiving package? A B&B in New Hampshire donated a weekend getaway. There was an all-inclusive vacation too."

"Oh, right. And we had that sick Bruins prize—the winner got to watch their morning skate," Whitney recalls, lighting up.

"Yeah, but that was because of G's dad," Demaine points out. "He arranged for it. I doubt we'll be able to get something like that on our own."

As expected, Whitney's shrewd gaze lands on me. "Can you work your magic and see if your dad or any of his famous friends will donate something cool?"

I nod. "I'll see what I can do. I'm sure he can hook us up."

"Must be nice," Ryder drawls.

I bristle. Really? First time we've spoken in a week, and that's what he comes up with?

I narrow my eyes at him. "Would you rather I didn't use my connections for the charity auction that we're all forced to plan?"

That shuts him up. I glimpse a hint of a smile on his lips before he ducks his head.

Camila says, "My stepfather owns a bunch of gyms in Boston. I'll ask him if he'll donate a gym package."

"Excellent," Whitney says, jotting it down.

An idea comes to me. "My cousin is launching a makeup line. Maybe I can ask her to put together, I don't know, a gift basket of products?"

Camila gives me a knowing look. "Hey, someone ask Gigi what her cousin's name is."

Beckett grins. "I'll bite. What's her name?"

I scowl at Cami. To Beckett, I say, "Her name is Alex, and it's really not a big deal—"

"Her name is Alexandra Tucker," Camila corrects. "Yes, that's right. The supermodel. So, you know, totally not a big deal."

Shane looks impressed. "Damn, you really do have friends in high places, don't you, Gisele?"

"She's my cousin," I grumble. "I can't help that she's famous."

From the corner of my eye, I notice Ryder is on his phone. Texting, I think. Which activates a jolt of suspicion. It suddenly occurs to me that maybe the reason he hasn't contacted me all week isn't because, like me, he was overwhelmed by how mind-blowing the sex was.

Maybe he's sleeping with other people.

The notion weakens my pulse, and not in a good way. For some reason, the thought of him in bed with another girl makes me feel—

My phone buzzes in my purse.

I wait a few seconds, trying to remain nonchalant, then fish it out of my bag. My breath promptly gets stuck in my lungs.

RYDER:

> I can't stop thinking about you.

I *did* not expect *that*.

Slowly, I lift my head to find him watching me. Completely expressionless. Then he turns his head away, but not before I spot the gleam of heat.

"Okay," Whitney says, "everyone start googling local businesses and pick some to contact. We can't leave here today without a solid list, so let's nail it down because I don't want to do this again. I have a life."

Beckett chuckles.

"I'm going to call my dad," I tell the group, scraping my chair back. "See what he might be able to offer. Maybe he'll be able to do a meet-and-greet or a private skate. I'll find out."

I grab my phone and leave the table. I walk down the European history stacks toward the back wall, heart drumming against my ribs.

Rather than call my dad, I text Ryder.

> Study Room B

Because I can see into Study Room B and it's empty. Beyond the narrow stack, I hear my group chattering quietly amongst themselves. They can't see me, though. I slip past two more rows and then duck into the study room.

I pull down all the blinds. And then I wait.

I don't know if he'll come. I don't know if I even want him to. This is crazy. All our friends are sitting right there.

Including Will, who's best friends with Case.

The reminder hits me, the realization of how bad an idea this is, just as the door opens and Ryder slides inside. He closes the door behind him at the same time he flicks the light switch, bathing the small space in darkness.

"This is dangerous," he says in a soft voice, speaking my own thoughts.

I bite my lip and search his expression in the shadows. "You can't stop thinking about me, huh?"

"Yes." He sounds perturbed. "It's a problem."

"I'm not sure I even believe you. I'm on your mind, yet it's been more than a week since I heard from you."

"Haven't heard from you either."

He's got me there.

Silence ripples between us, along with a ribbon of awareness that begins to uncurl, traveling through the room until I'm painfully aware of his proximity. The spice of his scent. His body heat.

"Why are we in here, Gisele?" His voice becomes low. Smoky.

"I don't know. We hadn't spoken since I came over that night, so I thought..."

"So you thought we would discuss it right now. In the library.

In a dark enclosed space. With our teammates about twenty feet away."

"I mean, I didn't say I thought it through."

He lets out a quiet chuckle and moves closer.

I tilt my head to meet his eyes. I can't see their vivid blueness in the darkness, but I can sure feel the heat of them on me.

"Do you regret what happened?" I ask him.

His hand finds my waist, lightly curling around it. My heart beats faster when his thumb dips beneath the hem of my loose long-sleeve shirt in search of bare skin. He finds it and I shiver at the rough pad of his thumb scraping over my hip.

"I don't," he answers. "Do you?"

There's something about the lazy way he's touching me. Almost indifferent, but I know every caress is deliberate.

"Should we do it again?" I find myself whispering.

That gets me a slight smile. "Yes, but not now. I can't fuck you here."

"Why not?"

"Because there's no way you'll be able to stay quiet. They'll hear every sound you make when I'm moving inside you."

The dirty visual summons an involuntary moan, and Ryder's mouth crashes down on mine to swallow the throaty sound.

I melt into him and welcome his kiss, gasping when he suddenly lifts me off the ground. I wrap my legs around him to stop from tumbling over. We stumble backward toward the wall. There's a slight crashing sound when the blinds hit my knee.

We both freeze.

The voices beyond the door carry on normally. Nobody comes barreling through the stacks of books to barge into the study room and demand answers.

With a rough groan, Ryder starts kissing me again. I love the taste of him. It's addictive. And every time I inhale, I experience a dizzying rush, as if some airborne drug is being injected into my system.

I've heard about pheromones, but never quite believed in their power before now. Whenever I breathe Ryder in, it destroys me.

My legs slide down his muscular body, finding solid footing again. My back remains pressed to the door, while Ryder's hand seeks out the waistband of my jeans. He deftly undoes the button.

"I thought you said not here, not now," I say breathlessly.

"No, I said I wasn't going to fuck you. I didn't say I wasn't going to do anything else."

He eases my jeans down, along with my panties, which are soaking wet. On a smile, his white teeth gleaming in the darkness, he slides to his knees.

The second his lips brush over my clit, I moan again.

Ryder's mouth promptly disappears. He looks up at me, his handsome features creased in the shadows.

"You have to be quiet. Otherwise I'll stop. You don't want me to stop, do you?"

"No," I manage to shudder out. My eyelids flutter shut when his mouth finds me again.

I'm shameless as I grind against his face. His hiss of appreciation is barely audible. So much quieter than the noises he made last weekend. Those guttural groans when he was licking me. The rough moans when he was filling me so thoroughly.

But silence is almost an aphrodisiac in itself. I'm painfully aware of every twitch in my body. Every quivering muscle. The trembling of my thigh when one warm palm strokes over it. Just when I think I've gotten a handle on this silence thing, he starts licking in earnest, and I can't help but moan again.

"Yeah, no. Definitely," a familiar male voice says behind the door.

We instantly stop, Ryder's hand digging into my thigh to quiet me.

"It's great to catch up. I'm glad you called."

I realize it's Shane. Who for some reason has decided to take a phone call right in front of Study Room B.

Ryder looks amused. I like it when he smiles. I like it more when he's licking my pussy until I can't see straight. Which is exactly what he proceeds to do, completely unbothered by the presence of his best friend behind the door. I want to worry that Shane is out there, but Ryder's tongue makes it hard to focus. He swirls it over the swollen bud between my legs, and the pleasure builds and builds. A deep ache.

The warmth of his mouth leaves me as he tilts his head back.

"I want you to come all over my face," he whispers. "Can you do that for me?"

I nod weakly.

He pushes one finger inside me, and my inner walls close around it so tightly that he groans too.

Now I hear a soft curse on the other side of the wall. Shane knows we're in here, I realize. Maybe he knew the entire time and the phone call was meant as a cover. Either way, I'm too turned on to care that he's standing out there. That he can likely hear every soft whimper exiting my throat. What Ryder is doing to me feels too incredible.

I want to come so bad. My core is on fire, breasts tight and achy, as I ride Ryder's more-than-welcoming face. He holds my hips to keep me steady. His tongue tends to my throbbing clit while his finger continues to work its magic. Then he adds a second finger and I cry out.

Shane's voice addresses the closed door. "Better come now, Gisele. They're starting to talk."

Ryder chuckles against my thighs.

I should be embarrassed. Mortified that not only is Shane listening to everything, he's invested in my impending orgasm.

But his presence has the opposite effect. I become impossibly wetter as I picture him standing out there. I wonder if he's hard, and a bolt of desire travels directly to my core. Ryder feels my inner muscles spasm around his finger, and his answering laugh sends vibrations through my swollen clit. I'm desperate for him to finish me off. My entire body burns for release.

I don't care that we're in the library, that our teammates are there, that Shane can hear us. All I know is this orgasm is coming and there's no stopping it.

I almost fall over, but Ryder holds me upright. I'm gasping by the time the waves of bliss subside. He releases me, looking mighty pleased with himself as he slowly pulls my panties up my legs. Secures them around my waist. He does the same with my jeans. Zips them up for me. I try to button them, but my fingers are shaking too hard. He takes pity on me and does that too.

There's a soft knock on the door. Then I hear, "Coast is clear," and I'm not sure whether to be embarrassed or grateful that Shane was doing us a solid. To my relief, he's not out there when I slip out. I don't think I could have looked him in the eye.

My fingers tremble as I unlock my phone. I bring up my dad's number because I need to show something for my disappearance.

Ryder lightly smacks my ass as he passes me in the stacks. It should be sleazy, but it only makes my thighs clench again. I stare at him in wonder until he disappears around the corner. How is he this good at making me forget my name, my surroundings?

Instead of calling my dad, I shoot him a text telling him we're doing a charity auction and could he get us any cool hockey shit? Then I wind my way back to the table where Ryder's already seated, ostensibly googling local businesses on his phone.

"Sorry, I couldn't get in touch with him, so I sent him a text. I was on the phone with my mom," I lie to the group.

Cami glances up at my approach, her dark eyes taking on that familiar gossipy gleam she always sports when discussing something particularly juicy.

"Holy shit, we were totally hearing sex noises coming from the European history stacks. Did you see anybody?"

"No. Oh my God." I pretend to twist around in search of the sex culprit. "Who do you think it was?" I force myself not to look Ryder for fear of giving us away.

"I'm guessing Shane," Cami replies, "'cause he's been gone quite a while."

As if on cue, Shane returns to the table with such nonchalance that *I'd* be questioning his absence if I didn't know better.

"Dude, were you banging someone down there?" Demaine asks, looking kind of impressed.

"We heard sex noises," Cami accuses.

"Oh. No." Shane settles into his chair, avoiding everyone's eyes. "I was, um, watching porn."

"In the *library*?" Whitney sounds horrified.

"Yeah, but, uh, I wasn't doing anything," Shane says. He's a terrible liar. And I feel guilty now because they have no idea what he's really lying about. "Someone sent me a clip and I just… I was stupid. I opened it and there was this girl moaning on it. You know," he finishes feebly, shrugging. "Porn stuff."

"Porn stuff," Whitney echoes in disbelief.

The meeting wraps up not long after, and everyone goes their separate ways. I walked to the library from the dorms, so I head outside prepared to make the trek back. As I button up my jean jacket, I hear my name. It's Ryder. He appears on the path, hands in his pockets, Briar jacket unzipped.

I wait for him to reach me.

"This is unexpected. I assumed we would go back to ignoring each other for at least another week."

Although he laughs, a flicker of guilt crosses his expression. "Yeah. About that, actually. I didn't get a chance to give this to you before." He reaches into his pocket. "I got distracted."

I grin because I know exactly what the "distraction" was.

"Anyway. Here."

An amazed laugh sputters out of my mouth when he holds out a crumpled daisy.

It must have been crammed in his jacket pocket this whole time. It's not in great shape, this poor flower.

"Oh my God. You're bringing me apology flowers again? Can't you ever apologize without all the pageantry?"

He smirks at me. "It's not an apology flower. It's to celebrate National Dessert Day."

"That is not a real day."

"Yup. I looked it up."

I think it over. "All right, I accept. I do love dessert." I offer an overly lascivious grin. "Seems like you do too."

"I mean, when the dessert is your pussy, I'll eat it any day of the month."

A hot jolt of lust tightens my core. Goddamn it. I know I started it, but he shouldn't be allowed to say things like that. They do my head in.

His humor fades, replaced with a slight flush of sheepishness. "I shouldn't have disappeared for a week."

I sigh and take some responsibility. "I didn't call either."

"Yeah." His lips curve mockingly. "What's your excuse?"

"I was scared. That was really good sex. Like, scary good."

He looks startled by my honesty.

"What about you? Why didn't you call?"

He's quiet for several beats. Then he bites his lip.

"Similar reasoning," he finally says.

My pulse quickens. "So what's next? Should we go back to being people who don't do naked things together?"

"I just went down on you, Gisele."

"I mean, starting now. Should we stop or keep going?"

Ryder searches my face. "Do you want to stop?"

"No," I admit. "But I also don't want to do this silent treatment thing again."

"Neither do I."

"And I don't want you doing naked things with anyone else," I find myself blurting out.

He startles again. "I'm not."

"Oh. Okay. But let's say you were wanting it to be an option, I don't think I'm comfortable with it. I mean, there's nothing wrong if you wanted that," I add hurriedly. "Lots of people don't want the exclusive label. They think it locks them into a relationship, which is not what I'm trying to do at all, I promise. I don't want us to be in a relationship. But…" I realize I'm babbling and force myself to articulate. "What I'm saying is, I know some girls don't care about not having exclusivity, and I don't judge them. But it's not for me."

He looks amused. "Are you done?"

"Yes."

"A lot of guys don't want to be exclusive right away," Ryder says roughly. "I'm not one of them."

I blink in surprise. "Really?"

"I barely have time for one woman, let alone multiple ones." Somewhat awkwardly, he moves closer and tucks a strand of hair behind my ear. "My dick belongs to you."

There's no way that could ever be considered a classically romantic line, but it makes my heart skip a beat nonetheless.

"Okay?" he prompts.

I nod slowly. "Okay."

I'm still thinking about the exchange when I get ready later to meet Diana for dinner in Hastings. My resting heart rate is dangerously high as everything Ryder said to me this afternoon continues to run through my mind.

Eventually, I grab my phone, unable to stop my own feelings from spilling out.

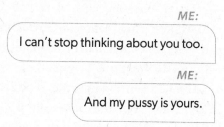

ME:

I can't stop thinking about you too.

ME:

And my pussy is yours.

Hockey Kings Transcript

Original Air Date: 10/15
© **The Sports Broadcast Corporation**

Jake Connelly: We'll continue to keep an eye on the situation over in New Jersey. Losing Novachuk will be a massive hit, but I will say, the Devils have always been able to bounce back from unlucky incidents. They had that nasty streak of injuries about five years ago—remember the season where their entire starting line was out with injury?

Garrett Graham: They'll recover, no doubt.

Connelly: Moving over to the college world now. Obviously, it's still early in the season, so all these games aren't necessarily indicative of which D1 schools will be at the top of the pack come February. But UConn is looking so good.

Graham: Phenomenal.

Connelly: Three consecutive wins and shutouts. They're off to a great start. Your alma mater, not so much.

Graham: Well, this is something we discussed in July. The so-called superteam and how they'd perform.

Connelly: Well, this superteam is off to a devastating start—lost their first three games. With that said, did you see the stickhandling from Luke Ryder against Boston College last night? Wow.

You've got these other guys, the flashy stickhandlers, who are all pop and dazzle but not necessarily the most effective. Ryder, meanwhile, is effective as hell.

GRAHAM: He is.

CONNELLY: So quick with the puck. Kid possesses the keen ability to throw defenders off with these cool deceptive moves, setting up passes they don't even see coming. Which is astounding considering his size. For such a big guy, with that kind of reach—and he uses a tall stick too—he shouldn't be able to stickhandle the way he does.

GRAHAM: All the stickhandling in the world won't help Briar if they don't start to gel.

CONNELLY: Three consecutive losses can't be good for morale either.

GRAHAM: Well, like we said back in the summer, this is a super-team on paper. Which only goes to show that it takes a lot more than individually great players to make a great team.

CHAPTER TWENTY-SEVEN
RYDER

Baby

GISELE:

> How are you doing after that hit you took last night? All bruised up?

ME:

> Black and blue.

GISELE:

> Yeah, it looked nasty. They should've thrown that guy out of the game instead of giving him a 5-minute major.

GISELE:

> On the bright side, that penalty got you guys your first win of the season. Is it my turn to bring you flowers?

UNLIKE OUR LAST SEXUAL ENCOUNTER, GIGI AND I REMAIN IN constant contact after our library hookup. We haven't seen each other all week because our schedules have been hectic, and midterms are in full swing. But she's a constant presence in my phone. We're always texting. To the point that if I don't wake up and see a message from her, I'm genuinely disappointed. And my dick aches to be inside her again. Hopefully we manage to make something work tonight.

Beckett and I walk into the training facility, our gym bags slung over our shoulders. He taps his key card at the scanner by the front doors, which automatically buzz open for us. All the athletes have access to the facility, and every off-hour visit is logged in. Someone told me the precautions started after a drunken incident in the weight room a couple of years ago.

We're both engrossed with our phones as we enter the building.

ME:

I'll take a blowjob instead. I mean, as long you're offering a reward.

GISELE:

Maybe later. Right now I have a date with an ice bath. Just pulled up to the arena.

I laugh out loud when I read her message. Great minds think alike, it appears. Or rather, dedicated hockey players do. The doors buzz behind us, and then Gigi strides into the lobby.

She stops in her tracks at the sight of us, but recovers quickly, eyeing us in humor. "Is this really how you're spending your Sunday morning? You losers."

I snort. "You're literally doing the same thing."

"Morning, Graham." Beckett lifts his head to smile at her before his attention returns to his phone. He keeps snickering to himself.

"What's that all about?" I ask suspiciously.

He clicks his lock screen on. "What?"

"You dating someone?"

"Of course not. I'm a free bird, mate. Can't be caged." He winks at Gigi.

"Are you guys lifting today?" she asks.

"That'll be me, solo," Beckett answers. "This brave fucker is all about the cold immersion."

The three of us head down the wide hallway toward the locker rooms. Halfway there, I say, "Hold on," and duck into the team kitchen to grab an apple. I usually carbo load the day after a game, and I'm already hungry again despite the huge breakfast we ate at the house and the two muffins I scarfed down in the Jeep on the way here. My stomach is insatiable this morning. Since the facility doesn't stock any junk, I have to settle for fruit.

"Nice wins this weekend," Beckett is telling Gigi when I return.

"Thanks. We're killing it so far. Got our second shutout in two weeks." She pats him on the arm. "And look at you guys, squeaking out your first win! How adorable."

He snickers, while I roll my eyes. Though I must say, that win did feel nice. It wasn't pretty. It sure wasn't anything I'd want on a highlight reel. But the fact that I was able to score on net…after two and a half periods of dropped passes, lousy communication, and festering animosity between my own teammates…well, it was not only a much-needed ego boost, but a bona fide miracle.

The win didn't come without a price. The bruise on my right side sends pain skittering through me any time so much as a breeze hits it. Nothing a good ice bath won't fix, though.

"So, you're crashing my tub time?" Gigi says to me, eyes narrowed. "Because I'll have you know, ice baths are *my* thing."

"That so? Are you sure you can handle it?" I look her up and down. "Because there's not a lot of meat on those bones. The chill will go right to them."

"I do this after every game." She plants one hand on her slender hip. "I might even do twenty minutes today."

"You rebel," I drawl.

"You think I won't? Because I could stay in there for an hour if I wanted to," she declares, but I think she's only playing.

"Hypothermia is hot." Beckett gives her another wink.

"I highly advise you don't stay in there for an hour, Gisele," I say politely.

"Stop trying to curb my dreams, prom king."

"Look at you two, with your cute little nicknames." Beckett grins at us. "You should hook up."

Gigi coughs into her hand. "Yeah, not going to happen," she replies, and I smirk at her when Beck's not looking.

"Seriously, why not?" he insists. "Now that you've decided not to ride the Dunne train—"

"Don't refer to yourself as that," she orders.

"—this guy's the next best thing. Plus you'd have good-looking children." Beckett pauses in thought. "Colson would shit a brick, though, so… Probably a good call not to drink from that well."

He wanders into the men's locker room, oblivious to Gigi's troubled face.

"Does he know?" she hisses when he's gone.

"I don't think so. It's just Beckett being Beckett," I assure her.

"Whatever. I'm going to change."

I do the same, changing into a pair of swim trunks while devouring my apple in five bites. I toss the core into the trash can, then slide my feet into flip-flops and head for the tub room. I'm all about cold-water immersion therapy, although it's not for the fainthearted. The first time you sink into the chilled water, you almost stop breathing. But eventually you build up a tolerance for it. They're still not pleasant, but a short ice bath works miracles on aching postgame muscles and speeds up recovery times.

Gigi's already in the therapy room, wearing a one-piece black Speedo that's modest and shouldn't be as sexy as it is. The way my body reacts, you'd think she was naked.

Approval flares in her gray eyes as they sweep over my bare chest. But when I turn to set my sports drink on the ledge across the room, she gasps.

"What?" I glance over my shoulder and realize her attention is on my bruise. "Yeah, it's not great," I agree.

She sips her water before setting down her own bottle down.

"How does fifteen minutes sound?" I suggest, drifting toward the timer at the door. "I know you'd prefer an hour, but I think fifteen is a solid start."

"Good call." Her voice is distracted.

I turn to see her fussing with her phone and a small external speaker.

"Just setting up my playlist," she tells me.

Dread rises inside me. "No," I say instantly.

"Yes," she confirms with a broad smile. "*Horizons.* Trust me, it's the best thing to listen to when you're shivering your ass off in that tub."

"I don't trust you and I believe that to be a lie."

"I've narrowed it down to two tracks. I'll even be nice and let you choose. What'll it be? The African bushveld or the reeds of North Carolina?"

"I fucking hate North Carolina."

"Africa, it is."

A moment later, we're both sliding into our respective cold tubs. Gigi lets out a shriek of despair the moment her body is submerged.

"Confession," she wheezes out.

I look over in amusement, resting my arms on the edges of the tub.

"As much as I like to brag about my cold-water proficiency, I hate ice baths with the chill of a thousand glaciers."

I wholly agree. But the things that make you great don't always feel great.

"In my early twenties, the African bushveld came calling. She welcomed me on a provocative journey, promising an unfiltered feast for my ears. Even now, decades later, I have never forgotten her raw, distinctive chorus."

"Oh God," I groan. "Why."

"...*I remember the trumpeting of an elephant mother, calling to her calf across the savanna. The relentless buzz of the African cicada as I smoked my pipe around the campfire. That night I learned that the hadeda ibis gets its name from the very sound it makes. The haa-haa-haa-de-dah...so penetrating and distinct. Making it one of the rare birds to earn itself an onomatopoetic name. I cannot begin to describe the unforgettable symphony I discovered in the African bush. And now...let me take you there.*"

We sit there for several silent seconds, the African bush serving as the backdrop for our cold therapy.

"Why do you hate North Carolina?" Gigi finally asks, curious.

I shrug. "I got stranded there once."

"Care to elaborate?"

"Nah."

She laughs. "Man, you really hate talking."

"Thank you for noticing."

"Sweetie. That wasn't a compliment. You know who else doesn't talk? Serial killers."

"I disagree... Seems like a lot of those crazy fuckers love to hear themselves talk."

The water laps the sides of the tub as she sinks lower. Her face is pained. Pale from the cold. "Did you see my dad's show last night?"

I flick her a dark look. "Yes."

"What's with the grumpy face? He complimented you."

"He did not."

"He said you were effective and praised your stickhandling."

"No, that was Jake Connelly. Your dad looked like he was holding his nose and forcing himself to go along with it."

"I promise you, if Jake thinks you're good, my dad thinks it too. You just need to find a way to make him overlook what happened at Worlds. He has a thing about fighting." She quiets for a moment. "I don't know how much you know about his past, but one of the reasons his foundation works with so many domestic abuse charities is because he was a victim of it."

I nod slowly. "Yeah, I did know that." A lot of articles were written about that situation, particularly since Graham himself hailed from hockey royalty. His father, the abuser in question, was a legend in his own right.

"I think where his concern lies is that you weren't fighting on the ice," Gigi tells me, her expression serious. "It wasn't part of the game, where you're dealing with…controlled aggression. Athletes can let out their aggression within the confines of rules, you know? But you did it in the locker room."

"Yeah, I did." I keep talking before she can push for details, which I know she's clamoring to do. "Maybe you can put in a good word for me with Connelly instead," I say dryly. "'Cause I'm starting to think your dad is a lost cause."

"Sure thing, kid. I'll be seeing his family for the holidays, so I'll make sure to talk about nothing but you."

Hearing it brings a rush of envy that I try to ignore. Not because she's surrounded by famous people. It's the family part that activates something painful deep inside me. I didn't have any of that shit growing up. Always wondered what it'd be like to have a real family.

It sounds nice.

She shifts in the tub. The water sloshes over her, and she shudders.

"God, this is cold," she gripes.

"One might think it's an ice bath."

"Listen, as much as I'm digging the sarcasm. Can it."

"I can't win with you. If I don't say anything, I'm a serial killer. If I do say something, you tell me to can it."

"By the way, it's your turn. I want to hear the North Carolina story."

"No, you don't."

"Come on. Humor me."

"I don't know how much humor you'll find in it." I give her a sidelong look. "You sure you want to hear it?"

Gigi nods.

So I shrug and give her the bare bones. "One of my foster families in Phoenix decided it would be fun to rent a minivan, pile all the kids into it, and go on a road trip to Myrtle Beach. The mom had a sister there. We'd just crossed over the state line into North Carolina when we had to stop for gas, and—I think they made a movie about this, where they forget the kid at home? Well, they forgot me at the gas station."

"How old were you?"

"Ten."

"Poor little buddy."

"At first, I figured they'd be back in a few minutes. They'd get on the road and then realize I wasn't in the van. So I just sat there by the door, playing a video game that their real son lent me."

"Real son?"

"Yeah. Most of the foster parents had their own biological kids too. They just tacked on a whole slew of other children to get the money from the government. But the foster kids were always second-class citizens. Real kids come first." I see Gigi's features soften and hurry on before she showers me with sympathy. "Anyway, I'm playing his video game, waiting around. An hour passes. Then two, three. Eventually, the gas station clerk comes out for a smoke break, notices me there, and calls the police. Tells them there's some abandoned kid out there."

"Damn."

"The cops showed up and took me to the station, where I waited there for two more hours. They couldn't track Marlene down. Her cell phone was dead, and I didn't know the sister's name because it wasn't actually my family, you know? Finally, seven hours after they drove off, Marlene and Tony noticed I was gone. And the only reason they noticed was because their kid was crying and complaining that

I took his handheld video game. They returned to the gas station, and the clerk was like, *The cops took him.* They came to the precinct to pick me up, and Marlene started yelling at me for making her son cry." I laugh to myself. "I got in trouble for taking his video game."

"You got in trouble," Gigi echoes in astonishment.

"Pretty bad too." I keep my gaze straight ahead. "Her husband liked to use the belt."

"Oh God. And you were only ten?"

"Yeah." I lean my head back, closing my eyes.

"There's no scenario where my parents wouldn't notice if I was gone for hours and hours. One hour, tops, and they'd freak out and send the entire neighborhood on the hunt for me. I can't even imagine how awful it would feel being completely forgotten by people who are supposed to take care of you."

There's a slight break in Gigi's voice.

I open my eyes and look over. "Don't," I warn.

"What?"

"You don't have to feel bad for me. It's over and done. I'm an adult."

"Doesn't mean I can't feel bad for the child you used to be."

"Trust me. That was one of his better experiences. Besides, it wasn't all bad. The family I lived with after that is pretty much the reason why I'm going to be playing professional hockey. The dad was a huge hockey guy, and when he realized how good I was, he basically took it upon himself to foster that, no pun intended. Bought all my gear, drove me to all my practices and games."

"How long did you live with them?"

"Three years. But after I had to move again, my coach was already invested, so he took over and filled that mentor role."

The conversation is suddenly derailed by a series of grunts from the speakers. Followed by snorting noises, then a cry that sounds like it's coming from underwater.

"What the fuck is that?" I demand.

"That, I believe, is a hippopotamus." Gigi flashes a big smile.

"You smile too much," I accuse.

"Oh no. Arrest me, officer."

I roll my eyes.

"I think the real issue is—you don't smile enough."

"It makes my face hurt."

"But you're hot when you smile. And it makes you look more approachable."

I blanch. "Baby, I don't want people approaching me. That sounds awful."

Her mouth falls open in awe. "Did you just call me baby?"

"Did I?" I didn't even notice.

"You did."

Well…shit. I need to watch myself.

A brief silence falls. Well, not quite. The symphony of Dan Grebbs's field recorder fills the therapy room. The timer should be going off any second.

"So, this thing we're doing," Gigi starts.

A chuckle slips out.

"What?" she says defensively.

"Nothing, I was just waiting for it. I called you baby. This was bound to happen."

"Waiting for what?"

"For the what-are-we talk. I swear it's encoded into chick DNA. Always need to know where they stand."

"Is that such a bad thing, knowing where we stand? I mean, I know we only had sex once—"

"Does it count as once when the first night involved about a hundred rounds?" I ask, genuinely curious.

"You're right. It's like a dog years thing. One night was the equivalent of two years of dating."

I snort like one of the hippos in the African bushveld.

"But…there's no feelings involved, right? It's just a physical release." She waves a hand between us, then winces when the water laps over her chest. "Another tool in our training arsenal to keep ourselves loose. Right?"

When I don't respond, she pushes the issue.

"Well?"

"You want to know if there's feelings involved?" I offer a shrug. "I mean, it felt really good when I was inside you."

"That's not what I mean." But I succeed in bringing a blush to her cheeks.

"It felt really good when you were coming on my face," I continue. She's squirming in the tub now. It's cute.

"Oh, stop that," she grumbles. "We're in an ice bath."

"So?" I reach my hand beneath the water and rest it on my groin. Her gaze doesn't miss that. "Don't tell me you're capable of having an erection while submerged in ice water. Is your dick actually hard right now?"

"No," I answer with a chuckle. Then I get serious again because I know she'll take us right back here if I don't. "Look. I don't do feelings."

"Ohhh. He doesn't do feelings," she says sarcastically. "Gosh, Ryder. You're so cool and tough."

"I'm baring my soul and you're making fun of me?"

"Baring your soul, my ass. All I'm saying is, you can't 'do' feelings or not do feelings. Sometimes feelings just sneak up on you."

"Not on me." Although lately I've been wondering.

She's quiet for a beat before heaving a sigh. "I guess it doesn't matter either way. I can't see feelings developing either."

There is no conceivable explanation for the disappointment that hits me.

I should be thrilled to hear those words.

So why the hell does it feel like a switchblade to the gut?

"We're too different. For example, my favorite thing to listen to is this—" She gestures to the speaker on the ledge. "These beautiful, soothing nature sounds. Meanwhile, you probably listen to death metal songs."

The timer goes off.

"Thank God," she cries, shooting to her feet a nanosecond later. A full-body shiver visibly rolls through her as she races to grab her towel.

I get out of the tub and find my own towel.

"I usually do five minutes in the sauna now," Gigi tells me.

Her gaze meets mine, and I can't control my lips from tugging upward.

"Lead the way," I say.

We go two doors down to the dry sauna. The heat feels like pure heaven on my face when we step inside. Gigi sets the timer for five minutes, then gives me a curious look.

"Have you ever had sex in a sauna?"

Damned if my dick doesn't jump at the idea.

I play it cool, though. "Very presumptuous of you to think I'm going to have sex with you in here."

Her jaw drops.

With a mocking grin, I walk past her and sit on the top bench. This heat is perfect after the cold tub. My pores burst open and it's a fantastic feeling. I'm still sore from last night's hits, but not as much as before. The body is an incredible machine.

As if to punish me, Gigi sits on the other bench. We face each other in the small space. My gaze focuses on the firm thighs emerging from the sides of her black one-piece.

"I like that suit," I say.

"Bullshit. It's downright Puritan."

"That's what I like about it. It completely covers you up. Makes me imagine everything underneath."

"You've seen everything underneath."

I smirk. "Damn right I have."

"What are you doing after this?" She pauses. "Wait, let me guess.

I bet you're going home to write sad poetry and then listen to your death metal."

I bark out a laugh. "I'm working on a paper for British history and that's about it. I'd ask you to come over, but the guys will be home." One eyebrow quirks up. "I could come to your dorm if you want."

"Maybe later tonight? I have plans after this."

"Yeah, what are you up to?"

She looks at me for a second. And then, "I don't want to say."

Which, of course, piques every shred of curiosity in my body.

"Well, now you have to tell me."

"Nope. Because you're going to make some kind of snarky comment about it, and it's one of my favorite things in the world, and I will not have you besmirch it."

"Look at you, using fancy words."

"You think *besmirch* is a fancy word? Do you need help with your vocabulary? If so, I'll make you a list of words. I can lend you some non-picture books too, assuming you can read."

I snort. "I read a ton."

"Uh-huh."

"I do. You came over to my place. There were books on my desk."

"Those all looked like textbooks."

"Some of them were. The others were nonfiction books. History stuff."

"History! Okay," she says, nodding in encouragement. "There you go. That's how you get in with my dad."

"What do you mean?"

"He's such a history buff. He makes us watch these boring-ass documentaries all the time. Like this summer in Tahoe he forced every-one, even the guests, to watch a two-part series on old aircraft carriers."

I sit up straighter. "Holy shit. That was such a good—"

"Oh my God," she interrupts. "See? You two would be best friends."

"I'm not talking to Garrett Graham about history. Only hockey."

"That's your problem. Next time you see him, I want you to be like, *Hey, so about those female ambulance drivers in World War One.*"

I can't control a sharp bark of laughter. I don't think I ever laughed this much with anybody else.

"I'm not doing that," I inform her.

"Just throwing it out there."

Our timer goes off and we both get up. When she turns toward the door, I admire her ass, unable to stop myself from stepping up behind her.

I cup those perky cheeks, resting my chin on her shoulder. "I love your ass."

She twists her head to smile at me. I can't help but kiss the perfect curve of her mouth while I cup the sweet curve of her ass.

Gigi tries to face me, but I keep her in place. "No. Stay just like that."

I hear her breath shudder when I inch even closer. My groin presses against her ass now, and she squirms against it. I slip a finger under the strip of fabric covering her, stroking it along one plump ass cheek. So smooth. Perfect.

I guide her back toward to the benches. Grab my towel and stretch it over the wood-slatted seat.

"Bend over," I whisper. "Hands on the towel."

"What if someone…?" Her gaze darts to the door.

"Then we'll have to be very, very fast, won't we?"

Which likely won't be a problem for my throbbing cock.

I'm raring to go, and I know she feels it straining against her ass. An erection I couldn't hide even if I tried. I thrust forward, a gentle push against the barrier of her swimsuit. She tries to turn again, and I expect her to tell me to stop. To say it's too dangerous. Yes, it's Sunday and the building is mostly empty. But it's not completely empty. There are people here, and any one of them could walk in at any moment.

But she surprises me. When she twists around, her eyes are on fire. She licks a bead of sweat off her lips and says, "Use me."

A smile spreads across my face, because it's the same thing I said to her before we had sex. And then again during it.

There's something so primal about hearing those two words escape her lips.

Use me.

I draw a breath and no oxygen gets in. But it's not the hazy air in the sauna that's suffocating me. It's the unadulterated lust clogging my throat.

I rub myself over the front of my trunks. The thick ridge strains against the material. I'm as hard as granite. Then I push aside the crotch of her swimsuit and drag a single finger along her slit. She's wet for me.

Gigi inhales sharply. Droplets cling to her collarbone, sliding down her face. With her ass jutted out, she's all but presenting her sculpted body to me. At my mercy. I want to fucking maul her.

I pull my cock out and drag the heavy length of it between her ass cheeks.

"You want to be used?"

"Mmm-hmm."

"Yeah? You want me to take what I want from this hot, tight body? You're going to bend over like a good girl while I get off inside you?" I let out a heated breath. "Maybe I won't even let you come. Maybe this one's all about me."

She releases an anguished whimper.

"That might be a problem," she chokes out.

"Yeah?" I rub my cockhead along her slit. She's dripping wet, and not just from sweat. Her arousal pools at her opening, soaking the tip of my cock. "Why's that?"

"Because I'm going to come the second you get inside me."

I make a low urgent sound and thrust inside her. It's such a perfect fit that a shudder overtakes me.

Christ. It only seems to get better with this girl. And I didn't think anything could be better than the first time, the night I lost myself in her over and over and over again.

But it's happening again. I'm losing myself again. So is she. She bites her knuckles to keep from crying out. I've forgotten where we are and stopped caring if anyone walks in. Let them.

I pull back, then slide back in. Once, twice, three times, and Gigi is gone. Gasping from an orgasm, riding the throes of it while I keep thrusting into her. Hard and fast. Gripping her hips, pulling her ass up against me. It's a true definition of a quickie. Not even ten seconds later and I let out a strangled moan, my balls drawing up tight.

I'm about to come when I realize I'm not wearing a condom.

Holy shit.

This has never happened to me before. Not ever in my life. Even when I was a teenager banging anything in my path, I would remember to use a condom.

Gigi Graham makes me lose my head.

It's too late to stop the climax, but I manage to pull out in time. Pleasure explodes inside me and then erupts as I shoot all over her ass. Getting it on her bathing suit too.

Panting heavily, I manage to get the words out. "We didn't use a condom." I curse to myself, reaching for the towel to wipe her up.

Her chest rises on a deep breath. "Oh, no. I'm sorry."

"Not your fault. On me."

She takes the towel from me and finishes cleaning herself. "If you're worried about me, I'm on birth control," she assures me, her tone slightly awkward. "And no STIs. You?"

"I get tested after every partner," I admit.

"Really?"

"Yeah, I'm very good about that. I'm a cautious person, in case you hadn't noticed."

"I got tested at the beginning of the summer. So it's been a while. But I also haven't had any partners since then."

I believe her. And I hope she believes me because I really don't mess around regarding sexual health.

Gigi chews on her bottom lip, as if she wants to say more. Then she walks toward the door. "I should go. Need to shower and change before I head out."

I secure the waistband of my trunks before following her out of the sauna. "Are you really not going to tell me where you're going?" I complain.

She hesitates. Then she shrugs. "Fine. Why don't you come with me?"

CHAPTER TWENTY-EIGHT

GIGI

What's cooler than butterflies?

WHEN WE GET INTO THE SUV, MY PHONE CONNECTS AUTOMATI-cally, playing the next track on my playlist.

"As a new father whose wanderlust could not be contained even with a squalling infant at home, I was eager to teach my son the auditory magic that nature has to offer."

In the passenger side, Ryder drops his face in his hands.

"We journeyed, my wife, Helen, and our son, Steven, to a place that may not spring first to mind when craving a pure auditory experience. The Northern Atlantic. Yet we were delighted by the happy chatter of the St. Lawrence humpbacks and piercing cries of the seabirds. Little Steve particularly enjoyed the symphony of the Northern gannet. We spent hours imitating the throaty vibrato that escaped their beaks as they foraged at sea. And that's only the gannets! Nothing can possibly prepare an eager toddler for the sheer volume created by thousands of seabirds at dinner time. And now…let me take you there."

Ryder inquires, "What do you have against music? Honest question."

I give him the finger.

Putting the car in drive, I leave the Briar campus and head for the interstate. At a red light, I notice a frown digging into Ryder's forehead as he texts something on his phone.

"Everything okay?" I ask.

He sends the message and rests the phone on his thigh. "Yeah. Fine. Just another update about the Dallas GM. Julio Vega. I guess he's not thrilled about Briar's performance this season. Although he did tell Owen he enjoyed my goal."

"Owen?"

"McKay," Ryder supplies. "He's the guy in the pros I was telling you about."

My jaw drops. I tear my gaze from the windshield to gawk at him. "Are you serious? You've been busting my chops about my famous dad and his famous friends, and meanwhile you're best buds with *Owen McKay?*" McKay is one of the hottest players in the NHL right now. "Who's friends with superstars now? Can you introduce me?"

He narrows his eyes.

"I'm serious. I'm a huge Owen McKay fan. How do you even know him?"

"We grew up together in Phoenix." Now he shifts his gaze out the window.

"That's really cool. Hey. You should see if he'd donate something to the auction. A signed jersey! We could get it framed."

Ryder shrugs. "I might be able to arrange it."

"I'll text Whitney and tell her. Seriously, that item would slay."

Thirty minutes later, I pull into a familiar place. The colorful signs in the parking lot guide me to the appropriate place to park.

Ryder exhales in resignation. "The butterfly gardens?"

I beam at him.

He sighs.

"If I told you, you wouldn't have come," I protest.

"Well, obviously. I thought it was going to be something cooler."

"What's cooler than butterflies?"

"Are you kidding me right now?" He diligently studies me. "I can't figure out if you're being serious."

"Dead serious. This is my favorite place in the whole city."

I shut off the engine and the sounds of *Horizons* disappear. We get out of the car, Ryder with visible reluctance. There's a small hut outside of the building where you can buy tickets, but I gesture for Ryder to bypass it. I reach into my wallet.

"We don't need tickets. I'm a member. And you're in luck—my annual fee covers one guest per visit."

"You have a yearly membership to the butterfly gardens."

"I told you, it's my favorite place. I come here all the time."

I flash my card to the person at the gate, and then we walk into the indoor conservatory, a.k.a. six thousand square feet of sheer heaven. Immediately, I feel my entire face light. I happily take in the sight of butterflies against a tropical backdrop. The beautiful colors all around us. Shimmery pastels to iridescent blues, with browns and yellows and reds thrown into the stunning array. I brought Mya here once, and she said it made her feel like she was inside a rainbow. I *think* she meant it as a compliment?

"Honestly, this is how I picture heaven to be," I tell Ryder, the lightness in my chest creating a spring to my step. "Look at it. Have you ever seen anything prettier?"

I glance over to find his blue eyes, vivid in their own right, fixated on my face.

"What?" I say self-consciously.

He clears his throat. "Nothing. You're right. It's nice here."

I grab his hand and urge him forward. "Come on."

We amble past a koi pond framed by lush vegetation and a bubbling waterfall. Lots of people decided to visit the gardens today. We pass a group of parents with their young children bounding along the winding paths. We dodge a hand-holding couple standing at one of the feeding stations. They're watching a small orange and black monarch sip on some nectar.

"I don't get you," Ryder says gruffly.

"What's not to get?"

He shrugs.

"No. Tell me."

"You're just…not how I figured you'd be," he admits.

"Okay. And how did you figure I'd be?"

"You know, this super serious hockey player with a one-track mind."

"I can be serious about hockey and still have other interests."

"Like butterflies," he says dryly.

"Why not butterflies?" I gesture at all the beautiful creatures fluttering over our heads. "Look how gorgeous they are."

We wander toward a new path, this one quieter because there's no children. A few feet ahead, a pink-haired lady is photographing a yellowish-brown butterfly perched on a leaf.

Ryder gives me a sideways look. "I just realized…I've never seen you take any pictures."

"Should I?"

"It's weird. I usually can't go one day without seeing a chick taking a picture for social media. I saw a bunch of cheerleaders the other day posing in the quad for, like, a million shots. One of them kept poring over each picture and then ordering her friends to redo it."

"Don't get me wrong, my camera roll is filled with a gazillion shots. I just don't take pictures here anymore because I'm pretty sure my last butterfly pic count was ten thousand, and I'm not joking. As for posting the pictures I take, nah. I'm not a social media girl." I cock my head at him. "I assume you don't have any social media either?"

He starts to laugh.

"Yeah, dumb question."

"You know better, Gisele." He shrugs. "I'm surprised you don't have it, though."

"Why is that surprising?"

"Because you're a chick."

"So that automatically means I need to be posting bikini pics and selfies? Fun fact: sometimes you can take pictures and just keep them for yourself without including the rest of the world."

"I'd like to be included in the bikini pics. How do I opt in?"

I grin. "I'll start sending you weekly shots."

"Thanks. I appreciate that."

"And I used to be on social media," I remind him. "I still have the accounts, but they're either private or deactivated. My old friend went after me pretty hard. That's when I realized I don't want my whole life online. All these moments belong to me. Not anyone else." I wave at the butterflies and moths floating freely around us. "This is just for me."

We keep walking, and I begin to feel the heat. The conservatory is made almost entirely of glass, and the October sun shining through the panes heats up an already tropical environment.

"It's like we're in the sauna again," he grumbles, rolling up the sleeves of his gray Under Armour shirt.

I sort of wish we were. Because then he'd be inside me again.

"The butterflies need the warmth to fly. Do you not want them to fly, Ryder? When did this vendetta against butterflies begin?"

"At a very young age," he says solemnly.

I love it when I get him to be playful. I'm starting to crave it on a level I'm determined not to overthink.

We stop in front a feeding station, where I read the information plaque on a nearby tree. No matter how many times I come here, I still manage to learn something new. There are too many paths and vegetation patches to keep track of.

"Aw look, you have a new friend," I say in delight.

Ryder cranks his neck to squint at the blue butterfly that just landed on his shoulder.

"Poor guy," I tsk. "He doesn't know you well enough yet to figure out you're an asshole."

With a laugh, I dance down the path. I'm in a spectacular mood today. First the sauna sex, and now I'm here. This place always revitalizes me. And, maybe…as grumpy and uncommunicative as he can be…a tiny part of me enjoys spending time with Ryder.

"So what else are you into?"

I stop in my tracks.

"Are you trying to get to know me?" My jaw is literally at my feet.

"Forget it." He walks past me.

I scamper eagerly after him. "No, let's do this. Ask me anything. But," I warn, "anything you ask me, you have to answer yourself."

"This feels like a trap."

"That's how it works."

"Fine," he finally relents. "What's your favorite color?"

"Wow. Such a thought-provoking question."

I swear, this guy is reticent to share even a single significant detail about himself. Favorite color. Ha. Total cop-out right there.

"Green," I tell him. "What's yours? Wait, let me guess—black to match that enchanting disposition?"

"Gray."

"That's pretty much the same thing. What shade? Light gray? Dark?"

"A deep slate gray. Stormy, like your eyes."

My heart does a little somersault. He's not trying to be romantic, but I liked that line. I liked it way too much, in fact.

I'm starting to worry I might be in trouble.

I keep reminding myself this is supposed to remain casual. He said he doesn't do feelings. And, really, it's hard to picture myself going out with this guy. He's notoriously tight-lipped. It's like pulling teeth to draw personal details out of him. Exhausting just convincing him to tell me a sad story about his childhood.

Granted, if *I* had a whole bunch of sad childhood stories, maybe I wouldn't want to share them either.

"Favorite sound?" His question interrupts my thoughts.

"Sound? That's a weird one." I ponder it. "The rain. I love the sound of the rain. What's yours?"

"A puck striking the boards."

"Oh, that's good too."

"Favorite sex position?"

My head swivels toward him in accusation. "You can't discuss sex in the butterfly gardens."

"Why not?"

"This is a very PG place."

"Yeah. Well. I just turned it X-rated. Got a problem with that?"

He moves closer and I gulp for oxygen. It's difficult to breathe, and that has nothing to do with the stifling tropical air pushing a hot breeze through the gardens. All around us, butterflies hover. Chase one another through the flowers. A few of them dance past Ryder's head. It's the most Disney moment possible, yet the gleam in his eyes is downright pornographic.

"Favorite position?" he prompts.

I swallow through my suddenly dry mouth. "I like being on top."

"Why's that?"

"It hits a good spot, inside and out."

He smiles knowingly. "You like grinding your clit against me while you ride?"

I can scarcely breathe. "Oh my God. You're not allowed to talk dirty right now."

"You think this is dirty talk? That's sweet."

I croak out a laugh. "Fine. What's *your* favorite position?"

"Anything that lets me be inside you is going to be my favorite position."

Yeah, I'm in trouble.

CHAPTER TWENTY-NINE
RYDER

Porn addiction and you

SHOWERING AROUND OTHER DUDES IS ALREADY NOT AN IDEAL situation. Showering with dudes who hate your guts is a whole other story. The epitome of discomfort. And I can't think of anything more painful than making small talk while naked.

Colson and I were the last ones off the ice this morning because one of the skills coaches wanted to practice some passing drills with us, so now we're the last ones in the showers. We need to be fast because we're due in the media room in ten minutes for a last-minute meeting. At least it's not the auditorium, which means Sheldon and Nance aren't there to torture us today. I hope. I'm half expecting an ambush from them where they show us their wedding video and possibly home videos from their joint childhood.

We stand in our respective stalls with the waist-high partitions, so I still see him from the corner of my eye. That's how I can sense his eyes on me as I drag both hands through my wet hair to wring the water out.

"What?" I say irritably, looking toward his stall.

"Would it kill you to be a little more complimentary during practice?"

"Toward you? What, you want me to stand there and stroke your ego?"

"No, not toward me. I don't need that shit. I mean the other guys."

"Really."

"Yes. Woody and Tierney were nailing those face-off drills. And Larsen killed it during our last game with that laser beam of a shot."

"Yeah, and how often do you compliment the Eastwood guys?" I counter.

"There is no 'Eastwood guys' anymore," he says in frustration. "You're all Briar."

"Cool—how often do you compliment the new Briar guys? Because from where I stood, Lindley was doing the sickest moves in practice yesterday to deke you out. Were you patting him on the back for that?"

Case has the decency to look contrite. "Whatever," he mutters.

"Just saying." I shrug. "It goes both ways, bro."

"Fine. I'll make an effort too. Is that what you want to hear?"

"I don't want to hear shit. You're the one who started talking."

"All right, got it. Great chatting with you as always, Ryder."

I turn my gaze away. I simply can't bring myself to be amenable to this guy. The truth is, it's his responsibility, because at the end of the day, this is his house. We're still the trespassers. He's the one who needs to bridge the gap, not me.

I towel off, quickly going to change into my street clothes. Case does the same, pulling a tank top over his head. He's got a couple of tattoos on his arms. After two months sharing a locker room with him, I've seen them before. The one on his right bicep is a cross but doesn't give an overly religious vibes. It's Celtic style with lots of ornate flourishes. Case puts on a black and silver Briar hoodie, turning his back to me.

I wonder if that's what Gigi's into, dudes with tattoos. Although I suppose it doesn't really matter, because she isn't screwing him anymore, now is she?

Nope. She's certainly not.

I lace up my shoes and grab my backpack. I sling it over my shoulder and head to the media room, Case at my heels.

Coach Jensen stands at the projector. Everyone's already seated, chattering to each other. As Case and I take our seats, Coach starts the meeting.

He opens his laptop. "Something's come to my attention," he says, his gaze conducting a sweep of the room. "Normally, I wouldn't address this because it's none of my goddamn business."

Okay. Curiosity piqued.

"But I was informed, because of the new rules regarding both appropriate campus conduct and potential mental health issues, we have to provide you with adequate information if something like this should arise."

"What the hell's happening?" Beckett sounds amused.

Jensen gives us a grim look. "Let's begin. Firstly, I didn't create this PowerPoint. I just want you to know that. I've got better ways to spend my time."

Chuckles echo through the room.

He clicks the laptop, and the header slide comes on.

PORN ADDICTION AND YOU

Someone hoots loudly.

"The fuck is this?" Trager demands.

"I was not born yesterday," Jensen begins. "Sex is a thing. Porn is a thing. It's available on every phone. I get it. I can't say I think it's healthy, because, you know, go find a real woman. Or man," he throws out. "Or both. Whatever you're into. I don't see how watching porn for hours on end is good for you, but as long as it's in the privacy of your bedroom, fine. Go nuts."

"Pun intended," someone says.

"Pun not intended. I don't make puns. To summarize—in

your bedroom? Great, I don't give a shit. But the consumption of pornography on university grounds, which includes libraries, is not something the faculty condones."

"Dude, he's talking about you," Rand blurts out, his head swiveling toward Shane. Then he starts laughing his ass off, and for some reason, Coach allows it to happen.

Rand is in hysterics, curled over the tabletop, broad shoulders shuddering.

Even I can't fight it. I hide my own laughter behind my fist.

Shane levels me with a murderous glare.

I press my lips together. Though I do feel a spark of guilt along with the humor. We both know this is my fault. Word of his library porn exploits has gotten around. Meanwhile, he was only covering for Gigi and me.

"Gonna fucking kill you," he whispers ominously.

"With that said, a point was raised that someone who does do this on university grounds might not possess the proper impulse control and perhaps there might be a deeper issue here, so, and I'm not going to name names here—Lindley," he says pointedly.

The room breaks out with laughter.

Coach holds up his hand and eyes Shane. "Pay close attention, son. Someone took the time to put this PowerPoint together for you, so let's not be an inattentive asshole."

He gestures to the team doctor, who steps forward.

"Good morning, boys. Let's talk about dopamine, shall we?" Dr. Parminder begins in his clipped, efficient voice. "Take a look at this first slide. Dopamine is a neurotransmitter, acting as a chemical messenger between neurons in the brain. It's also part of your internal reward system, meaning when you're doing something that makes you feel good, dopamine is released."

Shane drops his head in both hands. I do my best not to reach over and pat him on the shoulder. I anticipate getting a fist to the face if I attempt it.

Dr. Parminder goes on. "And when you masturbate, you feel good."

Patrick Armstrong yowls out a laugh.

There's no way we're getting through this entire thing without at least one person pissing their pants.

———————

Later that night, I've got Gigi in my bed, and I'm recapping the events of the day, which started off hilarious and ended up depressing. We tied our game against Boston University. Better than a flat-out loss, I suppose, but they're not the strongest team in the conference and had no right keeping it that close. It's infuriating. Yes, there are nearly thirty games to go, so we can still turn things around, but this season feels like such a bust already.

"I cannot believe Jensen did that." Gigi's cheek trembles against my chest as she shakes in quiet laughter. "Was Shane pissed?"

"Furious. You should have seen the text he sent me afterward." I grab my phone off the nightstand because this is a message that requires reading verbatim.

Curled up beside me, Gigi watches as I open the messages app. She suddenly stiffens as if someone poked her with a cattle prod.

"What?" I say in concern.

"Nothing."

"Gisele." She won't look at me, so I pry her chin up to see her face. Hurt and anger crease her pretty features. "What's wrong?"

After a drawn-out moment, during which the hostility in her eyes only intensifies, she finally taps the screen and mutters, "If you don't want a woman to know you're lying to her, maybe don't flash the lies right in her face."

What in the actual fuck is she talking about?

I look at my phone, trying to understand what—

Then I burst out laughing.

"You think this is funny?" she snaps.

She tries to sit up, indignantly pushing my hands away when I reach for her.

"It's not what you think. I promise."

"That message is pretty clear. Either you sent it and you're aching for someone who isn't the woman you're supposed to be exclusive with, or some girl is aching for you and you enjoyed the message enough to save it on your phone where anyone could see."

"It's my group chat," I croak. I can't stop laughing.

"Your group chat." Her tone hasn't given an inch. Hard as stone.

"The Eastwood group chat," I clarify. "All the guys are on it. And that's our standard message before a game." I click on the thread and show it to her. "See?"

She scrolls through the dozen identical messages.

BECK:

I'm aching for you

POPE:

I'm aching for you

KANSAS KID:

I'm aching for you

NAZZY:

I'm aching for you

She quits scrolling. "I don't get it."

"It's too stupid to even explain."

"Please try."

"Patrick—the one we call the Kansas Kid—has this pathetic habit of falling in love after knowing a chick for, like, ten seconds.

And once he falls, he does this love bombing thing with romantic messages and flowers—"

"Don't judge him. You get me flowers all the time."

"Twice," I growl. "That doesn't count as all the time."

"It's two times more flower-giving than I would ever expect from you."

She's got me there.

"Anyway, last year, it was the first round of the playoffs and not a single person expected us to pull out a win. We were playing the number one team in the conference—they were on a twenty-game winning streak at that point. So an hour before the game, Patrick accidentally sends a message meant for his new true love to our team chat. Goes without saying that we all ragged him mercilessly for it."

"But you won the game," she guesses.

"Yup."

"Hockey players and their superstitions."

She scrolls through the thread again, giggling. "Do you seriously send this message before every game?"

"Unfortunately."

She props herself on her elbow, remorseful. "I'm sorry I accused you of lying to me."

"I don't lie," I say simply. "Hell, my honesty gets me in trouble with chicks almost all of the time."

"I'm an ass for thinking it."

"I'm always going to be honest with you. I don't know how to be anything else."

"I know, and I love that about you." She sighs. "I may…have overreacted a little."

"A little?" I smirk. "PS jealous Gigi is hot."

"I wasn't jealous—"

She squeaks happily when I flip her onto her back and press my lips to one bare breast. A moment later, I'm sucking on her nipple.

I swear, keeping my hands and mouth and dick off this woman is truly impossible.

I nuzzle a path down her body until I'm lying between her legs, my cock pressed against the mattress. I kiss the smooth skin of her inner thighs, leaving a trail of kisses on my way to my destination. I slide one finger inside her to test how ready she is. She whimpers in response.

"*As a young lad,*" I narrate, "*I met a hockey player with the tightest pussy. She would make the hottest noises when I fingered her. And now... let me take you there.*"

Gigi looks delighted. "Admit it. You love *Horizons*."

"Nah. I love *this*."

I push my finger in deep, which causes her ass to rock off the bed, sending her core directly into my face.

I waste no time capturing her clit between my lips, licking gently. My efforts are rewarded with another whimper, followed by soft, anxious moans when I start licking her in earnest. I make her come, and she barely gives herself time to recover before she grabs at my shoulders and yanks me up so I'm on top of her. Nobody's even touched my dick and it's ready to burst. I'm painfully hard.

"I don't have any condoms," I mumble, kissing her neck. "We used them up yesterday." She's been over a couple of times this week already. "Didn't get a chance to restock."

"Oooh, I bet someone is dying for my value pack now," she teases, beaming up at me.

"Bring them over next time," I agree, because I genuinely never expect how many times I end up inside her when we're in the same room together.

"Or..." She bites her lip.

I wait for her to go on.

"After our sexual health talk in the sauna, maybe we can go without."

My dick wholly approves, judging by the pre-come leaking out of it.

We spend the next hour in bed. I hold off on finishing because I'm in the mood to torture myself a little. So I fuck her nice and slow, making her come a second time before I finally reward myself. Gigi is on her back, her tits bearing a rosy flush as she gasps in pleasure. She looks so sexy that when I feel the pleasure build, I pull out and stroke myself instead, getting off to the sight of her perfect tits and gorgeous face.

Afterward, we lie there, me in my boxers, her buck naked, and discuss tonight's respective games.

"Those were some crazy moves you did in the third," I tell her. "Someone posted a couple clips online. Shane and I were watching them on the bus ride home."

"Hmmm. But were they Olympic moves?" I love the way her voice sounds after sex. Drowsy. Lazy like molasses.

"You and your lofty goals."

"Actually, my original goal—at least when I was a kid—was to win the Stanley Cup."

I chuckle.

"I mean, I already had the nickname. Did I tell you my whole family calls me Stan? God, it's obnoxious."

"You got the nickname because you wanted to win the Cup?"

"No, I got it because I thought Stanley Cup was a person until I was six. I've been Stan ever since. But it wasn't until I was around eight that I realized I could never actually win it."

She snuggles closer. I run hot and she runs cold, so it's perfect. Her body cools me down and I heat hers up. I'm not a spiritual man, but in my sex-loosened brain, I suddenly wonder if somewhere, somehow, maybe someone designed us to fit this well together.

"Boston won the Cup that year, and I was so happy. I told Dad how excited I was to get older and win it myself. And that's when he broke the news that as a girl, that wasn't really an option." Gigi laughs quietly. "Man, I just started bawling. There's a trail behind our house, and I ran off crying my eyes out. I wanted to be left alone, but I was a kid and obviously my parents weren't going to allow it. Dad found me and sat me down on a log, wiped away my tears, and promised I'd have something even better than a Stanley Cup win: I was going to be the best female hockey player ever to walk the earth."

I smile at the story.

She snorts. "Then he's like, oh, and do I want to see the Cup? Turned out it was in our living room because every member of the team has the chance to take it home, and as the most valuable player that season, Dad had first dibs."

"Goddamn, your life is incredible."

"Anyway, having that aspiration taken away from me made me focus on the opportunities that were available. What was the highest mountain I could climb, if it wasn't the Stanley Cup? And I decided it was Olympic gold." She shrugs. "So that's the most important thing now."

"To you or to your dad?"

"He never pushed me to aim for Team USA. I did that for myself. And I want it for myself. But I guess, yeah, a part of me wants it for him too. I want to make him proud."

"I'm sure he already is."

"No, I know he is." Her hand strokes my pecs, and I feel her demeanor change, grow frustrated. "I want to make that team, Ryder. And I should be able to make it! But I haven't heard from Brad Fairlee since the beginning of the semester."

"From what I know about that selection process, it's vague and not always on a timeline. All you gotta do is keep playing the way you're playing, and you'll get your shot," I assure her.

"What if I don't?" Her body clenches, and I run my hand over her back. She relaxes slightly. Then her tone hardens with resolve. "No, I will. Because the alternative is unacceptable and something I refuse to allow. It *will* happen. I'm going to will it into fucking existence if I have to."

Her ferocity is sexy.

Gigi sits up then, yawning. "Ack, I should go. I don't want to be dragging at morning skate tomorrow."

Wincing, she looks down at her chest. Her breasts are sticky with my semen.

"You came on me," she accuses.

I snort. "Yeah, you saw it happen."

"Can I take a quick shower? I don't want to put my bra on over this."

"Only if I can join you."

"Deal. Are you sure we're in the clear?"

"We should be. I'm pretty sure Beckett is out. Shane's home, but he knows about this. Although I can't say he'll be covering for us anymore after the whole porn addiction seminar." Another wave of laughter spills out. "Christ, I wish you were there."

I tug her off the bed, hauling her naked body over one shoulder in a fireman's carry.

"No, wait," she protests, giggling as she scrambles back to her feet. "I should put something on."

"The bathroom is literally across the hall. We're walking three steps."

"Yeah, but you've got boxers on. You don't have to be embarrassed if Shane pops out of his room."

She snatches my discarded T-shirt from the desk chair and pulls it over her head.

"Oh, so you can wear my shirt and get it all sticky, but not yours?" I challenge.

"Exactly."

I reach for the doorknob, then pause because I could've sworn I heard soft footsteps. But when I open the door a crack and peer out, the hall is empty. Maybe it was just Shane wandering around downstairs.

I give her a little smirk as we step into the bathroom. "If you're good, maybe I'll fuck you in the shower."

"Promises—"

Gigi suddenly shrieks.

It takes me a second to register what I'm seeing.

She's just moved the shower curtain aside to expose Will Larsen hiding in the bathtub, fully clothed.

"What the hell!" Gigi shouts at him.

"Gigi?" he says, blinking in bewilderment.

"Will? What are you doing in there?"

"Seriously, bro," I growl. "Why are you in my house?"

"Um." He looks at Gigi. "Why are *you* in his house?"

"Jesus Christ," I snap. "Answer the question."

But he's too busy gaping at Gigi. His suspicious gaze lands on her oversized T-shirt, which clearly belongs to a man. To me. Climbing out of the tub, his eyes flick to her bare legs before returning to her face.

"You're hooking up with this guy? Does Case know?"

Gigi pales. "No. And you cannot tell him."

"Why are you in my house?" I repeat firmly. I'm getting tired of the lack of answers.

"He's with me," says an awkward voice.

I swivel to find Beckett in the hall.

"What do you mean he's with you?" I ask warily.

"Uh…" Beckett hesitates.

Will hangs his head. "We've been hanging out."

Silences crashes over us.

"Like dating?" Gigi asks in confusion.

Yeah, I'm confused too. As far as I was aware, neither of these dudes is gay.

"No, like hanging out. We're watching the *Timeline* franchise," Will says, as if that explains anything.

"You mean those stupid movies with the time-traveling scientists?"

"They're only stupid on the surface," Will mutters. "If you just forget about, like, the dinosaurs or whatever, the actual time travel theories are super solid. They adhere to the Novikov principle—"

I hold up my hand. "No." I already suffer enough of this shit from Beckett.

"So you two are secret friends?" Gigi sounds increasingly baffled.

"Yeah." His gaze flits toward Beckett. "I mean, it has to be secret. You really think Colson's gonna let me hang out with him?"

"What, Case is your mommy now?" she says sarcastically.

"Oh, you're right. I should tell him everything." Will's eyes are defiant. "You first."

Another voice joins the cauldron of confusion.

"Thank God!" Shane appears in his bedroom doorway, wearing a pair of sweatpants and a look of relief. "Is it all out in the open now?"

"You knew about these two?" I grumble at Shane, pointing toward Beckett and Will.

He nods. "Oh yeah. I caught them bro-ing out together a few weeks ago. Smoking a joint and talking about quantum mechanics."

Beckett sighs. "You make it sound so fucking nerdy." He implores Gigi with his gray eyes. "I just need you to know—I'm a fuckboy. I get a lot of sex. A lot of it."

As if something occurs to him, Beck's accusatory gaze swivels back to Shane.

"Wait. Are you saying you knew that these two were boning?"

"Of course," Shane shoots back. "Do you really think I'm jerking off in libraries like some creepy sex addict? I was covering for these assholes."

Beckett releases a huge sigh of relief. "Oh, thank God, mate. Because I'm the one who told Coach about your porn problem."

Shane hisses out an outraged expletive. "That was you?"

"Look, it seemed like a serious problem," Beckett says defensively. "The fact that you're getting off to porn in a library and then just acknowledging it to a group of people like jerking off to porn in a library is a normal occurrence—"

"Yeah, but I wasn't doing that!"

"Cool, great. And now we all know you're not a pervert."

"Will." Gigi grows tired of their exchange and refocuses her attention on Larsen. "You cannot tell Case about this."

"Same goes for you," Will tells her.

"You being friends with Beckett Dunne is nowhere near as catastrophic as me hooking up with Luke Ryder. You get that, right?" She stares at him. "Because I don't think you're grasping the gravity of this."

"I mean, mine is kind of bad," he insists. "Do you think I *want* to like an Eastwood guy?"

"Thanks," Beckett says dryly.

"That's not on the same level. At all," Gigi stresses. "This could really hurt Case." Her voice is soft now.

That sobers him up. "Okay, yeah. No, you're right."

Head bent, she covers her face with her palm for a moment, strands of dark hair falling onto her forehead. Then she sighs and looks up.

"Please," she says to Larsen. "Just keep this between us."

"Fine."

"Will."

"I said fine." His mistrustful gaze shifts from Gigi to me. "It won't leave this bathroom," he promises.

But I don't have a good feeling about it.

CHAPTER THIRTY
RYDER

This is your stop

"ALL RIGHT. HERE'S ONE. YOU'RE GIFTED A PET TIGER—"

"Nice," Nazzy says.

"What's his name?" Patrick asks.

Beckett rolls his eyes as he tapes up his stick in preparation for tonight's away game against Brown University. "He doesn't have one."

"What kind of tiger doesn't have a name?" demands Patrick.

"That's a good point," Shane tells Beck.

"Are you jackasses going to let me finish or no?"

"Fine, go," Nazem says, waving his hand in permission. "We get a pet tiger. A nameless pet tiger."

I snicker under my breath.

"Anyway," Beckett continues, "this tiger is great. Round the clock protection, top-notch wingman because all the chicks want to rub his ears or whatever. Basically, he's a net positive in your life."

"But...?" Shane asks, because there's always a but in these things.

"But for three hours every day, you have to hear him bitch," Beckett finishes.

"About what?" Rand asks curiously, pulling his jersey over his chest protector.

"About everything. I'm talking the most mundane, trivial, petty stuff." Beckett nods. "Basically, for three hours every day, he turns into Micah's girlfriend."

"Fuck off," Micah says, flipping him the bird. "Veronica doesn't complain that much."

Shane cackles. "Dude. All she does is complain."

From the locker at the end of the row, Jordan Trager turns with a scowl. "Why are you assholes always doing this thought experiment shit?"

"Oh, that's actually a funny story," Nazem pipes up, tossing out a rare olive branch. For the most part, the Eastwood and Briar guys religiously avoid each other. "We were on the bus coming back from a game against Dartmouth, and there was an incident—"

"I don't give two shits about your funny story," mutters Trager. "I'm just saying, this is fucking childish."

"Says the guy with the cartoon tiger tattooed on his back," Beckett replies with a chuckle. "Staring at that godawful thing is what gave me the idea for that thought experiment."

"You're seriously trashing my tattoo?" Trager snaps. "A man's tattoos are sacred."

"So are a man's eyes, and your tattoo is hurting mine," drawls Beck.

Across the room, I notice Will Larsen trying to hide a smile.

The memory of last night's mayhem promptly returns. Finding Larsen in my bathroom was…bizarre. His secret friendship with Beck is of no concern to me, though. I only care that he keeps his goddamn mouth shut about seeing Gigi there.

I notice Austin sitting on the bench, his curly hair falling into his face as he tightly laces up one skate. He's been quiet lately. He's always leaned toward the shy side, but he's usually a lot more talkative during practice and in the locker room.

I realize it probably falls under the purview of cocaptain to check in with everybody, so I clap a hand on his shoulder and lean toward him.

"You doing okay?"

Pope gives me a suspicious look. "Yeah. Why? Did I do something wrong?"

"No. Nothing. I was just checking in."

"Why?" he asks again.

Shane starts to laugh. "Dude. You're so bad at human interaction that people get suspicious when you inquire about their well-being."

"Fuck off," I grumble and start taping my own stick. See, this is why I didn't want the captain title to begin with. Leadership skills continue to elude me.

And, evidently, teamwork continues to elude us.

The game remains scoreless for the first two periods, which is more than one could hope for, considering how many shots they take on net. Kurth is a rock star. And Beckett and Demaine work so well together in the defensive zone that Coach keeps them on a few shifts in a row. They return to the bench utterly spent. Will helps to heave Beckett through the door so Pope and Karlsson can pop out. Beckett collapses on the bench, sweat dripping down his face.

Will gives him a consolatory look and passes over a squirt bottle of water. Colson catches the exchange and frowns, and Will then pretends to study his gloves, picking at an elusive loose thread.

There are too many secrets on this bench.

I'm banging Colson's ex-girlfriend.

His best friend is watching time travel movies with the enemy.

What has the world come to?

At the beginning of the third, we're ahead by one goal, after Austin releases a one-timer that makes it past Brown's goalie. It's the first gear shift we've had all game, but the momentum doesn't last. Next time we're in the defending zone, Colson misses a pivotal pass at the face-off that leads to a costly opposition goal.

The score jumps to 1–1.

When Colson returns to the bench, Rand gets in his face. "Good going, captain," he says sarcastically.

"Fuck you," Colson spits out.

"Fuck *you*."

"Enough!" Coach snaps, holding up his hand. He turns and calls for a substitution.

Meanwhile, I'm as pissed as Rand, because I clearly communicated I was going for the slot. All Colson had to do was fucking listen and the puck would be on his stick right now.

Still, it's probably not the smartest move on my part, as we skate into face-off position on our next shift, when I scowl at Colson and mutter, "Maybe listen this time?"

That gets his back up. I blink and he's in my face. His arm comes out, not quite to the point of a shove. More of a tap.

I stare down at his glove on my arm. Then I look up. Shocked and angry. "What the fuck are you doing?"

"Keep your goddamn commentary to yourself," he snaps at me. "We're trying to play a game here."

Except these five seconds of bickering get us the whistle. The referee calls delay of game.

Jesus Christ.

We took a fucking penalty.

"What the *hell*," Demaine growls as he shoots off toward the bench so Coach can get the penalty kill team on.

"Are you kidding me right now?" The vein on Jensen's forehead looks like it's about to explode. "Delay of game?" he screams toward our penalty boxes.

Colson and I both duck our heads. He's right to scream. There are many penalties that can be avoided, and the one we took is definitely one of them. Especially when it's called because you're arguing with your own teammate. No, worse—your cocaptain.

Coach's eyes tell me we're in grave danger right now. Brown capitalizes on our error and scores on the penalty.

2–1, Brown.

Case and I are out of the sin bin and return to the ice to do damage control. With two minutes left, a beauty from Larsen brings the score to 2–2. The five-minute overtime period ends scoreless, so now we've got a second tie on our record. It's not a loss, but it might as well be the way Coach fumes in the locker room.

Luckily, he spares us a prolonged verbal ass-kicking. He simply walks in, snaps his index finger from me to Case, and barks out one word: "Deplorable." Then he addresses the rest of the room. "Shower and change. I'll see you on the bus."

Fuck.

This season is off to a tragic start. Only one win so far. And now, tonight, our latest game ends in a tie because the damned cocaptains took a penalty they shouldn't have. I don't blame Coach for being mad. He's used to winning the Frozen Four, and that's starting to look like a pipe dream this season.

We reconvene on the bus. The mood is glum. It's a ninety-minute drive back to the Briar campus; about ten minutes in, I notice Jensen get up to talk to the driver.

Ten seconds after that, the bus stops on the side of the road.

Shane, my seatmate, lifts his head from his phone. He was texting with yet another cheerleader, who he's been hanging out with all week. "What's this?"

"Colson. Ryder. Get up."

Case and I exchange a nervous look at the forbidding command. We rise from our seats.

"This is your stop."

I turn toward the window. All I see is pitch blackness. This side of the two-lane highway offers nothing but a gravel shoulder and a dark stretch of forest.

"What do mean this is our stop?" Colson echoes. He's puzzled. "You want us to walk home?"

Jensen's smile is all teeth and no humor. "Think of it as another team-building exercise."

"Abandoning us in the middle of the woods to a serial killer is team-building?" Tristan Yoo blurts out.

"First of all, there is no 'us.' It's them. So calm down, Yoo." Coach nods. "But you raise a good point."

He extends his gaze over the sea of male faces until it lands on someone a few rows behind Beckett. A sophomore named Terrence who isn't a starter.

"Boy Scout, you always carry that Swiss army knife around. You have it on you?"

"Yessir."

"Hand it over."

"Yessir."

Coach scans the bus again. "Let's not pretend none of you smoke or have smoked a substance in your life. I need two lighters. Pass 'em up."

A couple of lighters make their way up the rows until they're in his hands. Jensen slaps one in my palm, the other in Case's. The army knife also goes to Case. I make a mental note of that. I guess between the two of us, Jensen believes I'm the one more likely to murder the other and thus shouldn't possess the weapon. Not sure if I should take that as a compliment or insult.

"You have your phones. You have fire. You have protection. You've got your jackets." He plucks a bag of chips out of a startled Nazem's hands. "And some food. All the tools you need to survive the night. The bus will pick you up from this location in the morning."

"Coach, come on. This is insanity," Colson protests. "You can't just—"

"I can't just what?"

Case falls silent.

"Because the way I see it, *I can't just* have my team captains taking delay-of-game penalties because they're squabbling like toddlers who haven't had their naps. Clearly your time with the Laredos isn't working."

"Yeah, because they're batshit crazy," Patrick mumbles.

Choked laughter echoes through the bus.

"At the end of the day, what happened tonight—this game that we *should have won* and didn't—is on you. Both of you." He looks from me to Case, his mouth pinched in a tight line. "It's about forty miles to Hastings, and if you choose to walk, it's going to take you all night. I personally suggest you hunker down and camp out for the night. Use the time to squash the beef. Make it right. The bus will be back here at 6:00 a.m." He bares his teeth and points to the door. "Get moving."

CHAPTER THIRTY-ONE

RYDER

She's fucking me, bro

"THIS IS BULLSHIT." CASE KICKS A ROCK AS WE HUDDLE ON THE side of the highway like a pair of Dickensian orphans.

So far, we haven't ventured into the woods. We're still loitering on the gravel shoulder, where Colson keeps alternating between kicking pebbles and looking at his phone.

I frown at him. "You should save your battery."

"Come on. He's not actually going to leave us out here all night."

"Pretty sure he is, bro."

Case narrows his eyes.

"He gave us a Swiss army knife and lighters," I say with a harsh laugh. "Of course he's not coming back. We pissed him off good tonight with that penalty."

"Yeah. We did."

Colson steps forward and peers down the dark road. Not a single car has passed since the bus left us in its rearview mirror.

"Are there any active serial killers out here?" he asks. "Wasn't there, like, a highway killer a while back on the West Coast? Do you think there's an East Coast one?"

"Why? Are you scared?" I mock.

"No. I just feel exposed here. You know what. Fuck it. I'm going to start a campfire."

At that, Colson takes off toward the woods. The silver stripes on his black hockey jacket glint beneath a shard of moonlight that's escaped a patch of clouds.

"You coming?" He glances over his shoulder.

"Yeah, whatever."

I shove my hands in my pockets and follow him. We let the moon guide the way. Since we're literally on the side of the road, there isn't an official path, but there are some trodden areas, so we manage to weave our way deeper into the woods without tripping on the undergrowth.

"Did you want to try to walk back to Hastings?" I ask.

"God, no. Do you?" he counters, incredulous. "I can't destroy my legs like that. We gotta be in the weight room tomorrow. I need to be able to do deadlifts."

Good point.

"It's only eight hours. We'll live." He stops in a small clearing in the trees and nods his approval. "This spot'll do. C'mon. Let's go look for some fire-making supplies."

We split up to scour the immediate area. I poke around on the forest floor in search of kindling and twigs, also finding some thick broken branches that would serve as decent fire logs. When we reconvene in the clearing, Colson's already constructed a pit using a bunch of hefty stones.

"Nice," I say, impressed.

"Thanks. I'm a pro at this. My family goes camping a lot. And not fake camping, like G's family. They're all like, We're *roughing it*, and then rent a mansion in Lake Tahoe. Nope. My family needs to be sleeping on literal rocks, or my dad says it doesn't count."

I can't fight my laughter. Then it fades when I realize by "G's family," he's referring to the Grahams. Meaning he's likely spent a lot of time with them.

Gigi brought him around her family. And here I am, fucking her in total secrecy.

"I got a bunch of shit." I drop the supplies on the ground near the stone pit and start building the fire.

He probably wouldn't believe it, but I know how to start a fire too. For other reasons, though. I didn't have a family to go camping with.

"You set that up nicely," he says, nodding. "You've done this before?"

I nod back.

"Scouts? Camping?"

"Hiding," I say wryly.

"What does that mean?"

I shrug. I'm not a big sharer, but for some reason I decide to elaborate. Maybe Gigi's rubbing off on me.

"I lived in this one foster home growing up where the dad got violent with his wife a lot. Sometimes it got pretty bad, so whenever that happened, I'd grab a tent and take my little foster sister and brother out to the woods behind the house. Some nights it was cold, so we'd start a fire to keep warm. Most of the time it was more smoke than flames, though. We knew how to start it, but not how to maintain it."

"Don't worry, I got the maintaining part down pat."

He pulls the lighter out of his pocket, bending over the fire. He blows on the spark and soon he's nurturing a flame that rises taller and taller. Within minutes, we've got a blazing fire going.

I peel out of my coat and lay it on the ground before sitting atop it. Case does the same. And then we sit there in silence. Well, not total silence. My stomach is producing a Dan Grebbs–worthy symphony of growls and rumbles. I usually load up on protein after a game and I'm famished.

As if reading my mind, Case says, "Should we go try to hunt a cheetah or something?"

I chuckle. "Yes, all those cheetahs out here in the New England forest."

"We could forage," he suggests. "I think some berries are still around in October. And black walnuts should still be in season."

"Dude, I'm not foraging. That's a you project."

He snickers.

"We can survive until morning. I think I've got a granola bar, though. We can have it with our bag of chips."

"Awesome," he says glumly.

And so we split a late dinner consisting of potato chips and the peanut butter chocolate granola bar from my jacket pocket.

This is gonna be a long night.

Not surprisingly, it's Colson who eventually brings up our issues. He seems to like talking more than I do.

"We can't keep doing this shit."

I shrug. "I know. But I can't make the Briar guys welcome us."

"It goes both ways. You need to want to be welcomed." He hesitates. "When you guys first got here, we were worried you'd take our slots. And—let's face it, you did. Fuckin' Miller's gone. He was a good friend."

I nod. "So was our old captain. Sean. He transferred when he heard about the merger because he didn't want to deal with exactly what we're dealing with right now."

"Then we both lost good guys. But that part's over now. We're all starters. And we're all good," he says, albeit grudging.

"All of us?" I say dryly.

"Yes. Fishing for compliments?"

"No, I know I'm good." I pause, grimacing. "You are too."

Case grins. "Hurts to say it, huh?"

"A little."

"All I'm saying is, we're cocaptains. We need to set an example for the other men. And a little flattery and encouragement goes a long way."

"Maybe we can change Jensen's mind about the no-pet decree," I say mockingly.

That gets me a loud snort. "Highly doubtful. Gigi's dad told me the story behind that."

My interest is piqued. "Dude. Tell me."

"I guess a couple decades ago the team had a pet pig, and one of the guys entered him in an event at a county fair in New Hampshire. He thought the pig would just get a ribbon for being the cutest or whatever. Plot twist: the winning entrant got turned into bacon."

Holy shit. Shane was right. They *did* eat their pet.

"That's traumatic," I say.

"For real."

We fall silent for a while, staring at the fire. Case adds another log, poking it with a skinny branch.

"What happened on the bus?" he suddenly asks. "That story Nazem was trying to tell before Jordan shut him down. Why do you guys do that thought experiment thing?"

I chuckle to myself. "Oh. That's all thanks to our resident idiot. So, Patrick, right, the Kansas Kid, falls in love every other day. At the beginning of last season, he meets this chick at a party, and of course within seconds he's planning to marry her. He accidentally ends up with her phone—I guess he was holding it for her because she didn't have a purse. Somehow it ends up in his backpack, which he's got on him when we're on our way to play St. Anthony's. We're halfway there when the cops speed up, sirens blaring, and pull the bus over."

"Because they thought he stole her phone?" Case looks incredulous.

"No, even better," I say on a chuckle. "I guess she took off with some friends to Daytona and didn't realize Patty still had the phone—she thought she just lost it. But her dad down in Rhode Island hasn't heard from her in more than twenty-four hours, can't get in touch with her, and the dude panics. He calls the police, and they use that find-my-phone app and discover her phone is traveling along the interstate. They immediately assumed she'd been kidnapped and sent three cruisers after us. It was a whole thing. Got stopped for hours, bro. We missed our game."

"Wait, I think I remember this. It was right before the playoffs and Eastwood had to forfeit. They said everyone had the stomach flu."

"That was a lie. We were literally all being interrogated about the whereabouts of this chick."

"That's wild."

"I know. Fucking crazy. No one's ever let Patrick forget it. Although I'm pretty sure he's forgotten all about *her* considering he's fallen in love at least sixty-five times since then. But yeah, as our punishment, we weren't allowed to use our phones on the bus for the rest of the season, which is stupid because it wasn't our phones' faults that Patrick is a moron. But suddenly we didn't have phones to entertain us, so we started asking these questions like *would you rather*, or *what would you do if*, and it sort of became a thing we do now before games. Once a superstition sticks, it's there forever." I narrow my eyes as something occurs to me. "I just realized—both our superstitions have to do with goddamn Patrick. Kid's a menace."

"What's the other superstition?"

"One time he accidentally texted 'I'm aching for you' to our group chat." I snort. "So that's a thing now too."

"Wait, that's what I always see you guys texting before a game?" Colson's jaw drops as he glares at me. "This is why we keep losing! Because the whole team isn't doing it."

I'm not at all surprised to learn he's as superstitious as the rest of us.

"We did win one," I point out.

"Yeah. And then lost the rest." He stubbornly sticks out his chin. "I don't acknowledge the ties. A tie is a loss."

"Agreed. I hate it when people say otherwise." I let out a breath. "I don't know. Maybe we'll do a new group chat, then."

Words I never thought I'd hear exiting my mouth because I hate both chatting and groups.

"Well, we have to try now," Case insists. "We can't keep losing."

I agree with that too.

He tends to the fire again. Pale orange embers dance and float away in the darkness.

Then he says, "I'm not usually such a dick."

"Oh." I pause. "I usually am."

He snickers. "I figured that. But...me...not so much. It's just been tough lately. I went through a breakup."

A thread of discomfort travels through me. "We're going to talk about women now?"

He checks at watch. "Well, it's eleven o'clock and I'm not ready yet to get mauled by a bear while I sleep, so...yes, I guess we are."

"You and Graham, huh?" I keep my tone casual.

"Yeah. We were together since the start of freshman year. Broke up this past June." He bites his lip. "It's really messed with my head."

"What happened? She dump you or the other way around?" I'm selfishly eager to gain some insight into the breakup. I'd never ask Gigi, but Case is fair game.

"She dumped me," he says flatly. "A week after she told me she loved me, no less."

I wrinkle my forehead. I'll admit, I'm not super adept at navigating the I-love-you landscape, but it seems odd that neither of them expressed that sentiment until more than a year into the relationship. Maybe that's normal, though? I've never uttered those three words to a woman. For all I know, it takes a while for people to say it.

"I screwed up. And I honestly thought we'd be able to get past it, but she doesn't trust me anymore, and it fucking kills, you know?"

I feel sympathy for the guy. Because there's genuine pain in his voice.

Then I feel like a total ass. Because he has no idea my dick was inside her last night.

"I threw it all away," he says in a sad, faraway voice. "Fuckin' idiot."

"You cheated on her?" I ask. I'm not the man who plays around with subtext.

He drops his head in his hands, groaning into his palms.

"Whatever. Yes. I cheated. And I don't think she's ever going to forgive me." Another groan. "I don't know what to do anymore. What am I supposed to do? I think she's the one."

If she were the one, he wouldn't think it. He would know it.

And if she were the one, he wouldn't have messed around with somebody else.

But I keep the thoughts to myself. I'm an asshole most of the time, but even I can't kick a man when he's down.

"So, yeah. I've been a prick lately," he admits. "I don't know how to let out all this frustration, you know? She's pulling away from me. And I miss her. I'm constantly wondering where she is and what she's doing."

She's fucking me, bro.

I keep that to myself too.

CHAPTER THIRTY-TWO
RYDER

Butterfly mating habits

THE NEXT MORNING, WHILE ALL THE GUYS ARE FRESH AND ALERT after sleeping in their own beds—or a sorority girl's bed, in Beckett's case—Colson and I look like we just got stateside from a survival show. After the bus picked us up, I managed to sleep for two hours at home before catching a ride with Shane for our lifting session. I was too tired to drive.

At Eastwood, we could lift based on our own schedules, but Briar requires a training regimen where we lift together as a team. Everyone is already in the weight room when I walk in.

"He lives," Beckett says, grinning when he spots me. He must have come here directly from the sorority house. "I was expecting to see you walk in wearing a squirrel-skin hat or something."

"We almost did kill a cheetah," Case says, smacking my arm good-naturedly.

More than a few sets of eyebrows soar at that.

"Double Cs," Trager says, wandering over to fist-bump Case. "You good, bro?" He shoots me a wary look.

Colson notices and sighs. "All right, everyone. Listen up." He claps his hands.

Guys stop what they're doing, sitting up on their weight benches, to focus on Colson. Demaine, who was spotting Joe Kurth, returns the barbell to its position. Near the back mirror, Rand and Mason set down the dumbbells they were deadlifting.

"We wanted to apologize for what happened during the game last night," Colson starts. "Brown shouldn't have scored that goal. The penalty was on us, and it wasn't captain behavior." He glances at me, and I nod my agreement. "Going forward, we need to be a team. A real team." His face becomes pained. "As much as I hate Nance and Sheldon, I think they have a point about this communication stuff."

Several skeptical looks are exchanged.

"So, I'll start." His gaze lands on Shane. "Lindley. Your slapshots are beautiful, man. I've never seen that kind of power."

Shane is startled. "Oh. Thanks."

Case tips his head at me.

I lock my gaze on Trager because he seems like one of the better options to try to win over. "Trager. You nailed that penalty kill yesterday."

He narrows his eyes at me. Then, noticing Case watching him, he gives a brisk nod.

Colson crosses his arms over his chest. "All right. Somebody else go. We're going to shower each other with fucking compliments until we're all swimming in goddamn dopamine."

"Lindley knows all about that," Nazzy says solemnly, and Shane flips him the bird.

After a beat of hesitation, Will Larsen addresses his secret best friend. "Beckett. You use the edges better than anyone I've ever seen."

Beck nods. "Thanks, mate." In response, he says, "Your shot is a goddamn laser beam."

And on and on it goes, everyone complimenting one another. It's definite progress.

Not everyone has been won over, though. Later, when I'm heading for the showers, Rand pulls me aside, speaking in a low voice.

"Is this for real? You're friends with Colson now?"

I shrug. I wouldn't call us friends, but I can't deny we had a fun night, despite being marooned in the wilderness. Dude's funny.

Really, now that we've called a ceasefire, the only thing hindering a true friendship between us is the girl who texts me when I leave the locker room twenty minutes later.

GISELE:

> I think I left my necklace at your house. Can I come over and look for it?

I grin at the phone. This chick is the best.

ME:

> Actually, I'm on campus. Want me to come to you instead?

GISELE:

> Really?

ME:

> Why not? Does your roommate know about us?

GISELE:

> Yeah. Come over.

I park my Jeep in the lot outside Hartford House and make my way to the dorm, reaching the front entrance as a willowy Black woman steps out. It's Gigi's roommate, Mya. I recognize her from the day I showed up here with flowers.

Which she doesn't let me forget.

Amusement gleams in her eyes. "Flower boy. How's it going?"

I give her a pained look. "Let's not make 'flower boy' a thing. I have a reputation to protect."

"That's not a promise I'm willing to make. G's upstairs."

Mya steps back to the door and pokes her head into the lobby.

"Hey, Spencer, he's not a murderer," she calls to the security guard at the desk, jabbing a finger at me. Then she gestures for me to enter. "Later, flower boy."

Gigi's room is on the second floor. She greets me in a pair of black booty shorts that are barely visible beneath a purple hockey jersey that's clearly custom made because when she turns, the back reads only her initials, *GG*, stitched on in white.

Her bedroom is as girly as I expect from her, considering she's a rabid fan of butterflies. There's a patterned bedspread and colorful throw pillows. Pictures of her with friends and family tacked on a bulletin board above her desk. And a couple of framed prints featuring, of course, butterflies.

I wander over to the glass frames. "So I was looking up butterfly mating habits the other day, and I discovered—"

"I'm sorry, no," Gigi interrupts. "You can't just gloss over that. You were looking up *butterfly mating habits*?"

I shrug out of my jacket, draping it over the back of her desk chair. "Don't read too much into it. Honestly, I was only trying to figure out how they fuck. Like what part goes where."

She howls in laughter. "Oh my God. Did you learn anything interesting?"

"I did." I flop down in the chair and swivel around. "There's this one tropical species where the male mates with the female and then sprays her with this, like, antiaphrodisiac chemical so other males can't get with her."

"Is this leading to some weird dirty talk where you say you want to spray me with a Ryder chemical?"

"You wish."

"Remember when you told me not to read too much into this?

Well, I am. You're totally trying to show interest in my interests," she accuses. Still laughing, she throws herself on the bed and rests her head on a pile of decorative pillows. "So, when do I get the details of your wild night?"

I tense. "How'd you hear about that?"

"Case texted this morning."

The resulting jealousy that surges through my blood has me clenching both fists.

Shit. That's not good. I'm not supposed to hate the guy anymore. But the idea of him texting Gigi, maybe even winning her back, reactivates all my former acrimony.

"He said you two worked things out."

I shrug.

"He also told me he confided in you about our breakup."

I shrug again.

Gigi gives me a pensive look.

"What?"

"Do you think kissing is cheating?"

I don't expect the question. "What do you mean?"

"If you're in a serious relationship with someone and they kiss someone else—do you consider that cheating?"

"One hundred percent."

"Really?"

"Sure. If you love and respect someone, you shouldn't be kissing someone else. End of story."

Gigi smiles at me.

"What?" I say awkwardly.

"Sometimes I struggle with how black and white you are. But in this instance, I love it." She licks her lips. "It's actually a huge turn-on."

"Is that so?" I drawl.

"Uh-huh."

And then she's climbing off the bed and into my lap. She locks her fingers behind my neck and dips her head to kiss me.

When our tongues meet, it's like a shock to my system. Desire radiates through my veins. My balls tighten and my ass cheeks clench. Then Gigi deepens the kiss and rocks her hips, summoning a strangled noise from my throat. All her squirming is pure agony. Fills me with an ache that only her tight warm heat can ease.

Noting my labored breathing and impatient hands, she laughs softly and slides off my lap, eliciting another groan, this one laced with frustration.

"You seem agitated," she says innocently.

"I wonder why."

"I think I can help."

"Mmm?"

A dazzling smile lights her face.

Then she gets on her knees and takes my cock out.

"You never let me do this enough," she says as she wraps her fingers around the hot aching shaft. "Always just want to fuck me, you terrible person."

"Awful," I agree.

My heartbeat becomes irregular when she lowers her head and swirls her tongue around the head of my cock. The way I get impossibly harder tells me I'm not going to last long. Especially not when she draws me into her mouth and eagerly starts to suck.

I lean back in the chair, head thrown back as I thrust my fingers through her hair and enjoy myself. The sensations she's creating are mind-blowing. Every inch of me feels hot and tight, every muscle coiled in anticipation for the next deep suck, the next firm stroke of her soft hand.

"You're going to make me come," I warn.

She simply tightens the suction of her mouth as if baiting me into orgasm. It's not long before she gets her wish. My hips move restlessly as she sucks me so fucking good. While her tongue scrapes along my length on the next upstroke, her braid falls forward and tickles my balls, and that's all it takes to unleash the rush of pleasure.

Afterward, she grabs some tissues and cleans me up. Then she flips her braid so it's hanging down the center of her purple jersey, looking mighty pleased with herself for destroying my dick like that.

And in that moment, I'm reminded of what Shane said weeks ago. That she's girlfriend material. That I'm not boyfriend material.

I brushed it off because it didn't matter then.

Now, I'm revisiting his assessment.

Maybe it's not true. Maybe I *can* be a boyfriend.

I mean, why not?

Well, other than the fact that Gigi has never once expressed interest in me being her boyfriend.

As if sensing my troubled thoughts, she wrinkles her brow. "What's wrong?"

"Nothing." I swallow through my suddenly dry throat. "What do you think if we went out somewhere?"

The groove in her forehead deepens. "Somewhere where?"

"I don't know. Like on a date."

She blinks. "You're asking me on a date?"

I shrug.

"Do you not remember that whole speech you gave—"

"Gonna interrupt right there, Gisele, because we both know I've never given a speech in my life."

That gets me a grin. "Fair point. I'm talking about that day in the therapy room when you said you don't 'do' feelings." She air-quotes me.

"This isn't about feelings," I lie.

"Okay, then what would be the purpose of the date?"

"I don't know. It might be nice to spend some time together when we're not naked."

Although now that I say it out loud, being naked is goddamn fun. Why do I want her with clothes on?

Gigi goes quiet for a moment before letting out a soft laugh. "I'm pretty sure you wouldn't want to date me. Not for real."

"Why do you say that?"

"I'm too girly for you."

"You play hockey."

"And I love butterflies. And flowers. And…um, opera."

"Opera," I repeat, and I can see what she's trying to do. Lighten the mood again. Give me the opportunity to back out this preposterous door I tried to open. Preserve some of my dignity.

"Yep, opera," she confirms, lips twitching with humor. "See? I can tell from your expression that it's not your thing. Totally understandable, though. I forgive you."

"You don't actually like opera," I say, because now I'm starting to wonder.

"I love it. In fact, it's the *only* date I will ever consider going on."

Now I know she's lying, but before I can dig deeper into this, she gives me a gentle smile.

"Come on, Ryder, we don't want to date each other. It'll only complicate things."

She says this as if the complication ship hadn't sailed a long time ago.

PUCKBOYS

SHANE LINDLEY

I'm aching for you

RAND HAWLEY

I'm aching for you

LUKE RYDER

I'm aching for you

CASE COLSON

I'm aching for you

BECKETT DUNNE

I'm aching for you

JORDAN TRAGER

I'm aching for you

WILL LARSEN

I'm aching for you

CHAPTER THIRTY-THREE
GIGI

Hockey players like it rough

On a weekend in mid-November, the men and women's team schedules line up where we're both playing the University of Maine. There are only a few dozen Division I schools in women's hockey, which means we're constantly playing the same teams throughout the season, often on back-to-back nights. So it's always refreshing to face a new opponent like Maine. The men play Saturday, while the women play both nights. Either way, it's a long enough drive from Briar that it means…

"Road trip, baby," Camila says happily as she flops onto the twin bed next to mine. Our team manager is the one who comes up with the room assignments, and this season I've been paired with Cami. I don't mind it, except that sometimes she talks in her sleep and doesn't believe me when I tell her.

It's game day, so I just finished a low-protein, heavy-carb meal, and now I'm nursing a sports drink until we need to go down to the bus. The hotel is about twenty minutes from the rink. It's an early game, starting at four thirty, so we'll have the rest of the night to ourselves, which Camila is all about.

"Should we hit up a club?" she suggests, rolling onto her stomach and scissoring her legs as she scrolls through her phone.

"Does Portland have any good clubs? I've never actually bothered to check."

"I say we go to the club after tomorrow night's game. We should do dinner or something low-key tonight."

"Sounds like a plan."

She answers a phone call, so I head downstairs without her. Coach Adley and his staff are probably already in the lobby waiting to herd everyone onto the bus. When I step out of the elevator and start walking, a stocky man with glasses and a beard intercepts my path.

"Gigi Graham."

I look over. "Hi." He looks vaguely familiar.

"Al Dustin." He extends his hand. "Assistant coach for Team USA."

My heart speeds up. Oh my God.

I try to hide my eagerness. "Right. Yes, sorry. Good to see you again. I think you were at our exhibition game back in September. With Coach Fairlee."

"Yes, we were."

"Are you just visiting Portland, or here to watch our games this weekend?"

"Here for the games. But don't worry, Brad's not with me." He winks. "So you can relax, let your guard down."

I laugh sheepishly. "Yeah, he makes me nervous. Is it that obvious?"

"Nothing to be nervous about, kid. I caught some tape of your last game," Dustin tells me, nodding in approval. "Excellent puck protection behind the net."

I feel myself blushing with pleasure. Yes. Someone's noticing. I make a mental note to thank Ryder.

"And while I'm not the one with the final say on our roster…" He smiles again. "I don't think you have anything to worry about. Just throwing that out there."

I force myself not to break out in a happy dance, but it's difficult. Because if he's implying what I think he's implying, then I'm going to be receiving a call from Brad Fairlee one of these days.

"Anyway, looking forward to seeing you play live this weekend. Good luck out there."

"Thanks."

I'm still riding the high of that conversation during the game, which ends up being far less competitive than expected. Meaning, we kick their butts. I don't know if it's the cloud of exhilaration I'm on, or if Whitney and I are just in perfect sync, but we're making the kind of plays you see on a professional level. By third period, Coach Adley benches the first and second lines. He gives the third and fourth lines the extra ice time, because there's no way Maine is going to make up a five-goal deficit in the time remaining.

There's loud celebration in the locker room afterward. When I check my phone, I find a text of congratulations from my dad. Our games might not be televised, but they're all taped, and Dad always manages to call in favors so he can watch them live from home.

When the bus returns to the hotel, I get a message from Ryder.

RYDER:

> Hey. Are you able to get away from the girls? I've got something to show you.

ME:

> Is it your dick?

RYDER:

> Of course, but we'll do that later. I'm in Portland.

ME:

I thought you weren't arriving till tomorrow!

RYDER:

I came up early.

Next thing I know, he calls me. I step away from my teammates, who are all filing into the hotel lobby.

His husky voice fills my ear. "Sorry. Easier to call. I told Jensen I had an appointment in Portland, so the school sprung for an extra night at the hotel for me."

"Wait, you're in the hotel?" My heart skips a beat. "Right now?"

"Yeah. Did you pack a dress by any chance?"

"Yes…" I say suspiciously.

"Go put it on. And be quick. We don't want to miss it."

"Miss what?"

"Meet you in the lobby in fifteen," he says without answering.

I'm intrigued.

Ryder is not Mr. Spontaneous, so I definitely want to see where this is going.

I tell the girls I'm bailing on dinner, and fifteen minutes later I stride into the lobby in a little black dress, very little makeup, and with my hair down. His eyes flare with appreciation when I approach. He's wearing black pants and a dark gray sweater, his dark hair artfully tousled as usual.

"Come on, we gotta get out of here quick," I urge, already heading across the lobby. "My teammates are coming down for dinner soon. Someone might see us."

He trails after me, hands in his pockets. "God forbid."

"Oh, are *you* ready for Case to hate you five seconds after you two called a truce?"

Ryder flinches. "Good point."

As we quickly exit the hotel, I'm sure to keep three feet between us in the event that we *are* spotted.

"I can't believe you actually brought a dress with you," he says with a grin.

"I always have one on hand these days. My aunt Summer is a fashion designer, and she has this strict rule that any time you travel, you should bring an LBD with you. Little black dress," I clarify at his raised brow. "I used to think it was a silly rule, but a couple years ago I was in New York for the weekend, and my cousin Alex and I were invited to a runway show at the last minute. The only outfit I had with me was jeans and a shirt that said…wait for it…*Hockey players like it rough*."

He throws his head back and laughs. "You're lying."

"Nope. Google it. It's actually on all those official stock photo sites. Me sitting in the front row with my aunt and cousin, and I'm wearing that ridiculous shirt. They've never let me live it down."

He's still chuckling as we slide into the back seat of an Uber. I still have no idea where we're going, and I don't know Portland well enough to recognize any of the streets we drive on.

"Where is this mystery ride taking us?" I ask him.

"Nowhere, really." He's the epitome of innocence, his large warm palm against my bare knee.

And he's freshly shaved, when normally he'd be rocking a five o'clock shadow. I check him out from the corner of my eye, resisting the urge to run my fingers over his smooth jaw. It's so chiseled. I think I like him clean shaven. Although I also wonder what he looks like with full facial hair. Like a scruffy, glorious god, I bet.

When the car comes to a stop and I notice where we are, my jaw drops. The bright, shining marquee in front of the theater advertises we're here for a production of *Samson and Delilah*.

My mouth drops open. "Oh my God. You're taking me to the opera?"

Ryder shrugs. "You said it's the only date you're interested in going on."

"I was lying."

"Yeah, I know." His eyes gleam. "And now you're being punished for it."

"You are such an asshole," I say, but I'm laughing.

I'm also downright astounded. I can't believe he brought me here.

"It already started, though. Curtain was at seven thirty. We missed a lot already."

I'm not sure I care. I'm more interested in the fact that we're here in the first place.

Ryder pulls up the tickets he purchased and passes his phone to the ticket taker at the door. The suit-clad man scans the barcodes and lets us into the theater. We walk down the empty red-carpeted lobby, following the signs to our seats. I'm startled to realize we're not sitting in the mezzanine, but on the second level in one of the opera boxes.

"How the hell did you swing a box?" I whisper.

"Baby. We're in a tiny theater in Maine. These seats cost like fifty bucks and almost every box was available."

He called me baby.

It happens very rarely, but when it does, my heart turns into a pile of goo in my chest. I think it might be time to start examining what this means. But not tonight. Right now, I'm too focused on this completely unexpected outing.

We have the box all to ourselves and are provided with a perfect unobstructed view of the stage. As we settle in the plush seats, I lean closer to Ryder and whisper, "I've never actually been to the opera."

"Me neither."

Since we're so late, I have no context for what's happening on the stage. A woman in a beautiful gown and a man dressed as a priest sing a duet, her high voice blending perfectly with his rich tenor. There's a frenetic feel to it, as if they're outraged about something.

"I wish we had a program," I murmur. I would search the details on my phone, but despite Ryder mocking it, the theater is at least at eighty percent capacity, and I don't want to disturb any of the other operagoers. "Do you know the story of Samson and Delilah well?"

"Sort of? If memory serves, Delilah is a total cocktease and spends all her time trying to figure out the source of Samson's power." Ryder speaks in a low voice, his gaze fixed on the action below.

"This is actually kind of incredible," I marvel, as Delilah releases a series of high, perfectly tuned lilting notes that bring actual goose pimples to my bare arms. "I regret missing the beginning."

"Me too." He sounds sincere.

As we watch, he reaches for my hand, interlacing our fingers.

"I think this guy is the one who bribes her to seduce Samson." Ryder brings his mouth close to my ear so I can hear him over the woman's haunting wails. "And then at some point, Samson falls asleep and she cuts his hair. And then he gets his eyes gouged out, which is pretty punk rock for a Bible story."

I laugh quietly.

Down below, the tone shifts as a new set is revealed onstage. It's a bedchamber. Delilah now wears a white nightgown that, at some angles, appears almost sheer beneath the stage lights. A new character joins her. A beautiful man who I presume is Samson because he's sporting a long luscious wig with golden waves cascading down his back. Either that, or it's his real hair and I'm jealous.

Delilah starts singing to Samson in a sweet soprano that is belied by the sensual movements of her body. I assume this is the seduction. Something about the way she's rolling her hips and blatantly attempting to bang the beautiful man elicits an odd tug between my legs. Never thought I'd be turned on by an opera, but here we are.

"What kind of pornography have you lured me into?" I whisper to Ryder.

"Like you're not into it." His voice is a soft, teasing whisper.

"I'm not."

"Uh-huh."

Before I have a chance to react, he slips his hand beneath the hem of my dress.

My heart stops.

"Not into it, huh?"

"Nope."

His fingers dance along my thigh before he curls them to rub the knuckles over my suddenly damp core.

"Really?" One teasing finger skims under the crotch of my thin panties. I gasp when the tip pushes inside me. "Then why are you so wet?"

All the oxygen has left my body. And all the blood has pooled between my legs, throbbing in my clit.

"I'm not," I croak out the lie.

"My finger disagrees."

He eases it out, and I squawk when he lifts it to his lips and sucks.

"Manners!" I hiss.

"What? I'm not the one who's dripping all over the seat."

"I am not," I say weakly. "I'm wearing underwear."

"Yeah, speaking of those. They're a problem. Take them off."

I can't stop the thrill that shoots through me. "People will see."

"It's too dark and their eyes are on the stage, anyway. Take them off."

Something has possessed me. Maybe it's the unfiltered lust burning in his eyes. Maybe it's his deep, commanding voice. Maybe it's the excitement surging in my veins.

Drawing a deep breath, I discreetly slide my hand under my dress. I hesitate when I reach the waistband of my skimpy underwear.

Ryder watches my every move. Waiting.

I grip the material with trembling fingers, lift my ass off the seat, and then slide the panties down my thighs. The entire time, I keep my gaze straight ahead in case anyone in the opposite boxes is paying attention to us. But the other patrons' gazes are rapturously focused on the sensual spectacle below and not the one above.

I drag the panties down my legs, then step out of them, one high heel at a time.

Ryder holds out his hand.

Without a word, I place the scrap of lace in his palm. His lips curve as he tucks it in his pocket.

"So obedient," he murmurs. "I like this new Gigi."

I narrow my eyes. "You're pushing your luck."

"Nah." He shifts closer. "Luck has nothing to do with this."

Then his hand is under my dress again, seeking out the warm, aching spot between my thighs. He rubs me with the pads of his index and middle finger. The first contact makes me gasp.

"Quiet," he warns. "Or I'll stop."

"Stop now, and I'll rip your head off."

"You're so violent. I love it. Spread your legs a little."

I can hardly hear the command over the sudden wailing below. Delilah's voice rises in pitch, the music gathering, building to a crescendo. Meanwhile, Ryder strokes my pussy until I'm quivering in my chair, a live wire about to explode. He pushes his fingers inside me, hitting spots that make me impossibly wetter. Bringing me closer and closer toward orgasm.

His lips are at my ear again. "Say my name when you come."

"What—"

Then the heel of his palm applies pressure on my clit, and I shatter, reflexively giving him what he ordered.

"*Ryder.*"

The sound of his name is drowned out by the aria below and the thunder of my pulse in my ears. I come hard enough my vision wavers.

When I crash back to earth, I find him grinning at me. Satisfied with himself.

"Should we bail on this and go back to the hotel?"

I finally manage to find my voice. "Yes."

Later, we lie tangled together in his sheets, sated and sleepy after the best sex of my life. Because every time with Ryder is the best sex of my life. I've stopped trying to figure that out. I just know I'm addicted to it.

I tell him about running into Al Dustin, trying to not be too hopeful, to curb my excitement. Though I can't fight my happy grin as I say, "It's not a done deal yet, but he sounded pretty confident Fairlee was going to pick me."

"Told you he would." He strokes my lower back, pressing his lips to the top of my head. "Olympic gold, here we come."

His words remind me of something, triggering a confession that's been nagging at me for a while now. A flash of reluctant comprehension I hadn't wanted to put into words yet. Because it still feels like...betrayal, I guess.

"Do you remember the last time we talked about the Olympics?" I run my fingers over the defined muscles of his chest. "You asked me why I'm so desperate to make the team. Whether it's for me or my dad."

"I remember."

"Well, it's been bothering me ever since. I thought about it. A lot." I lick my dry lips, still hesitant. But I've already come this far, so I force the rest out. "I want something he doesn't have."

Ryder tenses slightly, as if surprised to hear it. Hell, I'm surprised to say it.

"I've never said it out loud. I don't know if I've ever even thought that deep into it, but... He has everything. The Cup, the awards, the all-time records, MVP titles, almost-certain Hall of Fame induction. I will never come close to achieving even half of that." I swallow the lump in my throat. "But one thing he never did was compete for Team USA. And that's the one thing I can do."

Ryder rolls over so we're lying face to face. He watches me, his expression indecipherable.

Sometimes I hate that he's able to draw things out of me without even trying. He doesn't ask or beg or push me to talk to him. It just happens when he's around. All my secrets spilling out with abandon.

"I want…to feel important in my own life," I admit. "Achieving this is a way for me to finally step out of his shadow. I can be an Olympic gold medalist. Something my dad will never be." I groan in desperation. "It feels so petty to say it. Is that awful?"

"Depends on whether it's the *only* reason you want to compete. Is this nothing but a *Fuck you, look at my medal, old man*?"

"Of course not." I flinch. "It's like the teeniest part of it. A sliver of a percentage that pokes at the back of my mind sometimes. Competing on the world stage is so much bigger than him. It's exciting."

"Good. Focus on the excitement. But also acknowledge that the sliver exists."

"I feel bad acknowledging it," I admit, closing my eyes.

I jerk when I feel his thumb stroking my chin.

"You really need to get over this," he says gruffly.

I frown. "Wow. I just shared something really important and—"

"No, that's not what I mean." He shakes his head at me. "You need to stop feeling bad about the way you feel. You hate that chick Emma and feel bad about hating her. You want something your father doesn't have and feel bad wanting it."

For some reason, my throat tightens. The sting of tears burns my eyes. Oh my God, I better not cry.

"It's like you refuse to voice even a shred of negativity; otherwise it makes you a bad person. Or you feel like you need to be eternally grateful for being born wealthy and gifted." He wraps his arm around me, his lips gently brushing mine as he strokes his hand down my bare arm. "Just feel what you feel. It's okay."

I blink to keep the tears at bay, but they're threatening to spill over. And not because I'm ashamed by everything I've confessed.

It's the undeniable awareness that I'm developing feelings for this guy.

"I…" I take a breath, attempting to steady my voice. "I've never met anyone I felt comfortable sharing all that with." I peer into his bottomless blue eyes, always floored by how vivid they are. "I don't feel like you judge me. About anything. Ever."

"I don't."

"Do you feel like I judge you?"

"Never," he says simply.

Then he visibly gulps, and I know precisely how he feels.

This is fucking terrifying.

Ryder rolls us over so that he's on his back and I'm draped over his bare chest. He runs his fingers along my naked skin, from my shoulder to my tailbone, before resting his palm on my hip. I shiver from his touch.

"Gisele," he says.

"Mmmm?"

"Are we dating now?"

A smile tickles my lips. I rise slightly on my elbow and gaze down at him. He's biting his lip and it's adorable.

"Yeah. I think we are."

CHAPTER THIRTY-FOUR
GIGI

The world is scary sometimes

I sneak out of Ryder's hotel room at an ungodly hour because I'm terrified the Briar men's bus will show up early and somehow Case will see us.

I'm going to have to tell him eventually, I know that. I just hate the idea of hurting him. We were together almost two years. There's history there.

I assumed Ryder and I would hook up a few times and then it would end. Case would be none the wiser. Never even need to know. But Ryder and I can't keep hiding anymore. It's been months now. Which floors me, because it feels like I've known him forever. I can't remember a time when one of his drugging kisses didn't fog up my brain.

We win our afternoon game, remaining undefeated thus far this season. Then we have an hour to grab an early dinner before going to watch the men play. I haven't seen any of their games since Ryder and Case went camping in the middle of the road. They've racked up four consecutive wins since then, and from what I've heard, they've been an unstoppable force, but this is my first time experiencing it in person.

Right off the bat, I see the difference. Especially with those two.

They're gelling like I've never seen before, a deadly attack squad with Will serving as the third forward. Beckett and Demaine are the d-men, the pair of them also on fire.

"Oh God," Cami groans. "He has such soft hands."

She's talking about Beckett. It's true—he doesn't have the speed of Case or Ryder, but man, the ease with which he wields that stick…

"He's magnificent," she sighs.

"Have you still not hooked up with him?" Whitney says in amusement.

"No!" Cami whines. "Can you believe this? It's unacceptable."

The score is tied 1–1 for most of the game, until midway through the third period, the craziest play I've ever seen goes down.

Case takes a hit from his opponent, and as he goes falling to the ice, he manages to tip the puck. And Ryder, who just got checked himself and is in the process of spinning around from the impact, somehow manages to scoop the puck, do nearly a complete 360, and stuff the puck in between the goalie's leg pad and blocker.

Goal.

The entire rink loses it, even the home crowd. Because that was truly the coolest thing on the entire planet. There's an explosion of cheers and hollers as my teammates and I jump to our feet screaming our lungs out. An amazed and ecstatic Ryder thrusts both arms over his head just as Case throws his own arms around him. Flashbulbs go off, and I suspect that iconic victory pose is going to be blasted all over the sports blogs tomorrow.

"God, when he smiles…" Whitney says, shivering.

I realize she's admiring Ryder, who skates past the plexiglass and tips his head in our direction. I told him where we were sitting, and although I don't know if he sees me, the devastatingly handsome grin he flashes the stands sure feels like it's for me.

Five minutes later, the final buzzer goes off and Briar wins 2–1.

"Come on. Let's go wait for the boys," Cami says, hopping to her feet. "We gotta drag them out to celebrate."

We follow the people in our row toward the end of the aisle, but it's slow going. And once we get there, we join another line inching its way to the bottom of the bleachers. I take a step, then stop abruptly when Cami stops, which causes the person behind to bump into me. I glance over to apologize.

"Sorry," I tell the beefy blond guy.

"All good." His eyes then widen in appreciation. "Hi there."

"Hey," I say politely, then face forward again.

I jerk when I feel a tiny tap on my shoulder. I glance over again.

"You ladies have any plans for the rest of the night?"

"Just going to meet our teammates." I keep my gaze straight ahead and will the line to move faster. I can already tell this is not going to go in the direction he wants.

"Teammates? You mean the Briar dudes? You play too?"

"Yep."

A slimy grin spreads across his face as he moves a bit closer. "That's hot. I love female athletes."

I try to shuffle faster to get away from him. He's invading my personal space now and I don't like it.

Cami twists to look at me, lifting a brow as if to ask if I need help. I give a slight shake of my head.

"I really mean that," he tells me, as if I care whether or not he does.

"Cool." Relief hits me as we reach the bottom row. "Well, see you around," I say, and anyone capable of picking up on social cues would know I don't mean it.

This guy is not capable. "I'm looking forward to it," he drawls, winking at me.

Case texts as we reach the lobby of the rink.

CASE:

> We're all hitting up a club downtown later.
> Some place called Smooth Moves. You
> ladies down?

I check with the girls, and they all nod.

Back at the hotel, Cami and I dress for a night out. My only option is the little black dress I wore last night. When Cami's in the bathroom, though, I hastily examine the fabric to make sure I didn't leak all the way through it when Ryder was fingering me at the opera.

A shiver runs through me. I honestly don't think I will ever, ever get enough of him. Not the sex, which only keeps getting better. But the company's growing on me too. Every prickly, grumpy part of him.

My teammates are all ready to go when my phone rings. I check the screen and wave Cami through the door.

"It's my brother," I tell her. "I'll meet you guys in the lobby."

"*Undefeated,*" Wyatt crows when I answer the call. "I just heard."

"Yeah, the season's going really well."

"You think you'll make it to the championship?"

"I mean, it's still super early. There's like twenty more games to go. But I hope so." I bite my lip to stop the excitement, because I told myself not to get my hopes up, but I can't help sharing the potential news with him. "One of the assistant coaches from Team USA is here this weekend. He stopped me in the hotel yesterday and told me I don't have anything to worry about. Basically implied I'd make the final roster."

"Fuck yeah. I told you." Wyatt laughs. "Emma might be a total whack job, but her dad's clearly got a good head on his shoulders."

"One would hope. Anyway, I gotta bounce. We're going out tonight with the men's team to celebrate both wins."

"All right, cool. Just wanted to say congrats. Love you, Stan."

"Love you too."

I tuck my phone in my purse and zip up my jacket on my way to the elevator bank. I press the down button, then wait until the doors swing open with a chime. I'm stepping into the car when someone says, "Hold the door."

My stomach sinks when the blond guy from the rink follows me inside.

Fuck.

Of all the people to run into.

"You again!" he says, his face brightening.

"Yep." I plaster my back to the wall, hoping my body language is obvious enough.

But he of no personal space doesn't receive the memo. He stands directly beside me so that our arms are almost touching. Then he abruptly angles himself so I'm effectively trapped against the wall.

"I'm Nathan."

I glance at the lights over the doors. I've already pressed the button for the lobby, but for some reason the elevator is still not moving.

"You don't have to be scared of me," he teases, chuckling.

I jam my finger on the *close door* button, even though the doors are already closed. Maybe that will speed up the process.

"I'm not scared," I say lightly. "Just in a hurry. I have somewhere to be."

"Well, you're in luck, because I have nowhere to be." A lecherous smile appears. He even licks the corner of his mouth, which I suspect is his attempt at looking sexy. It's not working. "Why don't I tag along with you?"

"Sorry, it's a Briar hockey thing. Just for our teams."

"That's a shame." He's unfazed. "Maybe we can meet up after?"

"Oh, I don't know when it'll be done," I reply, when deep down I want nothing more than to say, *No, we cannot and will not meet up after. Ever.*

But saying no to men isn't always an easy task. I'd love to be direct. Confrontational. Look him right in the eye and say NO.

The problem with being a woman is that you never know what a NO will get you. Is it going to earn me an understanding nod and an *Okay, well, have a great night; it was nice talking to you?*

Or will it get me a *You entitled bitch, what, you think you're too fucking good for me?*

And I've experienced the latter multiple times.

The world is scary sometimes. So, no, I'm not going to shoot this guy down directly, at least not in this specific circumstance, where we're alone and I'm trapped. I'll vaguely dance around the issue until I'm able to escape this enclosed space and find the safety of a crowd.

The elevator finally begins to move, and relief blasts through me like a gust of wind. I track the numbers as they go down.

Normal guys would usually get the hint. This one doesn't. He leans in, and I wince when I feel his hot breath near my ear. I also smell a whiff of alcohol on it. I realize he was probably drinking at the game.

"I'd *really* like to meet up with you after," Nathan tells me.

I try to ease away, but now I'm stuck between the wall and the number panel, trapped in the little corner.

"No, thanks," I reply, finally opting for honesty. "I'm super tired. Won't be going anywhere after the team event."

"That's a shame. I think we could have a lot of fun together." He trails the tip of one finger against my cheek.

I flinch and try to sidestep him, but there's nowhere to go.

I give him a deadly look. "Okay, seriously. You need to step back," I warn.

And there it is, that telltale flashing of his eyes. The entitlement.

"You don't have to be a fucking cunt about it."

I ignore him.

"I'm just saying, we could have fun."

The elevator stops five floors below mine to let someone else on. The doors start to open just as he digs his fingers into my waist, trying to pull me closer.

I experience a flicker of honest-to-God fear. "*Get off me, asshole!*"

"Stop being such a—"

Before he can finish, he's hauled out of the elevator and into the wide hallway. I catch a blurry glimpse of Ryder's furious face. Shane's concerned one. And I almost sag with relief.

"She said get off her," Ryder growls.

I jump out before the doors close on me. Ryder has his hand on the creep. Not overly aggressive, but a controlled threat. A hand of warning on Nathan's chest, right near his neck as if prepared to yank him by the collar and shove him against the wall.

"Ryder, it's okay," I say, touching his shoulder.

"You sure?" He searches my face. "Did he hurt you?"

"Hurt her? I'm not a goddamn rapist!" Nathan snarls.

"Really? Because it sure looked like you were touching her without her consent."

"She wanted—"

"Don't finish that sentence," Shane suggests coldly. "Seriously, bro, just don't."

Ryder steps away from the guy and points to the stairwell door. "Get the hell outta here."

"We're on the fifteenth floor! I'm not taking the stairs—"

"I don't care. Go."

Nathan's thunderous gaze shifts between the two men. And suddenly three more bodies appear without warning. Case, with Will and Beckett in tow.

"What's going on?" Case demands. "Is everything all right?"

"This guy was harassing Gigi," Ryder mutters. "Tried to put his hands on her."

Case lunges forward. "Are you fucking kidding me?"

"We've got it handled," I assure my ex-boyfriend. "Seriously, it's fine." To the red-faced Nathan, I frown and say, "Would you get out of here already? You don't even know what can of worms you've opened."

We've gone from two to five strapping hockey players in the matter of seconds, and no matter how big his biceps are, they're no match for the Briar guys.

His gaze flits around in a visible panic. Then, without another word, he darts toward the stairs. We hear his footsteps echoing in the stairwell. I don't know if he has the stamina to descend all fifteen flights, and I hope to God we don't run into him on an elevator on our way down.

"You okay?" Case says urgently.

I can only guess how stricken I look. I won't deny I was scared, especially when his fingers dug into my hip. I'm strong, have taken multiple self-defense courses, but you never know if you're going to be able to fend someone off, especially a drunk guy who's twice your weight and inches taller.

"Yeah." I huff out a breath. "I am. I'm fine."

From the corner of my eye, I see Ryder watching me. He steps closer, as if sensing I'm about to fall apart.

I offer a slight shake of the head, and he stops abruptly. I don't think Case notices, but I know Will does, and I hear his resigned sigh before he speaks.

"We'll give you guys a minute," Will says to Case and me, as the elevator dings open again. "Meet you downstairs."

When Case turns to exchange a brief word with Will, I feel Ryder's hand lightly graze my arm. I crave his hug, but I can't have that right now. A moment later, he disappears into the elevator.

And I get Case's hug instead.

CHAPTER THIRTY-FIVE
GIGI

Friendsgiving

"I HAVE GATHERED YOU ALL HERE THIS EVENING BECAUSE I HAVE A secret to share," I announce.

"I thought we were gathered here for Friendsgiving," Diana replies with a grin. She's lying on the bright burgundy area rug in her living room, gripping both legs in a yoga stretch.

"Well, that's the other reason," I amend.

Mya and I are at Diana's condo for our friends' Thanksgiving the day before the real holiday. It's our only chance to hang out before we all head off to our respective homes. Diana and I are both from Massachusetts, although her family home is right on the Vermont border. Mya's dad is in Malta on his ambassadorial post, but her mother is meeting her in Manhattan for the long weekend.

I was tempted to invite Ryder home with me, but that's...a scary move. It feels too early. Besides, I suspect he would've flat-out said no. Not sure I'd blame him. My father would only be grilling him the entire time. Plus I haven't even told my parents that Ryder and I are together, and that's a conversation I wouldn't mind putting off a while longer. Nobody in my life knows other than Mya, Diana, and Will Larsen. I've even kept my own teammates in the dark.

I don't love sneaking around, but the idea of announcing to the world that I'm dating Luke Ryder… it's anxiety-inducing. Especially when my own feelings on the matter continue to be a jumbled mess.

"So, what's the secret?" Mya asks, glancing up from her phone. For the past ten minutes she's been filtering the photograph she took of our perfectly set table in Diana's dining nook, preparing to post it on social media.

"I think I'm an exhibitionist."

Diana rises from her stretch and purses her lips. "I don't believe you."

Mya nods. "Agreed."

I glare at them. "You haven't even heard why I think this!"

"Fine. We'll be the judge," Mya says. "Present your evidence, counselor."

I bring my legs up to sit cross-legged on the floral-patterned couch that looks like it belongs in a Victorian parlor. The apartment Diana inherited from her late aunt Jennifer came with all her aunt's furnishings. And Jennifer's décor style is what I like to call thrift store chic. This doesn't look at all like a college girl's apartment. It's got a quirky older cat-lady vibe, and yet Diana, in her booty shorts and Briar Cheer crop top, weirdly fits right in.

The aroma wafting in from the kitchen makes my stomach grumble. Rather than cooking a turkey for only three people, we opted for a rotisserie chicken that's roasting in the oven. I haven't eaten anything since before morning skate and I'm famished.

I don my most professional expression and commence with my opening statement.

"Exhibit A: I received oral sex in the library back in October. Well, in the study room."

Mya raises a brow. "Door open or closed?"

"Closed." I smirk at her. "But, like I told you after it happened— his friend Shane was behind the door. Practically participating."

Diana's eyebrows fly up. "What! I didn't know this part. Define *participating*."

"Well, covering for us. But he could hear everything, and at one point he told me to come."

"Okay, that's hot," Diana relents, impressed. "Well, except for the fact that it was Shane Lindley."

"What's wrong with Shane?" I protest, grinning at her dark expression. "He's hot."

"I don't care. He's officially on my shit list. Dude's slept with three of my teammates already this year, and counting. The last one, Audrey, fell so hard for him, figuratively, that when he dumped her, she was so upset she started falling, literally, during practice. Almost broke her damned ankle." Diana flips her platinum ponytail. "Tell that guy to leave the cheer team alone. We're trying to win nationals."

I snicker. "I'll pass that along."

"What's the rest of your evidence?" Mya says, gesturing impatiently.

"Exhibit B: Sauna sex. Anyone could have walked in," I hurry on when they both look ready to object.

Diana shrugs. "Everyone has sauna sex. You're not living on the edge there. But the library is an acceptable exhibition. I'll allow it into evidence."

"I've never had sauna sex," Mya says.

"You're missing out," I tell her. "Okay. Exhibit C: He fingered me at the opera." I give them a smug look. "That was one hundred percent public. Right in the box."

"Oh, he was in the box, all right," drawls Mya.

Diana howls. "Nice."

"And then yesterday, Exhibit D: I blew him in the car behind Malone's," I say, naming the sports bar in town.

Now that the Eastwood and Briar guys are openly fraternizing, they go out all the time, and Malone's is their watering hole of choice. Whitney, Cami, and I met them there yesterday for a few drinks, where Camila finally lived her dream of going home with Beckett Dunne.

"All right. I'm actually quite impressed with all this," Mya says frankly. "This is unlike you."

"Very," Diana agrees.

"That's the thing—I don't think that's true. I think this is very like me. I just didn't realize it."

Mya grins. "So the enemy Eastwood captain made you realize you enjoy public sex."

"I think yes, maybe he did."

Like my sex life is a video game and then Ryder shows up and unlocks a new level, helping me discover a whole new kink.

In fact, he's helped me discover a lot of things about myself. Like my tendency to refuse to voice my darker thoughts or complain about my problems for fear of being judged or told I have no right to complain because my life is too good. Thanks to him, I've been forcing myself to dig deeper into why I feel the things I feel, and why I do the things I do. Like the fact that I want something my dad doesn't have. A medal. I always believed acknowledging that sort of stuff made you weak or, worse, turned you bitter.

But I've felt a strange sense of lightness ever since I released all of that.

Maybe what I really needed was to find the right person to release it to.

"Case would've been so uncomfortable with all this public stuff," I admit. "He's such a Boy Scout. He was okay with car sex sometimes, but I can't possibly envision him getting me off at the opera. I would've felt weird asking him to."

"But you're perfectly cool asking Luke Ryder."

"I'd ask him anything. I'm never worried, not in the slightest, that he'd judge me. He never does. He accepts me for exactly who I am."

They both stare at me.

"What?"

"Oh my God. This isn't about sex," Diana accuses. She glances toward Mya. "This isn't about sex."

"Nope," Mya confirms.

I wrinkle my forehead. "No, it is. Of course it is."

Diana offers an oddly gentle smile. "Gigi. You're in love with this guy."

My jaw drops. "I am not."

I'm almost angry at them for suggesting it. It catches me completely off guard, because here we were having a lighthearted sex chat, and they had to turn it into a discussion about stupid feelings.

Ryder and I don't "do" feelings.

So why do you feel all of them?

Sometimes I really hate that voice in my head.

Fine. Maybe I feel *some* things. Urgency. Fascination. Hunger. Confusion. Desperate, raw need. Pure, bone-deep contentment.

Oh no. Those last two sound a lot like...

Nope.

I push it out of my mind and shut down the conversation when my friends tease me about it again over dinner. Later, while I'm washing the dishes and Mya wipes down the table, my phone buzzes near her hand. She peeks at the screen and says, "It's your true love."

"Oh, stop it," I grumble.

I dry my hands on a rag and go over to read the text.

RYDER:

Can I come over tonight? Need a change of scenery.

And a couple of hours later, we're in my bed driving each other crazy. His strong hands roam my body, warm lips trailing over my skin. My palms skim the defined muscles of his chest as I crawl lower and take him in my mouth. I suck him slow and deep, while he makes husky noises of approval, stroking my hair.

"You look so pretty right now," he mumbles, peering down at me.

I smile around his thick shaft before releasing him. Then I wrap my fist around him and lazily move it up and down, loving the way his gaze thickens, goes hazy.

"Why don't you come up here and sit on my dick." His features crease with agitation, hips lifting as he tries thrusting faster into my hand.

"You need it that bad, huh?"

"So bad." He's not even joking. His long muscular body quivers on the bed.

I have mercy on him and climb up to straddle him, except now I'm the one mindless with desire. He fills me so completely. A sense of belonging, of pure rightness washes over me, making me sag onto his strong chest. I grind against him, the need building until black dots dance in my vision and my clit is swollen and hot. He grips my hips as I ride him.

"Fuck, Gigi. Keep going, baby."

I'm lying on top of him now, rocking wildly.

"I love this so much," I whisper, my hips totally beyond my control. They're moving on their own.

"That's it," Ryder encourages roughly. "Show me how much you want it. Take what you need."

So I do. I ride him, while he palms my breasts and squeezes, rubbing my nipples with his thumbs. I moan his name as a tight knot of pleasure gathers in my core.

Approval fills his eyes. "Yes. Keep saying my name. I want everyone in this building to know who's making you feel this way."

That's all it takes for the knot to detonate. I collapse on his chest and ride out the orgasm, and I'm still gasping when he flips us over, pulling me onto my knees. One muscular arm locks around my chest, keeping me flush to him.

He thrusts upward, nuzzling my neck before he breathes a warning close to my ear.

"I'm coming."

I moan in response and he lets himself go. With a strangled

sound, he shakes with release, lodged deep inside me. His grip tightens, my breasts crushed beneath his forearm.

Then he brushes his lips over the side of my throat and whispers, "You're a goddamn dream."

While I desperately try to convince myself that I'm not in love with him.

CHAPTER THIRTY-SIX
RYDER

National Cotton Candy Day

COLSON AND I ARE FRIENDS NOW. THE KIND OF FRIENDS WHO CHILL outside of the rink and hang out at each other's houses. Sometimes he even crashes here if the guys are partying too hard and he's too drunk to walk home. Will's always here too, but that at least makes sense. He and Beckett are joined at the hip. The good thing about Will is, he doesn't incite any feelings of guilt, so it's a lot easier to have him around.

Colson, on the other hand... I've always been skilled at burying my emotions, but it's becoming a challenge to ignore the guilt. I'm starting to really like the guy. But Gigi doesn't want him to know about us yet, so I need to follow her lead on this. He's her ex, not mine.

They're both over right now, Will sprawled on the couch next to Beckett, while Colson sits next to me.

Shane is in the armchair texting a chick who for once isn't a cheerleader. He met her in Hastings and brought her over the other day. I think she said she was a prelaw student. They went to a party last night, where apparently her ex showed up drunk and sloppy and got in Shane's face. Now she's apologizing profusely to Shane via text.

"There's always that one obnoxiously wasted guy," Will says, rolling his eyes. "What's up with that?"

"It's the age-old rule of the party," Beckett explains. "Every party has a role that must be fulfilled. Sloppy Guy is one of them."

"Dude, that is so true." Case chuckles, then leans forward to grab his beer. He pauses for a moment, then laughs again. "Okay, here's one. You show up at a party and you're only allowed to hang out with one of these people. For the entire night, no breaks. Who do you pick—Crying Mascara-Streak Bathroom Girl or Annoying Acoustic Guitar Guy?"

Beckett groans. "That's pure torture either way, mate."

Shane sets down his phone and thinks it over. Then he fires a series of questions at Colson. "Do I get to fuck the bathroom girl?"

"No."

"Can I make song requests?"

"No."

"What's she crying about?"

"Sobbing too incoherently for you to figure it out."

"Can I do drugs?"

"No."

"Drink?"

"One beer."

Shane shrugs. "Acoustic Guitar Guy."

Will, who's in charge of the remote, stumbles upon that reality show channel Gigi is obsessed with. His eyes light up.

"Yo. *Plate Pleasers.* I love this show."

"Are you kidding?" Colson says. "This show is fucking nuts. Nothing good can come out of giving children this much power."

"That's what I always say," Beckett chimes in. "There's only one way this ends."

Shane eyes them both. "Please, finish that thought. What kind of apocalyptic future are you envisioning because a reality show allows children to judge food dishes?"

Colson looks at Beckett. "He doesn't get it."

Beckett nods.

"All right. I gotta go to class." I slap Colson's shoulder as I get up, then nod at the other guys. "See you later."

My Entrepreneurial Studies class is the only late one this semester. It annoyed me at first that I had to drive all the way back to campus for five o'clock classes three days a week, but the last few times, I met up with Gigi after class let out, and now it's become a routine. Sometimes we grab a late dinner. Tonight, she says she wants a hot tub and steam. She tweaked her shoulder during her game on Saturday, and I guess it's still bothering her.

After my lecture, I drive to the performance center, walking up just as Austin Pope is leaving. The kid's been putting in extra training now that the World Juniors is coming up.

"Hey, captain," he says, but his head is down, and he sounds distracted.

"Hey. How's the training going? Ready for the big game?"

"Not really." His tone is lined with exhaustion.

I frown. "What's going on, Pope?"

"Nothing." He continues to avert his eyes. "Just nervous, I guess."

I get that. Pope is usually rock-solid before games, but the stakes are much higher here.

"It's scary," I admit. "Knowing the whole world is watching you. Literally the entire world."

He hesitates for a moment, then says, "Plus there's this extra pressure."

My frown deepens. "What do you mean?"

"Just all these profile pieces about me being gay and how I'm the first openly gay player to participate in the World Juniors. Stuff like that. Just makes me feel… I don't know. Like it's taking away from my talent, I guess. My skill as a player. Focusing on my sexuality when it makes zero difference for this game."

"I'm sure they mean no harm. I bet they just want you to be a role model for other kids like you," I point out. "Guys who might still be too afraid to come out. That's not a bad thing."

"I get it. But like I said, just more pressure. How did you feel before your Worlds?"

"Scared shitless. And, dude, trust me, I know what it's like to have your talent take the back seat. I played one of the best games of my life, and the only thing people remember is I broke some guy's jaw in the locker room."

"Yeah," he says wryly.

I clap him on the shoulder. "You got this, Pope. Try not to focus on all the noise."

"Thanks, Ryder."

He heads off and I walk into the lobby. I notice the bright red flowers in the planters near the main desk, and when the security guy isn't looking, I nonchalantly pluck one of the scarlet blooms and keep walking. Then I search on my phone, grinning to myself.

Ten minutes later, Gigi walks into the hot tub area, wearing the Speedo that never fails to make me burn for her.

I stick out the flower. "Here."

She sighs. "Oh God. I'm scared to ask, but…what international day is it?"

"National Cotton Candy Day. Seemed like one you'd celebrate."

She releases that melodic, feminine laugh, and I pretend it doesn't affect me when the truth is, everything about her does.

We settle on opposite ends of the hot tub, as the jets swirl the water around us in a foamy eddy. We both know what'll happen if we sit too close together, and for once we're on our best behavior.

"I really thought I'd hear something about Team USA by now," Gigi grumbles. "Like, why did Dustin bother hyping me up in Maine, telling me I had nothing to worry about, if they weren't planning on contacting me soon?"

"I know it's frustrating, but you need to have more patience," I advise. "I remember it took forever when they were putting together the World Juniors team." I lick a drop of moisture off my top lip. "I think the more important question right now is—what are we gonna do about Colson? I keep going back and forth about whether we should tell him about us."

Her features strain. "You guys are really starting to get along, huh?"

"We are. I like him," I say begrudgingly.

She grins. "That was painful, wasn't it?"

"Very." I pause. "I don't know, though. Maybe we shouldn't say anything to him yet. This last month has proven that camaraderie is what the team needed. I can't fuck that up."

"So let's keep it on the down-low for a while longer." She sounds relieved.

The timer beeps, and we towel off, slip into our flip-flops, and move to the sauna. Afterward, stepping back into the corridor is the most refreshing feeling, the normal temperature instantly cooling my face.

Gigi's face is still flushed from the steam. She looks so pretty, gray eyes sparkling and cheeks rosy, that I forget where we are. I lean down and kiss her.

The tip of her tongue touches mine when someone clears their throat and we jump apart.

It's Coach Jensen.

Shit.

"Graham. Ryder," he greets us warily.

She jerks away from me, not at all discreetly. "Coach," she says with a nod of greeting. "Um. I need to grab a shower and change. Good night."

Then she dashes away.

Coach watches her fleeing form, then shifts his gaze back to me. I resist the urge to close my eyes so I don't have to face that scowl of condemnation.

"You really want to go there?" he asks, dragging a hand over his salt-and-pepper buzz cut. The guy's hairline looks the same as it does in pictures of him in the lobby from twenty years ago.

When I don't respond, he sighs.

"These fucking guys always thinking with their dicks," he mutters to himself. "Can I just have one season where this shit doesn't happen?"

"It's more than…whatever you think it is," I finally say.

He looks unconvinced.

"We're together. There's, ah, feelings involved."

Goddamn feelings. How did it even get to this point? I thought I would fuck her a few times and we'd both be on our way. Now, the idea of never seeing her smile at me again feels like someone ripping my heart out of my chest.

"All I can say is, tread carefully. Don't do anything to hurt the team."

"I'm trying not to. Look, you know we had a rough start, but I've been doing what I can to change that. Colson and I have been trying to unite everyone."

"I've noticed," Jensen acknowledges.

"So then you know that the last thing I want to do is screw that up." I shrug, a tad helplessly. "I didn't plan for this."

He lets out another heavy breath. "Look. Kid. I don't give a shit about other people's lives. I only care about a few things. My wife, my daughters, my grandkids. And my men. Once they leave Briar, that doesn't change. They still belong to me, you understand?" He nods in the direction Gigi went. "Her father is like a son to me, which means she's like a grandkid to me. Which means don't fuck around."

I gulp.

"I know you've had a tough go at it from a young age," Jensen says gruffly. "And I know I gave you a hard time when you first got here. But I've noticed the difference in you, Ryder. You're doing a good job as cocaptain, and the team is showing improvement because of that. If you keep this up, you boys are going to go all the way to the end." He shrugs. "So…I just want you to think about whether that's something you're willing to jeopardize."

CHAPTER THIRTY-SEVEN
RYDER

Don't call me that

THE LAW HAS FINALLY CAUGHT UP TO ME.

Or rather, the lawyer. I've been dodging his calls since September. More than three months and he still hasn't gotten the hint. In fact, he's only accelerated his get-in-touch-with-Ryder campaign. Emailed multiple times this week, left two more voice messages, and I've finally realized if I don't suck it up and rip the Band-Aid off, I'm going to be running from this guy for the rest of my life.

It's Wednesday evening and I'm on my way to the dorms to see Gigi. We made plans for dinner and a movie. When I pull into the parking lot, I stay in the Jeep and call Peter Greene back without listening to the message he just left.

"Peter Greene," comes his brisk greeting.

"Mr. Greene. It's Ryder."

"Finally." He sounds a bit annoyed. "I was beginning to think you pulled a disappearing act and changed your name."

God, the dream.

"Sorry for not returning your calls sooner, but…" I trail off, then opt for brutal honesty. "I didn't want to."

That gets me a rueful chuckle. "Look, trust me, I understand.

I really do, kid. But no matter how badly you want to avoid this, it doesn't change the fact your father is up for parole."

"Yeah, explain that one to me again," I mutter, trying to tamp down my anger.

But he hears it in my voice. "I get it," Greene says. "I'd be pissed too. But I wasn't the original prosecutor on the case, and I didn't make that plea deal. But it was made, and he qualifies for the hearing, provided he's exhibiting good behavior. And according to reports from the penitentiary, he is. He has a job. He's involved in the prison church."

"Good for him," I mutter sarcastically. "Just be real with me right now—is there a chance he gets out?"

"A very slim one. So, no, I wouldn't worry too hard about it. But…a spoken statement from you at the hearing will go a long way in ensuring that slim chance becomes zero."

"No." My tone is emphatic. Cold.

"Ryder."

"No. If you want a written statement, I'll send you that. But I'm not going in person. I don't want to see him—ever. Got it?"

"And you'd be willing to take the risk he gets out?"

"I don't give a shit if he's in or if he's out or wherever the hell he is. He doesn't exist to me. You got it? Don't ask me again," I warn.

"Luke—"

"Don't call me that."

This isn't the first time I've had to correct him. Greene and I met when I was thirteen, while Dad's various appeals were making their way through the courts. Luckily, the door was effectively slammed on each one of them. And I truly didn't foresee we'd be talking about parole so soon.

"Sorry, Ryder. I know this is difficult, but I urge you to reconsider."

"Not interested."

Then I hang up.

I take a breath. Fuck. I'm keyed up now. Wired. I didn't expect to talk to Greene tonight, and I gather my composure as I walk toward Hartford House. I tell the security guard I'm there for Gigi, and he buzzes me into the lobby, where I sign in and then head for the stairs. The dorm is only three floors and has no elevators.

Gigi greets me with a smile. I try to return it, but inside, I'm seething.

The nerve of this asshole. Greene knows exactly what's going to happen if he puts me in the same room as my dad. I had to attend one of his appeal hearings when I was twelve, then again when I was fourteen, and both times I wanted to kill him. Death is too good for him, though.

"Are you okay?" Gigi asks as I follow her into the kitchen. Whatever she's cooking smells good, but I've lost all my appetite.

"Yeah, fine," I lie.

She puts her arms around me and I'm not feeling it at all. I realize too late that I should have simply turned the Jeep around and gone home. But I'm here, so I put on the best face that I can, because Gigi doesn't deserve anything less.

While we wait for dinner to be ready, we sit on the couch, and she surfs the various streaming sites for a movie to watch. I absently nod at all her suggestions. My head is elsewhere and she knows it.

"All right. What's going on?" she demands.

I shrug. "Nothing."

"You're lying. Did something happen at practice this morning? Trouble in one of your classes?"

"No, none of that."

"Then what?"

Another shrug. "Look, if it's all the same, I'd rather not talk about it."

There's a beat.

"Okay, whatever you want." She hops off the couch. "Let me check on the lasagna."

I get up too. "No, you know what? I should go."

She blinks in surprise. "What?"

I'm already pulling my jacket off the hook in the hall. "I'm sorry, G. I'm really not feeling it."

Concern fills her eyes. "Luke."

"*Don't* call me that," I snap.

My tone is so harsh she actually flinches, which brings a twinge of remorse.

"Sorry," I mutter, avoiding her worried gaze. "Just…don't call me that."

"It's your name," she says softly.

"Yeah, well, fuck that. I told you before not to use it."

"Okay," she says in a careful tone. "Do you want to explain why?"

Frustration claws its way up my throat. "Now I owe you explanations?"

Gigi frowns at me. "You don't have to be an asshole about it."

"I'm sorry." I rake both hands through my hair and avert my eyes. I can't stand the way she's peering at me right now. Trying to burrow her way into my mind. "I told you, I'm not feeling this tonight."

"Then you shouldn't have fucking come." Now she's angry. "You could have just sat in your own house and sulked and left me the hell out of it."

I clench my teeth, my gaze returning to her.

"But you *did* come, so why don't you take this opportunity to behave like an adult and tell me what's wrong?"

There's a part of me that wants to do that. Just sit back down and confess everything that's weighing on me. But then I envision her face, her pity, and all the other questions she'll inevitably have, and the words refuse to come out.

After a long beat, Gigi huffs out a breath.

"Forget it. Just go. Even if you wanted to stay and talk, now I'm not in the mood to hang out with *you*. So get out."

CHAPTER THIRTY-EIGHT
RYDER

You silly, stupid man

GIGI'S NOT TALKING TO ME. AS IN, SHE'S STRAIGHT-UP IGNORING ME.

All right, that's not entirely true. She did text to say she doesn't feel like seeing me right now.

That was four days ago. I've felt like an ass ever since I left her dorm, but I'm not great at this shit. Talking. Apologizing. After my calls kept going to voicemail, I sent her three different apology texts. Each increasingly more frustrated, as evidenced by our third exchange on Sunday morning.

ME:

> I don't get it. I said I was sorry. I was in a bad mood that night. Didn't realize I wasn't allowed to be in one.

GISELE:

> If you still think that's why I'm mad, then you're never going to get it.

ME:

> Can I please just call you?

She's typing. Then the three dots disappear, and her name appears on the screen.

As my pulse speeds up, I duck out of the living room, where my roommates and I were watching football, and into the kitchen.

Fuckin' finally.

"Hey," I say, a little too eagerly.

"Hi."

My heart clenches at the sound of her voice. It's crazy how much you can miss someone's voice when you're no longer hearing it every day.

I lean against the kitchen counter, letting out a breath.

"I don't like that you're ignoring me," I say roughly.

"Yeah, well, I didn't like getting yelled at."

Regret fills my chest. "I know. I'm sorry. I was in a shitty mood and I shouldn't have taken it out on you."

There's a long pause.

"Is that it?" she asks.

I blink. "Um. Yeah?"

She makes a frustrated noise. "We're together now, right? Dating?"

"Yes…" I say warily.

"People talk to each other when they're dating."

"Aren't we talking now?"

"You know what? Apology not accepted. I have to go."

"Gigi—"

"No, I'm going to lunch with Mya and then for a run. And clearly you have nothing worthwhile to say, so…"

She ends the call without saying goodbye.

My jaw drops. I'm still staring at the screen wondering what the hell just happened, when Shane saunters in to grab a bottle of water.

I'm completely mystified. I apologized. What the hell else does she want from me?

"What?" He eyes me from the fridge.

"I pissed Gigi off and she won't accept my apology."

"Women, amirite?" he says, then wanders back to the living room.

I trail after him, grumbling irritably. "Seriously, like what the fuck?"

"What's this now?" drawls Beckett.

"Gigi is mad at him," supplies Shane.

"Am I not allowed to have a bad day?" I demand.

"Women, amirite?" Shane says, refocusing his attention on the Patriots game.

"Are you just going to say that to everything I say?" I ask him.

"Yes." His gaze remains glued to the screen. "The Pats are playing and your problems don't really interest me."

Will chuckles from his perch on the couch.

Desperate for any insight, I turn toward him. "You've known her the longest. Can you help me out here?"

"No way. I'm not getting involved in this," Larsen declares. "Bad enough that I'm in the middle of this Gigi and Case thing."

"She and Case are not a thing," I reply in a deadly voice.

He chuckles at my ominous face. "No, but they used to be. And she was my friend first, so after *that* breakup, I suddenly had to navigate the minefield of those two friendships."

"This is not a breakup," I growl.

"Just keep apologizing," Shane says absently. "You'll wear her down eventually."

"Make her a playlist where all the songs are about sex," suggests Beckett. "Get her horny enough to forgive you."

"You know what? Fuck off. None of you are helpful," I say.

Beckett looks at me, then blinks and turns to Will. "Let's do shots. I too am bored of his problems."

"Same."

The two assholes go to raid the liquor cabinet, while Shane watches the game, indifferent to my current state.

I don't know why I'm even bothered by this. Whatever. We were dating and I guess now we're done. For a stupid fucking reason, mind you. But fine. It's over.

Okay…that's not fine.

I don't want it to be over.

God fucking damn it.

It's in this moment I wish I had some female friends. There was one foster sister I was close to in high school, but we drifted apart after graduation. Other than that, any time I've tried to be friends with a girl, she just wants to fuck me. Probably conceited as hell to say, but it's true. I realized a long time ago there's no such thing as platonic. These days, I only allow myself to be friends with my friends' girlfriends. Very little risk there, although every now and then a girlfriend will totally hit on me.

An idea suddenly brightens my mind. *That's* the solution.

I scroll through my contacts until I find Darby's name. Nick Lattimore's girlfriend. I have her number from when she was planning Nick's surprise party last year.

I compose a quick message, keeping it as vague as possible. Only the people in this house know about Gigi and me, or that I'm even dating someone, and I'd like to limit that information as much as possible.

A couple hours later, I get a text that Darby's on her way. Not long after that, the doorbell rings. I throw open the door.

"Hey," I say awkwardly.

"I don't understand this," she says in lieu of greeting.

I don't understand it either.

She comes in, smacking a quick kiss on my cheek. She's wearing combat boots and a tight sweater beneath her winter coat. Darby's a cool chick. Confident, energetic. Always wondered what she was doing with a serious bastard like Nick.

"Called in the cavalry, I see," Beckett mocks when we pass the living room. "Hey, Darby."

"Beck."

"Let's go to the kitchen," I tell her. "You want anything to drink?"

"Tea, please."

I'm pretty sure nobody in this house drinks that, but I rustle around in the cabinets because Shane's mom is the one who stocked them. Knowing her, she'd have made sure we had some of everything. Sure enough, I find some herbal tea and get the kettle going.

"I know this is weird," I tell Darby.

"Literally the weirdest thing ever."

"But I just needed a chick's perspective on something."

She flops down at the kitchen table, eyes alight with curiosity. "On what?"

"It's, ah, a woman problem."

"You called me here to talk about your love life?" she shrieks. Then she lets out a calming breath and speaks in a reverent voice. "This. Is the greatest day of my life."

"It has to stay between us," I warn.

"Luke Ryder has a girlfriend."

"Why is that so shocking?"

"Oh my God. You don't even know how excited I am right now. You're seeing someone?"

I nod.

"Is it serious?"

"I think so."

"Oh my God."

"Stop saying that."

Darby narrows her eyes at me. "So how did you screw it up?"

"Who says I did?" I grumble.

"Did you?"

I pause. "Yes."

Grinning, Darby kicks out another chair with her foot.

I carry her tea over and set it in front of her. After a beat of reluctance, I sit down, sigh, and proceed to give her a quick rundown of my fight with Gigi. Leaving out names, locations, and any pertinent details that might be used against me in a court of law.

When I finish by voicing my irritation that my apology supposedly wasn't sufficient, she starts to laugh.

"What?" I glower at her. "You think she's right to be mad at me?"

"Do you even know why she's mad?" Darby counters, echoing Gigi's sentiments from the phone call.

I swear, do all women belong to some sort of telepathic network where they just know why they're angry?

"Because I snapped at her."

"Oh, Ryder. You silly, stupid man."

She's still chuckling as she reaches for her tea. The steam rises into her eyes when she takes a sip.

"Okay, let's recap. Something happened to put you in a crabby mood."

"Yes."

"So you went over there in a bad mood."

"Yes."

"She asked you what was wrong and you said to drop it. Then she pushed and you snapped at her."

"Yes." Guilt pricks me at the reminder that I snapped at my woman.

"And you apologized for snapping."

"Yes," I say in frustration.

"But she's telling you she's not mad that you snapped at her. She's mad because…?" Darby lets that hang, waiting for me to fill in the blanks.

"No, you don't get it. She hasn't *told* me why she's mad."

"You should know why!" Darby sputters in amazement. "Dude. She's upset because you wouldn't fucking tell her why you were in a bad mood. What was the thing that happened to upset you? What, do we live in some mystery land where we don't talk about things? The whole point of dating someone is to get to know them and share in all their moods. Their good moods, their bad moods. If I have a bad day, you damn well know Nick's going to hear about it. He's going to know every single detail."

"You realize you're a chick, right?"

She snorts. "You think Nick doesn't tell me things too? Like, when he and his younger brother got in a huge fight last month, that's all he talked about."

"I'm not a talker," I mutter.

"Then don't be in a relationship."

I sigh.

"Seriously, Ryder. There are different rules in play now. If you're just hooking up with someone, banging here and there, you don't have to talk about important things. But the second you start dating them, the expectations change."

I rub my forehead. "I don't like that."

"Well, hate to break it to you, but that's how relationships work. You have to talk. If something's wrong, the other person wants to hear it. They *need* to hear it."

My stomach churns. The idea of telling Gigi about the prosecutor's call or my dad's whereabouts, his parole hearing...it twists my insides.

But then I think about Gigi and how easily she tells me how she's feeling, even when it makes her uncomfortable. And I realize I don't give her anything in return other than orgasms.

Darby grins at me over the rim of her teacup. "You know I'm right, don't you?"

"Yes," I grumble. "I know you're right."

A sudden commotion sounds from the hallway. A loud crash, as if the front door flew open and smashed the wall. Thunderous footsteps then barrel down the hall.

I jump out of my chair just as Nick Lattimore comes tearing into the kitchen. He looks at me. Eyes Darby at the table. Then, before I can blink, he pulls his fist back and sends it flying toward my face. I dodge at the last second, so the blow only grazes my cheekbone, but there's no dodging the accompanying jolt of pain.

"What the fuck?" I demand, as Shane, Beckett, and Will run into the kitchen.

"Lattimore, stop," Shane says, pulling him away from me. "What the hell's wrong with you?"

"Me?" he roars. "He's making a play for my girlfriend, and you're asking what's wrong with *me*?"

"Are you crazy? I'm not after your girlfriend," I growl.

"You sent her a text that says, and I quote: *Come over to my place and don't tell your boyfriend.*"

I falter. "Oh, in hindsight, that was worded poorly."

Beckett doubles over in laughter. "Jesus. That's fucking priceless, mate."

Darby rises from her chair. "Sorry, Ryder, I know you told me not to say anything, but Nick and I don't keep secrets." She punctuates that with a look.

Point taken.

CHAPTER THIRTY-NINE
GIGI

He led me to you

I RETURN FROM MY POSTDINNER RUN TO FIND RYDER SITTING ON my couch. I jolt in surprise, tugging my earbuds out. "Hey. What are you doing here?"

He gets up. "Wanted to see you. Mya let me in before she headed out. She said to tell you she's meeting some Tinder guy for drinks in Hastings."

As I get closer, I notice a red mark on his left cheekbone. Not quite a cut. Maybe a slight bruise.

"What happened here?" Despite myself, I reach out to touch his face. "Did you get hurt during one of your games this weekend?"

He shakes his head. "Nick Lattimore punched me."

"What? Why on earth would he do that?"

"He thought I invited his girlfriend over for sex."

"Do I even want to ask?"

Ryder shrugs. "Darby came over because I needed advice on how to make you not hate me."

I know I shouldn't laugh, but I do. His gruff, sheepish admission instantly warms me over. God, this man.

"And I think I figured it out." Another shrug. "I was hoping we could talk. For real."

Sweaty and sticky from my run, I unzip my hoodie and take a step toward my side of the suite. "Do you mind if I grab a shower first?"

"Yeah, of course. I'll wait."

A moment later, I dunk my head under the hot water and let it wash down over me. I think about everything I want to say to him. Everything that's been weighing on my mind these past few days.

Do I want us to keep going?

Is there even a point?

Because I can't be in a relationship with someone who shuts down. Someone who doesn't let me in.

Except then I think about how rewarding it is to get a smile out of him. How my heart flips when he laughs. The way that he listens to me and shows me no judgment, only acceptance.

I quickly dry off and throw on a pair of flannel pants and a hoodie. It's the least sexy outfit ever, but the way he admires me when I walk out makes me feel so stupidly pretty.

I sit next to him, drawing my knees up and hugging them.

"My father's name is Luke."

It's not at all what I expected to hear.

I furrow my brow at him. "It is?"

"My mom named me after him."

"So you're a junior?"

"Not exactly. I don't have his last name. They weren't married, so Ryder is my mother's maiden name." He looks sick. "I'm glad I don't have both his names. Christ. Then there'd be no escape from it at all. At least I have Ryder."

"Why do you need to escape it? You're not close to your dad?"

"He shot my mother in the head and killed her."

Shock slams into me.

I'm given zero preparation and have no idea how to react.

I gawk at him, blinking. Until I realize he's just shared something so deeply personal and harrowing, and I'm here staring at him like an idiot.

"W-what?" I stammer. Again, not the most coherent response. But at least my voice works now. "Your dad killed your mom?"

Ryder nods.

"How old were you when it happened? Did you…?" I trail off.

My brain can't comprehend this. It literally cannot wrap itself around the fact that Ryder's mother was murdered by his own father.

"I was six. And yes, I saw it happen."

I reach for his hand and find it cold. I entwine our fingers, infusing his with warmth, urging him to continue.

His eyes grow strained. Features tight with pain.

"You don't have to talk about it if you don't want to," I finally say.

That gets me a dry laugh. "Really? Because the whole reason I'm here, the whole reason you're upset with me, has to do with me not sharing. So, what, now it's okay not to share?"

"I just mean, you don't have to give *all* the details. It's enough that I know—"

"That my father's a murderer?"

I feel horrible now. I barely spoke to him for four days because he refused to tell me why he doesn't want to be called Luke. And now I know the answer and it's fucking heart-wrenching. Maybe I shouldn't have pushed him to talk.

"It's fine," he says, noting my dismay. "I'll talk about it. It's just… there's no point. It's in the past."

"A past that affected you. Severely enough that you can't even use your own name."

Ryder's answering exhale is unsteady. He's quiet for so long I think he's done talking. But then he speaks.

"He wasn't a violent man. I know, it's ironic to say that, considering what he did to her in the end. But he didn't beat us. Never laid a hand on her, at least not in front of me. I never saw bruises or bloody noses. Sure, he could be an asshole when he drank, but it's not like I lived in fear of him."

"So he just snapped?"

"I don't know. I was six. I didn't know the inner workings of their relationship. I know they argued a lot. I don't think she was happy, but she would put on a brave face for me." Ryder rakes a hand through his hair. "Hell, maybe he *was* beating her and she just hid it really well. Honestly, I don't know. The night it happened, I remember waking up to shouts. I snuck out of my room, poked my head into their room, saw the suitcase. It was half-packed, so I think she was planning to leave him. And I guess, yeah, he snapped. When I came to the doorway, he'd already pulled the gun on her. He was telling her that if she walked out the door, he was going to put a bullet in her brain."

My heart starts pounding. I picture a six-year-old boy standing there, watching his father point a weapon at his mother, and it's unimaginable.

"Neither of them saw me at first. But then he noticed me and shouted for me to go back to my room. But I was frozen in place, too scared to move. She tried to go to me, but he ordered her not to move. And then they started fighting again. She told him that pointing a gun at her only proved why she had to leave. That he was too jealous and possessive and unstable. She said she couldn't do this anymore. He asked her if she still loved him, and she said no. That's the part that's etched into my brain. Like, why did she say no?"

He shakes his head in disbelief, then barks out a harsh laugh.

"Why didn't she just lie? This guy's pointing a fucking gun at her head. I get it, people aren't always thinking clearly in scary situations, but…Christ. Tell the man with the gun you love him. But she didn't, and it got her killed. The second she admitted she didn't love him, he pulled the trigger. Just like that." Ryder snaps his fingers, amazed. "It was so loud. I've never heard anything that loud. My ears were ringing. Mom's body fell to the floor."

My heart rate is dangerously high. I wasn't even there, and I feel the fear, visceral in my bones. "Did he try to hurt you too?"

"Not at all. He just walked out of the bedroom, told me to follow him. We went to the living room, and he sat on the couch, gun on his knee. He asked me to come sit beside him."

"Oh my God."

"So I did. He picked up his glass of whiskey from the coffee table and just started sipping it. Someone must have heard the shot and called the police, because it wasn't long before we heard the sirens. It was only about five minutes before they showed up and took him away." Ryder uses air quotes to repeat himself. "'Only' five minutes. Longest five minutes of my life. Five minutes of sitting on the couch with him while Mom's body was in the other room, bleeding all over the floor."

I feel like throwing up. Gulping through the nausea, I wrap my other hand over his hand, trapping it between both my palms. "What happened after that?"

"He was arrested. Child services got involved." Ryder offers a shrug. "Dad didn't have any family, and the few family members on Mom's side didn't want to step up. So I got thrown into the system."

"Did it go to trial?"

"No, he pled out. Life in prison with the possibility of parole. I had to give a witness statement to the police, though. They asked a million questions, and I didn't really understand any of them because I was six years old. All I knew was that my mom was gone."

His eyes become misty. Before I can stop myself, I reach up and stroke the underside of my thumb over the moisture there. He flinches, just slightly, but doesn't push me away. He leans forward, pressing his forehead against mine as I wipe away the tears.

"Anyway, that's it. That's the story. I share a name with the man who took my mother away. And every time someone calls me that fucking name, I hear her screaming it that night. When I was in the doorway and Dad suddenly noticed I was there, he spun around and pointed the gun at me. Not as an intentional threat. Just instinct, I think. But Mom screamed, *Luke, stop.* And Christ, I still have nightmares about it. I hear her screaming my name. His name."

I climb into his lap and lock my arms around his neck. Holding him. But I don't know if it's more for his sake or mine. This chilling glimpse into his childhood has shaken me.

"So that's why I hate it, all right? I don't want to think about him. I want to pretend it never happened."

I pull back and meet his red-rimmed eyes. "You can't, though. Because it did happen," I say quietly. "I can't even imagine how painful it was, how painful it still is when you think about it. But pretending it's not there doesn't help anything. Isn't that what you always tell me? To just let myself feel things even if they're not pleasant?"

Still, I get it now. The reason he put on that aloof front. This catastrophic event that shaped his childhood left him in self-preservation mode. Protect yourself at all costs. I don't blame him one bit.

"Trust me, I felt it all," Ryder says hoarsely. "I felt it all the time. And then I was done feeling it. It was time to move on. I decided to go to school on the East Coast and get the fuck away from Arizona. Put it all behind me—my dad in jail, my mom dead, those godawful foster homes. All fucking behind me." He gives a dark laugh. "The one thing I can't put behind me, though, is my own name."

"Yes. Your name," I repeat and cup his face, forcing him to look at me. "Your name is what you make it. I'm sure there are many, many people out there who were named after a parent that was a monster. You just have to do something better with that name. Be better than the monster."

Ryder's gaze locks with mine. "I'm not like him."

"I didn't think you were."

"No, I mean that's not the reason I avoid the name. I'm not worried I'm going to end up like him. I know I won't." He speaks with strong conviction. "I don't think I'm going to snap and kill someone. I know myself and what I'm capable of. It's the reminder, that's all. The reminder of this shitty place I came from. This shitty person I'm forever tied to, at least genetically. I hear my name, and the past comes rushing back, when all I want is to leave it in my dust."

"You can't outrun your history. It doesn't disappear just because you leave Arizona and move out east and go by the name Ryder. No matter what you do, it's still there. That is where you come from."

"I know." He bites his lip.

"And whenever you're reminded of it, instead of shutting down, burying it deep, pushing everyone away…all you have to do is this." I stroke his jaw with both thumbs. "Just be open and honest with me, and I'll do my best to help."

"I'll try," he says roughly.

"And, honestly, if you truly hate the name, you could always change it. But we both know you're not running from the name. You're running from shame."

His eyes look wet again. I bend down and kiss him. Just a soft caress against his lips, which I feel trembling beneath mine.

"There's nothing for you to be ashamed of," I whisper.

Ryder goes quiet for several long beats. "He's up for parole."

I jolt in shock. "What!"

"That's why I was in such a foul mood the other day. I'd just gotten off the phone with the prosecutor in Phoenix. I told you he pled out, right? Well, it was a sweet fucking deal. Eligible for parole after fifteen years—they didn't think he was a danger to society. Just a crime of passion unlikely to be repeated." Ryder laughs bitterly. "Until he gets into another relationship and decides to blow her brains out too."

I flinch. "He can't actually be released, right?"

"The DA says it's unlikely. But he wants me to come speak at the hearing. Said my statement would help keep him behind bars."

"Are you going?"

"No. I never want to see his face again."

I don't blame him.

"Anyway." This time he kisses me, another gentle touch of our lips. "I'm sorry for snapping at you the other day and shutting you out. Thank you for listening."

"Thank you for talking."

There's another long stretch of silence. Then Ryder throws me for another loop.

"I totally understand if you want to go and, ah, I don't know, be with Case."

I blink. "Where on earth did that come from?"

"I was just thinking about it. Colson's a good guy. And I'm sure he doesn't have this amount of baggage."

"You know, a few months ago you would've swallowed glass before admitting he's a good guy."

"I know, but...he is. He's a decent guy." Ryder sighs. "Do you still want to be with him?"

I don't hesitate. "No."

"Did you love him?"

"I did. But I've been thinking about it too. And the more I do, the more I realize I wasn't devastated when he cheated on me."

"Really, because it hasn't sounded like you were too happy about it."

"Well, no, I wasn't happy. And, yes, I was upset. I cried. A lot. But it didn't rip me apart, you know? I feel like it should have. I feel like if I truly loved him and wanted to be with him, get married, have kids, build a life...then that kind of betrayal would just destroy me. And it didn't, which tells me maybe it wasn't as right as either of us thought it was." I rest my chin on Ryder's shoulder, pensive. "Besides, if he hadn't cheated, you and I wouldn't be here right now. So in a way, he..."

He led me to you.

I can't bring myself to say it because I'm terrified it'll lead me into saying other things, and I'm not telling anyone I love them anymore. Last time I did, the guy freaked and ran.

"Why are you really bringing up Case?" I ask, lifting my head. "Are you feeling insecure?"

"No. I…I guess I just need to know you want me."

"I want you."

Smiling, he tugs us backward and onto our sides so we're lying on the couch facing each other. His fingers stroke my cheek. Toying with my hair. I love how he always needs to be touching me, even though he plays it off cool. Nonchalant.

My hand drifts up his chest and I can feel him trembling. I bring my palm to his left pec, press it against his heart, and instantly it starts beating faster.

"You feel this too, don't you?" His eyes are on mine. Dark blue and bottomless.

"Yeah. I feel it."

CHAPTER FORTY
GIGI

There's something different about you

THE HOCKEY DEPARTMENT FUNDRAISER IS HELD THE FOLLOWING week, on a Saturday night when neither of our teams has a game. I show up with Whitney and Camila, wearing a dress I picked up shopping with Diana this weekend. It's pale silver, floor-length, and features a plunging vee, which makes me slightly uncomfortable because I don't usually show off the girls. I feel like they're not big enough to dazzle. But Diana told me it wouldn't kill me to be a bit bold. So I extended the boldness to my hair, wearing it loose in big waves, and my makeup, opting for a smoky eye.

I hear a low whistle when we approach the arched doorway of the ballroom. The event is being held at a small convention center in Boston.

I turn, expecting to see Ryder, but it's Case. Then I remember Ryder and I aren't public yet. We couldn't even attend this charity ball together.

"Jesus. Babe, you look amazing."

I want to tell him not to call me babe. But Cami and Whitney are standing there, and I don't want to make things awkward. So I let it slide.

"Thanks. You look good too." He really does. He's in a tailored black suit, blond hair styled perfectly and clean-shaven face emphasizing his pretty-boy looks.

He flashes me that familiar smile, but there's no flutter in my chest anymore. No quickening of my pulse. Any romantic feelings I had for him are completely gone.

I'm all in on Luke Ryder, of all people.

Who would have thought?

"May I escort you inside, my lady?" Case holds out his arm.

I take it and hope he doesn't sense my reluctance. I also hope Ryder's not in there already and, if he is, doesn't see Case walking me in on his arm.

"See you guys in there," I tell my teammates.

When we enter the crowded ballroom, our conversation is momentarily drowned out by the sound of the eight-piece orchestra band. They're playing a classical version of a popular pop song.

Case speaks close to my ear so I can hear him. "I feel like I haven't talked to you in ages."

"Yeah, I've been busy. You know what it's like in December. Final exams, gearing up for the holidays."

"How've you been, other than that?"

"Good."

He searches my face. "Good," he echoes.

"Would you prefer I say *bad*?" I laugh.

"Sort of," he admits. "I want you to say you've been as miserable as I am." He bites his lip, visibly unhappy. "But it seems like you're doing really, really well. There's something different about you."

"Different how?"

"I don't know. You're kind of…glowing. Are you pregnant?"

I snort out another laugh. Then, as if to prove the point, I grab a glass of champagne from a nearby tray. "I most certainly am not," I say before taking a sip.

He chuckles too, but he appears relieved. It's almost as if he actually believed the reason I could be glowing is that I was knocked up.

"I'm just happy," I add. "Our season has been unbelievable. We're a lock to win our conference."

Case sighs. "I wish I could say the same."

Those early losses didn't do them any favors, and they faced some tough opponents the past couple of weeks. They're currently behind UConn in the conference. UConn's been playing some damn good hockey and isn't keen on relinquishing that lead.

"You'll get a bid," I assure him. The teams that don't make it by winning their conference can get a bid from the selection committee, which picks ten teams to advance to the postseason. I can't see how Briar doesn't make it.

My peripheral vision catches a flash of movement. I turn my head just as Ryder, Shane, and Beckett walk past us, wearing suits and rocking them. They nod in greeting before carrying on toward the open bar.

"Do you have that magazine picture of you and Ryder framed in your room?" I tease.

That infamous shot of Ryder with his arms thrust in the air and Case throwing himself at him in an astounded hug actually made it into an edition of *Sports Illustrated*. Printed alongside a three-page spread about college hockey.

"My dad does." Case snorts. "He bought a ton of copies and handed them out to everyone in town."

"If it makes you feel better, my dad bought a copy too."

Case's expression brightens. "It does, actually. I miss him."

"Yeah. I know."

Breakups are tough. And I feel bad that he's no longer part of our family. He fit in well. My parents loved him. Wyatt thought he was great. But we're not together anymore, and eventually Ryder will be the one attending my family events. At least, I hope.

But that means we need to tell Case about us, and I'm still dragging my feet about it. I'm not leading him on. I made it clear our relationship is over. I don't text him. I don't flirt. If anything, Case is leading himself on because he refuses to admit it's done.

Still, I know I could make it easier, nudge him closer to the road of acceptance by telling him I'm with someone else. But the idea of hurting him is so upsetting.

My phone buzzes in my sequined silver clutch. I pull it out, taking a sip of champagne as I read the text.

RYDER:

> I want to fuck you so bad right now. That dress is fire.

I cough loudly.

Case looks concerned. "You okay?"

"Yeah. Sorry." I cough again. "Just went down the wrong tube."

I know Ryder's watching, so I make an exaggerated show of sticking my phone back in my purse. I refuse to allow any exhibitionist shenanigans tonight, no matter how badly I enjoy them. This event isn't the place for it. Not with Case here.

"Gigi," he says softly, and I know he's about to bring up our breakup.

Thankfully, we're interrupted by more people who, this time, don't walk past us. Trager, Will, and several others join us. Cami then drags me away to browse the items our committee procured for the silent auction.

My dad outdid himself this year. His contribution was a private lunch with him, the lucky bidder, and…the Stanley Cup. I swear, when Garrett Graham calls in a favor, people in the hockey world race to grant it.

I'm three glasses of champagne in when my bladder says enough. I'm not drunk, though. Slightly buzzed and enjoying this party much more than I thought I would. But that's probably because Ryder is wearing a suit and I've been secretly ogling him all night.

I emerge from the ladies' room at the same time Jordan Trager is stumbling out of the men's. Unlike me, he *is* drunk. Visibly.

Someone's been taking advantage of that open bar, I see. I don't know whose idea it was to offer free booze to a bunch of college guys. They should have a cash bar next time. Keep guys like Trager in check.

He grins at me and swings his arm around my shoulder. "Goddamn, G, you really do look good tonight. That fuckin' dress."

"Thanks."

We head down the hall together toward the doors of the ballroom.

"When are you going to put my man Case out of his misery?"

I smother a sigh. "Come on. It's a party, Jordan. Let's not get too deep."

"I'm just saying, you two are perfect for each other."

"Yeah, well, things happen. And sometimes relationships end."

"He still loves you."

As my heart squeezes, I finally release that sigh. "Can we not talk about this?"

But Trager's not listening. "Hasn't he paid his dues already? Like, damn. He got a blowjob from some chick at a party. It's not like he actually fucked her."

His words are a splash of ice water to the face.

A blowjob?

Um.

This is the first I'm hearing of it.

I want more details, but I don't want Trager to think he's done something wrong and clam up. So while all the muscles in my body are trying to stiffen, I forcibly relax them and play it off like I knew.

"I don't know, maybe he did have sex with her," I say, tipping my head mockingly. "Guys always try to downplay things like that."

Like the time Case told me they just kissed and I'm now finding out some girl went down on him.

He lied to me.

The cord of anger that whips through me has nothing to do with ego, with the fact that Case hooked up with another girl. Maybe before it would've been. But right now, the betrayal I feel is all about the lie. He *lied* to me about it. He made such a big show about being honest when he sat me down, gave me those sad eyes, and confessed he'd kissed somebody else.

And I pushed him, damn it. Demanding to know if he did anything else. He looked me right in the eye and said no.

And now I'm here trying to protect his feelings? Keeping my current relationship under wraps so that poor Case doesn't feel bad about himself?

"Case and I are done," I tell Trager, my voice coming out colder than I intend. "Both of you are just going to have to accept that."

I shove open the doors. I'm halfway across the ballroom when a familiar song starts playing. It's so unexpected that I stop for a moment, turning my gaze toward the band. Hearing an orchestra play the rock song I grew up with brings a spark of warmth.

Followed by a jolt of irritation, because I would love to dance to it and I can't, at least not with the man I want.

And now I'm angry. At *myself*. Angry for not letting myself live my own life. All this time I was trying to spare Case's feelings, and now I realize what a crock of shit that was.

I'm not a petty person—I honestly don't think too hard about what I do next. I'm just tired. Tired of watching Ryder from across the room all night and not being able to talk to him.

Tired of having to send sly texts about how much we want to bang each other.

Tired of not being able to hold his hand.

Tired of not being able to throw my arms around him, like the night he protected me from the creepy elevator guy. I should have hugged him then, but I didn't. All because I was trying to be respectful of my ex-boyfriend's feelings.

My gaze drifts toward Ryder's group. They're howling over something Shane just said. Well, Beckett, Case, and David are howling.

Ryder, of course, is chuckling quietly because he's not a howler. No, he's too cool for that.

So, no, I truly don't mean to be petty, but this song is beautiful and the sight of him takes my breath away, and soon my legs, of their own volition, carry me toward the group.

"Hey," I interrupt, touching Ryder's arm. "Come dance with me."

CHAPTER FORTY-ONE
RYDER

One hundred percent

WELL.

I sure wasn't expecting that.

Gigi has spent months hiding me from the world and now she's asking me to dance in front of all our teammates?

I'm stunned speechless for a moment.

Then I shrug and say, "Sure?"

I keep my expression shuttered and my response vague, because I don't know how I'm supposed to react. If I'm supposed to treat it like a friend asking another friend to dance. Or a peer asking a peer.

Or my girlfriend asking her boyfriend.

Case's eyes narrow as Gigi takes my hand.

She tugs on it, and I follow her instinctively. I'm so crazy gone for this woman that not following her isn't even an option.

When we reach the dance floor, I dip my head close to her ear. "I don't dance, baby."

"You'll be fine." She places one hand on my shoulder and clasps the other in mine.

She peers up at me with the most beautiful smile, and I'm dumbstruck again because she's so gorgeous I don't even know how to function in the face of that smile.

"Put your hand on my waist," she says, so I do.

She moves closer, the top of her head tucked beneath my chin. The flowery scent of her shampoo drifts into my nose. I breathe her in and get high.

"What is this?" I ask, trying to concentrate on pressing matters rather than how good she smells and feels in my arms.

"Just dancing with my boyfriend," she answers.

I don't even want to look in the direction of our friends. I can feel their stares on us. I imagine that particularly prickly sensation tightening my skin is courtesy of Colson.

"Is this some sort of power play?"

"No."

We move to the slow tempo set by the orchestra. I recognize the song as a classic rock ballad.

Gigi tips her head back to look at me. "This was my parents' wedding song."

That startles me. "Really?"

"Yeah. It's the first song they ever danced to." She moistens her lips, blushing before averting her eyes. "I heard it just now and...I don't know. I knew I wanted to dance to it with you."

That does something to my heart. I don't know what. I don't understand half of the emotions she elicits in me. Whatever this one is, it just feels right.

We continue to sway, doing a little turn, during which I catch a glimpse of Colson's blond hair and suspicious eyes.

"Case is going to have questions," I warn.

"I don't care. I came to the realization tonight that I can't live my life worrying about his feelings."

She's right.

But she's also very wrong, because he's my cocaptain and I *am* worried about his feelings. We've only recently become friends. And I'm already grieving the loss of that friendship as Gigi and I turn again and my gaze locks with his. I can feel the surrender that pervades my face. The defeat. Because I can't hide how I feel about this woman anymore. And he knows it.

His blue eyes darken. Suddenly, he's breaking off from the group. Stalking toward the dance floor. I expect him to confront us, but all he does when he gets within earshot is hiss, "Fuck this," and then brush past us and march out of the ballroom.

The song changes to something more up-tempo, as if the violins and cellos also feel the urgency of the situation.

"Shit. I gotta go talk to him," I tell Gigi.

She bites her lip. "I know."

"He's my teammate."

"I said I know." She drops her hand from my shoulder and pulls me away from the floor. "Let's go."

We catch up to him at the valet stand, where Case spins at our approach and glares.

"Case—" Gigi starts.

"Fuck you both," he interrupts. His face is red with fury.

"Hey," she says sharply. "Come on."

"How long has this been going on?" He angrily gestures between us before his gaze fixes on me. Accusation burns there. "How long were you pretending to be my buddy while you were going after my ex?"

"That's not how it happened," I say quietly.

"When did it start?" he demands.

I glance at Gigi. I don't know how she plans to play this. If she's going to lie or not. I'll back her up either way.

But she's honest. "September," she tells him. "After my exhibition."

Case recoils. "That long?"

She nods.

And I'm momentarily floored myself because I can't believe it's been three months. It simultaneously feels like I just met her yesterday and like I've known her forever.

Case looks like he wants to hit me. I know it because he plasters his arms to his body, fists clenched to his sides. He's doing everything he can to control the violence simmering beneath the surface.

"You fucking asshole," he spits out. "You warned me you were a dick. I should've believed you."

I swallow a sigh. "I barely knew you three months ago, man. We weren't friends."

"Yeah, until we were."

"It's my fault," Gigi intervenes. "I told Ryder not to say anything, okay?"

His incredulous gaze shifts to her. "I can't believe this. He's my teammate, Gigi."

Regret floats through her gray eyes. "I didn't plan this. It just happened."

"You could've stopped it once it did. Taken a step back."

"Why would I take a step back? You and I aren't together anymore." She sounds frustrated. "I made that more than clear every time we talked. I didn't lead you on."

"I know that, but did you even consider showing me a modicum of respect by not banging my teammate?"

"*Respect?* Are you kidding me right now?"

She lunges forward, and since I know how strong she is, I swiftly put my hand on her shoulder. Easy there, partner.

"You cheated on me and lied about it!"

The valet chooses that moment to approach with Case's keys. He takes one look at the confrontation in progress and wisely steps away, trying to meld into the background.

"I didn't lie. I came clean the day after it happened."

"You told me you made out with her when she fucking gave you a blowjob."

Oh, Colson. You stupid bastard.

Case freezes. "That's not…"

"Not what? Not true?" Gigi snaps. "Can you look me in the eye and tell me it's not true?"

I see the wheels turning in Case's head as he calculates what *his* play is here. Whether he should fess up and admit he lied (because, hell, of course he lied) or try to maintain his moral high ground. If he picks the former, he sinks right back down to all our levels, and he knows it.

In the end, he proves to be a smart man.

"I knew you would never forgive me if you thought it was anything other than a kiss," he says in a hoarse voice.

"You had a better chance of forgiveness if you'd been completely honest."

"Bullshit. You think *kissing* is cheating."

"Kissing *is* cheating," she argues. "And let's not talk about respect right now. You disrespected *me*. All I did was try to spare your feelings by not flaunting my relationship with your teammate. Maybe it wasn't the smartest move on my part, but I'm not fucking perfect. Nobody is. Least of all you, with your secret blowjobs."

"Who even told you?" Case mutters.

"Why? So you can go yell at them? Bullshit. Own this. *You* made the mistake. *You* lied to my face."

"And *you* told me you still cared about me and wanted to be my friend," he throws back.

"I did."

"Really, this is you being my friend?" Sarcasm drips from his voice. He glares at me again. "Yeah, Ryder? You really wanted to be my friend?"

I don't answer. But yes, I did want to be his friend. I like the guy and I feel bad. This is a shitty situation all around.

"Well, excuse me if I don't bask in the glow of either of your friendship." Noticing the cowering valet, he stalks toward him and grabs his keys.

Without another word, Case gets in his car and speeds off.

I stare at his disappearing bumper, then give Gigi a dry look. "So it *was* a power play."

"It wasn't. I mean, yes, I just found out he lied to me. But I swear I asked you to dance because of the song."

"Are we lying to each other now, Gisele? Because my favorite thing about us is the honesty." I raise a brow. "Was it just the song?"

She sighs. "Ninety percent the song. Ten percent scorned woman."

I chuckle and reach for her hand. "Fuck. That was rough."

"I know." She gives me a glum look. "Should we get out of here?"

When I nod, she signals the valet.

"Let me pop inside and hit up coat check. Oh, and I need to make sure Whitney and Cami can get a ride with somebody else. Do you have a coat ticket?"

I hand it over.

She leaves me in the brisk December night, and I breathe in the cool air and wonder what the hell practice will be like on Monday. Probably not good.

But then Gigi returns, and I'm not sure I care whether Colson hates me or not. She's a walking wet dream with her high heels and plunging neckline. I want that dress off her so bad.

"My place or yours?" I drawl.

She winks when she notices the look in my eyes. "Your place is closer."

"Good call."

The next morning, I roll over to find a naked Gigi in my bed. Strong limbs spread out on my sheets. Long dark hair fanned over the pillow. Her hand and forearm are tucked beneath her silky cheek as she quietly breathes in slumber.

Not wanting to disturb her, I tiptoe out of my room to go take a leak and brush my teeth. I'm just stepping out of the bathroom when Beckett's door swings open.

I'm startled to see Will Larsen walk out wearing nothing but boxers.

Eyebrows soaring, I gaze past his shoulder and glimpse a naked Beckett and an equally naked blond sprawled on Beck's bed.

Will follows my gaze and speaks in a soft, sheepish voice. "It was…kind of a night."

"Yeah, I see that," I say dryly.

It's none of my damned business, so I slip back into my bedroom, where Gigi is stirring.

I climb into bed and plant a kiss on her nose. She gives a sleepy laugh when I try to kiss her lips and squirms away from me.

"No kissing," she protests. "You just brushed your teeth. I still have morning breath."

"Fine. I'll kiss you other places." I bury my face in her neck and breathe in her sweet, feminine scent. It gets my blood going. Everything about her is so stupidly sexy. I want her all the time.

"What are your plans today?" she asks, pushing me onto my back so she can snuggle up beside me.

"I was planning on spending the whole day in bed with you."

"Sounds like an excellent plan, but I have to drive into the city today. Doing some last-minute Christmas shopping. Do you want to come?"

"Oh boy. You want me to come shopping with you? Will you dump me if I say no?"

She snickers. "No. But don't you have to buy Christmas presents?"

I think it over. "No."

"Wait, do you celebrate Christmas?"

"I did growing up, and most of the foster homes I lived in did stuff for the holidays. But it depends on the year, I guess, and whether I have anywhere to go. Last year I was with Owen and his family in Phoenix."

"What are you doing this year?"

"Staying here."

"Alone?" She's aghast.

"Yeah. Shane asked me to go home with him, and Beckett's

fucking off to Australia for two weeks. Tried to get me to go too. But I'm not feeling either of those invitations."

She hesitates for a moment. "What about this invitation—do you want to come home with me?"

"Home," I echo.

"Yes."

"With your parents."

"Yep, that's what *home* means."

"Will your father be there?"

"He lives there, so yes."

"Your father, Garrett Graham."

"Okay, you know what? I revoke the invitation."

I sit up, thinking it over for a minute. "Do they even know we're together?"

"No, but I'll make sure to tell them before I bring you home. If you want to come, that is." Gigi sits up too, running a hand through her sleep-mussed hair. "For what it's worth, I think you should. You'll have a full week to make him like you…" She trails off enticingly. "Plus, my mom is a great cook, and she and my brother can harmonize on every Christmas carol ever written, so it makes for some awesome singalongs. Oh, and I forgot the best part: the Boxing Day Beatdown."

"What's that?" I ask in amusement.

Rather than answer, she lifts her T-shirt by the hem and pulls it off.

My mouth waters the moment her breasts are exposed.

"What's happening right now?" I croak.

"Are you ready? I'm going to try something."

"I like this already." My gaze is glued to her beaded nipples.

"You like this, right?" she prompts, cupping those perfect tits.

My dick twitches. "Yes."

"How hard are you, percent-wise?"

"Right now?" I reach down and cup my semihardening cock. "Forty percent?" I estimate.

"All right, are you ready for this? The Boxing Day Beatdown. TD

Garden. Private ice time." She pauses for dramatic effect. "Garrett Graham." Another pause. "John Logan."

I swallow.

She doesn't miss the response, faintly smirking at me.

"Hunter Davenport."

My dick twitches again.

"Jake Connelly."

"Oh my God, stop," I groan. "Are you saying you spend Boxing Day skating with all those guys?"

"Oh yeah. It's a tradition. All the kids play too. We pick captains. It gets intense." She gazes south. "What's the percentage now?"

I squeeze my cock. Appraising it. "Eighty percent."

She breaks out in gales of laughter. Then she shucks her tiny boxer shorts and bright-red panties and climbs on top of me, tits swaying.

"Wait. I left out the best part." She beams down at me. "Gigi Graham."

"One hundred percent," I growl, and then I lift her ass up and guide her down onto my rock-hard dick.

DAD:

Your mother just told me what you've done.

GIGI:

Oh my god. You are so dramatic

DAD:

You can't date Luke Ryder.
I don't like this, Stan

GIGI:

Great! Then You'll be thrilled to know I'm bringing him home for Christmas

GIGI:

Can't wait to see you! 😊

CHAPTER FORTY-TWO
RYDER

You can call me Mr. Graham

THE GRAHAM HOUSE LOOKS LIKE SOMETHING OUT OF A HALLMARK movie. It's a sprawling brick colonial in an affluent neighborhood, set far back from the tree-lined street, with a four-car garage and pillared entrance. Inside, the front entryway is intimidating, but once I venture deeper into the house, I realize it's actually cozy in here. The furniture isn't modern and sterile, but warm and lived in, and the décor is mostly family photographs and framed achievements.

"Have you always lived here?" I ask after Gigi gives me the tour.

It's Christmas Eve and we got here about an hour ago. We're the only ones in the house right now; her folks stepped out to grab something from the store, and Wyatt hasn't arrived yet. His flight from Nashville doesn't get in till the afternoon, according to Gigi.

"No, after Wyatt and I were born we spent the first couple of years in a brownstone downtown. But my parents wanted more space." She rolls her eyes. "The house they picked is probably overkill for a family of four. Six thousand square feet, eight bedrooms, four bathrooms. It's a bit intense."

She leads me into the cavernous living room, which she calls the great room. I stop at the wall of windows overlooking the yard, admiring the carpet of white and the threads of frost clinging to the skeletons of the trees. It started snowing last night and Gigi was thrilled, raving about how much she loves a white Christmas.

A wet nose nudges my hand. I peer down and grin at Dumpy the golden lab. The dogs have been following us around since we got here.

"They really like you," Gigi remarks.

"Why are you so surprised?"

"With your prickly demeanor? Seems like you'd scare animals away, send them fleeing in terror."

I bend down to rub behind Dumpy's ears. "Nah, man. We understand each other." I look at Bergeron. "Right?"

The husky tilts his head, listening intently.

"Are you sure you're cool staying in the guest room?" Gigi says. "It's the only way my dad would let you stay here."

I want to ask if Case stayed in the guest room when he visited, but I don't want to sound like I'm bitching about the sleeping arrangements. Truth is, I wouldn't step foot in Gigi's bedroom even if her parents rolled out a red carpet in front of it. I don't have a death wish.

As if reading my mind, she says, "Yes, Case always stayed in the guest room. But if you're good, I'll let you sneak into my room after everyone is asleep."

"Hard pass."

"Seriously?"

"Seriously. I don't want to get murdered by Garrett Graham."

Then again, judging by the way he frowns at me when he and his wife get home, murder is looking like a likely option, regardless of where I sleep.

"Mr. Ryder," he says coolly.

"Please don't call him mister," Gigi orders, rolling her eyes at her dad.

Mrs. Graham is a lot friendlier. "Welcome, Luke. I'm glad you're spending Christmas with us."

She flashes a smile that sparkles in her forest-green eyes. And since I don't want to correct her for calling me Luke, I suppose I'm going to be Luke this week, whether I like it or not. Because there's no way I'm doing anything to alienate the Grahams.

"Thanks for having me, Mrs. Graham."

"Oh, call me Hannah, please," she insists.

Her husband offers a deceptively pleasant smile. "And you can call me Mr. Graham."

So that's how it's going to be.

"Do you need help preparing dinner?" I ask, because it's officially time for the awkwardness portion of the day to commence.

It's always like this the first time you spend a holiday with people. I went through the same thing with Owen's family, Lindley's family, Beck's. You're just kind of standing there, not really part of it, but pretending to be. It's fucking brutal.

I've always wondered what it would be like to fit in somewhere.

Hannah tries damn hard to include me, though. When I offer my services, she puts me to work chopping vegetables and peeling potatoes for dinner, while Gigi and her father watch football in the great room.

"You know you could go watch with them, right?"

I blanch. "Oh, God, please don't send me out there." I'm only half joking.

She laughs. "Oh hush, he's really not that scary."

"I need you to think about how scary you believe him to be and then multiply that by five million." I reach for another potato to peel. "Is he protective of Gigi's brother too, or just Gigi?"

"Oh, trust me, Wyatt's not exempt. There's a reason he never brings girls home. He did it once when he was nineteen. Poor girl spent the weekend being interrogated by my husband, and then flew back to Nashville and never spoke to Wyatt again. The morning she left, Wyatt walked into Garrett's study, said, *Never again*, and walked right out. Swear to God, that boy isn't introducing us to anyone else unless they've already eloped."

I chuckle. "All right, so I'm not the only one intimidated."

"He'll warm up to you, don't worry."

I allow myself to feel hopeful, but then Gigi's brother arrives, and suddenly I've got two dudes staring me down.

Wyatt and Gigi are twins, and while I see the resemblance, there are more differences than similarities. His hair has more of a wave to it and is a lighter shade of brown. He's got green eyes like his mother, while Gigi's are gray. Gigi's short. Wyatt isn't—I'm six-five, and he and I are nearly eye to eye. He gives off a total musician vibe with his ripped jeans and black T-shirt, a leather band on one wrist, and a few other bracelets on the other. I can't judge the bracelets, since I've been wearing the same string around my wrist since I was sixteen. For some reason, that damn thing never came off. Owen and I assumed the bracelets would fray and fall off in a few months, yet here we are, five years later. I guess that says something about our bond.

Dinner's delicious, just as Gigi promised. I don't say much, despite her looks of encouragement. The only time things really get animated is when we discuss my teammate Austin Pope's performance in the World Juniors yesterday. For one glorious moment, Garrett Graham acknowledges my existence.

"Is his skating really that good, or was that a fluke?" Garrett asks. "I don't remember seeing that speed in his game film."

"He's that good," I confirm. "His speed is deceptive. He fools you into thinking he's slower, just moseying along, and then he shifts into a whole other gear and you're like, *What in the actual hell?*"

I take a sip of my water, then set down the glass.

"If you're not against picking freshmen for your Hockey Kings camp, Pope would be a great pick," I tell Garrett. Hesitant, because I don't want him to think I'm bringing it up for my own selfish purposes. Truthfully, I've given up on being selected as a coach.

"Yeah?" He sounds skeptical. As expected, he's eyeing me like I'm running some con on him.

"Definitely. I know he's young, but he's a good kid. Patience of a saint. He stays late at the rink all the time to help his teammates improve their game. He'd be an asset to any camp."

Garrett nods, the suspicion fading from his expression. "Oh. Well, we do try to avoid freshmen because they're too close in age to some of the boys at camp. But I'll keep him in mind when the time comes. Thanks."

I'm just thinking we made progress when Gigi reaches for my hand. As I instinctively lace my fingers through hers, her father's gaze tracks the movement. Then he gets all irritable again, as if suddenly remembering I'm dating his daughter and not just some dude with whom he's discussing the World Juniors.

The finger interlocking was probably a boneheaded move on my part, but I can't just pretend she's not my girlfriend, so I let her squeeze my hand. I notice Hannah watching us with an indecipherable expression.

"All right, you know the drill. I cook, you guys clean," Hannah says after we've demolished our meals. "I'm going to pour myself a glass of wine and start a fire."

Gigi has to use the bathroom, so now I'm in the kitchen gathering dishes with her dad and brother. Both of whom eye me like I'm an international terrorist who somehow wound up in their house.

After a prolonged silence, Wyatt crosses his arms and says, "What do you want with my sister?"

"Wyatt," Garrett says.

Gigi's twin glances at his dad. "No, I got this. I'll tag you in if I need you." His green eyes return to me. "Well?"

I smother a sigh. "We're together. Not sure what else you want me to say."

"Together," he echoes. "What does that mean?"

"It means we're together."

"I'm tagging in," Garrett says. His arms cross too. "Where do you see this going?"

Everywhere.

But I don't want to say that. I'm not used to talking about my feelings in general, let alone with two men I barely know.

"I'm not exactly sure how to answer that. We've been together a while now. It's going good." I force myself to meet their respective gazes. "I consider it to be serious."

Wyatt narrows his eyes. "I looked you up. You beat somebody up in the Juniors."

I nod. "Yeah, I did."

"Got an anger problem? Is that what this is?"

"Wyatt," Garrett chides. Then he raises an eyebrow. "Although I am curious about that particular incident."

"Guys, stop grilling him." Gigi walks in, annoyance clouding her face. "Stop it. You don't have to answer any of their questions, Ryder. In fact, Ryder helped Mom cook, so he doesn't have to clean. He's excused." She jabs her finger at them. "You two do it. We're going to hang out with Mom, a.k.a. a normal person."

Then she drags me out of the kitchen.

"Jesus Christ. Thank you," I murmur when we're out of earshot.

"Sorry. They can be a little overprotective."

"A little?"

"Now aren't you glad you went shopping with me? It's always good to have some bribery in your back pocket."

Well, technically, she picked out all the gifts because I don't know her family well enough to go beyond generic. But my presents do seem to be a hit, especially the sheet music I got Wyatt, which came in a cool metal box. He grudgingly thanks me, looking pleased.

"So, if you have dinner and open gifts on Christmas Eve, what do you do tomorrow?" I ask the Grahams. We're sitting in the great room, the twinkling lights of the tree casting shadows on the walls. Of course, they have a bunch of old sentimental ornaments, tiny plaster casts of Gigi and Wyatt's baby feet. It should be nauseating, but I don't mind it.

"We get lazy." For a moment, it's as if Wyatt forgot there's a fox in his henhouse. He answers me like I'm a normal person and not someone who's trying to despoil his sister. "We eat leftovers. Break open the boxes of Grandma's holiday cookies."

"Maybe we'll get a skate in at the pond down the street," Gigi pipes up. "I want to see a shootout between you two—" She flicks her finger between Wyatt and me.

He scowls at her. "Please don't force me to play hockey."

"You're *good* at it." She sounds exasperated.

"Yeah. Do you know how exhausting it is to be good at something you don't want to do?"

Garrett snickers. "Ungrateful little shit. I give you all my talent, and what do you do with it? You sing songs."

"Hey, that's my talent," Hannah says.

He's quickly shamefaced. "Sorry, Wellsy. Your talent is way better than mine. Hands down."

I think he truly means that. And the sheer love in his eyes almost has me feeling like a voyeur. I never saw my parents look at each other like that. I've never seen *anyone* look at each other like that.

I wonder what people see when I look at Gigi.

Eventually we all head up to bed. I walk her to her bedroom, and she stands on her tiptoes to whisper, "Sneak in when everyone's asleep?"

"Absolutely not."

"Come on."

"I already told you, I'm not touching you under your father's roof. This situation is precarious enough."

"What about sexy texting?"

I stubbornly shake my head. "What if he and I accidentally switch phones?"

"Why would that ever happen? Come on, just one dick pic."

"What is your obsession with me?" I drawl. "Do I need Jensen to send you his PowerPoint on sex addiction?"

I kiss her good night—on the cheek—and go to the guest room. The bed is insanely comfortable, but for some reason I can't fall asleep. I toss and turn for a while, finally deciding to raid the liquor cabinet and try to *force* sleep. One of the dogs follows me silently into the kitchen. The other dog is already down there. Lying on the floor in the adjacent dining room, where Hannah is wrapping presents.

I poke my head in there. "I thought we opened presents already," I say dryly.

"Oh, this is the second part of the tradition. We pretend all the gifts are gone, and then the kids wake up the next morning and find something extra waiting for them on the kitchen table."

"That's a really nice tradition." I shrug awkwardly. "Mind if I grab a drink? Something harder than water or milk, I mean."

"Having trouble sleeping?"

"Yeah. Unfamiliar surroundings, I guess."

"Come on. I got just the trick."

She leads me down the hall toward the den, which Garrett must also use as his office because there's a commanding desk and shelves full of awards and framed photographs. There's an actual shot of Garrett shaking hands with the president, yet my total lack of interest in politics has me moving toward a different photo. A group shot featuring around two dozen people on the dock of a lake.

Hannah follows my gaze. "That's from our annual Tahoe trip. Garrett always insists on taking a group photo. Nobody is ever prepared, and someone usually falls in the lake." She shrugs. "You'll see for yourself this summer."

"Who says I'll be there?"

"You will."

She pours two glasses of whiskey, and we settle on opposite ends of the brown leather couch.

"You love my daughter."

My head jerks toward her in surprise.

She sips her whiskey, looking amused. "You've figured that out, right?"

I gulp my own drink. "It's still...early."

"So? When you know, you know." Her lips twitch as she examines my face. "Got it. We're still fighting it. Don't worry, Luke—we'll save this for another time." She laughs softly. "Give your head some time to catch up to your heart."

CHAPTER FORTY-THREE
GIGI

Owen McKay

IT'S NICE HAVING RYDER HERE FOR THE HOLIDAYS. I CAN'T SAY MY dad and Wyatt have fully warmed up to him, but Mom certainly has, and it's kind of adorable to see the two of them together. They walk the dogs in the snow. He carries her groceries into the house. Listens in rapt attention when she talks about the new singer she's producing. It's really sweet.

I wonder if he longs for a maternal figure. He lost his when he was six, and it couldn't have been easy growing up without his mother. Even worse that his replacement for her was a series of foster moms who never stuck around long enough to care.

On our last night of the break, we hang out alone in my bedroom...with the door open because Ryder wears a chastity belt now. I only managed to convince him to have sex with me twice this week, and that's after he received multiple assurances that my family would be gone for an ample amount of time. He required a two-hour buffer on either end of the fornication period. His words, not mine.

I'm dating a crazy person.

Now, he's sprawled on my bed reading a book he grabbed from my father's study. I know Dad begrudgingly approved of his choice, but he's being stubborn and doesn't want to admit he and Ryder might have something in common, so he didn't comment on it.

My legs are stretched across Ryder's lap while I design a custom-made T-shirt on my MacBook. Tomorrow is my dad's birthday and I already got him a present, but I'm adding another item thanks to his behavior during the Boxing Day Beatdown. Beau Di Laurentis and AJ Connelly were named team captains that morning, and Dad was so outraged about getting picked fifth that he glared at the teenage boys and growled, "Is this a joke? Do you realize I'm Garrett Graham?"

"Do you think the *I'm Garrett Graham* line should be black or silver?" I ask, angling the laptop.

Ryder looks at it. "Black." Then he chuckles at what I'm working on.

My phone buzzes again, as it's been doing all day. I've been fielding texts from friends asking what I'm doing tonight. It happens to be New Year's Eve, but we decided to stay in.

I check the screen. It's Diana, who's spending New Year's with her older lover, Sir Percival.

DIANA:

> I kind of love how mature he is. I didn't feel like partying tonight and he was perfectly cool with staying in. NYE = wine, a movie, and very adult lovemaking. I think I'm getting swept away by the allure of the older man…

ME:

> I'm glad! But don't completely lose your head. It's early yet.

I'm as tactful as I can be. Truthfully, I've always thought there's something a bit off about a man who wants to date someone so much younger. Granted, six years isn't a huge age difference. But

Diana mentioned that Percival had a serious relationship with another younger woman before her. When he was twenty-four, he dated an eighteen-year-old. I find that icky. But he and Diana are both adults, and so long as she's happy, I'll reserve my judgment.

Another text pops up, this one from my cousin.

ALEX TUCKER:

> What do you mean you're staying in tonight?? NOT ALLOWED. You're coming to Manhattan.

In her last message, she mentioned she's making a paid appearance at a new nightclub in Manhattan tonight.

ME:

> This last minute? No way. It's too late for the train and any available flights will cost a gazillion dollars.

She disappears for a while, and I assume the subject's been dropped. But then she texts again.

ALEX:

> My friend will send his jet.

I cough out a laugh. Jesus. I thought *I* had friends in high places. Meanwhile, Alex is over here just hanging out with private jet owners.

ME:

> I can't.

ALEX:

> Yes you can. Come on, I miss you. And it'll be fun.

I think it over for a moment. It's rare I'm able to be impulsive with such a rigid hockey schedule, and I realize this might be my last chance to go a little wild. We're going back to school, where a new semester will commence, the season will resume, and playoffs will start soon. When will I ever have the chance to fly on a private plane to New York?

"Hey," I say to Ryder. "We've been invited to a New Year's party. You in?"

He looks up from his book. "Who invited us?" He's absently stroking my knee.

"My cousin Alex. She's going to a nightclub in Manhattan. One of those nauseating events where all the celebrities are paid to show their pretty faces."

"Is this the supermodel cousin?"

I nod. "Do you wanna go? She said she can send us a plane."

Ryder blinks. Then he snorts out a laugh. "Oh fuck off."

"I know." I sigh. "I can't help it, though. She's got serious connections. Uncle Tucker thinks it's pretty cool."

Another message from Alex pops up with a link to the event.

"Oh, these are the details." I pull it up and scan the information. Some hot DJ is headlining, and there's a list of the celebrities that are scheduled to show up. The name at the top of my list makes me hoot in laughter. "Dude. Guess who'll be there."

"Who?"

"Vizza Billity."

"The worst-named rapper of all time?"

"Yup. Oh man, if Mya wasn't in Malta right now, she would totally come with us." I keep scanning names. "Hey, look. Your buddy Owen McKay is supposed to make an appearance too."

There are a few athletes on the list, but McKay's name is the only one that jumps out at me.

"Okay, now we *have* to go," I tell Ryder.

He shifts, looking uncomfortable.

"Or we can stay here. Whatever you want."

His blue eyes fix on me. "You want to go, huh?"

"Kind of."

"Then I'll go." He cocks a brow. "But I will not be dancing."

"Yes, you will."

"And I'll also pretend I don't know you when you ask for Vizza Billity's autograph."

"You'll miss out then. I was planning on getting him to sign my tits."

Ryder grins.

And that's how later that evening, we board an actual private jet bound for Manhattan. The plane's interior is all white, from the leather seats to the plush carpets to the spacious bathroom. As much as I want to joke about it, it's kind of absurd.

Alex is Uncle Tucker and Aunt Sabrina's youngest daughter. She's twenty, so a year younger than me, while her sister is a lawyer and a few years older. It's so crazy to me that one daughter is toiling away to make partner, while the other is worth a hundred million dollars and rides on private jets.

"What, she's too rich and famous to pick us up?" Ryder growls in mock outrage when we step onto the snowy tarmac after descending the metal steps. It was only a forty-five-minute flight, and over much too fast. I would have liked to continue devouring that charcuterie spread the flight attendant brought out.

"Unacceptable," I agree.

Alex did send a car, though—a sleek black Escalade that whisks us away into the heart of the city. Luckily, we manage to avoid Times Square, because all the roads around it are cordoned off. You'll never make me understand it, the suffocating throng of bodies shivering in the cold waiting for a dumb ball to drop.

Ryder holds my hand in the back seat, but he's visibly distracted. He'd pulled out his phone on the plane a few times to check the screen, as if waiting for a message. But when I asked about it, he said he was checking the time.

Alex told me to give my name at the door of the venue. There's a line at least three blocks long. I feel like an ass for skipping to the front, where I receive mutinous glares from the young partygoers waiting in the endless line.

It's total chaos inside. Strobe lights, air humid with sweat and perfume, and deafening electronic music. Scantily clad women and thirsty men constantly flit in our path as we venture deeper into the club. I will say, it's kind of exhilarating. There isn't much of a night-life in Hastings, and I'm usually too exhausted from practice and games to drive to Boston during the season.

When I text Alex to say we're here, she tells me to come to the VIP lounge.

"Come on. This way." I tug Ryder's hand.

I notice him looking around at the crowd, a bit uneasy. Something still feels off about him, but I chalk it up to him being antisocial because, well, he's antisocial.

As we weave our way across the crowded main floor, the music begins to seep into my blood, making my hips move. Ryder's eyes focus on that.

He lifts the corner of his mouth.

"What?" I say.

"You look good."

We both ditched our coats in the Escalade after the driver said he'd be back for us later, so there's no hiding my skimpy dress. It's a shimmery silver with fringe at the bottom. Old-timey modern. I'm not wearing a bra, but the neckline is modest. Only a hint of cleavage. The dress does most of its work down below, showing off my legs.

The VIP area requires an elevator to get up to it. It's manned by two bouncers with earpieces and radios. I'm ready to drop Alex's name again when the elevator doors swing open and she appears herself.

It always startles me how beautiful she is. Growing up, I remember constantly thinking how pretty she was. Even as a ten-year-old, she made people take a second look. She started modeling officially when she was seventeen, and in three years, she's become one of the most recognizable models and influencers in the world.

She's stunning, with thick dark hair, big brown eyes, a perfect body. I notice Ryder checking her out and I don't even care because I'm checking her out too. A slinky red dress is glued to her tall willowy frame, showing off her huge tits, tiny waist, and perky ass. She has the kind of body that makes you cry in envy. I'm too muscular to ever look like Alex. Hockey does that to you.

"G!" She throws her arms around me. "They're with me," she tells the VIP guards.

The three of us step into the elevator. Everyone who's been lurking nearby, hoping to sneak their way up to the promised land, shoots us envious looks. Several women glare murder at me. I offer a rueful shrug as the doors close.

"Oh my God, you look incredible," Alex gushes. "That dress."

"Me? Look at what you're wearing. It's insane."

I introduce her to Ryder, who she checks out not at all discreetly. At nearly six feet, Alex has an easier time looking him in the eye. I realize they look good together, and although I know it's irrational of me, I experience a jolt of jealousy.

The VIP lounge is a whole other world. A long railing stretches across the entire space, overlooking the dance floor far below. There are a few mini dance floors up here too, but mostly it's plush black velvet booths, sensual lighting, and bottle service. In one corner is a raised platform offering another large booth cordoned off by velvet ropes. The Super VIP area of the VIP lounge. Holding court there is a tall guy wearing a white hoodie, white parachute pants, and white designer sneakers. I recognize the rapper instantly. For some reason I expected a lot more bling, but he boasts only a diamond-studded watch. Well, and the mohawk on his head is dyed gold, so I guess the bling factor is all in the hair.

When he notices me staring, he flashes a cocky smile and flicks his hand in a casual wave.

Alex follows my gaze. "You should go thank him," she says with a grin.

"For what?"

"You flew here on his plane."

My jaw drops. "Oh my God." I turn to Ryder. "We flew on Vizza Billity's plane." Although now it makes sense why everything was white.

"He's actually pretty cool," Alex says. "I'll introduce you in a bit. First I want to hear everything you're up to."

We haven't seen each other since Tahoe, but it's hard to catch up over the pounding music and we spend most of the time screaming in each other's ears. Meanwhile, Ryder stands there sipping a whiskey the server just delivered to him. I ordered my trusty scotch and soda, which made him grin.

"So, this is a thing," Alex remarks, her manicured finger dancing between Ryder and me.

"Yes," I answer, rolling my eyes.

"You're tall," she tells him.

"Thanks?"

"It's an observation, not a compliment."

Ryder chokes out a laugh.

"And you're both hockey players," she continues, giggling at me. "You and your hockey player fetish."

"It's not a fetish," I say with a loud snort.

"Wasn't the last one a hockey player too?"

Ryder narrows his eyes.

She flips her hair and touches his arm. "Don't worry, you're cuter. And taller."

My attention suddenly focuses on a familiar face in one of the other booths. I gasp when recognition dawns.

"That's Mac from *Fling or Forever!*" I exclaim. "And he's not with Samantha! Oh my God, I need to text Diana. And my dad." I grab my phone out of my purse.

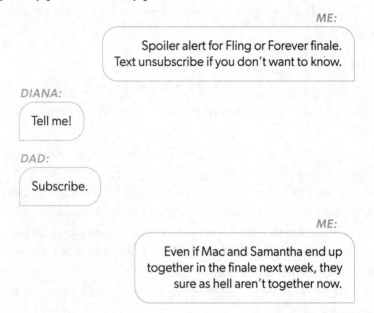

ME:

Spoiler alert for Fling or Forever finale. Text unsubscribe if you don't want to know.

DIANA:

Tell me!

DAD:

Subscribe.

ME:

Even if Mac and Samantha end up together in the finale next week, they sure as hell aren't together now.

I punctuate that with the grainy photo I manage to snap of Mac with his tongue down some girl's throat.

Eventually Alex drags me to the small dance floor. I feel bad abandoning Ryder, but he just waves us off. When I glance over at some point, he's chatting with Vizza Billity. I wish I had my phone so I could commemorate the moment, but it's in my purse, which is slung over Ryder's muscular forearm.

I have successfully managed to turn Briar's grumpy, bad-boy hockey cocaptain into a hold-my-purse boyfriend.

I've won the world.

We take a dancing break, and a waitress comes to take our order for another round. This time Alex requests champagne, and we toast and drink until she drags Ryder to dance while he pleads at me with his eyes to make it stop. But despite his pained look, there's no way he's not enjoying having her body rubbing all over him. This time

I don't feel jealous, though. Maybe because his heated gaze remains on me the entire time.

When he returns, he checks his phone and frowns before shoving it back in his pocket.

"Stop checking the time," I chide.

It's nearing midnight when a loud burst of noise echoes from the elevator and new arrivals stream in.

Alex glances over and laughs. "Your people are here."

I grin. "Our people?"

"Hockey crowd."

The group rolls in, ushered by the staff toward one of the roped-off booths, while half-naked bottle girls race over to serve the newcomers and stroke their egos.

Someone shouts, "Ryder!"

The next thing I know, Owen McKay strides toward us. He and Ryder are exactly the same height, so it's sort of intimidating when they're both standing there looming over us.

"Hey." Owen throws his arms around Ryder in an enthusiastic hug. He pulls back, arching a brow when he notices my cousin. "Hi, aren't you…?"

Alex bestows him her dazzling smile, and his eyes glaze over.

"Jesus Christ." He looks back at Ryder. "This is the company you're keeping now that you're on the East Coast? Supermodels?" He groans out loud, appreciation heating his eyes as he glances from me to Alex.

Call me a superficial bitch, but I enjoy being included in the category of "supermodel."

"What's going on?" Ryder says gruffly. "Didn't even know you were in town."

"I didn't know *you* were in town," Owen counters. "What are you doing in Manhattan? You said you were spending the holidays with a friend in Boston."

Ryder reaches for my hand. Tugs me toward him. "Yeah, this is the friend." He pauses. "Girlfriend, actually."

"Nice save," I tell him.

Chuckling, Owen stares at our joined hands. "Jesus, Luke, there's a lot you've been keeping from me. We have a girlfriend now?"

Ryder shrugs.

"I'm Gigi," I say, extending my free hand. "It's nice to meet you. And you already know Alex, apparently."

"Owen," he says.

He's still scrutinizing me, as if my presence in Ryder's life mystifies him. And when those blue eyes lock on my face, a strange feeling travels through me because I realize they're the exact shade as Ryder's. I don't think I've ever been in the same vicinity as two guys with the same dark sapphire eyes.

The suspicion that tickles at my brain is confirmed when Owen lifts a brow and says, "How long have you been dating my brother?"

CHAPTER FORTY-FOUR

RYDER

I want to be her hero

"Owen McKay is your brother."

Gigi voices the curt, unhappy words when we drag our worn-out asses into the hotel room around three in the morning. We're spending the night in her supermodel cousin's suite. The penthouse, of course.

I've been waiting for her to say something, but I'm glad she managed to hold it together until now. After Owen dropped his bomb earlier, I could tell she still had a million questions. But there was no way we could make small talk, let alone engage in deep conversation, amidst the deafening music in a nightclub on New Year's Eve. I was relieved when she didn't push, but knew she was only biding her time. She spent the rest of the night shooting uneasy glances between Owen and me.

Well, not the whole night. We also spent a decent amount of time on the dance floor. I didn't dance so much as let her grind all over me until the clock struck midnight, and then we made out on the dance floor surrounded by supermodels, professional athletes, and a rapper named Vizza.

Wild night.

Afterward, we piled into Alex's private car, Owen included. He and Alex disappeared into her room, and for a girl who made fun of Gigi for being into hockey players, she sure is screaming one's name right now.

I close the door, providing a barrier between the sexfest happening on the other end of the suite.

"All right. Let's have it," I say with a sigh.

"You lied to me," she answers flatly.

"I didn't lie." I bite my lip, forcing myself not to avoid her increasingly angry eyes. "I told you I knew Owen from Phoenix—I just left out the part that he's my brother."

Gigi leans against the door, arms crossed tight to her chest. "You lied by omission." She shakes her head in disapproval. "I just introduced you to my family, and you couldn't be bothered to tell me you have a brother?"

My teeth dig deeper into my lip. I force myself to stop, licking away the sting and taking a breath.

"I didn't intentionally keep it a secret," I finally tell her. "The first time it came up that I knew Owen, I hadn't told you about my dad yet, and I wasn't ready for all that shit to come out. So I played it off like we were just friends from Phoenix. And then later, it sort of slipped my mind."

"It slipped your mind," she echoes in disbelief.

"Because it never even came up again. We never talk about Owen," I point out.

"Yeah, and why is that?"

I sit on the edge of the mattress and run both hands through my hair. "Because I hate talking about my past. You know that."

"You also said you'd make more of an effort." She sounds frustrated.

"I know. I'm sorry. It's just…I'm not good at this." I let out a breath, regret flickering through me. "He's my half brother. We don't share the same dad."

Just the same dead mom.

I quickly swallow the lump in my throat.

As if sensing the pain building inside me, Gigi comes over and sits beside me, still clad in the shiny silver dress I couldn't take my eyes off all night.

"Why were you in foster care?" she asks in confusion. "I mean if you have a half brother. And Owen mentioned his parents more than once tonight. Why didn't his family take you in?"

A sick feeling crawls through me. "They just didn't."

"How much older is he?"

"Two years. He was eight when Mom died. But he wasn't living with us at that point," I explain. "Mom and Owen's dad got divorced when Owen was one. Then she met my dad and got pregnant with me almost right away. Owen lived with us until about a year before she died."

"Were you close?"

"Best friends. Still are." I hold up my wrist. "He's the BFF you like to rag me about. Got these fucking things when we were sixteen, and they still haven't fallen off."

She smiles. I can sense her anger melting away. "That's a good sign, I think."

"Anyway, when he was seven, his dad remarried. Really nice woman, Sarah. She had her own daughter from a previous marriage. Russ, Owen's dad, wanted them to be family, so he fought my mom for full custody. Told the courts he could offer a better environment for his son. He had a higher income, lived in a nicer area. Mom couldn't afford to hire a lawyer to fight him, and eventually she gave in. It wasn't like he was trying to keep her out of Owen's life entirely. He just wanted to be Owen's primary residence. So she agreed, and we got Owen on weekends and holidays. That hurt her a lot, though. She missed him." My voice thickens. "We both did. He went to live with his dad and stepmom, and I stayed with my parents. And a year later, my dad put a bullet in Mom's brain."

My chest clenches. Suddenly I find myself breathing hard, spitting out a ragged curse.

"What is it?" Gigi pushes.

"I will never forgive him for what he did." My throat is burning. "She wasn't a perfect mother, but she was mine."

Tears sting my eyes and I avert my gaze. But Gigi's goddamn perceptive, and of course she notices. She wriggles toward me, the fabric of her dress swishing, and forcibly lifts my arm so she can tuck her head underneath it.

I instinctively hold her.

She rests her head on my shoulder. "And Owen's dad just let you go into foster care after you lost your mother? That's cruel."

The frank assessment is sort of depressing. "I wasn't related to him, so he didn't care. Owen's dad is…" I try to be tactful, then wonder why I'm bothering. I'm not a tactful guy, so why start now? "He's a fucking prick. And Sarah, sweet as she is, is a total pushover. I think if it was up to her, she would have taken me in."

I think about the handful of holidays I spent with the McKays. It was only a few, and only because Owen begged his dad to let me come.

"Russ never liked me. I think I was just a reminder of my mom, his ex-wife. He claims she cheated on him with my dad, but I don't know if that's true. Maybe she did."

I probably wouldn't blame her if that was the case. Russ has always been a difficult, abrasive man. Strict, with impossibly high expectations for Owen. It's a damn good thing Owen was phenomenal at hockey, considering how hard Russ pushed him growing up. If Owen didn't possess the talent and the necessary passion for the game, he would've crumbled under that kind of pressure.

"Russ didn't want me," I say simply. *Nobody did.* I clear the sudden rush of emotion out of my throat. "I was a reminder of a life he'd put behind him."

"But Owen's been a good brother to you?"

"The best." Guilt squeezes my chest.

She doesn't miss the tension. "What?"

"Better brother than I deserve," I admit.

"What does that mean?"

"My father killed his mother, Gigi. That's not something either of us could ever forget."

"Does he hold it against you?" She sounds concerned.

"No, but he should," I say flatly. "If it weren't for my piece-of-shit father, he would still have a mom."

"Yes, but that's not your fault."

"All I'm saying is, I wouldn't blame him if he blamed me."

My throat feels tight again. Whatever. There's no point thinking about any of this. Talking about any of it. It doesn't change anything. Doesn't fix the past or—

"Don't do that," Gigi says softly. "Don't bury it down. I can feel you doing it."

I flinch when she grasps my chin. Forcing eye contact.

"You want so badly for this to not be your past, but it is. I understand how much that sucks, and I'm so sorry. But none of it was your fault. You're not responsible for it. Your father is."

"I know."

"Then stop taking ownership of his actions. Let yourself have a good relationship with your brother. You don't need to feel guilty."

"But I do feel guilty," I mumble, and it's the first time in my life I've ever said those words out loud.

I've never even told Owen how I feel.

It scares me that I can tell her everything. Just be vulnerable this way. And I'm not scared of her reaction. There's never even a trace of fear that she might judge me.

I wrap my arm around her waist and gently lower her onto her back. One hand cupping her cheek, I gaze at her gorgeous face. My heart's always in my throat when I'm with her. When I think about her.

I lean in to kiss her.

"I'm not good enough for you," I whisper against her lips.

Alarm fills her eyes. "Ryder—"

"I don't know if I'll ever be. But I want to try."

And I do. I mean that. I know I have my flaws. But I need to level up to be with this woman. She forces me to be better.

I *want* to be better for her.

I want to be her hero.

Emotion clogs my throat.

"Hey," she says, reaching up to touch my chin. "What's going on?"

"I love you."

Her breath hitches.

I've never said those words before. But I mean them with every fiber of my being. She's the one. She's the only one.

"Say it again."

"I love you, Gigi."

A brilliant smile fills her face. "I love you too, Luke."

That does something to me. The name I've loathed for so long, the name I've recoiled from, leaving her lips. Hearing it now, coming from that sweet voice and gorgeous face, accompanied by those three words, well, I guess I don't mind being Luke.

I'll be whoever she wants me to be.

———————

Pulling on a T-shirt, I duck out of the bedroom early the next morning and find my brother in the full kitchen of the lavish suite. Gigi's sound asleep behind the closed door of our room. Alex must be too because she's nowhere to be seen.

I walk toward my brother. "Morning."

"Happy New Year. You want a coffee?"

I nod. "Please."

The suite is equipped with an expensive coffee maker and the gourmet kind of coffee you find in those super bougie hipster cafes.

"Fancy," I drawl, and he chuckles.

A minute later, he hands me a cup, steam rising from the rim. We wander over to the living area and sit on the plush couch. We didn't spend any time in this room last night, so it's in pristine condition.

"So. You've got a girlfriend." He chuckles. "You neglected to mention that the last time we spoke."

"I was still wrapping my head around it."

"I like her."

"Me too." I nod toward Alex's closed door. "Is that gonna be a thing?"

"Yes, bro. I'm going to marry a supermodel. Come on now."

"Aren't you a famous professional athlete? Don't supermodels go hand in hand with that?"

"That girl is wildfire. She'll get bored of me in a week, tops. She's leaving for Paris tonight on a private jet."

"Yeah, and you're leaving on *your* jet back to LA."

"Oh fuck off. I'm flying commercial."

"First class?"

He hangs his head in shame. "Business."

I snicker. "How was Christmas with your parents?"

"All right. How about you? You spent it with the Grahams, huh?"

I sigh. "Remember when Garrett Graham hated me for being late to practice? Well, now he's got an even bigger reason. Dude can't stand me."

"I'm sure you're exaggerating."

"Trust me, I'm not."

I notice him eyeing me over the rim of his mug.

"What?"

"You look happy," Owen says. "Can't believe I'm fucking saying that. But you do."

"Hell's frozen over, right?"

"I mean…yeah."

Grinning, I set my mug on the glass table. "So what's your upcoming game schedule like?"

"We've got a stretch of away games." He runs a hand through his messy brown hair. "It's a grueling schedule. Being on the road is exhausting."

"You love it."

"I do." He pauses. "You're going to love it too."

"Yeah, if Dallas doesn't change their mind about me."

"They won't." He takes another sip. "We've got a couple games against the Bruins next month. You should come to one. Watch the game in the box and grab dinner with me and the team after."

"Sounds good."

"Bring your girlfriend." He winks.

"You really like saying that word."

"Yeah, 'cause it's you and you don't do girlfriends. I'm gonna keep saying it forever just 'cause I know it makes you uncomfortable."

Speaking of uncomfortable, I suddenly remember what Gigi said last night. About how I can't take ownership of other people's actions.

I hesitate for a long time, watching Owen sip his coffee and scroll on his phone. I would normally never discuss this. Never dream of bringing it up. But maybe my "normal" doesn't cut it anymore. Maybe it's time to change the way I handle shit.

"Do you blame me?"

He lifts his head, confused. "For what?"

"For Mom." I stare at my hands for several seconds, then force myself to meet his gaze. "Do you see him when you look at me?"

He recoils. "Fuck no."

I can't even describe the relief that shudders through me.

"You didn't hurt her," Owen says quietly.

"I didn't save her either."

"You were six. Trust me, if I'd been there, I wouldn't have done much either." Regret digs a crease into his forehead. "I'm the one who should be apologizing. I couldn't do anything for you after it happened. I begged my dad to let you come live with us, but he wouldn't hear it."

"I know. It's not your fault. I know what he's like."

"Yeah, but I still felt bad. I'll always feel bad about it, that I had a family while you got shuffled around to different foster homes. My dad's an asshole, but it's nothing compared to the hand you got dealt."

"It wasn't all bad," I assure him. "I got to play hockey, didn't I?"

"True."

A brief regretful silence passes between us.

"I can't believe he's up for parole," I say flatly.

"Me neither." Owen's tone is grim.

We texted about it a while ago after I finally returned Peter Greene's call. Like me, Owen was asked to—and has no desire to—speak at the hearing.

"And no, Ryder. Just to answer that question again. When I look at you, I don't see him—I see you. You're my little brother. I love you."

"I love you too."

We sit there in silence for a while, drinking the rest of our coffee as the sun begins to rise above the Manhattan skyline.

"You should be prepared," Owen eventually says, glancing over to grin at me.

"For what?"

"You're gonna marry that girl."

CHAPTER FORTY-FIVE
GIGI

We were best friends

AT THE END OF JANUARY, I HAVE DINNER WITH MY PARENTS AFTER the team plays Boston University. Normally, we're all expected to be on the team bus after a game, but I got special permission from Adley to stay behind. I swear, any request that has to do with my father, Adley will grant without blinking. He simply waved his hand and said, "See you tomorrow." Tomorrow is a home game against Providence, and I'm looking forward to it. We haven't faced Bethany Clarke and those girls since our exhibition in the fall. It's bound to be competitive.

Wyatt is back in Nashville, so the house is a little quieter. My parents and I order Chinese takeout and eat at the kitchen counter while I track a social media thread that's providing live updates of the men's game against UConn.

"Ugh," I say, squinting at my phone in irritation, "Why can't this one be televised?" It's actually super important for the standings, since UConn is only leading their conference by one game. Briar still has an excellent chance to edge them out.

"UConn's so solid this year," Dad remarks. "Connelly has them as the lock to win the Frozen Four. Don't tell Jensen."

"You think Briar doesn't have a shot?"

"No, they have a real good shot," he relents. "I'm impressed by how they managed to turn the season around."

"It's shocking that Ryder and Case are still playing so well together despite the complete silent treatment from Case."

Dad raises a brow.

"Case hasn't spoken to him in more than a month," I admit. "Not since Ryder and I went public with our relationship. Case isn't happy. He spent most of last year trying to win me back, but now he finally realizes it's not going to happen."

"And you're okay with that?" Dad asks carefully.

"What do you mean?"

"This choice that you made."

I sigh. "Look, I know you like Case. And he's a good guy, but it was never going to happen, even if Ryder *wasn't* in the picture. We were never getting back together."

Dad's mouth dips in a slight frown. "I still don't get why it ended in the first place, Stan. It never made any sense—"

"Because he cheated on me."

His jaw drops. Half a second later, anger floods his expression.

"No," I interject, holding up my hand. "See, this is why I didn't want to tell you. I didn't want you to think badly of him."

"How can I not?" he growls.

"He made a mistake. Honestly, he's not a bad guy. He freaked out because things were getting too serious. Just such a typical guy thing."

Except…Ryder hasn't freaked out on me once.

He was the one who told me he loved me. He said it first. He wasn't scared to, and he didn't run screaming when I returned the sentiment.

I don't know if Case ever truly loved me. Not only because he cheated. But because he was content—we both were—to date for nearly two years without exchanging *I love you*s.

"'A typical guy thing,'" Dad echoes, amused.

"Yeah, it's like the second they feel like they're being locked down, they experience this overwhelming urge to go and spray their seed everywhere."

"Stan, please don't say the words *spray* and *seed* in my presence again."

I snort. "Anyway. That's why it was never going to work."

"I get it." He shakes his head, chuckling. "If you'd just told me this months ago, I would have let it go."

"Oh, it's that easy to shut you up?"

"It is." He rounds the counter and slings his arm around me.

Mom returns to the kitchen and eyes us in amusement. "What's going on?"

"Case cheated on Gigi," reveals Dad.

She gasps. "No."

"Yes," I tell her, "but it's over now because I'm in love with somebody else. So, let's all just move on."

Dad starts to cough.

"In love with somebody else, huh?" Mom teases. She turns to Dad. "See? I told you."

He looks ill now. "Of all the men out there…"

"Come on. Ryder's great," I assure him.

He's more than great.

He's everything.

That hard exterior hides the kind of man I'm honored to be with. A man I trust enough to show every ounce of vulnerability to. A man who hears me when I gently point out a flaw and tries to alter his behavior. A man who makes me desperately happy even when I'm feeling sad.

"All right, Gigi, there's an hour before the mall closes," Mom says. "Did you still want to come along while I pick up Allie's birthday gift?"

"Sure," I say, and we head out.

We get to the mall at eight thirty, right before closing time.

While Mom ducks into the jewelry store to pick up the custom pendant she got for my aunt's birthday, I stand near a planter and text with Ryder, who's sneaking in messages during intermission.

"Gigi?"

I glance up, then freeze. Tension fills me when I see Emma Fairlee sauntering up to me.

Oh, man. I am so not in the mood for this. The last time we crossed paths was at a party thrown by a mutual friend the summer after I started college. Emma and I stood on opposite sides of the house the entire night. Neither of us seemed interested in approaching the other, so I'm surprised she's interested now.

She looks as beautiful as ever. Shiny hair. Perfect eyebrows. Pink lip gloss slathered on pouty lips, and designer clothing plastered to her perfect body.

Emma closes the distance between us. She has a couple of shopping bags dangling off one arm.

"Emma," I say carefully. "Didn't know you were in town."

"Yeah, I'm visiting my dad for the weekend."

The reminder of her father brings a clench of frustration, because would it kill the man to reach *some* sort of decision about the national team? It's taking ages and I'm getting impatient for news.

"How wild is it that he took over Team USA?" she gushes.

There's genuine pride in her eyes, and it succeeds in disarming me. Just slightly.

"Amazing news," I agree, nodding. "He's a great coach. He's going to do well there."

"How about you? Are you doing well?"

"Yep, you know, keeping busy as usual. I heard you got a role in a television pilot? That's cool."

Her eyes flash for a second. "It didn't get picked up."

"Oh, sorry to hear that."

"Are you?"

I smother a sigh. Here we go.

Her tone becomes chilly. "Because I'm sure it makes you happy to hear that."

"Okay, don't put this on me," I say, taking a step away. "I don't care what you're doing in LA. I was just being polite."

Her cheeks redden. One thing about Emma, she doesn't like to feel dismissed. And that's precisely what I'm doing right now.

"I have to go. My mom's waiting for me."

I've barely taken two steps when her voice bites at my back. "You know, you're a real bitch."

I turn, baring my teeth in a cheerless smile. "Oh, I am, am I?"

"You don't need to talk to me like I'm a piece of gum under your shoe. We were best friends, Gigi."

I stalk over to her. "Yes, Emma. We were best friends."

"We were supposed to have each other's backs," she spits out, eyes glittering. "And you just let your brother humiliate me."

I stare at her in disbelief. "Seriously? Tell me, how did he humiliate you? Did he dump you in front of everyone at a party? Did he tell you he loved you and then bang somebody else? Like how? Because if memory serves me, he was considerate enough to sit you down in person and tell you he wasn't interested in a commitment. *You're* the one who couldn't handle it and decided to try to destroy my entire family."

"Okay, now you're being melodramatic. I didn't destroy shit."

"Really. So you were doing me a solid when you got naked and crawled into my dad's bed?"

She has the decency to look embarrassed. "Look, I apologized for that."

"Actually, you didn't," I say with an incredulous laugh.

"Yes, I did," she insists.

"No, Emma, you didn't, and no amount of rewriting history will change that. You didn't apologize for *anything*. You went batshit on us. Shared personal messages, things that I told you in confidence, with everyone at school. Trashed me on social media. And now you're standing here telling me I'm somehow to blame for it? Not once did you show any remorse."

I'm so fucking frustrated. I force myself to draw a deep breath, suddenly realizing I don't want to do this. I don't owe her this conversation. I owe her nothing. Ryder's voice fills my head, reminding me I'm allowed to feel what I feel, even if it's hatred.

And the truth is, I don't want to make amends with Emma because some things just aren't mendable. She clearly hasn't matured at all in three years. Still trying to brush her own actions aside and make *me* feel crazy for being pissed at *her*.

"We're not friends, Emma." I let out a drained breath. "So, please, just leave me the hell alone. You do you and I'll do me. And let's keep our friendship where it belongs: in the past."

CHAPTER FORTY-SIX

GIGI

Hat trick

IT'S WEIRD BEING OUT IN THE OPEN WITH RYDER, ESPECIALLY IN the arena. Sometimes we show up together if our training aligns. We hold hands, and I don't miss the looks from his teammates or mine. Cami thinks it's fantastic. Whitney's always asking me what we talk about, refusing to view Ryder as anything other than the silent bad boy from the beginning of the year.

Then there's Case, who's not quite giving us the silent treatment, but not gung-ho to start a conversation either. If I see him, he nods. Says *hello, how ya doing.* Other than that, he's shut me out. I haven't seen his name on my phone since December. Not that I want him to be texting and calling constantly, but I was hoping maybe one day we could be friends.

And while his friendship with Ryder was short-lived, at least they're still performing on the ice.

We're definitely going to win our conference and make it to the championship. The Briar men probably won't win the conference, but they're in good shape get a bid for the tournament.

It's February and blisteringly cold outside when we leave the Graham Center gloved hand in gloved hand. I'm griping because despite what Al Dustin said, there's still no word from Brad Fairlee.

"I was hoping I would hear in January at the *latest*," I grumble, my breath coming out in white puffs. "Because then I could be training with them and maybe even play in Worlds."

The Worlds game is in May, only two months away. Unlike Ryder, I've never actually competed in an international event. And, yes, I knew it was going to be a long shot. They don't just put you on the team and throw you on the world stage. But I was still hopeful I'd receive some sort of news by now.

We walk to his Jeep and he unlocks the doors for us. I eagerly jump in the passenger seat and fumble for the seat warmers. It's freezing out.

"The guys are throwing a party tonight," Ryder says. "You in?"

"Sure. Can I invite Diana? We spoke earlier and she said she felt like going out."

"Yeah, of course. Ask Mya too."

"She has a date tonight."

Because of the frigid weather, the party is primarily indoors. But every now and then someone goes out to smoke a joint or a cigarette, and a gust of icy air slams through the house and brings a chill to my bones.

There's a competitive game of beer pong happening in the kitchen. A solo match between Diana and Shane. Diana, who must have been a polar bear in a previous life because she never gets cold, wears a short skirt and halter top, drawing the eyes of nearly every guy in the kitchen. She just landed a perfect shot that plopped in the cup in front of Shane. Beer splashes over the rim and soaks the front of his T-shirt.

"Did you have to put that much heat behind it?" he grumbles.

"Sure did," she chirps.

Their game continues with a fair amount of trash talk, ending after Diana beats his ass and saunters down the table toward him.

"Are you feeling under the weather tonight? Because I'm still waiting for you to flirt with me," Diana says, her sweet smile belied by her mocking green eyes.

"Why would I do that?" Shane drawls.

"I'm a cheerleader."

He narrows his eyes.

"I thought that was your thing. Bang anyone in a cheer skirt and then leave them brokenhearted and distracted, making me clean up your mess at practice."

Flicking up an eyebrow, she sashays past him without a backward look.

Shane turns to me. "Your girl's got a mouth on her."

"Stop breaking all her friends' hearts," I reply with a shrug, and Ryder chuckles.

Glaring at me, he wanders into the living room.

Beyond the doorway, I spot Beckett and Will in the corner with a dark-haired girl sandwiched between them. Will whispers something in her ear, while Beckett lazily runs his fingers along her arm.

I glance at Ryder. "I can't figure out if they're competing or teaming up."

"Probably the latter." He looks like he has more to say, then shrugs.

"What?" I demand. "Do you have gossip?"

"No. Because I don't gossip. I'm a grown man."

"Do Will and Beck ever hook up?"

I still don't know Beckett well enough, but I try to remember if I've ever caught any bi vibes from Will. No. He's always seemed solidly hetero.

"Do they?" I push when Ryder doesn't respond.

He shrugs again. "Nah, I think they're both into women." A pause. "They have a lot of threesomes."

"Oh my God, really?"

"Don't say anything," my boyfriend warns. "Larsen is such a choir boy. Shane commented on their extracurriculars once, and Will looked like he was going to throw up."

Yeah, that's why I'm surprised to hear it. Will truly is the boy next door. How on earth was he able to be corrupted like this?

Beckett Dunne is a powerful force, I suppose.

Then again, who am I to talk? I'm going around banging guys in opera boxes and saunas.

The next few weeks fly by. Before I know it, it's March and we're playing in the regional semifinal after handily winning our conference and moving on. The single-elimination tournament is being held in Rhode Island this weekend, and I'm not at all worried about tonight's opponent. My girls and I have been rock-solid since the season started.

In the locker room, before Adley arrives to deliver his pep talk, Whitney gives me a look.

"What?" I say.

"Team USA is here."

My heart jumps. "Really?"

"Yup, I saw Adley talking with the head coach and one of the assistants."

I'm not the girl who caves when an anvil of pressure suddenly crushes my chest. If anything, I use the nervous energy to my advantage.

And tonight, I proceed to play the best game of my life.

It's what we call a barnburner. High-intensity, fast-paced, both teams determined to score as many points as possible. Not unlike the exhibition we played in the fall.

"That's what I'm talkin' about!" Adley shouts when I return to the bench after lighting the lamp. He's slapping his clipboard in excitement.

It was my second goal, and it's only the second period. By the time the third rolls around, I've secured myself a nice little hat trick. I know my dad is probably screaming in our great room, watching the live feed at home. I wish Ryder was in the stands cheering me on too, but the men's team is in Vermont tonight, competing in their own semifinals.

I'm riding a high of exhilaration when the game ends. I've never been more accurate in my shots. Never shown the kind of speed I utilized tonight. It's embarrassing, but it's kind of the Gigi Show in the locker room afterward as we celebrate moving on to the regional final in a few days.

Teammates slap me on the shoulder, pat my back. One of the seniors lifts me off my feet, twirling me around.

"What the hell was that, Graham!" she crows, before going to the showers.

I get dressed in a hurry, because I have a feeling Brad Fairlee will be waiting for me outside the locker room. There's no way in hell he *can't* be waiting, not after the way I just played.

My prediction proves correct. Fairlee stands at the end of the corridor chatting with Coach Adley. Their heads turn when Whitney and I emerge from the locker room.

"Gigi," Adley calls. "Do you have a minute?"

Whitney pokes me in the arm, sporting a barely contained smile. She knows what's up. "Go get 'em, tiger," she murmurs.

When I reach the two men, Adley gives me a quick smile and says, "Come find me after."

Once he's gone, Fairlee offers a smile of his own. "That was extraordinary. Some of the best hockey I've ever seen."

I feel myself beaming. "Thanks. It's been a while since I was on fire like that."

"Hat trick, huh? Using some of your father's moves, I see."

No, they're my moves, I want to retort. There's no bodychecking in women's hockey. If I can't be physical, I must be tactical, which means I have the kind of moves my father never needed to keep in his arsenal.

But I'm not about to argue with the man who's about to be my coach.

"Anyway," he says, "I wanted to talk to you."

"Okay." I try to contain my rising excitement.

"My staff and I spent most of the fall putting together our team. You know, it's kind of a difficult process, which is why it's taken so long. Especially because Coach Murphy had his way of doing things. And I have mine. I'm more meticulous. Less worried about stats, and more interested in which players are going to gel on the ice. As you know, there are some talented women playing in the professional league. Most of them are older, more experienced. Many have already competed on the world stage and excelled there."

I nod. I expect the majority of the roster to consist of those women.

"And because there's so much talent available to us in that sphere, we're only taking on two college students for the time being." He smiles at me again. "You're one of the best players out there."

I ignore my quickening pulse. God. This man has mastered the art of drawing out anticipation.

"With that said, I thought I should tell you in person that all the slots have been filled. I'm sorry, Gigi. You won't be making the roster at this time."

CHAPTER FORTY-SEVEN
RYDER

You fall, I pick you up

THE BUS DROPS US OFF ON CAMPUS AROUND ELEVEN, AND IT'S CLOSE to midnight by the time I make it home. Shane and Beckett went directly to a party at the Kappa Beta sorority house, determined to celebrate our advancement to the finals by hooking up with as many women as humanly possible. But as thrilled as I am about the results of tonight's game, I'm exhausted and ready to go home.

When I pull up to the house, I spot the white SUV parked at the curb. Then I glimpse the yellow glow behind the living room curtains. Gigi must have used the key I gave her.

I find her on the couch. Sitting there silently, staring at an action movie on the TV.

"Hey, how long have you been here?" I say from the doorway. "Why didn't you text to say you were coming over?"

"My phone's dead." Her face is devoid of emotion.

Concern flickers through me.

"What's wrong?" I ask immediately. Her entire vibe is off, from her vacant expression to her empty voice. The women's team literally moved on to the finals tonight—she should be beaming from ear to ear right now.

I shrug out of my winter coat and duck out to hang it up. Then I come sit beside her, pulling her onto my lap. The moment we make physical contact, she buries her face in my neck and starts to cry.

"Hey, hey," I say in alarm, rubbing her shoulders. "What's going on? What's wrong?"

"Brad Fairlee showed up to our game tonight to talk to me." Her voice breaks.

And with a sinking feeling, I know there's no way she would be crying if it was good news.

"All the roster slots have been filled," she mutters. "I didn't make it."

"Oh, fuck, babe. I'm sorry."

I tighten my grip and she burrows her face deeper into my skin. Wetness coats my neck, a cold trail sliding down to soak the collar of my shirt.

"I played the best game of my life tonight," she moans. "And it still wasn't good enough for this asshole. He just fucking threw it back in my face."

"Did he say why?"

"He said I'm one of the best college players, but he's not looking at stats. He's trying to focus on some of the older players, the women out of the pros who have more experience competing on the world stage."

It makes sense, but I don't say that out loud. She's far too distraught to hear it right now.

"I can't believe I didn't make it." The words are spoken on a shaky, anguished moan.

I slide my fingers through her hair, stroking gently. "I'm sorry. I'm really fucking sorry."

She tips her head back, her bottom lip trembling wildly as she fights another onslaught of tears.

"I failed," she says weakly.

"You didn't fail."

"Am I on Team USA, Luke? Because last time I checked,

I'm fucking not." She drops her forehead in her palm, breathing unsteadily.

"You're not on Team USA *yet*," I correct gently. "You're still young."

She's doggedly shaking her head, refusing to accede to the point. "I failed."

And suddenly she's shuddering in my arms again, crying harder this time. Choked, breathless, hiccupping sobs. I've never seen her like this before. I've seen her tear up during sad movies. I've seen unshed tears of frustration. Welled-up tears of anger, like the time she kicked me out of her house after we fought.

But this is something else. This is agony. Deep, tortured sobs ripped from the depths of her soul.

And I'm utterly helpless. All I can do is hold her as tight as I can while she shakes in my arms.

"It's okay, let it out," I urge.

I don't know how long she cries for, but her voice is hoarse by the time she settles. Her eyes are swollen and red, and my heart breaks for her.

I'm so goddamn in love with this woman. Seeing her cry makes me want to find the person who did this to her and slam his head through a wall.

I inhale a deep breath, searching for the words to ease her pain.

"You didn't make the team," I finally say. "I know that hurts. But that doesn't mean you won't ever be on it."

She inhales too. Her breathing still sounds ragged to my ears.

"The average age of the current roster is, what? Twenty-six? Twenty-six, G. You have plenty of years ahead of you to make it."

"But the Olympics are next February," she says in a small voice. "Now I'll have to wait four more years. I'll be ancient by then."

I chuckle softly. "Their current team captain is thirty-two. You're not ancient, I guarantee it. Look, maybe you won't compete in these Olympics," I relent, and she releases another choked sob. "But the national team plays a lot of other significant games. There's Worlds every year. The Four Nations Cup. Maybe next year, Fairlee will have an open slot. Or maybe it'll happen the year after."

"Or maybe I'll never make the team."

She starts to cry again, and although it kills me to make it worse, we promised each other we'd always be honest.

"Maybe you won't," I agree softly.

She rears back, releasing a cross between a laugh and a wheeze. "You are so bad at this."

"Maybe you won't ever make the team," I repeat. "Doesn't change the fact that you're the single greatest player in women's college hockey right now. Fairlee said so himself. He's not looking at stats, because if he was, you'd be on that roster in a heartbeat."

"But why don't I have that other quality he's looking for? What the hell about me is lacking?"

"Nothing about you is lacking. Ever. You're perfect, exactly the way you are. Even with all your flaws. Like needing to be the best. And your taste in music."

Her answering laugh is a bit wobbly.

"Nobody likes failure, G. But I maintain that this isn't failure. This is just one moment in time."

"A moment in time," she echoes weakly.

"Yes, and right now, in this moment, you're down. But that's okay because I'm here to lift you up."

"Always?" she whispers, peering at me with those big gray eyes.

"Always. You fall, I pick you up. *Always.*"

Her tears are drying up, her breathing growing steady. She loops her arms around my shoulders and presses her face into my neck. "Thank you."

CHAPTER FORTY-EIGHT

RYDER

This is it, Luke

BOTH THE MEN'S AND WOMEN'S TEAMS DOMINATE THE REGIONAL finals. For the first time in a decade, both Briar programs will be competing in their respective Frozen Fours this April.

After crushing our opponent in the regional tournament, we're riding the momentum and eager to get into the arena with the final four teams. Minnesota Duluth and Notre Dame also made it through. But the real upset of the playoffs was Arizona State, who slayed the dragon known as UConn to advance forward. Luckily, they're facing Notre Dame next, and I pray we don't face them in the final. I haven't shared the ice with my former teammate Michael Klein since we were eighteen and I was cracking his jaw open with my fist.

We have two weeks off before the game. And we lucked out this year—our Frozen Four is being held in Boston. The women's tournament is a week before ours, and Gigi's lying in my bed when she suddenly rolls over and says, "Do you feel like coming to Vegas with me?"

"Are you asking me to marry you?" I inquire politely.

"No, I'm asking you to come to Vegas and watch us play. My parents will be there. My brother too."

"Gee, great. Can't wait to see them."

She lightly punches me in the arm. "Come on. They've warmed up to you a lot."

"Only your mom."

In fact, Hannah Graham is pretty much my best friend now. Gigi teases me about how frequently we text. It started after the winter holidays, and at first, I pretended it made me uncomfortable. Shrugged it off. Said it was weird she kept contacting me.

That was all talk. Whenever her mother checks in on me, it unleashes a flood of warmth in my chest. It's a totally foreign sensation.

But it's not entirely unwelcome.

A few days later, I'm boarding a plane with Gigi. Since I have the time off and we both have a good handle on our schoolwork, we decided to skip classes and go a day early to get in some tourist shit. She's never been to Vegas.

She seems to regret that decision within hours of our arrival, though, looking around the strip in dismay. "Oh God, these lights are the worst. Why are they all shining at me? It's the middle of the day! I feel like I'm on a spaceship." She glares at a gold fountain shooting ten-foot-high water arcs as if it personally insulted her. "This is not fun. I'm not this extravagant."

I link our fingers together, chuckling. "Not my cup of tea either."

Our gazes lock. I lick my lips.

"Should we go back to the hotel?" I drawl.

"Yes, please."

We spend the rest of the evening fucking. I go down on her in the huge shower in our room, tormenting her by denying her an orgasm for a solid forty minutes. She returns the favor by blowing me in front of the floor-to-ceiling windows. I don't care that everyone can see my bare ass and that someone's probably filming us and posting it online. All I care about is how warm her mouth is and how wet her tongue is, how silky smooth her lips are as they travel along my shaft.

We lie in bed afterward. I stroke her hair. Reach for the remote and flip channels until I land on TSBN. They're airing a countdown show touting the ten greatest hockey players of all time. Number one is Gigi's dad.

As his face fills the flat-screen, I chuckle. "I can't wait to see him tomorrow. I'm sure he'll be super delightful."

"I don't feel sorry for you at all. Now you know how it feels to be around a prickly asshole who doesn't want to make conversation with you."

"I wasn't that bad."

"You were worse. You communicated exclusively in shrugs. Infuriating jackass."

I grin. "Call me that again, and I'll go back to shrugging instead of talking."

"Nope. The floodgates have opened. You can't dam that back up, baby."

She's right. I can't.

I turn off the TV and move onto my side, propping up on one elbow. I bite my lip as I gaze down at her.

"I don't want anybody else. You know that, right?"

Gigi blinks. "Where did that come from?"

"I don't know. I just need you to know I don't want to be with anyone else. Ever."

A soft smile tugs on her lips. "Me too." She reaches up to touch my face, rubbing the stubble on my jaw. "This is it, Luke. I think we both know that."

Yes, I think we do.

I jerk when the loud growl of her stomach vibrates between our bodies. We skipped dinner because we were busy having sex.

"You doing okay there, Gisele?"

"I'm so hungry. Why does this hotel not have room service?" she moans.

"Because you specifically asked me to book one that didn't," I remind her, rolling my eyes. "To quote you, you're on a championship diet and must not be tempted by room service dessert."

"Why do you listen to me?"

"I'll start ignoring your wishes," I promise.

She snorts and climbs out of bed. "Well, I guess we're venturing onto the horrible strip again in search of nourishment. I need to put something in my belly."

"I'll give you something to put in your belly."

"I don't know what that means, Ryder. Are you talking about a baby, or is it a semen swallowing thing?"

I keel over in laughter. "Why do you always have to ruin my jokes by digging too deep into them?"

"Tell better jokes," she advises.

I haul her off the bed. "Come on. Vegas, take two."

Two days later, the morning of the women's Frozen Four championship game in which Briar will play Ohio State, I wake up with a huge smile on my face. Although that's what happens when there's a gorgeous woman in your bed and she's giving you a handjob. She brings me to the edge and then shoves me right over it, while I lie there panting. Gigi's equally giddy, beaming and bouncing with excitement as she gets dressed.

"I wish I could spend all day with you," she says, crawling back on the bed to throw her fully dressed body on top of my naked one.

After last night, I'm in full agreement. I just want to keep the high going. Stay naked with her forever, but she has a championship game to play.

"I need to get to the rink," she says reluctantly. "And my parents' flight lands soon."

I offered to pick them up, but Hannah said they're fine taking a cab. I suspect Garrett just didn't want me as his chauffeur because he hates me.

But there's nothing I can do about it now, nothing to change the way I feel about his daughter and the way she feels about me. She's mine and I'm hers, and he'll have to deal with it eventually.

After Gigi is gone, I shower and dress, then reluctantly leave the hotel to meet the Grahams for lunch. Garrett and Wyatt talk to each other the whole time, while Hannah and I have our own side conversation. I anticipate quite a lot of this in my future.

I'm drowning in relief when it's finally time to head for the arena, where we have excellent seats directly behind the Briar bench. The game is being televised, so cameras are everywhere. Flashbulbs going off. A hum of excitement travels through the rink and it's contagious. I rub my hands together as we settle in our seats. My gaze seeks out Gigi, landing on the back of her jersey. #44. Her long dark ponytail is sticking out of her helmet.

The game is fast paced from the get-go, but it's exactly what you'd expect from the championship. The best female college players are on that ice right now.

Halfway through the first period, Gigi twists around to grin at us from behind her visor. She's just heaved herself onto the bench after scoring a goal that sent the entire rink into a deafening frenzy.

"She looks feral," Wyatt remarks. "You guys raised a feral child."

I snicker.

"Hey, blame him," Hannah says, jerking a thumb at her husband. "He's the one with the hockey gene."

I'm fully on board for this matchup. On the edge of my seat the entire time. It's like a seesaw. First Briar has all the momentum, leading Ohio State around by their noses. Then a sudden momentum shift, and Ohio is wiping the ice with Briar. Then another abrupt shift, and Whitney Cormac is on a breakaway. She doesn't score, but Briar's on the attack. They're going hard—Whitney, Gigi, and Camila Martinez shooting bullets at the net like a trio of snipers.

I've never experienced more pride than when I see Gigi pivoting behind the net like a fucking professional. Distracting the goalie, creating an opportunity for Camila to get a shot in the back door.

2–1, Briar.

The second period is much of the same, although I notice a couple of the Ohio girls starting to get more physical than they should. Sometimes it's just incidental contact. Sometimes it's a surreptitious check cloaked in incidental contact. It usually depends on the refs whether they'll call it or not.

The opposing center, #28, is taking a lot of liberties, though. The chick's at least five-nine, so a decent bit taller than Gigi. But my woman holds her own. Angling her body with ease, winning every face-off against #28. And yet the chick is relentless.

At one point Garrett jumps to his feet, shouting at the refs. "The hell are you doing down there! Use your eyes! That was clearly checking!"

His outburst draws attention. Several pairs of eyes widen in recognition.

Hannah yanks him back to his seat. "Garrett, sit down. I didn't bring your fake beard and glasses."

Wyatt laughs.

As he resettles in his seat, Garrett exchanges a look with me. I can't deny I'm also a bit annoyed.

"This chick is too rough," I tell him.

He nods. "Those refs better start paying more attention."

Luckily, it's as if #28 realizes how close she is to earning herself a lifelong vendetta from Garrett Graham. She backs off. They're tied 2–2 now, after a goal courtesy of an Ohio winger.

Christ, this game is a nail-biter. I lean forward with my forearms on my knees, my eyes glued to the action below.

Gigi's got the puck and is crossing the blue line. She dumps it; then she and Whitney give chase, tangling behind the net with an Ohio defenseman. #28 throws herself into the mix and I'm instantly on guard. So is Garrett. Our hawklike gazes focus on the net.

"Get it out," Garrett is murmuring. "It's too dangerous back there with number twenty-eight."

I agree. Normally I'd want Gigi to hold her ground, but I don't like this girl. I breathe a sigh of relief when Gigi snaps the puck into the boards and skates toward the bench when Adley calls for a substitution.

She's trying to make the line change, but #28 is breathing down her neck, not letting her get off. Fucking asshole. I understand wanting to put pressure on your opponent, but come on. There's still honor amongst hockey players.

Two new forwards pop on, one of them coming to Gigi's aid against the boards. The Briar player wins the battle for the puck and careens off while Gigi gets in position in the slot. She's shouting something. The puck snaps out and lands on her stick at the same time she collides with #28.

It's a total accident. Even I, who now has a personal blood feud against #28, can tell she didn't mean to do it. Her stick breaks, knocking her off balance. And the abrupt shift in body weight sends her slamming into Gigi's back.

We all watch in horror as Gigi flies forward. My panicked eyes track the blurry streak of #44 as Gigi slams headfirst into the boards, helmet flying off.

She goes sprawling onto her stomach, one hand still gripping her stick, the other one outstretched on the ice near her discarded helmet. We're all on our feet. At first, the crowd continues screaming because they don't realize what's going on. Then the entire rink goes deathly silent when the fans realize she's not getting back up.

My heart stops. Just quits beating in my chest, a useless, motionless mass of pure fear.

"She's just winded," Wyatt says, his green eyes glued to the ice. He sounds like he's trying to convince himself. "She's fine—"

Before he even finishes speaking, I'm racing down the aisle. Pushing through people without excusing myself, Gigi's dad hot on my heels.

We practically vault over the wall below to the walkway between the bleachers and the plexiglass.

"Let me through," Garrett snaps at the staff member in front of the door to the bench. "That's my daughter."

I'm frantically peering at the ice, my heart still not beating because she's still not moving. There's a ref bent over her, as well as Coach Adley and some of her teammates. Finally, I've had enough of the man at the door. I step forward and attempt to shove him to the side. I think it's one of the Briar assistant coaches, but I don't give a shit about being polite.

"You can't go out there," he insists, getting in my face again.

A fucking stampede wouldn't be able to stop me from getting to Gigi.

"Like hell I can't," I growl. And then I give him another firm shove, forcibly moving him out of my way. "That's my wife out there."

CHAPTER FORTY-NINE
GIGI

We got married

"So. Um. Yeah. We got married."

You can hear a pin drop in the women's locker room. The team doctor and EMTs just left, satisfied I'm in no danger of a concussion. Despite what it looked like to the crowd, I didn't actually hit my head out there—the helmet came off after I already landed on the ice. But the wind was completely knocked out of me. Lying face down, ears ringing and lungs seized, I forgot how to breathe for a moment there.

Now, Ryder sits beside me on the bench, while my parents and brother stand in front of us. Speechless. Now that the doctors are gone, the bomb Ryder dropped before I went down can finally be addressed. There's no defusing it—that thing went *boom* the moment he broke the news to my parents. But I'm hoping the fallout of the explosion won't be too devastating.

I bite my lip in trepidation, waiting for someone to speak.

"G, I love you. You're my sister. But that's the most cliché thing I've ever heard in my life. *I got married in Vegas.* That's so generic I wouldn't even write a song about it."

"Wyatt," Mom warns.

Dad still hasn't uttered a single word. He's completely

expressionless. Not even anger on his face. Nothing. It's like staring at a brick wall, a cardboard box, some inanimate object that's incapable of telling you how it feels.

"Look, I know this is unexpected," I tell them.

Because it was. Totally and undeniably unexpected.

But not thoughtless.

Despite what my brother thinks, we didn't do the predictably tacky Vegas elopement. We weren't married by a jovial Elvis, spurred by alcohol in our veins. We were stone-cold sober. We applied for an after-hours license because, well, that's possible in Vegas. And then we had an entire night to think about it. To change our minds. We didn't have to go back to the courthouse the next morning, but we did.

Ryder's still hovering over me, running an agitated hand over my forehead because he doesn't believe I didn't hit my head. It's cute. I touch his cheek in reassurance, and the moment my fingers connect with his skin, the anxiety leaves his eyes. I have that power over him, and he has the same power over me.

Like the night I sobbed in his arms after Fairlee shot down my dreams like a well-trained sniper and left me bleeding from a bullet to the heart. Bang. Dream dead. Ryder made it better that night. He makes it better every night. And day. And minute.

We make each other better.

"I know everything you're going to say." I keep talking when it's obvious my parents won't. "You think we're too young. It's too fast. But you're wrong. And yes, I can imagine thousands of stupid, idealistic girls before me saying those exact same words after running off with their boyfriends. Wyatt's right, it sounds cliché. But Ryder and I aren't stupid." I shrug. "And in case you're just joining the party, neither of us has an idealistic bone between us."

My brother snorts softly.

"We know exactly what we're getting into. It's not going to be perfect. We're going to run into issues. Life's going to hit us hard from all directions, all the time. But we're choosing to do life together. We went into this with our eyes wide open."

I notice a sheen of tears clinging to Mom's eyelashes, and for a moment I revert into a little kid.

"Please don't be mad at me," I beg her, but deep down I know even if she stays mad forever, that's just something I will have to deal with.

I've made my choice. He's it.

Mom walks over and sits on my other side, putting her arm around me. "No, I'm not mad. I'm glad you recognize it's not going to be all rainbows." She touches my cheek reassuringly. "But this probably isn't the time or place to discuss…this…in any further detail." She stands up. "Are you sure I can't take you to the hospital?"

I shake my head. "I really don't want to. The paramedic said I didn't even need to go into concussion protocol."

I can't play the rest of the game, though, which is fucking brutal. But the team doctor wouldn't sign off on it, despite the EMTs saying it would probably be okay. It was the word *probably* that made Dr. Parminder frown. So now I'm benched. There's half a period left, and I should be out there, skating with my team. Or at least sitting on the bench, cheering them on. But Coach Adley made me change out of my uniform, so I'm not even dressed for that.

"I'm going back out there," I say firmly, rising to my feet. "Even if I can't be on the ice with them, I can still scream my lungs out."

Ryder takes my hand. "It's gonna be loud out there."

"My head doesn't hurt," I grumble. "I swear. It only took me a while to get up because I was winded."

I glance at my family again. At the brick wall that used to be my father. His prolonged silence finally triggers something in me. Impatience. Annoyance. Maybe a bit of anger too.

"Are you going to say something?" I move to stand directly in front of him, trying to force eye contact. "Anything at all? Because you're starting to scare me a little."

His gray eyes lock with mine.

And finally, he speaks.

"This is, truly, the stupidest thing you've ever done."

I flinch as if I've been struck.

"And I've never been more disappointed in you."

"Garrett," Mom says sharply.

But it's too late. The bullet that took me down when Fairlee kept me off Team USA finds its mark again.

This time, courtesy of my father.

CHAPTER FIFTY
RYDER

The father-daughter problem

MY NEW MOTHER-IN-LAW COMES TO SEE ME A FEW DAYS AFTER the Briar women win the Frozen Four and bring the trophy back to our college after three years in other hands. She calls ahead, so I'm not surprised when I find her on my doorstep.

"Hey, come in," I say, hanging up her coat for her. "Want something to drink? Coffee? Water? A shit ton of liquor to make up for these past three days?"

Hannah laughs. "Let's start with the water and save the shots for after."

She looks around as I lead her deeper into the house toward the kitchen.

"It's cleaner than I thought," she says with a grin. "I was expecting a bachelor pad."

"Nah, we're not total barbarians." I pause, offering a sheepish look. "Shane's mom sends a cleaning lady twice a month."

That gets me another laugh. In the kitchen, she sits at the table while I drift toward the fridge to grab some water.

"Is Gigi moving in? She said she hadn't decided yet."

I glance over my shoulder. "I think she'll just unofficially crash here until the semester is over. And then we'll find a place together in Hastings."

Shane and Beckett are still giving me serious grief about that. When I first got back from Vegas and told them I'd married Gigi, they were both highly amused. Ragged me about it for hours. Shane spent a full day referring to me as Mr. Graham. Beckett gave me honeymoon tips and some Viagra pills.

It was all fun and games until they realized this wasn't just a lark or a marriage-on-paper-only sort of situation. Eventually I'd be moving out. We won't be living here together for senior year. Since then, they've been a bit subdued.

When I pass Hannah the water bottle, I notice her eyes drop to the silver band on the ring finger of my left hand. Gigi and I grabbed the rings this morning from a small jewelry shop on Main Street. It still startles me every time I look down and see it there.

I don't even remember which one of us suggested we tie the knot. I think it might have been me? I just remember walking hand in hand down the Strip that first night in Vegas and thinking there's nobody else I want to hold hands with for the rest of my life. And for some inexplicable reason, Gigi agreed.

"Married," her mom says with an amused look.

"Married," I confirm.

It's pretty funny when you think about it. We haven't even been together a year.

"I know you think we're crazy," I say, shrugging.

"Actually, no. I don't. I know my daughter. She doesn't enter into things lightly. And I think I'm starting to know you too. You're not impulsive."

"No," I agree.

I'm the opposite, in fact. Calculated. Perpetually skeptical of people who jump first and think later.

"Look," I say roughly, after a short silence falls, "you don't have to pretend you're on board with this or that you even support it. I give you permission to react like your husband. Go full silent treatment on us."

"Hey, he's trying."

She's not wrong—for the past three days, Garrett has texted, called, and left multiple voicemails for Gigi, asking to talk. But his daughter is stubborn. She's the one refusing to accept the olive branch.

"He hurt her," I say quietly.

"I know. He regrets it. You two just caught him by surprise. Garrett doesn't like surprises. And no, I'm not secretly upset."

"Really?"

She reaches across the table and takes both my hands in hers. "I know you lost your mother at a young age," she starts.

I shift in my chair, discomfort tensing my shoulders because I don't know how much Gigi told her parents about my background. I didn't ask her to keep it a secret, what my dad did, but the idea of her parents knowing is still unsettling.

"It's not an easy thing growing up without a mother."

I shrug. "I had foster moms."

She searches my face. "Were they good to you?"

I give an abrupt shake of the head. My throat tightens.

"That's what I figured." She squeezes my hands. "And that's why I came over. I wanted you to know that I'm here for you. I mean it, Luke. I have no doubt you'll be in our lives for a long time to come, and I'm not at all bothered by that."

A thought tickles the back of mind. About my own mother. If she were alive and I brought home some girl I married, I wonder how she would react. If she'd be wise enough to recognize that Gigi actually isn't "some girl" but my entire life.

But I'll never know. And that bleak notion scrapes at something inside me. I blink. Blink again. The moisture in my eyes doesn't dissipate. It just wells up, distorting my vision.

"Hey," Hannah says gently. "It's okay."

I twist my head to avoid her gaze. I feel raw and exposed.

So she gets out of her chair and crouches in front of mine. "I'm sorry. I shouldn't have brought up your mother."

"No, it's okay." My voice breaks. I drag my forearm across my face, wiping my eyes with my sleeve.

Before I can stop her, Gigi's mom pulls me in for a tight hug and now I'm crying in her arms like a little kid.

This is so fucking embarrassing.

She reaches up and smooths a lock of hair away from my forehead, unfazed by my tears. "All I was trying to say is, you're family now. I know I'm not your real mom, but I think I did pretty well with my own kids."

"You did," I say thickly.

"So if you ever need anything, I'm a call or text away. I'll always be here for you."

I suddenly hear the front door opening. Shane and Beckett's voices. I quickly scrub my eyes, while Hannah gets up and sits back in her seat. She takes a sip of her water, then sets the bottle down and sighs.

"So. Now how are we going to solve the father-daughter problem?"

That is easier said than done. A week passes and Gigi still refuses to speak to her father. Garrett's gotten so desperate he even called me and asked me to intervene on his behalf. I said I'd try. Because one, he's my idol. And two, he's now my father-in-law.

But…she's my wife.

Wife.

It still feels surreal to say that. My whole life, nothing has ever felt entirely right aside from hockey. When I'm out there on the ice, chasing a puck, slapping a shot at net, that's when I've always felt most like myself. A sense of belonging, like I was exactly where I was supposed to be.

I've only felt that way one other time in my life.

When I said, "I do," to Gigi in the courthouse.

We've chosen each other. And she's right—I don't expect it to be easy. Life never is. But she's the one I want to face all the adversity with. She's my partner, and no matter what happens, we'll always have each other's backs.

So I need to have her back now, even though I recognize that her father regrets every word he said in the locker room that day.

But man, those words cut her deep. She's tried to please him her entire life, and he goes and tells her he's disappointed in her? No, that he's never been *more* disappointed in her?

It's going to take a long time for her to forget that. Garrett knows, and that's why he's at the point of desperation where he's turning to me. I know it must kill him. It's obvious he disapproves of our marriage.

Oddly enough, someone who doesn't disapprove—other than my mother-in-law—is my new brother-in-law. Wyatt texted me from the airport the morning he left Vegas.

WYATT:

> Hurt my sister and I'll hurt you. You feel me, Bill?

ME:

> Bill?

WYATT:

> Brother-in-law. Tried to write BIL but autocorrect didn't like it. So you're Bill now. Don't hurt her and we'll be good.

ME:

> I won't, and cool.

WYATT:

Welcome to the family. I figure we need to make an effort to get along. Now that we're stuck with you forever.

ME:

Thanks, Bill.

Wyatt isn't flying to Boston to watch me play in the Frozen Four tomorrow night, but Hannah and Garrett are coming. Garrett's probably hoping Gigi will have no choice but to acknowledge his existence if they're sitting together.

In another upset, Arizona beat out Notre Dame in their matchup two days ago, so we're playing them in the National Championship. I don't love it. I'm worried about playing with Michael Klein again. We didn't face Arizona this season, so who knows how he'll behave during play.

The entire team, including Jensen and the coaching staff, go out for dinner that night. Those of us who aren't minors are even allowed to order one pint of beer—and only one—as Jensen so graciously informs us. Then he adds that anyone who takes him up on the offer needs to drink three glasses of water to combat the unwise choice. Still, more than a few of us order that pint.

News of my nuptials has traveled through the roster, and I notice Colson eyeing my wedding band on several different occasions during dinner. The one time our eyes meet, he mutters something under his breath and turns away in disgust. Next to him, Jordan Trager glares at me in solidarity. I reach for my pint glass in resignation.

We've just returned to the hotel and are striding into the lobby when my father-in-law texts to say he's at the bar and do I have a minute.

"I'll meet you upstairs," I tell Shane, who nods and heads up to our room.

Some guys from the opposing team are milling in the lobby wearing their hockey jackets. Eyes widen and guys murmur in excitement when they catch sight of Garrett Graham striding across the lobby from the bar.

"Hey," he says when he reaches me. He must feel the stares because he rubs the back of his neck and grimaces. "I was going to suggest we grab a drink at the bar, but what do you say we go elsewhere?"

I nod. "Good idea."

We leave the hotel and give the street a quick scan. There's a bookstore at the end of the block with an adjacent coffee shop, so we walk toward it.

"I have no right asking you for favors," Garrett starts ruefully. "I know I haven't been very welcoming to you. When you came home with Stan for the holidays. When you showed interest in my camp. I probably could've been...less dickish."

I shrug. "All good. I don't hold grudges."

"I usually don't either. But I will say"—he offers a pointed frown—"I don't love that you didn't ask for my blessing before you married her."

I tip my head at him, curious. "Would you have given it?"

"No."

A snort slips out. "Then, better ask forgiveness than permission, right? Because I would've married her either way. I—" My jaw drops. "Holy shit."

"What is it—"

But I'm already venturing toward the partition between the café and bookstore. I stop near a table of nonfiction books in front of the easel that caught my attention. Displayed on it is a large poster print depicting a barren white landscape bisected by a rushing river. Block letters read:

HORIZONS: THE YUKON TERRITORY

Holy.

Shit.

"What are you doing?" Garrett comes up beside me.

I scan the interior of the store until I see it—the small line formed beside another easel holding the same poster. At the front of the line is a table with stacks of CDs sitting on one side and a pile of headshots on the other. Behind the table sits an elderly man in a red plaid shirt and corn husk–yellow suspenders. Rounding out his outfit are an old-timey cap and black-rimmed frames.

"Dude, that's Dan Grebbs," I tell Gigi's dad.

"Who?"

"The nature sounds guy your daughter is obsessed with. Come on, we need to get in line."

He's dumbfounded. "Why?"

"Because Gigi loves him, and I want to get her a signed photo. I'd get the CD too, but she probably already has this track downloaded."

Ignoring his bemused face, I get in line, which is surprisingly long considering this is an eighty-year-old man who records nature sounds with his own equipment. Dude doesn't even add instrumental to it, but I guess that's part of his charm.

Garrett sighs and says, "I'll go grab the coffee."

The line moves slowly, so I'm still standing there when he returns with two Styrofoam cups. He hands me one.

"Black okay?"

"Great, thanks."

He's staring at me again.

"What?" I mutter.

"Nothing," he says, but he keeps staring.

The line edges closer. Now I can hear what Grebbs is saying to the woman in front of him. She's in her fifties, which seems like the appropriate age to be waiting for an autograph from this man.

"...for a lad in his late twenties still craving excitement, the Yukon was desolate. Suffocating even, despite the vast openness all around me. But once I let my mind clear, once I embraced the rush of the Klondike and the brisk kiss of the air drifting toward me from Tombstone Mountain, I was changed."

"That is...incredible. Thank you for the work you do, Mr. Grebbs. I truly mean that."

"It's an honor to bring you these experiences, my dear." He hands her a CD and headshot.

The couple after her doesn't linger, just gets their shit signed and leaves, and soon I'm in front of Gigi's aural idol, feeling out of place and, frankly, stupid.

But Garrett nudges me, and I step forward.

"Uh. Hi. Mr. Grebbs. Huge fan."

From the corner of my eye, I see Garrett pressing his lips together to stop a laugh.

"Well, really, it's my wife who's the fan. She has all your... soundscapes."

Garrett coughs into his hand.

"Seriously, she listens to you religiously. In the car, on her runs, when she's meditating."

"How wonderful." Dan Grebbs has kind eyes. There's something as soothing about him as his sounds.

And I will never, ever tell Gigi I just thought of his sounds as soothing. She will use that against me forever.

"What is your wife's name, young man?"

"Gigi." I spell it for him.

He picks up a black felt-tipped marker and bends over, studiously inscribing what looks like an essay down the entire side of his headshot. He's wearing the plaid-and-suspenders combo in the photo. I'm pretty sure it's the same one.

He hands it to me. "So thoughtful of you to do this for your wife."

"Thank you."

We step away to make room for the next fan. I roll up the

headshot because I don't want to fold it. Garrett continues to watch me.

"Quit looking at me like that," I grumble. "I know it's stupid."

He just sighs, shaking his head to himself. "You really love her."

"Till the day I die," I say simply.

His fingers curl tight around his coffee cup. "Is she going to avoid me forever?" he asks miserably.

"I hope not. But you know her—she's stubborn." I shrug at him. "And she's spent her whole life trying to please you."

Guilt flashes in his eyes.

I'm quick to reassure him. "You didn't put the pressure on her, I get that. She puts it on herself and she's aware of that. But that doesn't change the fact that all she's ever wanted to do is make you proud."

"I *am* proud. And not just because she's good at hockey. Look, I said things in anger. But it wasn't actually anger. It was fear." He closes his eyes briefly. "Because I knew in that moment that I lost her. She doesn't belong to me anymore."

My head jerks in surprise.

"I don't mean belonging like property," he says gruffly.

"No, I know what you mean."

"She's my little girl. You'll understand what that means one day, if you two ever have kids. If you have a daughter."

He keeps talking as we make our way down the block toward the hotel.

"I wish she'd just let me explain things."

"She will. Eventually."

He gives a wry laugh. "That's not very encouraging."

"If you want your own personal cheerleader, I ain't your man."

"I figured."

"I will talk to her again on your behalf, though. I don't think anything good comes out of you two not talking—"

"Luke Ryder?"

A man wearing glasses and a sports coat appears in our path. Instantly, my guard shoots up ten feet.

"Yes?" I say warily.

A hungry gleam lights his eyes and suddenly he reaches into his pocket for a mini recorder that he shoves in my face.

"Do you have any comment about your father's upcoming parole hearing?"

CHAPTER FIFTY-ONE
RYDER

Media storm

A COLD, FLUTTERY SENSATION WHISPERS THROUGH MY CHEST. IT travels south, becoming a queasy churning that makes my gut clench.

I'm stunned speechless. Not that I'm a huge talker to begin with, but in other circumstances I'd at least be able to muster a *fuck you* or *get lost*.

But I've got nothing.

"My sources tell me you're refusing to speak against him at the hearing," the reporter pushes when I don't respond. "Are you in support of your father being released?"

He's not the only reporter circling. Several others lurk in the hotel lobby, sharks who've smelled my blood. A man holding a notebook and a woman with a cameraman in tow hurry over.

"Luke Ryder?" the woman says eagerly. "Do you have any comment regarding—"

Garrett notes my expression, and his own promptly hardens to stone. He barks, "No comment," and then lays a hand on my arm to usher me away.

In the elevator, he gives me a grave look. "What floor?"

"Nine," I say weakly.

A few minutes later, Garrett and I walk into my room. Word of the sharks downstairs has already spread through the Briar grape-vine, because several of my friends are already in the room. They alternate between eyeing me uneasily and trying not to gawk at Garrett Graham.

"Dude, there's a bunch of reporters downstairs asking questions," Shane says grimly.

"Yeah, just saw them."

I take a breath and go to the mini fridge. I grab a bottle of water, but I don't uncap it. I just press it to my forehead. I'm feeling hot. Tight with discomfort.

"What the fuck is going on?" I mutter to the guys.

Beckett speaks up from the small love seat across the room. "Your old buddy Michael Klein gave an interview last night. Clips of it went viral."

My jaw clenches. "What did he say?"

Shane meets my eyes. "Wasn't great."

"What did he say?" I repeat.

My friends give me the rundown. A sports blog ran video profiles on some of the Arizona players, including Klein. When asked about his previous relationship with me, he basically painted me as a goon with a temper who went after him for no reason in the locker. Oh, but don't worry, Mr. Martyr went on to say, "It's all water under the bridge," and "He's moved past it."

But that's not the part that went viral. When asked whether my actions after the World Juniors shocked him, Klein said he wasn't surprised at all, seeing as how violence runs in my family.

"Fucking hell," Garrett mutters in disapproval.

The reporter then took that statement and eagerly ran with it. Did some digging, found out about my past, and wrote a follow-up article. A source in the Maricopa Attorney's Office apparently told them I was refusing to attend the hearing, and now it's being posited that I'm not speaking against my father because I *want* him to be released.

What I want is to throw up.

Other bodies drift in, including Coach Jensen and Coach Maran, and soon there's a full-scale meeting in process. My entire body feels itchy, like there're ants creeping along my skin. Shane and Beckett know about my dad, about Owen, but nobody else does, and now I'm forced to stand there and discuss the darkest thing that's ever happened to me.

I don't offer details, not to the level I did with Gigi. I give my teammates only the gist of it. Dad had gun. Gun go bang. Mom dead.

They're all stricken. Even Trager looks upset.

"It's fine," I tell them, so uncomfortable I want to crawl into a hole.

I wish Gigi were here, but she's not coming until tomorrow. I'm sure if I called her, she'd hop in the car and break every speed limit to get here. But tonight was supposed to be about my team. Dinner, game tape, our last official night of a roller-coaster season full of ups and downs.

"Why is this Klein asshole giving interviews about shit that's none of his business?" The outraged demand comes from Rand Hawley.

"For real," Trager actually agrees with Rand. "I'm starting to think this dude deserved to have his jaw wired shut."

I shrug. "He did. Said a lot of nastier shit in the locker room after the game."

"What did he say?" Colson glances at me from his perch against the wall next to Garrett. They exchanged a hug when Case came in. I didn't love seeing that.

"Nothing that bears repeating." A sigh lodges in my throat as I look around the room. "You guys have played with me all year. You know I don't have a temper. It takes a lot to trigger me."

"So this fucking asshole was running his mouth back then, and now he's doing it again," Trager says. "You know what they're trying to do, right? They're trying to distract us with this superfluous bullshit so that our heads aren't in the game."

Angry murmurs go through the room. Me, I'm more impressed by the fact that Trager knows the word *superfluous*.

"Well, fuck that," Rand pipes up, nodding at Trager. "It's not going to work."

"No," Colson agrees. "It won't."

Coach Jensen finally speaks, his hard gaze landing on me. "We can skip the press conference tomorrow morning if you want. I have no issue telling the officials we're not interested."

There's always a pregame press conference between the two teams, usually comprising of the captains and assistants. Michael Klein happens to be the latter.

"It's fine," I tell Coach. "I'll do it."

His dark eyes focus on my face. "Your head will be where it needs to be tomorrow?"

"Always," I promise.

The coaches head for the door, along with Garrett, who claps me on the arm before leaving. Everyone else starts to disperse too. I walk various guys to the door and accept various words of encouragement that I don't want to hear. I just want to be left the hell alone. I even wish Shane weren't here right now, and he's my roommate.

Colson lingers, then gestures for me to step into the hall. I flip the lock to keep the door open and follow him out.

"You okay?" he says brusquely.

I offer a faint smile. "You really care if I am?"

"I do. Also..." Case lets out a breath. "I never thought I'd say this in my life, but... I sort of miss you."

"Bullshit."

He laughs. "Right? Who in their right mind would miss your prolonged silences and asshole remarks?"

I run a hand through my hair, and Case's gaze fixes on my left hand. Just like that, his laughter dies.

"Christ, Ryder. You married my ex-girlfriend," he says flatly.

"No, I married my wife."

He's quiet for a long moment, pale blue eyes focusing on his feet. Then he sighs again.

"I don't know if I'm ready to, like, hang out with you guys. Just the three of us."

"I wouldn't put anyone through that uncomfortable torture."

He snickers. "But I'll get over it," he says, shrugging. "You're not a bad guy, Luke. I know you didn't do this on purpose."

"I didn't." I sigh too. "Can't help who you fall for."

"No. You can't." He sticks out his hand. "We're good if you want."

"I want."

I shake his hand, but he surprises me by yanking me in for a side hug. I return it, giving him a determined look when we pull apart.

"I won't let this Klein bullshit screw with my head," I promise.

"Never thought you would." There's a steely look in his own eyes. "Those assholes are going down tomorrow. Don't worry, we'll make them regret pulling this stunt."

———

The next morning, I awake to a missed call from Julio Vega. I'm instantly sick to my stomach, because I highly doubt the Dallas GM is calling to wish me luck in the finals today. Just *happens* to coincide with the fact that my sordid family history suddenly became hot news.

My hand is shaking as I step onto the balcony holding my phone. Shane is still asleep. I woke up ahead of the alarm, as if my subconscious sensed I missed a call from the man who holds my future in his hands.

There's a chill in the air, and I wish I threw my hoodie on first. I stand there in a T-shirt and track pants, cold fingers scrolling to return his call.

"Luke, I'm glad I caught you. Sorry for the early hour."

"No problem. I was up."

"Some media storm you found yourself in," Vega says, cutting right to the chase. "Way to draw focus away from what really matters, huh? It's the Frozen Four. That's what they should be writing about."

My stomach twists into knots. "I'm sorry, sir. I had nothing to do with—"

"Oh, you misunderstand. I'm not laying the blame at your door. It's those vultures. And judging by the source of the initial article, it seems your opponent was trying to unnerve you."

"Seems so."

"Well, I wanted to touch base and let you know you have the full support of myself and the franchise on this matter."

I'm so shocked I almost drop the phone off the ninth-floor balcony. "I do?"

"Of course. Not only will you be part of the family soon, but it's just common decency. You lost a parent at a very young age. That shouldn't be made into a spectacle or a piece of gossip."

I swallow. "Oh. Well, thank you, sir. I appreciate that."

"I lost my mother at a young age too. Not under such appalling circumstances, but painful nonetheless. If you need anything—you want me to speak to the prosecutor in Phoenix, arrange for you to attend the hearing without it being a media circus—just let me know. We'll do everything on our end to help."

"Thank you, sir."

"And good luck today. We'll be rooting for you down here in Dallas."

After I end up the call, I'm embarrassed to realize I'm blinking back tears. But, Christ, the relief that gusts through me is almost an emotional release. I fumble with my phone to text Gigi, filling her in on the call with Vega. She's awake too and texts back immediately.

GISELE:

I'm so glad, baby.

She's still typing.

GISELE:

> Maybe now you can stop waiting for the other shoe to drop all the time? Dallas wants you. They're waiting for you. Stop doubting yourself.

ME:

> I'll try not to.

GISELE:

> Good. Now go get something to eat and try not to overdo it during morning skate. Save it for the game.

ME:

> I will. Love you.

GISELE:

> Love you too.

I do my best to keep my mind relaxed, my body loose. After a very light game-day skate, I make my way to the hotel conference room for the press event.

Dread rises as I near the door. Fuck. I don't want to do this. But I'm not going to run from it. I'm not a coward.

The moment I slide through the door, Coach Jensen pulls me aside and says, "Anything you don't want to answer, just say, 'No comment,' understood?"

I nod.

"Don't feel bad about it or explain why you're not commenting. 'No comment.' Period, end of sentence."

"Yessir."

Two long tables are set up at the head of the spacious room with a podium between them. I settle in a chair between Colson and Demaine. Coach sits at the far end of the table, a slim binder in front of him. Talking points courtesy of Briar's PR gurus, I assume.

At the Arizona table is their head coach, team captain, and two assistant captains, one of whom is Michael Klein. I don't even spare the curly-haired guy a look. I sense him watching me, but he doesn't deserve acknowledgment.

To my relief, the first question, posed by a college sports blog, is about Briar's season and how we turned it around to reach this point. Colson fields that one. He's good with the crowd. Easygoing and articulate. The next question is directed at the Arizona captain. I'm starting to think I'll get out of this unscathed when a female journalist addresses me.

"Some very shocking details were revealed about your family yesterday. Do you believe this will affect your mental state today?"

Jensen looks ready to intervene, but I lean toward the microphone to answer. "You say 'shocking' and 'were revealed' as if my background was a secret, something I was trying to keep hidden. It wasn't. Anyone with a computer or phone could have known about my family history prior to yesterday. The fact that a bunch of people are talking about it now makes no difference to me. My head is always in the game."

Shockingly, she drops it and nobody else asks about my parents.

One annoying reporter, however, does decide to bring up the other elephant in the room.

"Michael, the last time you and Luke were on the ice together, you were teammates in the World Juniors. That particular encounter ended poorly, is that fair to say?"

"Poorly?" he echoes derisively. "I ended up in the hospital."

"It's evident there's still plenty of residual tension here," the intrepid reporter hedges, looking between us. "Have you two spoken since Worlds, and have or are you willing to bury the hatchet?"

Klein just laughs into the mic.

The sound is grating and raises my hackles. Asshole.

I'm not the only one irritated by him. From the corner of my eye, I see Case lean into his microphone.

"I have a question," Colson says. With a raised eyebrow, he looks toward the Arizona table. "For you, Klein."

My former teammate narrows his eyes. His coach tries to intercede, but Colson speaks before he can.

"What'd you say to Ryder in the locker room to get your jaw broken? Because I've played with this guy all season, and he's got the patience of a saint and the composure of a brick wall."

There's a beat of silence. Klein notices the room watching him intently and realizes he needs to provide some sort of answer.

Finally, he speaks through gritted teeth. "I don't recall what was said that day."

A curious woman in the front row addresses me. "Do you recall what was said, Luke?"

I flick my gaze toward Klein. Normally I would keep my mouth shut. Avoid the petty temptation. But his mocking laughter still rings in my ears. And this stain on my record that's followed me for years has finally become too much to bear.

Being with Gigi has taught me that sometimes you simply need to let things out, so I shrug, moving close to the mic again.

"He said my mom deserved to die and that my father should've shot me in the head too."

My response brings a whole lot of silence.

A few of the journalists look startled; others appear disgusted. In his seat, Klein's face is bright red. His hand fumbles for the base of the mic, but his coach shakes his head in warning as if to say, *Not a fucking word*. Because nothing good will come out of Michael Klein trying to defend *those* statements.

I remember it vividly, though. Still hear it knocking around in my head sometimes.

Michael and I were always butting heads. Our personalities just never meshed from the get-go, mostly because Klein has a hair-trigger temper and an insecurity-fueled need to be the big banana. He wanted to be recognized as the best player on the team and was furious that I was better than him. We won the World Juniors because of the goal *I* scored. That ate him up inside.

I don't even remember what started the argument in the locker room. Just normal trash talk at first. I ignored him, which only pissed him off further. He grabbed my arm when I wouldn't pay him any attention. I shoved him off me. Told him he was a loud, whiny prick. Then he spit out that line about my mother and I snapped.

I don't regret it. Even now, having to endure a bunch of strangers asking me about it in a press conference, I don't regret wiring that asshole's jaw shut.

And I'm going to enjoy every second of beating him tonight.

Fired Up with Josh Turner

Excerpt from Owen McKay Interview Transcript

Original Air Date: 4/22

© **The Sports Broadcast Corporation**

Owen McKay: You know, Josh, I sort of resent that question. Briar University just won the National Championship. Shouldn't that be what we're focusing on right now? What we're celebrating? Why don't you ask me how it feels knowing my little brother scored the winning goal in the Frozen Four? Because I'll tell you—it felt damn good.

Josh Turner: I get where you're coming from, and I certainly don't begrudge their achievement. It's a great feat. I'm simply reading questions from the live chat, Owen. The audience is asking this, not me.

McKay: Understood, but neither me nor my brother owe your audience, or anyone else for that matter, a comment regarding our father. We were both young when he went to prison. We haven't had contact with him since, and we don't ever plan to. We also have no interest in rehashing our past with the world. And yes, I feel comfortable speaking for my brother right now.

Turner: I see… Hmm… Hank Horace from Tennessee wants to know if you can comment on the current state of the justice system in America, specifically the parole process—

McKay: No. Next question.

Turner: All right... Oh, here's a fun one. What is your go-to beauty routine, Sandy Elfman from California is asking. Are there any men's products you would recommend?

CHAPTER FIFTY-TWO
GIGI

Your husband

"I THINK IT'S WEIRD THAT YOU'RE MARRIED, AND I'M NEVER GOING to understand it," Mya declares as she watches me wander around our common room in search of my keys.

"It's weird, yes, but eventually it will stop being weird and you'll realize it makes perfect sense."

She stubbornly shakes her head. "You're twenty-one. Who gets married when they're twenty-one? This isn't the Middle Ages!"

"I'm pretty sure the chicks in the Middle Ages got married when they were, like, twelve. I'm a spinster compared to them. My mother would be fainting with relief, and Dad would be getting the smelling salts if they managed to marry off their old maid daughter."

But I get it. We're young. And it'll definitely take a while for all my friends to get on board. The only one who seems totally unruffled by my elopement is Diana, but nothing ever ruffles her. She's already talking about double dates with her and Sir Percival. Somehow those two are still together, though he's sounding more and more controlling the more details she gives about him. I don't love that.

"Oh my God, where are my keys!" I groan in frustration.

"Oh, is that what you were looking for? They're right there."

I glare at her in outrage and walk over to snatch them up. "You could have saved me so much time right now."

"Where are you going? Plans with the hubby?" she mocks.

"Nope. I got my sports marketing and psychology papers back on Friday and aced both, so I'm treating myself to an afternoon at the butterfly gardens."

An hour later, the car's parked, my membership card's been scanned, and I'm walking into my favorite place on earth. I stroll the paths for a while, enjoying the humid breeze and rainbow of wings flapping all around me. I smile when I hold out my hand and a blue morpho flutters down to perch itself on my finger. This is as close as I'll ever get to being a Disney princess, and it's glorious.

I admire how the butterfly's lustrous wings reflect in the sunshine streaming through the glass walls.

"You have such a good life," I tell him. "You don't have to write exams or decide if you want to take a summer school course so you have a lighter workload next fall. You just get to fly around in here all day. Play with your friends. Drink your nectar."

Then it suddenly occurs to me maybe he *wouldn't* want to be trapped in here. Maybe he wants to be out in the great big world beyond the conservatory, surrounded by a million things that could kill him. Like, I've seen Bergeron snatch a butterfly out of the air with his jaw and eat it whole.

"Would you want to be eaten if it means having your freedom?" I ask the blue morpho in dismay.

I hear a startled cry from a child nearby. Her mother scowls at me and takes her hand. Marches her away from me.

Wow. Apparently you can't have philosophical conversations with butterflies in front of children anymore. People are so close-minded.

I meander down another path and turn the corner.

My dad is standing there.

I freeze. Jaw dropping. Oh, come on. Seriously? I can't have one beautiful Sunday in my beautiful happy place without being reminded of the fact that my father has never been more disappointed in me in his life?

The memory whips through me like a hurricane. Rips into my chest, leaving nothing but pain in its wake.

He must see it seeping out of my face, the joy I usually feel here, because his features crease with unhappiness.

He walks over to me. "Hey."

"How'd you know I was here?" I say in lieu of greeting.

"Your husband told me where you were."

I lift a brow. "Wow."

"What?"

"You actually said the words *your husband* without flinching."

"Yeah, well…" Dad slides his hands in his pockets. He's wearing cargo pants and a white T-shirt, and I don't miss the way some of the women around us check him out. Dude's still got it going on in his forties. "I don't know if you've noticed, but Ryder and I are friends now."

Ryder keeps telling me the same thing, insisting they've cleared the air and all the tension is gone. Ever since the men's Frozen Four win, there's been something lighter about Ryder too. His teammates backing him up with the media was humbling for him, and he and Case are friendly again. He and my mom are even friendlier, practically best friends now. Even my brother is on board—those two have stupid nicknames for each other. So it wouldn't surprise me if he's made genuine headway with my father.

As for me, I've been making a diligent effort to avoid anything related to my dad. I'm still so mad.

Except I'm not mad.

I'm devastated.

"You were right," Dad says. "He's a good guy."

"I know." It's become a habit now, when I'm on edge, to twist my thin silver wedding band. It's like Ryder's presence washing over me, relaxing me.

We walk down the path and cut toward another one that's empty. There's a wrought-iron bench near one of the fountains. Dad gestures at it.

Once we're seated, he gives me a sad, earnest smile.

"Forgive me," he says simply.

I don't say anything.

"I know I screwed up. I reacted poorly."

"Very poorly," I mutter.

"It's just…a lot of things were happening in that moment. I was shocked, obviously. Totally didn't see that one coming." He looks over dryly. "You've always been so terrible with surprises, like when you tried to plan your mom's surprise party and sent her an invitation?"

A laugh pops out. "That was a mistake."

"Yeah, I'm just saying, you don't surprise me very often. But this came completely out of left field. So there was the shock. And I guess in the moment I felt angry that you made this life-altering decision without even consulting us."

"I'm sorry." Then I shrug. "It didn't need consulting."

"You really mean that?"

"Yeah. Nothing you could have said, or any advice you would have given—or Mom, or Wyatt, or any of my friends—would have stopped me from marrying him. He's it for me. He's the one." I twist my wedding band again. "Like I said, I don't envision it being perfect. I'm sure eventually the sex won't be as good—"

Dad coughs. "G!"

"Sorry, but you know what I mean. The honeymoon phase will fade. We'll get stuck in ruts and routines, and probably want to kill each other half the time. But it doesn't matter. He's the one I'm choosing to do all of it with. Like you and Mom."

He nods. I'm startled by the look in his eyes. It's not resignation, but acceptance. I note that difference, wondering if maybe he *has* come around to this.

"So that's why you were such a jerk?" I prompt. "Shock and anger?"

"No. I thought that's what it was at first, and then I realized there was something else too." His voice becomes rough. "I was hurt."

"Hurt," I echo, and experience a flicker of guilt. I don't like the idea that I hurt him.

"I always pictured myself walking you down the aisle."

The admission grips my heart and squeezes it tight.

Damn it. Now I know why my mom can never stay mad at him. It's because he goes around saying things like that.

"Let's be real," he continues. "Your brother's never getting married—"

"Fuckboy till the day he dies," I agree.

"But I thought I had a shot with you. You've never been super girly, but I heard you and your mom talking about wedding dresses before. I assumed yours would be this fluffy white thing. You'd look beautiful in whatever you chose, though. I was looking forward to seeing you in it. Walking you down the aisle. Dancing with you at your wedding." He looks over, hopeful. "I know you already tied the knot, but you should totally consider having a wedding. Your aunt Summer would kill to plan it for you, you know that."

I snicker quietly. "You'd have to talk to Ryder about that. The man has a problem sharing what he had for dinner—you think he's going to stand in front of hundreds of people and recite his vows? Because we both know you're not keeping that wedding guest list below five hundred."

"I can't help that I have friends. Jeez." His humorous expression quickly sobers. "And you're wrong about him. I think you'd be surprised what that man would be willing to do for you."

We go silent.

Then I turn toward him and lean my head on his shoulder.

"I'm sorry I disappointed you," I say.

"You didn't. I disappointed myself." He pauses. "I love you. You know that, right?"

"Of course." I pause. "I love you too."

Another silence ripples between us.

"I was inducted into the Hall of Fame."

"I know." I didn't send him a congratulations myself, but I did tell Mom to pass it along because I'm not a heartless jerk.

"There's a ceremony and party next weekend. I'd love it if you and your husband would attend."

After a beat, I nod and squeeze his hand. "We'd be honored."

CHAPTER FIFTY-THREE
GIGI

Just a moment in time

RYDER LOOKS LIKE SEX IN A SUIT, AND IT TAKES ALL MY WILLPOWER not to bang him in the bathroom at the Hall of Fame ceremony. I didn't realize how difficult it would be, having a hot, six-foot-five hockey player husband. I want to bang him all the time, and that's a real problem.

But tonight is about my father, so I keep my brain out of the gutter, chastely hold my husband's hand, and count the hours until we're in a bed.

The ceremony was more emotional than I expected. I cried during it, pride filling my chest when the former Boston head coach honored my father with a beautiful speech. Now it's the party portion of the night, and we're unfortunately stuck doing the part I hate the most: mingling. Luckily, I have Ryder and Wyatt to share in the torture with. Mom doesn't seem to mind the mingling. Or maybe she just had to do so much of it over the years, for both her career and his, that she's good at pretending.

"Greg, I'd like you to meet my kids, Gigi and Wyatt." Dad appears with an older gray-haired man in town.

The man looks vaguely familiar, and then Dad introduces him, and it turns out they played together for one season twenty years ago, when Dad was a rookie and Greg was the wily veteran.

"And this is my son-in-law, Luke."

It amazes me how in less than a month, Dad can now say the word *son-in-law* with such ease, as if Ryder's been part of the family for years.

"Oh, this guy needs no introduction," Greg says with a grin, reaching out to shake Ryder's hand. "Luke Ryder! Ah, man, I've been following your career since the World Juniors. Can't wait for you to head to Dallas and see what you do down there."

"Me too," Ryder says.

They chat for a few minutes, and then our group moves along to mingle anew.

This time it's a coach from Detroit. One of the other inductees this year is a former Red Wings player.

Dad once again introduces Ryder, although this time he adds a throwaway line that makes me raise an eyebrow.

"Luke is going to coach at the Hockey Kings camp in August," he tells the guy. He glances at Ryder. "Coach Belov will be assisting us one of the days on a shooting workshop. So you two will get to work together, get to know each other better."

"Looking forward to it," Ryder says, and I can see him doing his level best to maintain a neutral expression.

Once Belov wanders away, Ryder stares at my dad, who says, "What?"

"Was that your way of giving me the coaching slot at Hockey Kings?"

"Oh, do I need to do an official ask? I just assumed you'd say yes."

Wyatt snorts.

I sip my champagne. For once in my life, I might actually be enjoying myself at one of these events. So, of course, the universe decides to ruin it.

Brad Fairlee is making his way toward us.

"Shit," I mutter under my breath.

Ryder follows my gaze and instantly reaches for my hand.

Dad notices the new arrival and gives me a look of assurance. "It'll be okay."

And it is. At first. Fairlee just shakes Dad's hand, congratulates him on the honor. Then he congratulates both me and Ryder on our respective championships. I manage to stifle my resentment when he and Dad discuss the upcoming women's Worlds. It's in two weeks, and it utterly grates that I could have been playing in it. Still feels like a failure on my part, but I keep forcing myself to remember Ryder's words. It's just a moment in time. There will be other moments.

Everything's friendly and polite—until Fairlee brings up his daughter. It starts off innocuous, him telling Mom about how Emma is auditioning for roles on the West Coast. Then it turns into him glancing at me, his features tightening.

"Emma mentioned you two ran into each other this winter."

I nod. "We did."

"She was quite upset when she got home." His tone remains careful, but his eyes are accusatory.

"I'm sorry to hear that," I answer, equally careful.

There's a beat of silence.

Then Brad sips his champagne, lowers his glass, and sighs. "Of the two of you, I will say, I expected you to be the more mature one, Gigi. You could afford to show her some grace."

Oh no, he didn't.

And ironically, it's not *my* reaction he needs to worry about. He just called me immature and graceless in front of my asshole husband, my asshole brother, and my asshole father. That's bad enough.

But it's the mama bear he triggered.

"I don't think so, Brad," my mother barks in a sharp voice. "With all due respect—and I do respect you—don't try to parent my kid. Go parent your own. She's the one with issues that need working through."

His eyes flash. "Emma didn't do anything wrong."

"Emma crawled into my bed, naked, and tried to screw my husband," Mom says politely, while my brother coughs into his hand to stop from laughing.

Fairlee is stricken. He quickly turns toward my father, who nods and says, "True story."

"Jesus. Garrett." His chastened eyes return to my mom. "Hannah. I had no idea. I…apologize on behalf of my daughter."

"Brad. No. You have nothing to apologize for," Dad interjects, because at the end of the day Brad Fairlee didn't do anything wrong. He simply tried to be a good dad by spoiling his kid, making up for her mother leaving them both. "We just kindly ask you don't talk to our daughter about things you know nothing about."

"Understood." Fairlee nods, still looking mortified.

A moment later, he stumbles off in a daze, chugging his champagne.

Sighing, I glance at my parents. "You didn't have to tell him what Emma did. I feel—" I stop, remembering everything Ryder advised me. Then I shrug, smiling at my husband. "Actually, no. I don't feel bad. She made her bed."

Ryder grins. "That's my girl."

CHAPTER FIFTY-FOUR
RYDER

You love me too much

Shane is throwing himself a goodbye party. But I don't have time to dwell on how pathetic that is, because I'm busy banging my wife in the hall bathroom during said goodbye party.

She's bent over the vanity, skirt bunched up around her waist, hands gripping the edge of the sink. I pump into her from behind and watch her in the mirror, enjoying the dreamy look on her face as I fuck her hard and fast.

"Jesus, you're making my head spin," she moans. "Keep doing that."

"That good, huh?"

"So good."

I slam into her eager pussy, bringing my lips to her ear. "You always get me so hard."

I'm rewarded with another moan and her ass pushing into me to take me as deep as she can.

"You need to come," she tells me, breathless.

"Want to get you off again first."

"Someone will be pounding on that door any second." She's still rocking back against me, her face flushed.

"Fine," I grumble, and her reflection smiles at me. Then she intentionally squeezes her pussy because she knows it'll destroy me, and even if I wanted to hold out for longer, it's not humanly possible.

I press myself inside her and groan as release shudders through me. Afterward, I grab some tissues and we clean each other up. While Gigi fixes her yellow sundress, I wipe down the sink, because I'm not a total asshole.

She smooths the bottom of her dress over her thighs. Turns to check her hair in the mirror, tucking it behind her ears. Then she examines me.

"You don't look like you just got fucked," she says, nodding in approval. "Do I?"

"Yes."

She sighs.

I wrap my arms around her from behind and kiss her neck. "I love you, you know that?"

"Of course I know that. You tell me like every other second."

Now I pinch her ass. "Don't complain about my I-love-you frequency or I'll crank it down to zero."

"You would never." She twists her head to smirk at me. "You love me too much."

She's not wrong about that.

"It's okay," Gigi consoles. She stands on her tiptoes, and even then, she can barely reach my lips. "I love you too much too."

Finally that knock comes. The door rattles from the force of it.

"Seriously, assholes! People need to pee!" One of the female partygoers is not as happy with our quickie as we were.

We keep our expressions indifferent as we step out of the bathroom. But everyone out there knows what's up.

Shane catches sight of us and wanders over. "You realize there are two bathrooms upstairs, along with three bedrooms. One of which is yours."

I shrug. "Where's the fun in that?"

Beckett overhears and nods in agreement. "Ryder gets it."

The weather's nice enough again to take the party outside, where one of my drunk teammates is barbecuing, and I pray to God he doesn't burn the house down. At least wait till the lease is up. Although...Beckett is sticking around, so maybe no house fires. Will Larsen is moving in, claiming he's sick of the dorms, so it'll be just the two of them here unless they manage to find a third.

Shane, meanwhile, is moving into a condo his rich parents just bought him. Turns out it's in the same complex as Gigi's friend Diana. He's raving about it now, telling us about all the renovations his dad did in preparation for Shane's move-in date.

"Must be nice," Gigi drawls.

"Oh shut up," Shane tells her, grinning. "Your dad is rich and would buy you a fuckin' mansion if you asked."

He's got her there. In fact, her father has already been threatening to do just that. We said no. We can wait until I officially sign my rookie contract with Dallas next year and buy it ourselves.

"Hey, off topic," Shane says, sipping his beer. "You'll like this, Gisele—last night TSBN was showing highlights from the women's Worlds. They did a countdown of the top five plays. Four of the plays were Canada." He snickers softly.

Gigi rolls her eyes at him. "I appreciate the solidarity, but don't cheer for our country's loss on my behalf."

She and I watched the game together last month, though, and she was definitely throwing some shade. I don't know if her presence on the roster would have altered the results of that game and given USA the gold instead of Canada. But it wouldn't have hurt, that's for sure.

"Anyway, there's still a chance I'll make that roster one day." She shrugs. Unbothered. Which is a vast improvement from the night she sobbed about what a failure she was. But like me, she's learning to accept her limitations while continuing to hone her strengths.

"And if I don't," she says with a grin, "I'll just graduate from college and be Ryder's agent and land us multimillion-dollar endorsements."

"Solid plan," I agree.

Will, Beckett, and Case drift toward us, and we chat over beers and drunk-boy-prepared burgers for a while. At one point, Diana wanders over in a tiny skirt that barely covers her thighs and a T-shirt with the neckline cut away so it drapes low on one shoulder.

"Lindley," she says, eyes narrowed.

"Dixon," he mimics.

"I just want it to be known that Meadow Hill was my turf first, and you are to stay away from me at all times. In fact, we can draw a line down the center of the pool and assign sides."

"Well, that's mean." He feigns a pout. "Are you going to be rude to your own friends too? Because I plan on bringing a cheerleader or two over. Nightly."

She glares at him and saunters off.

"Do you have any big plans this summer other than tormenting my best friend with your fuckboy antics?" Gigi asks pleasantly.

Shane grins. "Nah. I'll probably split the time between here and my parents' place. What about you guys?"

"I want a honeymoon," she declares. Beaming.

He grins at me now. "Take the woman on a honeymoon, asshole."

"I plan to," I protest. "We're going to fuckin' Italy in August."

"That was highly aggressive toward Italy, mate," Beckett says, and Will and Colson laugh loudly. Case seems to have completely gotten over his issues with Gigi and me being together. He's spent most of the night flirting with Gigi's teammate Camila.

"He doesn't think he'll like it there," Gigi explains.

"It feels like a very lackadaisical place," I mutter.

Neither of us mention that we're going to Arizona in July. Gigi and I discussed my dad's parole hearing at length—Owen weighed in too—and eventually we decided the benefits to speaking at the hearing outweighed the costs. Owen and I would rather never see that man's face for as long as we live, but fifteen years isn't long enough. He deserves to rot in prison for what he did to our mother. And if there's even the slightest risk the parole board would let him out if they don't hear any dissenting voices, we can't take that chance. So the three of us are flying down there next month. Gigi's parents offered to come along too.

Life is…good.

That's not a sentiment I'm used to expressing. Or experiencing. But it is. I've got my health, my friends, my brother. My wife. Neither of us have any idea what the future holds. Nobody does.

But I can't imagine any future with Gigi not being bright.

ACKNOWLEDGMENTS

When I first wrote *The Deal* and subsequent books in the Off-Campus/Briar U series, I didn't expect these characters to have such an impact on me. Every single one of them has stuck with me over the years, especially my OGs—Hannah and Garrett. When I decided to revisit the Briar universe, I broke one of my own rules and chose to write a "next generation" story. I'm not usually drawn to those types of stories, but lately I've been driving myself mad wondering what Garrett and Hannah's twins from *The Legacy* would be like. And...*The Graham Effect* was born!

A quick note about some of the hockey plot points in this book—I usually fudge certain details in order to create a fictionalized hockey world so that certain plot elements can line up better. In this book, I played around with the NCAA hockey schedule and conferences, as well as certain elements about Team USA/the national team. All errors are my own (and often intentional).

As always, this book wouldn't be in front of your eyes right now without the support of some very important people:

My agent, Kimberly Brower, for always being there to hold my hand through minor, major, and imagined emergencies.

My editor, Christa Dèsir, for being my biggest cheerleader and even bigger champion for this series. And the rest of the rock-star team at Bloom Books/Sourcebooks: Pam, Molly, and the rest of the marketing and publicity team, the incredible art team, and Dom for being the coolest publisher I know.

Nicole, Natasha, and Lori for their social media wizardry and overall awesomeness.

Eagle/Aquila Editing for always dropping everything to proof-read for me.

My family and friends for putting up with me when I'm on deadline and forget to answer their calls because I'm lost in a different universe. And my little sister for feeding me when I forget to eat while I'm writing.

Sarina Bowen and Kathleen Tucker for lending me their ears and eyes and never failing to make me laugh. Oh, and Kathleen gives me plants. Gardening for the win.

And of course, you. My readers, the kindest, funniest, coolest, most supportive people on the planet. You're the reason I'm able to do what I do, and you're the reason the romance community is the most welcoming and engaging place to belong to. I hope you enjoyed Gigi and Ryder's book, and I can't wait for you to read the other stories planned in the Campus Diaries series!

ABOUT THE AUTHOR

A *New York Times*, *USA Today*, and *Wall Street Journal* bestselling author, Elle Kennedy grew up in the suburbs of Toronto, Ontario, and holds a BA in English from York University. From an early age, she knew she wanted to be a writer, and actively began pursuing that dream when she was a teenager.

Elle currently writes for various publishers. She is the author of more than fifty titles of contemporary romance and romantic suspense novels, including the global sensation Off-Campus series.

Website: ellekennedy.com
Facebook: ElleKennedyAuthor
Instagram: @ElleKennedy33
Twitter: @ElleKennedy
TikTok: @ElleKennedyAuthor